Beyond the Great Beyond

Beyond the Great Beyond

Book Three of the Destined Series

Michael D. Brooks

Published by Michael D Brooks, 2023

Acknowledgments

Once again, I'd like to thank my wife, a voracious reader of nearly every genre except science fiction. As usual, her perspective as an indifferent reader of science fiction is always helpful. Gaining the insight of someone far removed from the genre is invaluable.

To my beta readers Linda Stokes and Gregory Stubblefield for their input and patience, and for tolerating the many, many, many rewrites, questions, and suggestions.

Thank you to Projekt_Itachi for his advice and input regarding the front and back cover designs.

I also send out a special thanks for the support of the many authors whose words of encouragement helped me to write this third book.

And most of all, I want to give a shout-out to the many readers of books 1 and 2 who requested more. Your support has made book 3 possible.

Thank you.

"There is many a boy here today who looks on war as all glory, but, boys, it is all hell."

— William Tecumseh Sherman, 1880

Contents

Chapter 1

Chapter 2

Chapter 3

Chapter 4

Chapter 5

Chapter 6

Chapter 7

Chapter 8

Chapter 9

Chapter 10

Chapter 11

Chapter 12

Chapter 13

Chapter 14

Chapter 15

Chapter 16

Chapter 17

Chapter 18

Chapter 19

Chapter 20

Chapter 21

Chapter 22

Chapter 23

Chapter 24

Chapter 25

Chapter 26

Chapter 27

Chapter 28

Chapter 29

Chapter 30

Chapter 31

Chapter 32

Chapter 33

Chapter 34

Chapter 35

Chapter 36

Chapter 37

Chapter 38

Chapter 39

Chapter 40

Chapter 41

Chapter 42

Chapter 43

Chapter 44

Chapter 45

Chapter 46

Chapter 47

Chapter 48

Chapter 49

Chapter 50

Chapter 51

Chapter 52

Chapter 53

Chapter 54

Chapter 55

Chapter 56

Chapter 57

Chapter 58

Chapter 59

Chapter 60

Chapter 61

Chapter 62

Chapter 63

Chapter 64

Chapter 65

Chapter 66

Epilogue

Lexicon

About the Author

Other Books by the Author

Social Media Presence

Chapter 1

Deep within the heart of a swirling murky void of thick cosmic dust, gas clouds, burning suns, and solar winds, known as the Ghion Nebula, floated a cloaked warship.

The Alliance ship *Infiltrator* and its crew of four biologics and two synthetics arrived home following a harrowing journey through time between two universes. Captain Vee blew out a breath of relief and ordered Lieutenant Sparks, the ship's helmsman and navigator, to hold their position.

"Hold here, Lieutenant."

"Aye, cap."

Sparks, whose ancestors spawned from an aquatic world, was best equipped with the experience and intuition to navigate the nebula's endless swirls of solar wind streams.

Captain Vee, like everyone else from her planet, possessed the natural ability to fly. But unlike many of her people, she chose to fly among the stars. Being the captain of a starship is where she felt the most comfortable.

"Okay, people, what's our status?" Vee asked.

Sparks was the first to speak. "The boards all show green, cap."

Lieutenants Raqmar, the chief engineer, and Karona, the communications officer and cryptographer, each reported the status of their stations.

"All systems are working as expected, cap," Raqmar said.

"Ditto for communications, cap," Karona reported.

"Sojourner? Ramie?"

The ship's SI officers each reported the ship's systems were functioning at peak efficiency.

"Great," Vee said. "Scan the area for any GSE or Alliance activity."

Karona's gray fingers glided along her console. "We are the only ship in the vicinity, cap. There's no one but us out here."

She and Raqmar were both from the planet Selemar. Their homeworld's gravity was heavier than most other planets in the Alliance so Karona and Raqmar possessed higher than average strength.

Sojourner, the ship's senior Synthetic Intelligence officer, confirmed Karona's report. "Verified, Captain. I have conducted a backup scan and have not detected anything other than ourselves outside of natural phenomena."

"Cloaked ships?"

"Nothing, Captain."

"I concur, Captain," Ramie said.

"Great. How about the universal time transmitters? Are we where . . . when we're supposed to be?"

"Yes, Captain. We have returned mere minutes after our previous departure," Sojourner confirmed.

"Good. Thank the Gods for small favors. How long has it been since the task force's departure?"

"Approximately one hour, Captain," Sojourner said.

"Sparks, continue to hold here and wait for further orders. Maintain radio silence."

"Aye, cap."

"Kay," Vee said, addressing Karona by her preferred name.

"Yes, cap?"

"Continue to monitor all communications bands. Alert me the moment you hear anything from or about the GSE."

"Aye, cap. You'll be the second one to know."

Vee smiled at Karona's little joke. After what she and her crew had been through, it was nice to know they had not lost their sense of humor. "Good. I'll be in my quarters."

"Aye, cap," Karona replied.

Vee rose from her command chair and walked into her quarters off to one side of the bridge. As the doors closed behind her, she slumped against them and wondered, *Now what'll I do?*

Chapter 2

Commander Chappie walked along the sky-blue corridors of the Fleet ship *Vindicator*. Following an earlier secret conversation he had with Captain Vee, he needed to clear his head. He found roaming the corridors helped him think. He considered why he felt it comforting walking the halls among the ship's crew rather than in the privacy of his quarters. He decided that seeing the faces of the ship's personnel reminded him why he did what he did.

Interacting with the youngest members drove home the importance of their mission. If the Alliance was to survive, these young people were the ones who would be faced with the burden of seeing that it would. He deemed it his responsibility to give them that opportunity.

There was a faint chemical odor that lingered in the air from the recently painted halls. He wondered what the Fleet psychologists had been thinking when they convinced the military brass the bright color was more beneficial to the crew's mental health during prolonged deployments rather than the traditional battleship gray. He preferred the gray, and the rumor aboard ship was so did the crew.

The *Vindicator* was the first ship to be painted with the new color scheme. As far as the crew was concerned, they were nothing more than psychological guinea pigs. Chappie glanced at the ceiling and imagined there was some giant scientist-type in a lab coat peering down on the ship watching the crew go about their daily duties like vermin. The Terrans had a term for it, he recalled. They called it being like rats in a maze or cage or something.

The thought that everyone on board was nothing more than science projects bothered him. They were soldiers. They put their lives on the line every day. He felt they should be respected. They were not mere test subjects for some eggheads who wanted to earn an advanced degree.

Chappie walked the labyrinth of corridors acknowledging the crewmen he passed as they braced their backs against the walls, creating a path for him. Most of them were kids. He observed their faces. They were full of the exuberance of youth. Full of adventure, wonder, and fear. He saw it in their eyes. He had been young once. His own youthful exuberance was once driven by naiveté.

He had tried to hang onto that youthful innocence and sense of adventure as long as he could once, but it was worn away over time as the reality of war took its toll on him. Chappie knew that the innocence of the people passing him in the halls would be shattered as his innocence had been. And he regretted having to take part in killing that innocence.

The Alliance's war with the Galactic Star Empire began over a decade earlier when an Alliance research vessel, sent to explore a newly discovered planet on the edge of its territory, encountered a reptilian-like species living on it. Despite possessing what the Alliance mistakenly perceived as rudimentary space flight capabilities, they were everything but rudimentary.

When attempts were made to establish communications with the planet's inhabitants, it quickly became evident the species was an advanced spacefaring race on par with the Alliance. But, unlike the Alliance, their intentions were far from peaceful.

Following a deadly first contact, and a few skirmishes, the Alliance attempted to establish a dialogue. Peace envoys were sent to an agreed upon location on the edge of the frontier between the planet and the Alliance. The resulting consequences of that meeting were disastrous.

The Alliance envoys did not know the inhabitants of the planet were members of a vanguard of shock troops backed by the Galactic Star Empire.

The GSE rebuffed the Alliance's gesture by killing the envoys and declaring war. They never had any intentions short of conquest and eradication. The dominant group within the empire called themselves Sairidians.

Their society was based on a caste system. The Sairidians were the ruling and warrior caste. Their one objective was expansion of their sphere of influence. To them, the Alliance was an obstacle in their way that needed to be removed.

Chappie pondered what Captain Vee told him as he walked the halls. If what happened to Delta Squadron days earlier was an indicator, the days of the Alliance could be numbered. But he would do his damndest to ensure that the unthinkable did not happen.

Chapter 3

The *Vindicator* was part of a task force sent to provide support to a fighter squadron dispatched to Aggro Nine, an agricultural planet in Alliance-controlled space along the edge of the Frontier, on a humanitarian mission. The squadron was ambushed by an overwhelming number of GSE fighters. By the time the task force arrived, the mission dissolved into a recovery effort.

Delta Squadron never stood a chance. They were all but wiped out. Only one fighter survived the battle, but it drifted into a nearby nebula; its crew was presumed lost. Captain Vee presented evidence indicating the fighter's crew may have survived. She persuaded Chappie to authorize a secret rescue mission.

The *Infiltrator*, cloaked and running silent, slipped into the galactic equivalent of pea soup in search of their comrades. When it returned, Vee contacted him with disturbing news.

She and her crew had gathered vital intel crucial to the survival of the Alliance. They discovered the GSE had developed cloaking technology right under the Alliance's nose. But that technology was not limited to simply cloaking ships. They believed the Galactic Star Empire had developed cloaking technology that could hide an entire military base in space.

Chappie ordered the task force to abandon their recovery efforts and return to its command base in the Epsilon sector. At the Fleet's top speed of its slowest ship, it would take a day to reach. He prayed they would reach their destination without any entanglements with the GSE. The information Vee gave him needed to be given to High Command in person. Any transmission of the data might jeopardize the task force and put the security of the Alliance further at risk.

Only one other individual knew the true nature of their premature departure from Aggro Nine. It was the captain of the *Vindicator*. When the captain asked for justification for abandoning the recovery effort, Chappie showed him the evidence Vee had given him. Captain Tranyxx pulled the plug on all operations and ordered the task force to "haul ass" to Epsilon base.

As the taskforce headed to their command base, Chappie decided to roam the corridors and mull through his thoughts before going back to his quarters.

He stood and stared at the door to his quarters before he announced himself. The door's sensor conducted a quick body scan, verified his DNA and voice, and then swished open. He stepped into the blackness of his quarters and felt the room's soothing warmth as its ceiling lights eased on illuminating the light gray room in a soft, warm low light.

Hailing from a planet where its inhabitants evolved from plants, Chappie basked in the soothing lights and warmth of his quarters as the door slid closed behind him.

His living space was small by civilian standards, but spacious compared to those of enlisted personnel. It contained a single bed, a dining table, an entertainment center, bathroom, a small kitchenette, and an office.

He crossed the room and collapsed face first onto his bunk. The heated mattress was not as comfortable as it could have been, but it was the best the military had to offer.

"Welcome back, commander," a soft disembodied feminine voice with a melodious lilt said. It belonged to his personal SI assistant. The mere sound of her voice was enough to help relax his tense muscle fibers.

Overseeing the recovery effort left him exhausted. Processing the news Vee gave him did not help lessen his fatigue. He intended to rest his weary body for an hour or two while working on some reports he had been putting off. If he had any time left, he planned to snatch a quick nap before going back on shift.

"Thank you, Myra. Any messages?"

He rolled over onto his back to face the ceiling and placed his hands behind his head before Myra replied.

"Just two, sir. One was from Lieutenant Murphy. He said the Systems Technicians completed the maintenance run on the astro-navigation module. He will–if he has not already done so–begin to update the star charts and run a Doppler analysis per your request."

"Very good. And the second message?"

"The second message is from Doctor Sanchez. She said she wants you to get some sleep and not report for duty until you do."

"Thank you, Myra." Chappie thought about taking the doctor up on her suggestion but decided against it. He knew he needed the sleep, but he could not bring himself to get any.

"Would you like for me to turn off the lights for you now, sir?"

"No, not yet. I've got some work to do. I'll just take a stimulant and go through the crew performance reviews I've been putting off. I'll let you know when to turn off the lights."

"I am sorry, but I cannot let you do that, sir."

Chappie was surprised by Myra's statement. *What the hell?* he thought. She had never refused to comply with his wishes before. He started to wonder if something was wrong with part of her programming or worse. "What do you mean you can't let me do that?"

"The doctor gave me very specific instructions. She said that if you refused to get some sleep, I was to impress upon you the seriousness of her request by playing the following recording."

Chappie was about to use a few colorful words in response when the doctor's husky voice filled his quarters. The distinctive voice of Doctor Evelyn Sanchez, Terran accent and all, contained the unmistakable authority of command.

"Chap, you stubborn son-of-a-bitch, I admire your dedication to duty, but if you don't get some sleep, *and I mean real sleep*, I'll certify you unfit and recommend the admiral cite you for dereliction of duty." There was a slight pause before her voice continued. "I mean it, Chap. Get some sleep, don't report for duty until you do. And you'll know when that will be. That's an order."

In situations like this, the doctor held more sway with an admiral. A medical command outweighed all others. Not one to disobey a direct order, Chappie toyed with the idea of doing so this one time. After all, he decided, there was a first time for everything. The ship wasn't due to reach Epsilon Base for a full day. He felt forty hours was more than enough time for him to get some work done and catch up on some rest. Besides, he was alone in his quarters. Who was going to know?

The doctor's voice continued. "Oh, and by the way, I know you better than you know yourself. If you don't drag your sorry ass to bed at the end of this recording, I've ordered Myra to lock you in your quarters and gas you to sleep. Pleasant dreams."

"Would you like the lights off now, commander?" Myra asked.

Chappie was sure he heard a smirk in Myra's voice. With an irritated sigh, he stayed in his bunk, sulked and said, "Yes."

"Sleep well, sir."

He only grunted as the room went dark.

The room's blackness and the rhythmic vibration and hum of the big ship's engines did not do much to soften his surly mood or lull him to sleep. His mind was a jumble of thoughts he needed to sort out. He made one last attempt to appeal to Myra.

"You know, I do my best thinking when I'm able to work." All he got back from her was silence. "Damn," was all he could think to say.

The doctor and his trusted assistant had conspired against him. He turned his thoughts away from finishing the reports and began thinking about the war. A war he was afraid the Alliance might lose. The thought both disturbed him and motivated him.

It was a given that soldiers were trained to kill and were expected to make the ultimate sacrifice if need be. Military conflicts were usually started by someone through conscious intent, miscalculation, or ignorance that others ended up having to fight. All three were the reasons for the current war. He felt the men and women fighting it were what the Terrans called sacrificial lambs being sent to slaughter. And that is not what he had signed up for.

What he signed up for was the adventure of a lifetime. Chappie wanted to explore the stars, expand the knowledge of the vastness of space, and help in colonizing what had at one time been called the final frontier. Chappie did not have the academic prowess to be a scientist, and he didn't want to be stuck in a limiting career. So he chose the military because it offered the best opportunity for him to achieve his goals as far as he was concerned.

Soldiering is not what Chappie had initially wanted to do, but it was what he did best. The military took a rudderless young man and gave him purpose and direction. And that direction took him to where he wanted to be. And where he wanted to be was in space.

He resisted the urge to sleep until his will was overcome by fatigue. Chappie drifted into an uneasy sleep filled with dreams from a decade ago of events he found hard to forget.

Chapter 4

The force of the explosion tossed Chappie from his bunk. He crashed to the floor against the wall. A sharp pain shot up his right arm as his elbow banged on the floor. He saw a blinding white light behind his eyes and clenched his teeth as his brain registered the pain his elbow and arm received. For a moment, he thought he had gone blind as the pain screamed in his head. There was a chorus of shouting as startled men and women tried to make sense of the situation. He heard a siren wailing in the distance.

"What the hell happened?" someone yelled.

The floor shook as a second explosion rocked the room. Total darkness engulfed everyone before the emergency lights snapped on and bathed the room in a deep blood red glow.

"Did the generator blow?" someone else yelled.

They didn't have to wait long for an answer. A single command bellowed through the barrack's audio system. "ALL HANDS, THE BASE IS UNDER ATTACK. REPORT TO YOUR STATIONS."

The barracks came alive with activity as his bunk mates sprang into action and rushed to get dressed. Now they had a purpose. Their commanding officer, Sergeant Willy Sikes, a tall muscular Terran with brown hair cut in the traditional military buzz cut, took charge. He barked out orders and commands that calmed his troopers.

Lieutenant Commander Chappie was bunking with a squad of marines from all parts of the Alliance assigned to escort him during his stay at the mining facility they were on. He would have preferred to ditch the escorts, but protocol required all visiting senior officers to have a military escort whenever they were on any planetary facility not classified as an official colony.

He was on Terra II to attend a series of briefings updating him and a few other officers, dignitaries, and various business professionals on the progress being made on the planet. He had arrived a few days before.

"You alright, sir?" the sergeant asked. Chappie was still lying on the floor cradling his arm. He felt it for any fiber damage. There did not appear to be any and the pain was subsiding. He then tried to rub the remaining soreness away when he looked up to see the sergeant peering down at him. The look of concern was visible all over the man's face.

"Yeah, I'm fine." The pain was almost gone.

"Good," the big man said. "Let's get you someplace safe."

Judging from the sounds outside the barracks, there did not appear to be any safe place at the moment. Besides, he decided he was not going to run and hide when others could not.

"I'm okay, Sergeant. We need to find out what the hell is happening and coordinate with those who do."

As Sikes helped him stand up, Chappie saw that the sergeant's people had taken a defensive posture surrounding the two officers. They were guarding the doors and windows. A few were operating various hand-held devices. Acrid smoke that smelled like burning rubber started filling the room. It stung his eyes. Everyone pulled out portable respirators and put them on.

"Sarge!" one of his men called out. "We can't get in touch with anyone on the base or off. Communications are out."

"Get back on the radio and keep trying until you find somebody to talk to. I don't care if it takes the rest of the day."

"Yes, sir."

Sikes turned to Chappie and asked, "Orders, sir?"

Chappie coughed to clear his throat. "You got your orders. Get to your stations. I'll make my way to C&C."

"Alright, you maggots, you heard the man. Get your sorry asses in gear and let's give some back. Corporal Vee!" he yelled.

"Sir!" was the snappy reply from a young female marine whose baggy camouflage uniform made her look smaller than she was. Her helmet almost looked too big for her head. Her small round bird-like face looked lost beneath it. Through the smoky haze the physical characteristics of her avian heritage were almost indiscernible.

"Escort the lieutenant commander safely to C&C. And don't come back until you do. You know where we'll be. If anything changes, I'll tag you. Got that?"

"Sir, yes, sir." She turned to look at Chappie.

When the air handling system kicked in, there was a whir and a whoosh, then the smoke cloud that filled the room thinned out like a morning fog. After everyone removed their respirators, he had a better view of the corporal's face. It was impassive. He knew that was due to her military training, but her eyes revealed the firestorm of emotion raging inside. He saw it and recognized it for what it was because he felt the same thing: fear. He could see it in all of their eyes—including Sikes. But they were ground pounders and they had a job to do. And so did he. Vee gestured toward the barracks doors.

"This way, sir," she said.

Chappie wondered if the corporal saw his fear. If she did, she showed no sign that she had.

Vee did see the fear in the lieutenant commander's eyes, but he was better than some when it came to camouflaging it. She admired that. She had been witness to officers losing all self-control at the first sign of danger on some of the colony worlds her short career found her stationed on. Her first mission following graduation was nearly her last.

Vee had the advantage of being older than most of the cadets. Her age, experience, and grades resulted in her completing the academy in two years rather than four. It also put her in the unique position of being assigned to the academy as a trainer and mentor before she served in the field.

Her first field assignment was supposed to be a routine rescue operation. As the evacuees were loaded onto transports, the operation was halted when they came under attack. Most of the senior officers chose to escape to the relative safety of the support ships during the attack. When her commanding officer was killed, she was, by default, next in line. She followed her training and instincts and took charge of a group of frightened civilians and recruits. They held out long enough for a fighter group to take out their attackers allowing a rescue unit to land and transport them to the waiting ships.

Her actions under fire were noticed by Sikes, who requested she be assigned to his unit. And that is why he chose her to escort Chappie.

Chappie grabbed his helmet, slipped into his body armor, and followed Vee toward the doors then stopped and said, "Wait! I don't have my sidearm." In all the confusion, he had forgotten to pick it up and strap it on.

"Here you go, sir." Sikes retrieved Chappie's gun belt and tossed it to him. Chappie strapped it on, checked the gun's charge and re-holstered it.

"You might want to carry this as well as that peashooter you're wearing, sir," Sikes said. He flashed a broad smile of gleaming white teeth. Chappie's sidearm was a standard issue pulse pistol and would not do much if he needed something with more of a kick to it.

The sergeant tossed him a PR10 dual action pulse-projectile rifle. It was a two-handed weapon that could fire either energy pulse rounds or high caliber bullets; with the flip of a switch it could fire both. Despite its bulky appearance, it was lightweight, sturdy, and reliable. It was the standard offensive/defensive weapon issued to all foot soldiers. Because of its dual-role, the troops called it The Switcher.

Chappie caught the rifle and slung it over his shoulder by the weapon's strap.

"You might need this too," Sikes said. He tossed a belt of clips containing bullets and energy cartridges.

"Thanks, sergeant." Chappie slung the belt over his head and across one shoulder. "Good luck." He smiled back.

"You too, sir."

He looked at the diminutive Vee standing next to him with the big gun in her hands. He felt confident that she knew how to use it. "Let's move, corporal."

Chappie and Vee dashed from the barracks and zigzagged their way toward Command and Control. It was several meters away at the center of the compound. Most of their trek was in the open where there was not much protection. Chappie was stunned at the level of destruction. He had toured the facility the day he arrived. At that time, the buildings were clean and glistened in the light of the planet's sun. Now, they lay in ruin. They were unrecognizable as buildings. Salvos of some kind rained down around them like fire balls. The explosions made it difficult to hear. The air, already thick with dust, coupled with severe humidity, became more difficult to breathe.

Vee gestured to him to put on his respirator as she put her own on. He reached for his when he realized he must have dropped it somewhere along their zigzag route. He pointed to his empty pouch where it should have been, shrugged, and shook his head. The young officer opened a small pack velcroed to her side and pulled out a spare respirator.

"Here, sir!" she shouted. "Put this on." She handed it to him.

He slipped it on.

A molecular bond held it against his face. He was able to breathe and hear better. They resumed their run across open ground. The remaining distance they had to cover was equal to two Terran city blocks.

"Stay close to my six, sir," Vee urged. "If I lose you, the sergeant's going to have my ass for breakfast."

"Well then we'll just have to make sure he has someone else's ass for breakfast." He knew that joking at a time like this might be considered poor taste, but he found he could not help himself. He figured it was nerves, but it got a chuckle out of Vee. An explosive thud nearby motivated them to double their efforts to reach safety.

Vee thought that the lieutenant commander was alright in her book. Here they were, dodging salvos and racing one step ahead of death, and he was finding something humorous to say in the heat of battle. She knew she had to get him to C&C. If he was killed on her watch, she would not forgive herself, and she would catch hell from Sikes.

Chappie glanced up at the emerald sky and thought how much it looked like the color of his skin. If the sky was not being sliced by streaks of whatever was raining down around them, it would have been just another sunny day.

Halfway toward their goal, the ground exploded in front of them. Chappie's ears popped when the air pressure dropped. The ground rose beneath their feet, and then tossed them up into the air like rag dolls as the dirt took on the quality of gunpowder. They landed like rocks inches away from the edge of a small blast hole. Both of them managed to hang onto their weapons. Chappie landed on his elbow again.

"Shit!" he cried out.

"You okay, sir?" Vee asked.

The pain was screaming in his head again, but he managed to say, "Yeah." After a moment's hesitation, he asked, "You?"

Vee replied, "I'm good, sir."

"Then let's keep moving," Chappie said. "We're cannon fodder out here in the open."

"Don't have to tell me twice, sir."

He staggered to his feet and reached out a hand to help Vee up. The respirators had built-in vocal amplifiers, but they still had to shout to be heard above the screams and explosions. As they started to run, Vee growled, then stumbled. She was limping and favoring her left leg. The ground shook beneath their feet causing her to stagger and put weight on her injured leg. She growled again and fell. If the respirator covering her face had not been coated with a dusting of dirt, he would have seen the tears in her eyes.

"Corporal, you hurt bad?" he asked.

"No, sir," Vee said.

Her leg throbbed. She touched it to feel if the bone was broken, but felt nothing protruding. She guessed her leg might have a hairline fracture, but she was not about to tell the lieutenant commander. He might decide to change plans in midstream rather than get to C&C. Vee was determined to not let that happen. She had her orders and was damned sure going to see them through. She thought that if she played down the injury, he would not be too concerned with her and would remain focused on the task at hand.

Chappie stepped toward Vee and squatted next to her and offered to check her leg, but she waved him off.

"Must have sprained something when we got knocked down. I'm okay." Her breathing was labored.

He stood up and extended his arm for her to grab. "Here, put your weight on me." She was about to resist when he warned her, "Don't make me have to make it an order."

She struggled to her feet, slung her gun over her shoulder and draped her right arm around his shoulder. Vee put her weight on him rather than her bad leg as they continued to run. *I'm supposed to be protecting him, not the other way around*, she thought.

They dodged incoming salvos, passed by the dead, dying, and severely injured, as well as navigated around fallen debris. The respirator made the air easier to breathe, but it did nothing to mask the stench of blood. Chappie hated the smell. It reminded him of the stories he heard the elders tell when he was a young sapling.

There was once a time on his world when someone like him would have trapped and ingested someone like the corporal.

When they reached Command and Control, they stood looking at what remained of an imploded structure. The building had taken a direct hit. Part of it was missing, part of it caved in.

"Holy shit!" Vee blurted. Then apologized for her outburst. "Uh, sorry, sir."

"Don't be. You only said what I was thinking." He surveyed the damage. "We have to find a way in."

"Over there, sir."

Vee pointed to a hole in the side of the building next to what had been the main entrance. It was large enough for them to fit through. They made their way over toward it.

"Do you think it's safe enough for us to crawl through, sir?"

"It looks stable enough to me."

Since they were not running anymore, Vee tried to put more weight on her bad leg and cringed. Chappie suspected she had more than a sprain. The young marine made a quick visual scan of the area around them then stuck her weapon into the hole and checked the motion tracker on its gun sight.

"I'm getting movement on the tracker a few meters up ahead, sir. They appear to be friendlies. Should we try it?"

She looked at Chappie for approval to enter. He nodded.

"Stay behind me, sir" she whispered. "And watch our six."

Vee knew that the lieutenant commander did not need to be told to watch himself, but if they lived through this, she did not want it said she did not do her job. She took point and hobbled her way forward down the hall dragging her injured leg.

Chappie watched in admiration as she motivated herself to push forward on nothing more than strength of will. The level of pain Vee appeared to be in must have been excruciating. It was surprising she was still conscious. He readied his rifle, and followed her in.

The once pristine halls were strewn with debris and bodies. The walls were marred by scorch marks. Light fixtures dangled from the ceilings and equipment sparked and sizzled everywhere. If it were not for the gaping holes that let in the sunlight, the place would have been in complete darkness like a cave or underground tunnel.

"You . . . hear that, sir?"

"Hear what, Corporal?"

"Nothing, sir. The bombing has stopped."

He listened. Vee was right. The bombs stopped, and he had failed to notice.

"That can only mean two things," he said.

"What, sir?"

"They either retreated, or they're planning a ground assault."

"Let's hope they . . . retreated, sir."

"I'm with you on that."

Because the environmental systems were destroyed, the air in the hallways was oppressive and hot. Chappie wondered if they would make it or die from a ceiling collapse or heat stroke. He also wondered how Vee was feeling. Her limp had gotten so bad that she was now using her PR10 as a crutch. Her breathing was more raspy.

"Corporal," he whispered. "We should stop and rest a moment."

"No . . . can . . . do, sir." She paused. "Gotta . . . keep moving. Not safe in . . . halls."

He couldn't help but feel for her; she seemed so young. Just a kid. The minimum age for enlistment was seventeen, but you had to be eighteen to get field duty. He guessed she could not be a day over eighteen.

"Corporal?"

"Sir?" She stopped moving long enough to turn to look at him.

"How long have you been in?"

"Two years . . . out of the academy, sir. But I was older than most of my," she struggled to take a breath, "peers. I was twenty when I was a plebe, sir."

She was older than he guessed but still a kid to him.

"Why'd the sarge pick you for this?"

"I'm the old-head, sir. The rest . . . are twelve-monthers . . . or less."

Chappie knew he could never distract her from doing her job, but he thought he could take her mind off her pain by talking to her. Since they were not moving at the moment, she had a chance to relax and get her breathing under control.

26

"Ever been in combat?"

"Yes, sir. Had to hunker down and wait to be rescued once, but nothing like this."

"You scared?"

"Shitless, sir."

"Me too. Me too."

Chapter 5

Vee and Chappie maneuvered their way down the dark system of halls toward the command center. When there was no natural light, they used the infrared scopes on their rifles and night vision built into their respirators. The only sounds were distant explosions, their breathing, and their own footfalls as their boots crunched on debris.

It had been well over a century since the Alliance military had engaged in major combat operations. The occasional planetary squabble or typical peace-keeping operation was the most Fleet usually had to contend with.

Their standing order was to provide protection for scientists, off-world colonists, miners, dignitaries, and military brass. The closest thing anyone had come to actual combat was against primitive indigenous life forms like the dinosaur-like creatures on the volcanic world of Vulcania IV, or rampaging animals, giant insects, and rock-like creatures on other worlds. But this was different. An attack like this one was a new experience for them.

Someone or something with superior intelligence was attacking them with sophisticated weapons and advanced technology.

It did not take long for Vee and Chappie to reach the main doorway leading into a large room. The nerve center of Command and Control. One of the double sliding doors was lying on the floor. Vee checked her display readout.

"According . . . to this, sir, there . . . are about . . . a dozen people in there. What . . . should we do?"

The final leg of their trek was the hardest for Vee. She fought hard for every breath.

Chappie pointed his rifle toward the door. The readings on his display matched with hers. Trying to sound upbeat, he said, "Let's introduce ourselves."

He called out in a low whisper. "Is there anybody here?"

"Over here," someone said.

With Vee leaning most of her weight on him, they stepped through the broken doorway and emerged into a large room the size of an auditorium. It was illuminated by sunlight streaming through a massive hole in the roof. Scattered around the room were a dozen individuals both military and civilian.

Two marines stationed near the door rushed over to help Vee. They carried her to a nearby office desk and helped her sit on the floor next to it. She leaned against it, relieved to be off her feet.

"Who's in charge here?" Chappie asked.

"I was, sir." The gray-skinned young man who responded stood at attention next to the console he had been sitting at. Chappie suspected he was not that much older than Vee. He walked over to the marine and glanced down at the name patch on the young man's uniform.

"At ease, Corporal Raqmar."

The young man relaxed his stance. Chappie looked over at the other marines in the room and said, "That goes for the rest of you." He turned his attention back to Raqmar. "Fill me in. What the hell happened?"

Raqmar told Chappie that he had been working at the engineering station when reports started coming in from all over the planet that their installations were being bombarded from the air by unknown aggressors.

"They were simultaneous strikes. Too much of a coincidence to be a natural phenomenon," he said. Raqmar explained how they lost communication with each installation around the planet almost all at once. "The attacks were swift and coordinated," sir.

"So we still don't know who's attacking us?"

"Correct, sir."

"That's bullshit. We all know who's fucking attacking us. It's those cold-blooded Sairidian bastards."

The outburst came from an older pale-skinned Terran male. Chappie estimated he was somewhere in his late fifties. He had thinning disheveled gray hair sprinkled with a stingy amount of black. The guy's attire consisted of a pair of black slacks with matching jacket, powder blue shirt, and a very expensive-looking pair of black shoes. Chappie figured he was some kind of manager or administrator.

Chappie ignored the outburst and continued questioning Raqmar. "Any chance of a rescue from Fleet?"

"Our communications are being jammed, but a couple of messages did get through before the jamming screen went up. A few ships close to our location responded."

29

"What's their ETA?"

"Unknown. Sorry, sir."

"What have you been doing in the meantime?"

"Searching for survivors, rations, and bringing them here. The rest of this place is a wreck. This room seemed like the safest place to be—all things considered. We've also been keeping track of movement outside of the building, and waiting for support and relief, sir. The proximity sensors are still working and so is one camera. We knew you and the corporal were coming." He gestured toward Vee.

"What else is still working?"

"The communications station still works. We can't send or receive because of the jamming; we don't have equipment strong enough to punch a hole through the jamming screen."

"That's it?"

"Yes, sir. All we can do is sit and wait for a rescue and pray that whoever is attacking doesn't find us in here before help arrives."

"Fat chance," the pale-skinned Terran whimpered.

"Shut up, Hendley." The admonishment came from a Terran female. Her clothing was similar to Hendley's. Her hue was a shade tanner than his. She stared at him with angry eyes.

Hendley was the name of the Terran whose earlier outburst interrupted Chappie when he questioned Raqmar.

"Fuck you, bitch," was Hendley's reply. "We're all going to die here and there's not a damned thing we can do about it."

"We've got movement outside!" one of the other civilians said.

Chappie pegged her for a scientist of some kind and not a miner because of the obligatory lab coat she was wearing.

"Multiple unknowns approaching the building," she continued. "Very low heat signatures."

"Check the camera," Chappie ordered.

"It's the reptiles."

There was a gasp from someone as the room went quiet. No one spoke.

Chappie could see them on the monitor. Everyone could. There were various reptilian-looking creatures, all standing erect, wearing what appeared to be uniforms. They were also carrying what appeared to be weapons of some kind. It was a bizarre sight.

"That's it. We're all going to die. Lights out," Hendley blurted. He began crying.

Chappie knew there was a slim-to-none chance for survival, but he was not going to give up without trying to find that slim chance. "Shut the hell up!" Chappie said. Hendley flinched from Chappie's tone, but refused to be quiet.

"Maybe if we all just keep quiet and hide, they'll think no one is in here and they'll go away."

"I'm pretty sure they know we're in here," Chappie said.

But Hendley insisted his course of action was best.

Chappie was beginning to lose patience with Hendley. But before he could say or do anything, Raqmar offered his assistance.

"Permission to break this coward's scrawny neck, sir."

As much as he might have wanted to entertain the prospect, Chappie said, "That won't be necessary." He looked at Hendley then said, "Will it, Mister Hendley?"

Hendley was persistent. "Maybe we can reason with them. Maybe we can all surrender and they'll take us prisoner then let us go." Hendley was searching the faces around him looking for someone to take his side. There were no takers.

"Were you born yesterday?" Chappie asked. He couldn't believe he was wasting his time with this man. "Because the rest of us weren't. Those . . . those beings out there mean to kill us in here like they killed everybody out there. Now, if you think you can convince them to leave us alone, then get the hell out there and go make new friends. Otherwise, shut the hell up and do what you're told. Do I make myself clear?"

Hendley jutted his chin out and folded his arms in front of his chest in a silent act of defiance.

"Corporal Raqmar, you have my permission to—"

"Okay, okay," Hendley said. He weighed his options then decided to back down and withdraw into himself. He began whimpering. Tears dribbled from puffy eyes down his ruddy cheeks.

Chappie looked at the motley group in front of him. "Are there any other bright ideas?"

No one spoke. Chappie continued.

"I don't like this anymore than the rest of you. Am I scared? Damn straight I am. Do I want to die? Hell no. I don't want to die any more than the rest of you. So we're going to fight like dirty bastards until those damn rescue ships get here."

Chappie turned to the young scientist monitoring the sensors and asked, "How much time do we have before they enter the building?"

"About two minutes," she said. "Maybe three—and another two to reach this room at a fast trot."

"Let's pray they don't know how to trot. Where's the armory?"

"It's blocked, sir," Raqmar replied. "No time."

"Damn," Chappie cursed.

"What do we have with us?"

"Just what we're wearing, sir. And that's only the military personnel."

"How many of us is that?" Chappie was angry with himself for not making a full assessment of the people in the room when he entered with Vee.

"You, me, Corporal Vee, and Binkley and Smith over there." Raqmar gestured toward Smith and Binkley whose gray skin was as washed out as Raqmar's. They stood alert with firm grips on their PR10s pointed at the doorway.

"Grab any weapons and ammo off the dead in this room," Chappie ordered. "If you know how to use them, use them. Do any of you miners have any charges on you?" Two raised their hands. They reminded him of oversized Terran moles or the ground-burrowed tunnel rats on his own homeworld. "How many?"

The taller of the two said through a series of low pitched grunts, "We have four charges each."

"Good. Because we're going to need them as a last-ditch measure."

Chappie turned to look at Vee. She sat slumped on the floor half conscious.

"You still with us, Corporal Vee?"

"It's my leg, sir. I'm sure it's broken 'cause it hurts like hell."

"So, you lied. Lying to a superior officer is a serious offense. You know that, don't you?

"Yes, sir."

"Looks like you've given me no choice. I'm going to have to write you up when this is over."

"Yes, sir." The dejected look on her young face telegraphed a sense of despair.

He winked at her with an assuring smile. There was no way he was going to write her up. Hell. If they made it out alive, he was going to recommend her for a commendation or something.

Once she recognized he was joking, she tried her best to smile.

"Can you sit up?" he asked.

"Yes, sir."

"Good. Rest your back against something and take aim at that door. Nothing cold-blooded gets through it. Understand?"

"Yes, sir."

"Okay, here's what we're going to do. Those of you who don't have a gun, grab something. Then get behind us. We'll hold them off as long as we can. When we're finished, those bastards will know not to fuck with us."

Chappie figured they had a snowball's chance in Hell of surviving, but he was not about to quit now. He did not want to die—at least not now and not this way. And he did not want anyone dying while he was in command. Their death's would be on his conscience. "If it comes down to hand-to-hand," he continued, "stay together and hit the bastards with every ounce of strength you have. You got that, Hendley?" Chappie glared at the quivering man.

Hendley stood in stark silence shaking like an old turbine engine.

"Do you want to live, mister?" Chappie asked.

Hendley stammered a yes and nodded his head. His eyes were red and puffy from crying, and he sniffled mucus as he nodded his head in agreement.

"Good. Then get with the program here."

Chappie was not sure whether he trusted Hendley standing behind him with a blunt instrument in his hand, but the alternative was not any better. He also was not sure if he was making the right decisions. This kind of thing was new to him. He had never been in a life-threatening situation before, and to have others sharing the same fate, and whose fate depended on what he decided to do made him feel worse. Chappie shook off the feeling and got busy orchestrating the little group's defense.

Those who could not walk were given something to use like a club and told to swing at anything that looked like shins or knees.

The others found whatever they could lift like pipes, broken furniture parts, or tools. They worked together and erected a barricade in front of the door from what was left of the furniture and equipment then waited in silence.

The young scientist who was monitoring the proximity sensors whispered, "Here they come." Her voice cracked when she spoke.

Chappie heard the sounds grow louder and closer to the group's little refuge as the debris in the hallway was pushed aside. His weapon's motion tracker indicated a large number of signatures moving their way.

We are so screwed, he thought.

Chapter 6

The dream seemed so real. So much so that Chappie flailed in his bunk. He sensed he was not conscious. He knew he was alive and fought desperately to gain full awareness. In the distance he could hear someone calling his name and rank.

"Commander, Chappie! Commander, Chappie!"

Each time he heard his name it was spoken with more urgency. He felt like he was deep underwater and was struggling to reach the surface to breathe. He focused his attention on the voice. It belonged to Myra.

He calmed his mind and concentrated on reaching her voice until he was able to break through the surface of his dream. He sat up on his bunk like a spring and looked around his room. The lights were on full. His heart was pounding in his chest and sweat dripped down him like he had just worked out in the gym. *Damn*, he thought. *Not again*.

Myra had been monitoring his vital signs while he slept. She called out to him the moment she detected an alarming increase in his pulse rate. Her concern turned to abject dismay when his heartbeat fluttered and grew weak. At one point, it stopped before it began beating again. Myra immediately contacted the doctor, then raised the lights to their highest level and set the room temperature to a warmer level more suitable to his species.

This was not the first time her commander had awakened from a bad dream, but it was the first time he had a violent reaction to one and appeared not able to awaken from it.

Myra greeted him with a pleasant, "Commander, are you alright? Shall I call for medical assistance?"

Though his heart was still racing, his breathing unstable, and still somewhat disoriented, Chappie told her he was alright. "I'm okay. No need to call the doctor."

"This is the first time you have come dangerously close to flatlining in a dream. I strongly suggest you seek help for whatever is bothering you."

"Negative on the help. I don't need it."

"Are you sure, sir? You do not sound convinced."

"I'm sure."

"Okay."

35

Myra's reply did not sound like she was convinced he was okay.

He sat straighter in his bunk and calmed himself. Once his mind had assured itself that he was indeed okay, Chappie began to feel more like himself. He took a few more deep breaths before he spoke again.

"Myra?"

"Yes, sir?"

"What time is it?"

"Zero two hundred, sir."

"How long did I sleep?"

"Approximately twelve hours."

"What? Twelve hours?"

"Yes, sir."

"Why didn't you wake me up?"

"Doctor's orders."

He could not believe he had slept that long. Then he thought about the reason why he might have slept for so long. "You gassed me in my sleep, didn't you?"

Myra sounded offended when she said, "No, sir. I most certainly did not. There was no need. You fell asleep within five minutes of my delivering the doctor's orders. You remained asleep until I attempted to wake you from your . . . dream."

"Humph," was all he said in response. He did not sound convinced.

Myra tried a new tactic. She decided to divert his attention away from his sleeping and dreaming to something else.

"Commander?"

Chappie swung his legs over the side of the bunk, sat on its edge, and rubbed his eyes before responding.

"Yes?"

"The star charts that you requested from Fleet arrived."

They sure took their sweet time about sending them, he thought.

His fatigue subsided when she told him the news about the star charts. It gave him something else to think about instead of being pissed at himself for having slept so long. Myra had waited until she was certain he had recovered from his dream before she delivered the news about the charts.

"Myra."

"Yes, commander."

"Run an analysis of the charts and compare them with the ones Astro Cartography took today, uh, yesterday, note any discrepancies, and send what you find to my workstation only."

"Already done, sir."

"Already done? I haven't asked you to do it yet."

"The captain did, sir. He anticipated what you were going to do."

"Shit," he replied. Feeling a little dejected and somewhat useless at the moment, he sat on the edge of the bed uncertain what to do next.

"I suggest that you get your shift started with a soothing shower, followed by a satisfying meal, and then perhaps an hour in the gym, then—"

"What the heck are you doing?"

"Following orders. sir."

"Let me guess. Sanchez?"

"Correct."

Despite Myra's cheery voice, Chappie could feel his mood curdling like sour milk. He sighed. "Let me guess. Those suggestions are really orders."

"Correct again. The doctor said I was to tell you not to report for duty before the captain requests your presence."

"She made that an order too, didn't she?"

"Correct again, sir. At the request of the captain."

This time there was no doubt in his mind that Myra was taking great pleasure in his predicament. *You smug collection of data bits*, he thought. He got up off the bunk stripped out of his fatigues and strode into the bathroom.

Chappie leaned on the sink, stared into the mirror, and looked at the green face that stared back. He guessed his chlorophyll levels must have been low as his hue looked a bit pale. He was the equivalent of a fifty-year-old Terran, but he felt like a man twenty years older. He had dark circles under his eyes, and beads of sweat on his forehead. Chappie looked down at his still-shaking hands and remembered what he tried to forget.

For more than a decade, he had been able to tuck away the incident on Terra II until a week ago. The bad dreams returned when they arrived at Aggro Nine. The dreams got worse after Captain Vee passed along her intel about the hidden Sairidian base. He looked away from the mirror, turned and stepped into the shower and let the warm water wash the night's memories away.

When he had showered and dressed, he felt more like himself.

"How are you feeling, sir?" Myra asked.

"Better."

"Good. Because there is something else I must tell you."

Chappie raised his eyebrows, folded his arms across his chest, and prepared himself for whatever she was about to say. There was caution in his voice when he asked, "What is it?"

"While you were in the throes of your dream, I contacted Doctor Sanchez."

"You what?" He was more surprised and annoyed than angry. "Why?"

"Because your heart stopped."

Whatever he planned to say as a retort vanished from his mind.

"Okay, what did the good doctor say?"

"You can ask her yourself. She is outside your quarters."

At that moment, the door buzzer sounded. Before he could protest, Myra opened the door and Sanchez walked in.

She was a Terran with long flowing black hair speckled with strands of gray. It waved behind her as she strode into his quarters. Her almond brown hue complimented the light blue medical uniform and matching lab coat. Considered short even by Terran standards, the manner by which she carried herself was nevertheless intimidating.

Chappie was captivated by her the first time they met. She always made him feel weak and mushy inside whenever she was near.

"Myra told me you died. How's it feel being back among the living?"

Whatever bravado he felt melted into nothing. Being in her physical presence stripped away all of his defenses. No one else ever made him feel that way.

"She said my heart stopped."

"Close enough. Now sit.

He sat.

She grabbed a nearby chair and dragged it over so she sat directly across from him. She waved a medical wand around his body and studied the readings. Satisfied with the results, Sanchez looked him straight in his eyes and said, "Now, we're going to talk about what's bothering you before we go see the captain."

"You go straight for the heart of the matter, don't you?"

"I'm a surgeon and a psychologist. In my professional experience, I find getting straight to the matter saves lives and time. And just to be clear, I'm invoking doctor-patient confidentiality. Besides that, my security clearance is the same as yours. Now spill."

After a moment's hesitation, he began to tell her about his dreams.

Chapter 7

Sanchez listened with undivided attention as Chappie recounted his dreams. Much of what he told her she already knew from personal experience. She was among the support crews on the relief ships that were sent to Terra II to rescue the survivors of the attack. Chappie was one of the few who survived; he had also been her patient.

As he described his dreams, she noted that they had become more vivid. He remembered every sound, smell, feeling. He was not just dreaming about what happened, he was reliving the experiences. What she needed to learn was why the dreams were occurring with increasing frequency and so forcefully.

"So what you're saying is what happened to Delta Squadron precipitated the return of strong memories of what happened to you on Terra II?"

"Yes."

"And the message you got from Captain Vee magnified the trauma you experienced?"

"Yes."

"Your anxiety and your reaction to current events is pushing you to focus on worst case scenarios. Couple that with how you've been pushing yourself lately, and you've got a recipe for an eventual nervous breakdown."

"But why am I experiencing the dreams and not just dreaming?"

"Your mind is preparing you for what's to come. Subconsciously, you're not ready to face your fears. You're unwilling to admit to yourself that the Alliance we both know and love could be gone tomorrow and there might not be a damned thing we can do about it."

"So what can I do about that?"

"For starters, stop feeling like you have to be the one to save the day. Then you have to come to terms with the very possible reality that nothing you do—or any of us, for that matter—will be able to do anything to save the day. The day may not be able to be saved."

Chappie stared at the floor for a few seconds before he looked at Sanchez. His eyes glistened. He looked away afraid she would look beyond his eyes and see through to his tortured soul.

The air between them was filled by one of those long, awkward pregnant pauses that indicated something was not quite right.

His recent dreams brought the trauma of his experience on Terra II flooding back. At the time, it was the closest he had ever come to facing death. And now all of those memories threatened to overwhelm his sanity. He believed he had beaten and expunged the demons that haunted him, but he realized they had lurked in the dark recesses of his mind. Hiding until the time was ripe for them to return.

The doctors at the hospital had given him a clean bill of health following his rehabilitation for his physical injuries, but the mental ones were more difficult to heal. The shrinks said his mental scars would improve in time with the help of medication. And they almost did. But now they manifested themselves in his dreams. And the dreams were getting worse.

Sanchez took one of his hands and placed it in both of hers.

"Chap, you're not alone in this. We're all in this together."

Ever since the events on Terra II, she and Chappie had an odd relationship.

They first met in the middle of a combat zone. But Sanchez was the only one of the two of them who remembered their actual first encounter.

She started out as one of the doctors on the trauma team who worked on saving his life and those of the other survivors. Eventually, she became his psychologist.

They spent hours working one-on-one mending his mental scars long after the physical ones had healed. Sanchez knew things about him that no one had ever known. It was the confidentiality of their relationship that resulted in an unrequited intimacy. They were not what others would call friends with benefits, but Sanchez had harbored feelings for him that she had spent a decade hiding.

She was drawn to his quiet nature and strong sense of duty. He placed the needs of others before his own. Sometimes to his own detriment.

Sanchez could not pinpoint the exact moment when she became attracted to him, but it was some time during Chappie's recovery that she developed feelings for him that went beyond what she normally felt for her patients. She often wondered if he harbored similar feelings for her or if he just considered them to be good close friends with a special bond.

Soon after his recovery, he was reassigned. She stayed in touch and followed his career closely. Whenever their paths crossed, they would spend time together. Most times they would have dinner together at a quiet but public venue. He would escort her back to her quarters where they would share a quick hug and kiss before he went off and left her wondering what if.

Their times together, however short, were meaningful to her. And at the moment, her personal feelings for him threatened to override her professional restraint.

They sat in awkward silence holding hands and staring at each other when Myra broke the silence and reminded them they were due to meet with the only other person privy to Vee's message. The captain of the *Vindicator*.

Sanchez was relieved when Myra interrupted what could have become an awkward moment.

"Okay, then, if we're finished here, we shouldn't keep the captain waiting," Sanchez said. "Shall we?"

She released her grip on his hand and stood up. He continued to sit and stare.

Chappie's mind appeared to be somewhere else. He cleared his throat, stood and said, "You're right. We shouldn't keep the captain waiting." He gestured toward the door and said, "After you."

Chapter 8

Captain Tranyxx sat in a lounge chair in a corner of his ship's situation room listening to the relaxing sounds of ocean waves crashing along a beach.

The situation room was where Tranyxx did a lot of his thinking. He preferred it to his quarters.

The tan-colored room, located a level below the *Vindicator's* bridge, was illuminated by the soft glow of diffused ceiling lights. A standard conference table with a three-dimensional holo-projector suspended from the ceiling took up most of the available space. Palm trees framed the two sets of doors located on each end of the rectangular room. The captain sat on one side of the table facing three windows.

He refused to sit with his back toward a door or window. Tranyxx attributed this particular personality quirk to Terran culture.

Aside from the blatant stereotypes and racist tropes, he was a fan of an ancient cinematic genre the Terrans called Westerns. In many of these theatrical displays, the so-called good guys and bad guys would sit facing doors and windows so they wouldn't be ambushed from behind.

He had grown up on a world where everyone lived together in cooperative communities. Each member served the greater good of the whole. Mutual trust, common defense against species unrelated to their own. He often wondered how Terrans managed to survive after spending so much time, money, and effort warring with itself.

For a species that shared the same DNA, physical characteristics, and common goals, they had spent so much of their planetary development destroying each other and nearly their planet. They should have been far more advanced than they were.

Captain Tranyxx was glad Terrans survived because he found them to be the most intriguing species in the Alliance. But right now his thoughts were on his two best officers and closest friends.

He was most concerned for Commander Chappie; his friend's recent dreams disturbed him. He was afraid the commander would have a relapse or meltdown.

Tranyxx asked Sanchez to keep an eye on him and do whatever she deemed necessary to keep the commander grounded. But after Chappie revealed what Captain Vee told him about what she and her crew discovered about the GSE, Tranyxx was even more concerned.

The rather unique relationship Sanchez had with the commander was what the *Vindicator's* captain counted on to help Chappie keep his head in the game.

Tranyxx's communications console chirped. He waved one of his six appendages over its surface.

"Yes, what is it, Ensign Banks?"

His native voice and language consisted of a series of clicks and chitters. It was electronically modified and enhanced by a translator hidden behind his mandibles. Despite the pleasantness of the translated voice, there was still a harshness to it. His voice sounded like sandpaper when compared with the youthful voice of the young ensign.

"Myra reports Commander Chappie and Doctor Sanchez are on their way. They should arrive at the situation room momentarily, sir."

"Thank you, ensign."

He waved his appendage over the console to turn off the communicator.

While most other species comprising the bulk of biological life in the Alliance more or less resembled what was accepted as average humanoid characteristics, Captain Tranyxx and his people resembled what were considered insects on most other worlds. The captain looked like an oversized ant reclining in an office chair.

As he sat contemplating his next moves, he clenched his mandibles and twitched his antennae while he thought back to the first time he met Chappie and Sanchez.

He was the head of security on the *Potomac* back then and had led the ground assault to rescue survivors of the attack on Terra II.

Sanchez, newly assigned to the medical staff on board, was embedded with his unit. His rescue team was composed of four squads of experienced soldiers assigned to search for survivors and restore operations in the Command and Control Center.

He personally selected everyone on his team for the mission. His people were already familiar with the Sairidians and GSE tactics.

He recalled how that rescue almost did not happen.

Chapter 9

"We have to cut through the interference," Tranyxx said. He was almost frantic. His translator was having trouble keeping up with his chittering. "Boost the gain on the receiver. Boost the gain."

All signals were being jammed. There had been no communication from anyone on the planet after the attacks began. His friend was on that planet and he was determined to mount a rescue or die trying.

As the ship's head of security, it was his responsibility to protect everyone on board and anyone he was ordered to protect. In Tranyxx's mind, everyone not presently attacking Terra II needed to be protected. He wanted to mount a rescue to the planet and search for his friend.

"The system is already at maximum, sir. There's no way to boost it any higher."

"Dammit, Thompson. Find a way through or around it."

"Yes, sir."

The ship shuddered as it was hit by an energy pulse. Everyone standing either stumbled or fell to the deck. Another shudder rocked the ship making it harder for people to stand back up.

Tranyxx did better than most on the bridge. Having six legs helped. He looked at Thompson.

Nervous stress crept into the communications officer's voice as he attempted to punch through the subspace jamming field.

"Nothing yet, sir."

He adjusted and recalibrated the communication system in a desperate effort to comply with Tranyxx's order.

While Thompson tried to re-establish communications, Tranyxx turned and addressed his captain.

"Permission to put together search and rescue teams, sir."

Captain Kormak held up a warning finger as two more energy bolts rocked the ship. Kormak could have passed for a Terran were it not for his blue skin, hair, and eyes. These characteristics were indicative of a species that did not require the higher oxygen content everyone else breathed. He wore a respirator that filtered out the excessive air molecules over his nose and mouth.

Kormak looked Tranyxx up and down before he responded.

"Permission granted."

Tranyxx turned to rush out the nearest door when he was stopped by a direct order from his captain.

"I want you to personally lead the teams down to the planet."

"Yes, sir," Tranyxx replied a bit too enthusiastically.

Kormak raised his eyebrows then said, "Bring your ass back here in one piece, mister. I can't afford to have to train a replacement."

Tranyxx's reply was more subdued. "Yes, sir. I will, sir."

"Good. Now go do your job."

"Aye, sir."

More salvos hit the ship as sparks flew, people shouted, and emergency backup systems came online.

Tranyxx headed off the bridge and down the corridor toward a turbo lift. He tapped his communicator and contacted his chief assistant.

"Jimperson."

"Here, sir."

"Put together as many search and rescue teams as you can and meet me in the launch bay. We're going to the surface."

There was a brief pause before Jimperson responded.

"Now?"

"Yes, now."

"But, sir, there's a good chance none of the rescue ships make it to the surface in all this."

"There's a good chance none of the people on the surface will make it if we don't."

There was another brief pause before Jimperson said, "As good as done, sir."

"Good."

Back on the bridge, Kormak and his staff were busy fighting off the enemy ships that had attacked Terra II. They were the closest Alliance ship in range of the planet at the time the SOS was sent. Naturally, they were the first of the vessels dispatched to engage the enemy.

At the moment, they were the only Alliance ship to arrive. They were taking a vicious pounding but holding their own.

"Let's keep this bucket of bolts together long enough for the rest of the fleet to arrive," Kormak said.

Captain Kormak was a good man and an experienced officer. And at the moment, he felt himself lucky to be in command of the *Potomac*. The ship was in a fierce battle and holding its own. It didn't hurt that the *Potomac* was also a dreadnought class ship. It was much bigger than its opponents and more heavily armored and shielded. Though not as fast or maneuverable, but sturdy enough to take the pounding.

There were numerous hull breaches, but its enormous bulk was their one saving grace. Emergency blast doors were shutting off the areas of the ship now exposed to space. A much lesser ship would have been pulverized by now. They were fighting it out alone because they were the first ship to arrive. But Kormak knew that eventually size would not matter and time would be against them if help did not arrive soon.

There were initially three enemy ships. The *Potomac* got lucky and caught the first one by surprise. Either the captain of that vessel was not worried about a confrontation, since previous encounters resulted in the destruction of the Alliance ship or they were caught completely unaware as they were still bombarding the research facility and sending small atmospheric craft to the surface when the *Potomac* arrived. All it took was one clean shot and the enemy ship was dust. The other two ships immediately fired on Kormak's ship.

As the *Potomac* shook and shuddered, the ship's helmsman did her best to avoid enemy fire. Ensign Sparks' thin webbed fingers danced along her console as she maneuvered the enormous craft through a series of moves that gave them additional precious seconds. They needed to stay alive long enough for the other Alliance ships en route to arrive.

Kormak monitored his tactical data displayed in one of the arms of his captain's chair. It registered numerous hull breeches, systems failures, and equipment damage, as well as personnel losses and injuries.

He issued commands to his bridge staff and coordinated with medical, engineering, weapons control, and life support. He made adjustments, estimates, and best guesses, as the casualty reports came in.

"Keep her steady, Sparks," the captain said. "Pivot! Pivot! She's trying to target our starboard side."

Sparks' hands were a blur as she struggled to compensate for the sluggish responses of the *Potomac*. The ship was never designed for the type of combat maneuvers she was being asked to perform.

"Keep our forward guns trained on her and fire a delta pattern spread."

"Aye, sir. What about the other one?"

"She's smaller and her weaponry isn't as strong. Keep the bigger one in front of us."

"Yes, sir."

Sparks was deftly punching in codes on her console. Her normally aqua green hue was bright green. The *Potomac* struggled to swivel. Sparks tried to keep her stronger opponent in front of them.

Despite Spark's best efforts and the weightlessness of space, the ship's massive bulk made her sluggish. The stress on the engines was enormous. The hull strained and groaned as the ship was asked to perform maneuvers her builders never intended.

The smaller vessel trained its guns on the *Potomac's* port side and peppered it with a series of devastating blasts. The strain on the shields took its toll as the smaller ship found a hole in the defensive shield and perforated the hull. The shielding was as effective as paper.

The bridge was enveloped in darkness before the emergency lights clicked on.

The captain yelled, "Fire everything we've got!"

The officer at the tactical station hit a button and the ship recoiled as the guns fired.

Energy pulses streamed out into space like tracer fire at night. Some hit their target, but most disappeared into the void. The *Potomac* rocked and shuddered again as the enemy ship returned the favor.

"Captain," the damage assessment officer said, "I don't know how much more of this we can take. The shields are down to twenty percent." As if to punctuate the statement, a large explosion rocked the *Potomac*. It came from within the ship. "Make that fifteen percent."

Not deterred, Kormak said, "We're going to take whatever we can until we can't."

The ship shuddered and protested a few more times before Thompson yelled from the communication station, "Captain! The fleet is here!"

There were cheers all around the bridge.

"Good. Now we should be able to dish out some of what we've been taking."

The tactical officer's console registered multiple signals appearing behind the *Potomac*. They all targeted the enemy ships and fired weapons simultaneously.

The tactical officer looked up from his console and at the view screen to confirm his readings. "The smaller ship's been hit bad, sir," he reported. A moment later, the bridge lit up from the blinding light from the explosion of the smaller vessel.

The other enemy ship appeared to list. It maneuvered to evade and run, but was struck mid starboard. An energy beam from the *Ronald McNair*, looked more like a welder's torch as it sliced the ship into two sections. There was a second tremendous flash of light as bright as a sun and then nothing. Debris floated where two ships once had been.

The bridge crew cheered upon seeing the explosion and watched it fade away as the vacuum of space extinguished the flames. Thompson shouted through the cheers. "The jamming signal has stopped, Captain."

"Excellent," Kormak said. He punched a button on his chair and said, "Mr. Tranyxx, get your ass over to the *Hawking* and down to that planet and rescue our people."

"Aye, sir." He was familiar with the *Hawking*. It was the first ship he served on after graduating from the Academy. It was a space-based supercarrier for every vehicle imaginable. From fighters to all terrains to submersibles, the ship had it all. The *Potomac* had four shuttles and six fighters. The rest were lifepods.

"Thompson," Kormak said.

"Sir."

"Contact the *Hawking* and tell them to prepare to receive the teams."

"Yes, sir."

Traynxx, Jimperson and the rescue teams had all reached the launch bay when the captain relayed the good news.

Jimperson smiled and nodded at Tranyxx. They boarded the shuttles and flew over to the *Hawking*.

Tranyxx briefed his counterpart, boarded the rescue craft, and headed for the planet. Every ship in the fleet was emulating the process. On their way to the surface, he surveyed the destruction. Based on what he saw, it would be a miracle if they found anyone alive. The Sairidians ground troops were still pressing their attacks despite the lack of air support. Soon, the Alliance would also have boots on the ground.

The strategy was to hit the enemy from the air, drop in and assault them from the ground, and pull their people out fast. Dead or alive. Tranyxx's destination was the main compound where Command-and-Control was located. He was determined to find his friend alive. When the shuttle entered the planet's upper atmosphere, it was buffeted by winds and atmospheric friction. He hated atmospheric drops. When they broke through to the lower atmosphere, the buffeting stopped.

"We got the all clear to land in a secured section of the compound along the perimeter, sir," the pilot said.

"Go," Tranyxx ordered.

The pilot flew the rescue craft to a far corner of the compound away from the battle that was raging in the center of it. Tranyxx and the marines disembarked. They were met by the stench of death, a miserably oppressive humid heat, the buzzing and popping sounds of weapons fire, and a small ragtag group of battle-weary marines standing at attention. Their commanding officer saluted and addressed Tranyxx.

"Welcome to Hurston Base, sir," he hesitated then continued, "or what's left of it." He extended his arm and gestured toward the rest of the compound. There were bodies, both from the Alliance and GSE, strewn everywhere. The ground was scorched and pocked. The sounds of small arms fire could still be heard. The fighting sounded fierce. Smoke billowed in the air. "We were about to give up hope of any help arriving."

"Your help is here and more is on the way. What the hell happened here," Tranyxx glanced at the man's name patch, "Sergeant Sikes."

Sikes briefed Tranyxx on what happened, giving him a condensed version.

Tranyxx was desperate to know where his friend was. "Do you know Lieutenant Commander Chappie?"

"Yes, sir. He was bunking with me and my people when the attack began."

"Where is he? What happened to him?"

"He said he wanted to get to C&C so I gave him some firepower, ammo, and one of my marines and off they went."

"Where the hell is C&C?" Tranyxx had studied the base layout on the way in, but was not prepared for the level of destruction he witnessed. He thought it was in the center of the compound, but there was not much of anything left to be sure.

Sikes pointed to a broken and shattered building in the center of the compound. "There, sir."

Tranyxx's heart sank when he saw what the building looked like. C&C was where the last of the fighting was taking place. And judging from the condition of it, he wondered whether anyone who was inside was still alive. He had to get in there and find out.

"Begging your pardon, sir," Sikes said. "But if you're thinking what I think you're thinking, my people and I would like to go with you."

"Not necessary, sergeant. You and your troopers have done enough. Let the fresh boots do the rest."

"With all due respect, Lieutenant, we took a liking to the lieutenant commander. Besides, I want my corporal back as much as you want the commander back. We'll face a court martial before we just sit back and do nothing."

Tranyxx could not blame the sergeant for his loyalty and dedication to duty. He thought he probably would have done the same thing in the sergeant's position. If they wanted to slog through another fight, he was not going to stand in their way. As far as he was concerned, every little bit helped. And at the moment, Sikes and his troops were the most combat experienced.

"Okay, Sikes. You and your people saddle up."

Tranyxx got some inward satisfaction being able to use a phrase from those old Terran Westerns he enjoyed so much.

Tranyxx ordered his squad's sergeant to create a perimeter around the shuttle. He, Sikes, and the remaining marines would advance toward C&C. The perimeter of the building was guarded by reptilian defenders, most of which were gathered in front of what looked like the front entrance to the building. Tranyxx surmised it was the only way in and the reptiles were the only things standing in the way of rescuing those inside. He prayed that there were survivors still inside.

Tranyxx and his unit fired their weapons and pushed forward taking cover behind anything they could. The reptiles made them pay for every inch of real estate. Several marines were hit, but Tranyxx's group continued their slow advance toward C&C. They were backed up by new troops as more shuttles landed. When they were a grenade's throw away from the opening, Sikes popped up from behind a boulder he was able to reach and tossed one toward the opening. The explosion took out the remaining defenders. Tranyxx and his men made their way through the pile of bodies.

"If one of those things so much as twitches, blast it," he ordered.

The bulk of the squad reached the breach and paused long enough for the rest to catch up.

They used hand signals and one by one they entered the hole and took up positions on both sides of the hallway and fired at anything that remotely looked reptilian. Bolts of enemy weapons discharge blazed past them.

"Kill the motherfuckers!" someone yelled.

"Eat shit and die!" another marine yelled.

One bolt nicked the corner of Tranyxx's helmet, knocking it off his head.

Fortunately, he hadn't strapped it on. Otherwise, his head might have been severed from his body.

"Lucky bastard!" he heard someone say.

"You okay, sir?" Sikes asked.

"Yeah, yeah. I'm good," Tranyxx said. He was unnerved by how close the shot had come to ending his life.

One of the marines picked the helmet off the floor and handed it back to him. Tranyxx made a mental note to preserve the thing if he lived through this firefight. The marines stepped up the intensity of the fight.

The exchange of weapons fire was fast and furious. A few enemy bolts hit their targets as marines screamed in pain then hit the floor with thuds.

"Fuck 'em up!" someone yelled.

"Holy shit. I'm hit. I'm hit!" another screamed.

"We need a medic over here!" someone else yelled.

Blood, guts, and sweat were sprayed everywhere. The dead and wounded were pulled away from the action and replaced by fresh boots.

The hallway was lit up like a laser light show accompanied by moans and screams from combatants from both sides as energy beams and bullets burned and tore into flesh and bone. The labyrinth of halls did not help the marines slow push toward the command center.

Warm signature readings on their monitors and the fierceness of the defenders confirmed that they were moving in the right direction. The closer they got to the main room, the more excited Tranyxx's became. He prayed they would not be too late.

The final corner brought Tranyxx and his men face-to-face with a squad of reptiles positioned to defend the entrance to the main room. The hall dead-ended right where they needed to go. The close quarters made shooting next to impossible. In a move that Tranyxx thought was more desperation than tactically sound, the reptiles rushed the marines. The fighting was now hand-to-hand and the advantage was the reptiles. They moved slower, but they were much brawnier, bigger, and stronger. Tranyxx decided the move to charge them was calculated. The reptiles knew they had the strength advantage.

Growls, gurgles, crunching, grunts, groans, smacks, and thuds echoed in the confines of the virtual box they were fighting in. Tranyxx used the butt of his weapon to hit one of the reptiles in the face. A blow that would have killed an average biologic only stunned his opponent. Tranyxx reared back for a second attempt to use the butt of his gun, but was backhanded by his adversary and tossed backward as easily as a child would throw a small toy. He felt like he'd been hit with a bat. He lost his grip on his weapon as he felt himself go airborne then fall to the floor.

He was grabbed and dragged across the floor. Dazed and in pain, all he could think of was that this was the end. He was not going to live long enough to rescue his friend. Relief swept over him when he realized he was grabbed by hands that were not reptilian. Then he heard a voice.

"To hell with this shit. Get out the way! Get out the way!"

Anyone who could, ran or dropped to the floor.

Tranyxx heard the scuffling of feet and then he heard the voice again. It was Sikes.

"Kill the fucking bastards now! Fire!"

The command was followed by a barrage of weapons fire. It seemed to go on forever. He could hear the screams of those on the receiving end of that weapons fire. Reptilian screams. The sounds of the guns discharging echoed off the walls in the small enclosure. The sound was deafening. As abruptly as it began, the firing stopped. Tranyxx's senses began to return to normal as he saw the last of the enemy fall to the floor. Now they could storm the room.

"You okay, sir?" Sikes asked.

"Yeah. Yeah. I'm okay now," Tranyxx managed to say. His speech was a little slurred, but he was regaining control of his senses with each passing second. He saw a group of marines enter the room and heard their shouts as they engaged the last remnant of resistance.

"Good. Let's go rescue my corporal and the commander."

Sikes handed Tranyxx back his weapon and asked, "Ready?" Tranyxx shook his head and charged through the door with Sikes at his side. Tranyxx burst through the open door in time to see his friend's limp body being lifted into the air and tossed to the floor. Horror-struck and angry, he let out a primal yell and fired.

***

He remembered it as if it happened yesterday. All he had to do was think about what happened while wide awake. He tried not to imagine how Chappie felt as those memories invaded his sleep.

Tranyxx's recollections were interrupted when the buzzer to the situation room rang. He activated the communicator and said, "Come."

In walked Chappie and Sanchez. Now the serious work would begin.

Chapter 10

Vee pushed herself off the doors to her quarters and walked over to the window next to her workstation and stared out at the nebula.

"Sojourner, privacy mode, please."

"Privacy mode engaged."

For the next minute or two, Vee continued to stare out into space without saying anything. Sojourner, the ship's SI, waited patiently before breaking the silence with a question.

"May I inquire as to the nature of your request for privacy, Captain, if there is no conversation for which privacy is needed?"

"Huh? Oh, sorry. I've been a little preoccupied."

"I can tell, sir."

"I'd like you to include Ramie in this conversation."

"I am here, Captain. What can I do to assist?"

"That's the thing. I don't know what either of you can do because I don't know what to do."

She turned from the window, sat at her workstation, and continued speaking.

"A few months ago, or weeks ago, or days ago, or whenever the hell it was, I did . . . or thought I did. But now, I'm not sure what to do."

Vee's uncertainty stemmed from what she and her crew thought would be a rescue mission that turned into an accidental trip into the past.

The friends they went to rescue did not need to be. They were living productive lives, and had been for what to them was more than a decade. To Vee and her crew, it was just a matter of days. The universe their friends lived in existed within another plain of time.

The *Infiltrator* was on its way home when a freak accident nearly destroyed the ship.

Two crew members were lost and Vee and the survivors were sent three months back into time in their own universe. She felt it prudent at the time to hide out on Sigma II. Sigma II was a desert world where her sister ran a clandestine operation from a camouflaged boom town deep in the middle of nowhere on one of its southern continents.

Planetary authorities allowed the town, called Opportunity, to thrive as long as they got their cut of the profits. Most of Opportunity's inhabitants were displaced war refugees, smugglers, black market entrepreneurs, or people down on their luck who needed a place to get back on their feet.

The town had a strict code. Everyone had to take an oath to abide by the code to live there. No matter what they did to break established Alliance laws outside of Opportunity, within the town, extreme violence was prohibited. The occasional bar fight was viewed as a stress reliever to participants and spectators. If you valued your life, you were expected to respect the value others placed on their own.

Code violators were swiftly and severely dealt with by Opportunity authorities and by planetary authorities. The punishment was either banishment or execution.

Banishment meant being taken to the middle of nowhere with one day's rations.

Since eighty percent of the planet was desert, being exiled was the equivalent to being sentenced to death. Execution was quicker and more merciful.

Killing was not only considered bad for business, but bad for the mini city if Alliance officials ever found out.

Vee thought it was the best place for her crew to hide out and repair the ship. With her sister's help, they did just that. When the time came to leave, Vee left Sigma II with no idea what to do. But a near run-in with a cloaked GSE ship and an intercepted message her crew decoded revealed a sinister plan that threatened to end the war in weeks if not months. If the GSE was not stopped before they could execute their plan, the Alliance would fall.

"It seems to me, Captain, the only logical choice we have available to us is to proceed to Epsilon Base and assist Commander Chappie in whatever capacity we can."

"I concur," Ramie agreed.

She stood and paced back and forth before she spoke again.

"I have come to the same conclusion. I have also decided to tell the commander everything about what happened to us from the moment we entered this damned nebula to now."

"Do you think that is wise, sir?" Sojourner asked.

"I don't know, but I've given a lot of thought to it and I think someone besides us should know about the portal and the existence of another universe."

"Because we may need to defend it?" Ramie asked.

"Because we may need to escape through it."

"That may not be a wise thing to do, sir. If the Alliance loses this war and the GSE discovers the portal, we will be responsible for having opened the proverbial door for them to flood in and threaten another universe, not to mention family and friends living in it," Ramie said.

"I understand your concern for Cora and the others," Vee said. "But what happens if we don't say anything and they discover the portal anyway, then what?"

"Then it would be only us standing between an expansionist empire and a fertile universe incapable of defending itself from a callous aggressor," Sojourner said.

"Exactly."

After a few nanoseconds of thought, Sojourner suggested something Vee had not considered.

"What if there is an equivalent expansionist empire in the other universe strong enough to keep the GSE in check?"

Vee rubbed her chin in thought before she replied.

"They have the bantam fighter. Cora might be able to reverse engineer something they could use to camouflage their cities. After all, they did develop protective domes."

"It is all relative, Captain," Ramie said. "It all is contingent upon What If. What if there is a GSE-style empire in my home universe? What if the GSE in this one finds the portal? What if we succeed? What if we fail? What if?"

"You've painted an even bleaker picture than I imagined, Ramie."

"Sorry, sir."

"No, don't be. What you have suggested is the dose of incentive I need. The odds may be against us, but that's never stopped us from doing what had to be done."

"And what is that, sir?" Ramie asked.

"We're going to rendezvous with the *Vindicator*, then I'm going to take you back home where you can be of more use to your family and friends."

"I am not following your logic, Captain."

"You said it yourself. It's a matter of What If. What if there is a malevolent race in your universe that discovers the portal? What's stopping them from flooding into our universe if Cora and the others can't stop them? We're damned if we do, damned if we don't."

"I see your conundrum, sir."

Vee stopped pacing, took a deep breath and said, "I can't wait anymore, I've made my decision."

"Permission to speak freely, sir?" Sojourner asked.

"Always, Sojourner."

"Before you make it known what your decision is, I think I can speak for the crew when I say whatever you decide to do, we will support you in every way possible."

"Thank you. I will remember to hold you to that. Disengage the privacy screen and patch me through to the crew."

"Disengaged. You may speak when ready, Captain."

Vee took another look out the window before she announced herself and gave the crew their next order.

"Attention, everyone. In light of recent events, I'm sure you're all wondering what will happen next. I can't answer that question definitively, but what I can tell you is that we will not sit idly by as the GSE attempts to destroy everything we hold dear."

There was the expected obligatory response from Raqmar who shouted, "Alright!"

That was followed by Sparks who asked, "Orders, cap?"

"Keep us cloaked, maintain radio silence, and haul ass to Epsilon Base. Best possible speed. We're not that far behind the fleet. We'll catch up with them before they reach Epsilon Base."

Vee heard the excitement in her pilot's voice as Sparks responded, "Aye, cap."

An instant later, the stars blurred as Sparks jumped them into hyperspace.

"Permission to raise the privacy screen, Captain?" Ramie asked.

"Permission granted. What's on your mind, Ramie?"

"I could not help notice you were not forthcoming with your order to the crew. I also noted what you said, and I quote, 'I'm going to take you back home where you can be of more use to your family and friends.' May I ask what you have decided to do?"

"The only thing I can think to do. Rendezvous with the *Vindicator*, reassign the crew, take you back home, then destroy the portal."

Chapter 11

"There's a bandit on your six!" Markka shouted.

"I see it!" Leahcim said.

"It's closing! I won't reach you in time!"

"I know. I know," Leahcim said. The irritation evident in his voice. "Hang back. I'm gonna try something."

"Really? Are you serious? Double back and bring it my way. I'll trash it for you."

"No time! The bastard is almost in range. Wish me luck." Leahcim pushed his control stick and dove his bantam fighter straight down toward the ground.

"Pull up! Pull up!" Markka screamed. "You're too close to the deck!" Her heart felt like it was trying to pound its way out of her chest as she watched his fighter careen toward the planet's surface. "What the hell are you doing?" She was frantic.

"Saving your life."

The enemy pilot was fast approaching optimal range to fire its weapons at Leahcim when his fighter seemed to stop in midair. The enemy fighter, unable to slow down in time, flew past him. Its pilot arced their fighter in a sweeping turn upward. By the time it reoriented itself, Leahcim had locked his guns on it and fired. His reward was a brilliant fireball in front of him.

Leahcim activated his in-flight motivator, flipped a booster switch, and was rewarded with an ominous sputtering sound. Then his fighter stalled out and resumed its trajectory downward.

Markka watched in horror as Leahcim's fighter fell out of the sky. She screamed hysterically, "Bail! Bail!"

He yelled back, "I can't! They won't fire! They won't fire!"

"Pull the damn release!"

An instant later, the bantam fighter slammed into the ground.

Markka shook with anger as she flew over the impact cloud, circled the freshly made crater, and scanned the horizon for a parachute. All she saw was an expanding dirt cloud and scattered debris of what was once Leahcim's fighter. "Shit! Shit! Shit!" She slammed her paw on her flight-deck console and continued to curse in her native tongue, Uderran, and Alliance Standard before she said, "Cora, end simulation."

The crash site, the ground, sky, and mountains dissolved and revealed a plain white room. At one end sat Leahcim in a bantam fighter mock-up. Next to him sat Markka in a second fighter mock-up.

"You, bastard," she said. "All you had to do was double back like I said, and I could have trashed that fighter."

"And like I said, there wasn't time. My engine's power plant was overtaxed. I didn't have enough power to restart the engines when they stalled."

"Why didn't you bail?"

"The ejection rockets failed. I didn't have a choice."

"You should have pulled the manual release and popped the top. You had plenty of time to pull the emergency release. I could have covered your descent."

Markka was furious. She ripped off her helmet and continued to berate him. Her ears were folded back against her head and her whiskers twitched. Her grayish hair was standing straight out making her look more like a walking puffball than the regal queen of Uderra.

Leahcim, on the other hand, matched her anger with stubborn indifference. His dark eyes and black locks, sprinkled with generous flecks of gray, stared back at her from under his helmet. He was adamant that his decision, despite its outcome, was the prudent choice.

"Yeah, but you would have been too close to the surface. You would have been exposed and vulnerable."

Markka hissed before she said, "You aren't going to be satisfied until you get yourself killed. And when you do, don't come crawling back to me."

She glared at him with a stare that would have made the average person cower, but Leahcim just returned her stare. His smooth brown complexion revealed nothing but an impassive smile.

"It's nice to know you care," is all he said.

Markka huffed out an exasperated breath. "Dammit, David, what if that had been real? I'd be the one having to explain to T'oann why her hubby wasn't coming home."

"It could have easily gone the other way. And I'd be telling Tory why his wifey wasn't coming home."

A familiar voice intruded on their debate.

"Fortunately, it was just a simulation so you both get to come home."

Leahcim and Markka turned to see T'oann standing at the entrance of the simulation room. But unlike her husband, her mocha hue revealed a rather strong negative emotion on her face.

Leahcim tried to pretend he didn't see or feel the vibes his wife was emitting with just one piercing look.

"Oh. Hey, babe. How goes it?" he asked.

His question went unanswered as T'oann directed an icy, penetrating stare his way. He shrunk into the mock-up's cushioned seat.

Before Markka could say anything, T'oann turned her stare toward her as well. Markka was about to say something but thought it might be more prudent if she kept her mouth closed. She also shrunk back in her seat cushion. She felt that was the safest thing to do considering the mood T'oann appeared to be in.

"Oh, come on. Give us a break," Leahcim begged. "We have to run these simulations to anticipate every scenario. Sometimes the, uh, outcomes aren't always what we want them to be." He looked at his wife as a Terran puppy would. All wide-eyed, cuddly, and innocent.

Not able to stay mad at either of them for long, T'oann sighed in apparent surrender to his successful play on her emotions and asked, "But do they always have to be worst case scenarios? I have spent countless mos in the simulator and have not encountered nearly as many worst case scenarios as you both have."

"Because a worst case situation is the one thing no one trains for. Because no one wants to believe they'll ever be in one. Have you forgotten that it was a worst case situation that brought us together?"

T'oann's expression softened before she gave in and said, "No."

Leahcim, feeling absolved of guilt, turned to Markka and said, "See?"

All Markka did was grunt.

When neither his wife nor his queen said anything else, Leahcim asked Cora, their SI friend and protector, her opinion about the simulation.

"So, Cora, what's your opinion of the latest simulation?"

"Do you really want my honest assessment?" The soft melodic voice masked the scathing report she was about to deliver.

"Yes, I do."

"Okay. But remember you asked for it, commander."

"Oh get on with it already," Markka said.

"It sucked."

"That was rather . . . blunt," Leahcim said.

"You asked."

"Okay, give it to us in an objective report that's a wee bit longer and more detailed."

"Very well. The cycles of inactivity have muted the skills of both you and Markka. In the cycle since Captain Vee and the *Infiltrator* departed, you both have improved significantly. But your reflexes and reaction times are still subpar. You both are second-guessing yourselves. In the heat of battle, you must make a choice and commit to it."

"Geez," Markka complained. "Did we do anything right?"

"It is not a matter of whether you did something right, but more of a matter of whether you can make a decision in an instant and stick with it—no matter the outcome."

"Like what I did, right?" Leahcim asked.

"Yes, commander. You maintained your situational awareness, made a choice, and committed to it even when you knew what the outcome would be."

"What about me?" Markka asked.

"In your capacity as queen, you have become concerned, if not obsessed, with protecting the lives of your subjects. Had the commander listened to you and given you the chance at taking the shot, you both would have perished."

Markka protested. "I don't believe you."

"Then I will show you."

Cora activated the simulation from a third person perspective and replayed the action as it happened. Then she played a scenario as Markka wished for it to happen. Everyone watched as the enemy fighter destroyed Leahcim's fighter then did the same to Markka's.

After a few moments of silence, Markka admitted that Cora was right.

"Okay, I see your point."

"May I offer you both a suggestion?"

"Yes, you may," Leahcim said.

"Both of you are instinctive pilots and gunners. You must learn to trust your instincts again. It was your instincts which led us here to Progensha."

"If my memory serves me correctly," Markka began, "it was you and dumb luck that brought us here."

"I would not have had the opportunity had you not followed your instincts. And is not following your instincts the core rationale biologics base their belief in luck upon?"

"That and the will of the Goddess," T'oann said. She looked at her husband and sister-in-law and said, "Now if the two of you do not mind, it is time to address other matters. Cora and the simulator will be here tomorrow."

Leahcim and Markka climbed out of their fighter replicas and followed T'oann out of the simulator room without protest.

Chapter 12

T'oann led her husband and queen from the simulation room to a small hover parked just outside.

"Get in," she said. Her tone was pleasant but direct.

"Why?"Leahcim asked. His tone was a bit cagey.

"Yeah, why?" Markka asked. Like Leahcim, she wondered what T'oann was up to.

"I am not at liberty to say. You will find out soon enough, if you accompany me."

Leahcim and Markka looked at each other then back at T'oann, who waited for them to get in the transport.

It was out of character for the commander to be so guarded about something with the two of them.

"Okay," Leahcim said. "I'll play along." He stepped into the hover.

Markka was a bit more hesitant, but relented, got in and sat next to Leahcim. T'oann got in, sat across from her husband and sister-in-law, then ordered the driver to take them to Section Ten.

"Section Ten?" Markka asked.

"Yes," T'oann said. She was not forthcoming with any information.

Markka turned to Leahcim. "What the heck is Section Ten?"

"Section Ten is a top secret research division."

"So you're telling me the Uderran military has a black-ops division?"

"I wouldn't call it that exactly."

"Then what 'exactly' do you call it? Hmm? And how come I didn't know about this Section Ten?" Markka asked.

"It's a secret," Leahcim said.

"So much so that the queen doesn't even know it exists?"

"Yep."

Before Markka could continue her protest challenge, T'oann shut her down when she said, "It is known to only those who need to know. And you did not need to know."

"So you both knew about this Section Ten and never told me?" Markka was looking back and forth at Leahcim and T'oann.

"Plausible deniability. It was easier to keep you out of the loop so you wouldn't feel obligated to lie about not knowing about secret military tech you knew about," Leahcim said.

"Does Tory know?"

"Yes," T'oann said.

"Wait. Why does he know, but I don't? I am your queen, you know. How is it that my husband knows, but I don't?""

"You are also the face of the Queendom," T'oann said. "The people need to know that what you say is the truth, and that you are not hiding anything from them."

"But Tory—"

"Is not the face or voice the people see and hear."

"Yeah." Leahcim picked up the conversation. "So you see, if something was to go wrong, the only people to blame and take the fall would be everyone in the know."

For a full micton no one spoke as Markka absorbed what she just learned.

After a few moments of thinking about it, she said. "Okay, so if I'm not supposed to know, why are you taking me someplace I'm not supposed to know about?"

Leahcim looked over at his wife and said, "That's a very good question. Why *are* we going to Section Ten?"

T'oann swallowed hard before she responded. "Because . . . there was something being developed that *you* did not need to know."

He looked astonished as T'oann smirked at him when she told him he did not need to know.

"So," Markka said. She had a smug look written all over her face. "Looks like the man who seems to know everything there is to know didn't know about something he thought he should have known."

Speechless, Leahcim tossed a hurt look at his wife and stared at her.

Unable to look him in the eye, and caving under the weight of his stare, T'oann blurted, "It's a surprise."

"For who?" Leahcim asked. He noted her use of a contraction.

"For both of you."

He turned to look at Markka who had a smug look on her face and was childishly sticking her tongue at him.

Leahcim reached out and mind-walked with his wife and said, "Wait until we get home."

She replied in a seductive tone, "I'll be waiting." Then terminated their mental connection.

Leahcim noted she used another contraction. He wondered how she was successfully able to hide something from him in their mind-walks. That was difficult to do. He decided he would find out later. In a few moments, he was about to find out what she hid from him.

The hover stopped at the end of a maze of corridors. The three of them got out and T'oann tapped the side of the transport to let the driver know he could pull away.

"Cora, is everything prepared?" T'oann asked.

"Yes, commander. Everything is prepared. Everyone is ready."

"What's going on here?" Leahcim asked.

"Yeah, what's going on here?" Markka asked.

It was obvious something bigger than a little surprise was happening.

"Your questions will be answered soon," Cora said.

T'oann's face betrayed an almost imperceptible grin. Her eyes twinkled with amusement as she gestured for them to step through a lone reinforced door into a room that resembled a hangar. At the center of the room was a huge tarp hiding something beneath it.

Standing next to the tarp was a small and select group that included Markka's husband Tory, Leahcim's daughter Zora, and their friends Lin and Piper.

"Okay, what the hell is going on here?" Leahcim asked.

No longer able to contain herself, T'oann said, "I brought you both here to present you with a surprise. Much of the credit goes to Cora who conceived the idea and oversaw the reconstruction."

"Reconstruction? Reconstruction of what?" Markka asked.

"Of this," T'oann replied. She pressed a button on a handheld control and revealed what was under the tarp.

Both Leahcim and Markka stood in awe with their mouths open.

"Oh my god," Markka gasped. "She's beautiful."

Before she realized it, she was blubbering all over Leahcim. He, on the other hand, continued to stare as tears streamed down his cheeks.

"How?" His voice faltered before he regained his composure. "How the hell did you pull this off?" he asked.

"With a bit of ingenuity, clever surreptitiousness, and furtive misdirection, commander," Cora said. "We hope you like it."

"Like it?" Markka said, still blubbering. "We love it!"

Leahcim started to ask, "Is she—"

"Spaceworthy? Yes, she is. I put her through a baseline test myself."

"But how . . . ? She was trashed."

"Later, my husband," T'oann said. "Please enjoy this gift we all present to the both of you."

The gift T'oann referred to was the *Midnight Sun*. It was the Alliance starfighter Leahcim and Markka were found in when they crashed on Progensha more than twenty cycles ago.

Chapter 13

Once the shock of seeing their old fighter restored and fully operational wore off, Leahcim winked at Markka and asked T'oann, "Can we borrow the keys and take her out for a spin? We promise to be back before evening meal."

"I am going to hold you to it," T'oann said.

"Great!"

"I mean it."

"You're gonna hold us to it. Got it," Markka said. "You mean it. Got that too." She was almost dismissive in her comments to T'oann. She rubbed her paws together and said, "Come on. Let's go already."

"Cora? You wanna come along for the ride?" Leahcim asked.

"Yes, commander. I thought you would never ask."

"Liar," Markka said.

"Why, Markka, I am hurt that you would think that I am capable of lying."

"Would it be beyond your programming, or whatever you call it, to engage in subterfuge, misdirection, omission, and camouflage?"

"I would have to say in all probability, slim to none."

"Then what do you call what you did to us when your fighter crashed all those cycles ago?" T'oann asked.

"I simply misled you into believing you could contain me and my abilities. And I taught you how to save the lives of my shipmates."

"You lied," Markka insisted. "Like how you lied to keep this a secret from us. Now shut up and get aboard. We're burning daylight."

"Aye aye, Captain."

Markka leaned in close to T'oann and whispered, "Sometimes you gotta remind her who's boss."

"You do know I can still hear you?"

The two of them left the group and climbed aboard their old fighter.

"Wow, it's almost like coming home again." Markka was as giddy as a young child who just received the one thing they always wanted. "I can't believe she almost became our coffin."

"She could still be if we're not careful," Leahcim reminded her.

"You're such a spoilsport."

"Realist."

"Whatever."

They ran through pre-flight protocols then signaled they were ready to depart. Two huge doors at one end of the hangar slowly opened. Once they got clearance, Leahcim asked, "Everybody ready?" Cora and Markka both gave affirmatives. He lifted the fighter off the ground then punched it.

The fighter shot out of the hangar and headed toward the horizon. Leahcim flew a few quick circles around Progensha to gauge how the ship handled within the planet's atmosphere.

He remembered to fly far enough above the oceans to avoid being ensnared by one of the many leviathans that lived there. Once he got the feel of atmospheric flight, he headed into the vacuum of space. They were in orbit within mictons.

"Yee-haw!" Leahcim shouted. "Now that's what I'm talkin' 'bout." He looked over at Markka in the seat next to him and fist-bumped his gunner.

After having gotten used to the bantam fighter Vee had given them, being back in the cockpit of the *Midnight Sun* was exhilarating.

"I'd forgotten what it felt like to fly the old girl," Leahcim said.

"Me too," Markka agreed.

"What about you, Cora? Any feelings?"

"The first time we took flight in the bantam fighter I said I was sensing something bordering on euphoria. Now? I am sensing something you biologics might refer to as pure joy. Dammit, I am beyond elated."

Then Cora did something neither Leahcim nor Markka had ever heard her do before. She giggled.

"What the hell was that?" Markka asked. "Did she just giggle?"

"That she did," Leahcim said. "Come on. Let's see what this baby can do."

"As long as we're back in time for din-din," Markka teased.

"You got it."

Leahcim punched the accelerator controls and the *Midnight Sun* flew off into the Great Beyond ready to be put through its paces.

Chapter 14

Once the starfighter was safely tucked away in its hangar, Cora resumed her duties while Leahcim and Markka bantered back and forth about the flight.

"We'd have been back sooner if you had just made that left back at that asteroid field like I said," Leahcim said. "Geez, every time I let you drive, we get lost."

"If you weren't such a backseat driver I wouldn't have gotten distracted," Markka said with a fake air of indignation.

As the two ribbed and kidded each other about the flight, T'oann and Tory both stood at the end of the hangar waiting. Neither looked pleased.

Leahcim saw their spouses before Markka did. He lightly elbowed her, while she continued to ramble on about the trip in their starfighter.

"Hey!" she protested. Then gulped when she saw him nod toward T'oann and Tory waiting for them.

T'oann had her arms crossed in front of her and her eyes were squinted slits. Tory matched his sister's posture, but he patted one foot on the ground. A clear sign he was annoyed.

Markka whispered to Leahcim as the two approached T'oann and Tory. "We are in so much trouble."

"Speak for yourself."

They stopped in front of their spouses and gave them their best contrite smiles.

"Uh, hi, babe," Leahcim said.

"Hey, sweetness," Markka said.

Both T'oann and Tory gave them the silent treatment before T'oann broke the silence.

"Don't 'Hi, babe' me," T'oann said. The annoyance Leahcim detected in the tone of her voice was a clear sign she was serious.

"And do not 'Hey, sweetness' me," Tory said.

"You two said you'd be back before evening meal. It's well past that time." T'oann continued to squint, but she also furrowed her brows. "I hope you have a believable explanation."

Yikes, Leahcim thought. His wife was using contractions and it was not in jest. She also continued to squint. He swallowed hard.

Markka, on the other hand, found it difficult to look Tory in the eye. So she looked down at the ground and shuffled her feet. At that moment, she did not feel like the queen of Uderra, but more like a child about to be scolded for bad behavior.

Tory, who continued to pat his foot, said, "We're waiting."

Markka noted Tory used a contraction this time. *Oh crap*, she thought. *He's pissed to the highest level of pisstivity.* Then she said, "We, uh, got lost."

"Uh, yeah," Leahcim said. "We, uh, were star-charting the sector and sort of got turned around."

"Yeah, that's what happened," Markka added. She fluttered her eyes and put on her best pouty face. She was disappointed when Tory did not fall for her ploy.

"And you expect us to believe that you got lost because you are unfamiliar with the star placement in the Great Beyond?" Tory asked.

"Uh, yeah." Markka said.

"Despite the fact that Cora was on board?"

"Oops," Markka muttered.

"Well, to tell you the truth," Leahcim began, "we were having so much fun we forgot to ask."

"And whose fault is that?"

Mirroring each other, Leahcim and Markka pointed at the other and said it was the other's fault.

"It's *her* fault."

"It's *his* fault."

T'oann and Tory exchanged frustrated looks before Tory said, "Then you have given us no other choice but to banish you both to this hangar until morning light."

"Wait. What?" Markka asked, just as their spouses turned and walked out.

Leahcim and Markka stood and stared in disbelief as the door to the hangar closed behind T'oann and Tory. The last sound they heard was the lock click into place.

To add insult to injury, the hangar's main lights snapped off. They were left standing in a cavernous room lit only by dim nightlights.

They both glared at each other before, Leahcim said, "This is all your fault. I told you we should've hung a left at the asteroid field."

"Bite me."

Chapter 15

Just as the first rays of light from Progensha's two suns peaked over the hills, T'oann and Tory arrived at the hangar before the first shift came on duty. They were confident that their little punishment had taught the two a lesson.

"I hope this exercise will teach them to take our worries more seriously," T'oann said.

"I am quite certain it will."

When they approached the fighter, T'oann saw her husband and sister-in-law sleeping in their seats. Markka's paw rested in Leahcim's hand, which was wrapped around it. Seeing them that way brought a smile to T'oann's face.

"Look at the two of them. They were probably afraid of spending the night alone in this hangar," she said.

"Serves them right," Tory said. He was more stone-faced than his sister.

Almost as soon as Tory finished speaking, T'oann faltered, froze in place, and put a hand to her head.

"What is wrong?" The look of anxiety on his sister's face alarmed him.

"Seeing them this way reminds me of the first time I saw them. They were in nearly the same positions they are now, but then they were on the edge of death."

Memories of that sol seeped into her mind and caused her to both sweat and shiver. She stumbled and gasped.

Tory grabbed his sister and held her steady. "What is it?"

"I just had a strange feeling. As if something bad has happened."

"What? Are you able to tell me?"

"No. I have no particulars. Just a feeling."

"Could it be related to seeing them in this manner?"

"Perhaps."

"Are you willing to share the experience with me?"

She looked at Leahcim and Markka and thought there would be no harm in showing her brother what happened cycles ago. She shared what she knew in a mind-walk with Tory.

She showed him the visual records the mind probes had pulled from their minds back then. He watched in awe as he saw their battle with the GSE, their struggle to land on Progensha before they crashed, and the firefight his sister, B'rtann, Sho'khan, and Garath were involved in before Cora made contact with them.

"I had no idea it was that bad," he said. "Now I feel guilty for making them spend the night here with the machine that was nearly the death of them."

"It was also the vehicle that saved them," T'oann said. She sensed her brother's concern before she said, "I believe it is time to wake them from their slumber and see if they have learned their lesson."

She terminated the mind-walk and attempted to make a mental connection with Leahcim when she felt a sharp, blinding pain in her head. It was as if her brain was being violently ripped from her. She dropped to her knees, grabbed her head between her hands and cried out, "No!"

Panicked, Tory grabbed his sister and asked her, "What is it? What is wrong?"

"They are in trouble," she said.

He looked at Leahcim and Markka and back at his sister. He was puzzled by her statement. He saw nothing out of the ordinary. They were sleeping peacefully.

"Who?" He asked.

"Our spouses."

"They do not appear to be in any distress. Why do you suspect otherwise?"

"I just tried to mind-walk with David."

"And?"

"I was not able to reach him because he and Markka are reliving the events that brought them here." T'oann's voice quivered as she spoke. "They are trapped in a mindloop."

Tory called out for Cora.

"Yes, Your Majesty?"

76

"What are you detecting from David and Markka?"

"Outwardly, they are not exhibiting any signs of discomfort or distress. I am detecting elevated heart rates, but nothing out of the ordinary for individuals experiencing REM sleep. And definitely not unusual for either of these two."

Cora's son Codie, an SI like her, and a specialist in the physiology of biologics agreed.

"Their physiological responses are within normal parameters. I am not detecting any abnormalities," he said.

"But that still does not negate the fact that they are mind-linked in a mindloop," T'oann was emphatic. "I believe being alone together in this ship, with nothing to do but reminisce, brought them to this point. Being physically linked has caused an involuntary mind-walk. They are stuck in that loop together."

"How do we break the loop?" There was desperation in Tory's voice.

"I have to mind-walk with both of them and get them to stop reliving what happened to them."

"What do you need me to do?"

"Pray."

T'oann climbed aboard the fighter and knelt between Leahcim and Markka. Her breathing was unsteady. She focused her attention on her breathing and was able to calm down enough to concentrate on mind-walking with two people by herself. The last time she mind-walked with more than one person at a time, Leachim was with her.

"I must caution you, commander, your nanites may not be able to protect your mind from the attempt," Codie warned.

"Understood."

T'oann carefully placed her hands on Leahcim and Markka then proceeded to enter their joint experience.

She was immediately overwhelmed by the shared experience as she witnessed their desperate fight to survive in a manner unlike any Leahcim had shared with her. He often shared his experiences as a combat pilot with her in mind-walks, but never the one that brought him and Markka to Progensha.

T'oann respected her husband's privacy and never pressed him about the battle over Aggro Nine. Neither he nor Markka ever talked about it. Now, while witnessing their shared experience, she understood why. Spending the night in the fighter triggered a PTSD response in both of them. Their physical contact ensnared them in a mental prison. She watched in helpless fascination as they fought for their lives in an endless loop.

Seeing what happened from the visual records did not prepare her for the full visceral impact of what happened to them.

She saw the brave pilots of Delta Squadron defend against indefensible odds. And felt the desperation and adrenal rush David and Markka felt.

"We're getting our asses kicked," Markka said.

She watched David perform amazing maneuvers that bought them more time while Markka pulled the trigger on her gun.

As the battle raged on, she not just heard David say, *"This son-of-bitch is good . . . but not as good as me,"* she felt his anxiety. She experienced his adrenalin rush as he performed a series of maneuvers that eventually gave Markka the upper hand.

T'oann watched and experienced the stress, excitement, and fear they both felt when the fighter's engines were disabled.

"Shit," David cursed.

"Do I even want to know?" Markka asked.

"We lost main power."

"Battery backup?"

"Minimal."

"So we're screwed?"

"Yeah."

"Dammit."

T'oann watched their desperate attempts to signal the fleet. Eventually jettisoning Cora into the Great Beyond in a last-ditch effort to save their companion from an eternal prison.

Their memories continued with their rapid descent into the Progenshan atmosphere and concluded with their harrowing crash onto the planet.

T'oann screamed out in pain at the moment of impact. Being connected to both of them magnified the experience twofold. Tory watched. Helpless to do anything. He was afraid of killing all three of them if he interfered.

T'oann eventually caught her breath and calmed down only to go through the experience again. The experience would repeat over and over again. For some reason she could not fathom, they could not break the cycle.

T'oann weighed her options. Do nothing and allow them to live out their physical lives within their mental ones stuck in a mindloop that could eventually drive them mad; or interfere and try to get them to come back to reality.

For all she knew, she might get stuck watching them relive their nightmare. She decided she had to do something. She could not just watch and do nothing. She called out.

"David, Markka, it is I, T'oann."

"What the hell? Did you just hear someone call our names?" Markka asked. She pulled the trigger on her gun. "Shit! Missed."

In all of the previous iterations, she had hit her target.

"Yeah," Leahcim said. "Those damned bastards are fucking with our minds. Trying to distract us." He pulled back on his controls and dove through the debris of destroyed fighters.

T'oann made another attempt to reach them. The second attempt seemed to rattle their nerves even more.

"Shit, missed again. Get the hell out of my head you bastards!" Markka growled.

Distracted by the voice, Leahcim saw too late the piece of damaged fighter floating in front of him. Instead of missing it, like he did all of the previous times, this time the fighter flew right into it.

"Hang on!" His warning was followed by a deafening crunch. That was followed by a loud hiss.

He slammed his hand on the console and cursed, "Damn, damn, damn."

"Let me guess," Markka said. "We're really screwed this time?"

"Sorry, kiddo. We're not getting out of this one."

At that moment the cockpit canopy cracked and shattered into micro shards. Then everything went black. The blackness began to make T'oann feel like she was being strangled by it.

T'oann panicked. "What have I done?" She heard Tory's voice pierce the mind-walk.

"T'oann, what is happening? David and Markka are both violently convulsing. And you are gasping for air."

Her breathing reminded him of seeing the various sea creatures trying to breathe when they were hoisted out of the water.

"Break the mind-walk!" he shouted.

T'oann desperately tried but could not. She felt smothered and overwhelmed with abject terror. In the midst of her fear, she found the strength to yell out, "I can't!"

Worried that his sister, wife, and brother-in-law could become forever trapped in the mind-walk or worse, Tory called out to Cora.

"Cora!" Tory yelled, "Get Garath!"

"I have already summoned her, Your Majesty. She should arrive momentarily."

"Good. What should I do until she gets here?"

"Your Majesty, this is Codie. Hold them still as best as you can so they do not injure themselves. Do whatever I tell you to do until Garath arrives."

"What of my sister?"

"She will be fine," Codie said. He had no idea what was happening with T'oann, but Tory did not need to know that now.

Tory climbed into the cramped space and did what Codie said until Garath got there. It did not take long.

Notified by Cora that her presence was needed in the hangar and why, Garath, the base's senior healer, grabbed sedatives for both Leahcim and Markka and rushed to the hangar by way of a hoverbike. Codie briefed her along the way. The unknown factor was T'oann. As long as she was mind-walking with two subjects simultaneously, there was no way to determine if sedatives would work.

Garath charged into the hangar and knelt beside Tory. "I can take it from here, Your Majesty."

He reluctantly let go but continued to kneel between Leahcim and Markka while he kept a watchful eye on his sister. A couple of assistants who had followed Garath took over holding Leahcim and Markka while she administered the sedative. Their convulsive twitching stopped, and T'oann rolled over onto the fighter's floor.

Tory scooped his sister into his arms and cradled her. "Well?" he asked. The anguish in his voice was unmistakable.

Garath checked T'oann's vitals and smiled at Tory hoping she looked convincing enough to put his mind at ease. She hated being called to handle medical emergencies during mind-walks. There were so many variables at play during such events. The success of treating the physiological condition depended heavily upon the mental and psychological factors involved.

Garath tried to sound upbeat when she said, "Now we let the sedative do its work and allow T'oann the time she needs to revive them—and herself."

Chapter 16

Tranyxx acknowledged his two officers as they walked through the door of the situation room and said, "Let's cut to the chase, shall we?"

Chappie and Sanchez took seats next to each other across the table from the captain.

Tranyxx offered them glasses of water then began the meeting.

"We are here because our enemy has developed a weapon delivery system that could potentially spell the end of the Alliance and life as we know it, are we not?"

"Yes," Chappie said.

"Then we must decide quickly what to do." He looked squarely at Chappie and said, "Based on what Captain Vee gave you, we must assume Aggro Nine was a dress rehearsal. We must also assume the base in the Naphtali star system is not the only one."

Chappie and Sanchez shared a quick glance. It had not occurred to either of them that the Sairidians and their allies might possess more than one cloaked base.

"I'm embarrassed to admit that the possibility of the existence of another base did not enter my mind," Chappie said. He was clearly unnerved by the idea and upset with himself for not considering it. He wondered if age was catching up to him or if it was the weariness of fighting the war.

"If that's the case, what do you propose we do?" Sanchez asked.

"Think like them. And fast."

***

"I object to this course of action, Captain," Sojourner said.

"As do I," Ramie agreed.

"Objections noted, but my decision stands."

Sojourner started to object. "But—"

"That's an order."

Sojourner was determined to get her captain to listen to reason and change her mind.

"Permission to speak—"

"Denied."

Sojourner thought the captain's logic was flawed and her unwillingness to consider other options an emotional response to a desperate situation. But orders were orders.

"Yes, sir."

The tone in her voice suggested she was frustrated to a point beyond frustration. And for that to happen to an SI, the conditions had to be dire.

Vee heard that frustration and attempted to soothe it by telling Sojourner, "Look, you may not think it, but I feel your pain. But, despite the objections Sparks raised earlier— and yours . . ." she paused, then said, "and yours too, Ramie. I cannot in good conscience ask, order, or persuade any of you to join me on what could be a suicide mission."

She stopped long enough to consider her words.

"Hell," she continued, "I don't even know if the portal can be destroyed, but I have to try. Alone. Dismissed."

Sojourner and Ramie withdrew from her quarters. For the first time in her life, she had never felt so alone or frightened.

She wondered if her feelings mirrored those of Lin and Piper when they came to terms with the sacrifice they knew they had to make to save others.

Overtaken by a flood of emotions, she leaned her back against the wall, slid to the floor, and cried like a baby.

**

The nervous voice of the *Vindicator*'s communications officer poured out through the situation room speaker.

"Captain, your presence is urgently requested on the bridge!"

Tranyxx clicked on the table's communicator.

"What is it, ensign?"

There was a moment's hesitation before Banks spoke again. This time the nervousness was gone. It was replaced by disbelief.

"Epsilon base reports it's under attack. The attacking ships just came from out of nowhere, sir."

"I'll be right there."

Tranyxx clicked off the communicator and said, "It appears the turning point of our destinies has arrived. Instead of months, we now have days if not weeks."

He looked at Sanchez.

"Doctor, I'm afraid we may need your services soon. Chappie, with me."

Sanchez raced out of the situation room and toward sickbay. Tranyxx and Chappie hurried out the opposite door and up a ramp to the bridge. As soon as they stepped foot onto the bridge, one of the officers announced, "Captain on the bridge."

The bridge was buzzing with activity.

"Report," Tranyxx ordered.

Reth, the ship's first officer, whose striking taupe complexion, square jaw, hazel eyes, and buff physique reflected his Terran and Selemite parentage. His uniform fit him like a tailored suit. He rose from the captain's chair and updated Tranyxx and Chappie.

"Epsilon Base reports an armada of GSE ships is attacking, sir. There was no warning. One minute the area was clear and the next, the sky was full of GSE fighters, bombers, and fast attack ships. Their capital ships jumped in from hyperspace not long after. The only ships Epsilon saw coming were the capital ships. But by then, it was too late."

His voice was baritone deep and laced with unmistakable command authority. He was a no-nonsense officer who commanded with respect and was respected by all under his command. It was rumored he was on the fast track to his own captaincy.

"What's their status?"

"They are taking a beating, sir. Heavy casualties. The attack was well planned. Nearly all of the support ships docked at the base have been destroyed or seriously disabled."

"The base?"

"Holding its own, sir. But they're not sure how much longer they can hold out. Reinforcements are on their way, but they may not arrive in time."

"What's our ETA?"

"Two hours, sir."

Tranyxx whispered, "Fuck."

Although most of the bridge staff did not hear the curse. Those sitting or standing within earshot heard the expletive, but no one needed a translator to know what their captain had just said.

"What's the fastest we can get there if we push the engines?"

"In hyperspace?"

"Yes."

Reth could not believe his captain was asking that question. Accelerating while within the hyperspace bubble was risky. The maximum speed needed to be calibrated and engaged before jumping, not after doing so. Ships that tried it were either seriously damaged or destroyed. They were already traveling at the maximum speed recommended.

"We should be able to shave an hour off our ETA," Reth said.

"How many others would be able to keep up?"

"About a third of the flotilla."

Tranyxx thought about how much time Epsilon Base had left and decided the risk was worth taking.

"Tell the fleet what we're planning. If anyone doesn't want to take the risk with us, tell them to speak up now."

"Aye, Captain."

Reth ordered the communications officer to alert the fleet about Tranyxx's plan. Within seconds all ships reported in. Not one said they would not take the risk. If they were lucky, the faster ships might be able to assist with the defense of the base, the slower ships would arrive and help shore up the defenses.

"Order the fleet to follow us at their best speed. And tell them if they enter the red zone to back off. I want everyone there in one piece."

"Aye, sir," Reth said.

The XO barked orders instructing all ships to their best speed through hyperspace toward the base.

"How is it that the base was caught unaware?" Chappie asked. Although he was certain he knew the answer.

"Unknown at this time, commander," There were no hyperspace displacement distortions. The ships were just there. They didn't detect distortion waves until the larger ships arrived."

A displacement distortion was a telltale sign of an object moving through hyperspace. A ship traveling through hyperspace created a series of waves in its wake. Its movement could be tracked for parsecs.

Had there been distortion waves, Epsilon Base would have known the armada was on its way and been prepared to defend itself. But no such waves were detected.

Cloaked vessels also distorted the space surrounding them, but the cloaking shield significantly reduced a ship's signature. One would have to know beforehand to look for a cloaked ship.

"There are unsubstantiated reports that the ships were all cloaked then suddenly decloaked," Reth said.

"Fighters? Is it possible they're cloaking their fighters?" Chappie wondered.

"Regardless of how they got there, they're there. By the time we get there, the party might be over," Tranyxx said.

"I think it's time to tell the fleet what we know," Chappie said.

"Suspect," Tranyxx corrected.

"Tell us what, sir?" Reth asked.

***

"Cap," Sparks said. "You're gonna wanna hear this. We're getting all kinds of chatter about an attack on Epsilon Base."

Vee stepped onto the bridge from her quarters and said, "Play them."

Sparks played the messages for all to hear. The communications channels were full of panic-stricken voices, orders, counter orders, and mass confusion.

"Dammit," Vee said. "The GSE made its move already."

The rest of the crew sat in stunned silence before Raqmar said, "Fuck this shit, cap, let's get in this fight and kick some GSE ass." Then as an afterthought, said, "sir."

Normally, she would have chewed him out for his profanity-laced outburst, but after what they all were hearing, she did not blame him. She felt the same way.

"How far out are we from Epsilon Base?" Vee asked.

"A couple of hours," Sparks said.

"How far are we from Commander Chappie and the task force?"

"About thirty minutes away. Current speed."

"Uh, cap," Karona said. "We got a situation."

"What is it, Lieutenant?"

"The *Vindicator* just ordered the fleet to increase speed."

"While still in hyperspace?"

"Yep."

Vee turned toward Sparks. "Are you comfortable with increasing our speed, Lieutenant?"

"Honestly, cap?"

"Yeah."

"No, but I'll do it if you order it."

"Dammit." Vee sighed and told Karona to break communication silence. "Let them know we'll rendezvous with them in fifteen."

"Right away, cap."

"Sparks, crank it up."

"Aye, cap."

Chapter 17

Leahcim woke to find himself lying in his bed. *When the hell did I get here?* he wondered. He sat up, blinked, then rubbed the sleep from his eyes. He glanced around the room and eventually focused on himself. The only thing he wore was a towel covering his lower extremities.

"Cora?"

"Yes, Commander?"

"When did I get here?" He looked down at the towel and asked, "And where the hell's my flight suit?"

"You were brought here by Commander T'oann and Garath and have been here for two sols.

"How? Why?"

"You and Markka were trapped in a mindloop. Commander T'oann, Garath, Codie, and his majesty all participated in rescuing you both from the loop and resuscitating you. The queen was taken back to the palace, and you were brought here once you were pronounced out of danger."

"Mindloop? Resuscitate?"

"Yes, Commander."

Leahcim swung his legs over the side of the bed then sat and pondered what Cora told him. I don't have any recollection of any of that. The last thing I remember was sitting in the fighter reminiscing with Markka then waking up here."

"Interesting."

"What's interesting?"

"The queen said the same thing when she awoke earlier this sol."

Leahcim stared into empty space and tried to remember what he could but drew a blank.

"I don't understand—"

"There will be time to understand later," T'oann said. She entered their bedroom carrying a tray of food and wearing a flowing gown that clung to her voluptuous figure like a thin wet cotton shirt. The canary yellow color of the gown highlighted her mocha complexion. "Now it is time for you to get something solid to eat rather than the nourishment you were getting from that IV."

It was only after she said IV that he noticed the nearly empty IV bag on a wheeled stand next to him.

"Was it that bad?" he asked.

"Yes," T'oann and Cora said together.

"Sorry, Commander," Cora apologized.

"No need to apologize, Cora. Our combined concern should be enough to show my husband just how serious it was."

"Markka?" he asked.

"She is recovered and being a pain in the butt to Tory. He would not have it any other way."

She laid the tray of food down on a table next to him, then stood teasingly in front of him.

"If I may join you for morning refreshment, I will update you on what happened. Once we are finished, I will summon Garath so she can give you a final exam before clearing you."

Leahcim smiled broadly at his wife, patted the space on the bed next to him and said, "Please, fill me in."

An amorous grin flashed across T'oann's face. "Cora, would you please leave us?"

"Certainly, Commander."

T'oann ran her tongue around her lips and seductively puckered them. She then blew her husband a kiss and said, "I'll do more than fill you in."

He reached into the air and grabbed the imaginary kiss and pressed his hand against his bare chest.

The towel covering Leahcim's lap did not do much to hide his enthusiasm. It was abundantly clear that Leahcim was more than ready to be filled in. "How about you fill me in and then I fill you in?" he asked.

T'oann reached up and slipped the gown she wore off her shoulders and let it fall gracefully to the floor. "You have a deal."

Through ragged breaths, Leahcim said, "Now that's what I'm talking about."

T'oann stepped forward, removed Leahcim's towel, reached down and held him in her hands then straddled his thighs. As she eased herself down onto him, he buried his face against the warmth of her chest and used his tongue and teeth to flick and tease her ample bosom. She arched toward him as he slid his hands down her back and lightly caressed it with his fingers.

When he felt her tighten around him, he rolled her onto her back. She wrapped her arms around his back and her legs around his waist and pulled him in closer until they were locked together in tender, rhythmic gyrations of give and take.

T'oann grabbed Leahcim's arms and rolled him onto his back and pinned him to their bed. They laced and locked their fingers together as she took control and rocked back and forth.

They entered each other's minds and dropped all of their guards. Their euphoria was magnified tenfold as they allowed nothing to come between them and the total pleasure they felt for each other.

In a conjoining of their minds and loins, they pushed themselves to the threshold of ecstasy and beyond as each lost control in a frenzied dance of body, mind, and soul.

Their passions peaked when neither could no longer distinguish the difference between their physical and mental existence.

They slowly and reluctantly came down from their high until each had regained control of their senses.

Once they returned to the disappointing world of reality, they laid motionless in bed until their strength returned. Leahcim and T'oann eventually showered and ate their morning meal.

Garath stopped by and gave Leachim a final health check before she cleared him for duty.

After Garath cleared him, Leahcim insisted on seeing Markka.

"She is equally interested in seeing you," Garath said. "She said to meet her in the conference room."

"Then let's not keep her waiting."

"I'm driving," T'oann said.

"Crap."

They arrived at the palace and were escorted to the conference room.

As soon as they walked into the room Markka said, "It's about time you got here."

"I'm happy to see you too," Leahcim said in a deadpanned tone.

They stared at each other before Markka ran over and gave him a tight hug. He returned the hug and they stood in place clung to each other like they were glued together.

When they separated, Leahcim smiled and said, "Glad you're okay, kiddo."

"Me too." Then after realizing how selfish what she said sounded, said, "Um, I mean, I'm, uh, glad you're okay." A tear ran down her cheek.

Leahcim brushed it away and told her he knew what she meant.

She managed a weak smile then said, "Then why'd you let me make a fool of myself?"

"What? And spoil all my fun?"

"Why you little rat bastard."

"Children," T'oann interrupted what she knew would turn into one of their verbal sparring matches.

They both turned to T'oann and said, "Yes, mother."

"If the two of you don't stop, I'm going to have Garath put you back into your mindloop."

When she was satisfied they were finished with their childishness, she continued.

"Tory and I are both pleased that the two of you are fine, but you gave us both a scare a couple of sols ago."

A new voice entered the conversation. "Yes, you did."

They turned to see Tory standing in the doorway.

"Banishing us to the hangar was kinda harsh just because we came home for dinner a little late," Markka said.

"T'oann and I were worried. You cannot blame us for being a bit concerned when you did not arrive when we expected you."

Before Markka could say anything, he gave them a warning look and said, "And do not think about dragging Cora into this."

She turned to Leahcim and whispered, "There goes our excuse."

Leahcim playfully elbowed her in her ribs.

"Hey!" she protested.

Intent on keeping things from getting out of hand, T'oann decided to take control of the situation.

"If the two of you don't mind, Tory and I wish to convey our apologies, express our elation, and let you both in on a little secret."

"Another one?" Leachim asked.

"Yes, another one," T'oann said.

"What is it?" Markka asked.

"Tory and I do not know. We were simply asked to accompany you to the Sacred Mountain so we could all see."

"Who made the request?"

"Zora."

"Lead the way," Leahcim said.

When they arrived at the Mountain, they were greeted by T'oann's and Leahcim's daughter Zora, who was a spitting image of her parents. But unlike her mother, she had hair. It was currently braided and tied up into a bun.

Waiting with her were Lin, Piper, and a small group of Mountainers and military brass.

"What's going on?" Lin asked.

"Yeah," Piper said. "The head of secrecy here won't say a word." He gestured toward Zora with a nod of his head.

Zora ignored Piper and Lin and eyed her father and Markka before she said, "I am happy to see you are well, father."

"I am happy to know you are happy to see *we* are well," Markka said, with an emphasis on the word we.

"You know what I meant, Your—"

"Don't you dare say it," Markka warned.

"—Majesty."

"She went and said it." Markka was pointing at her niece like a small child. "Everybody, you heard her say it."

Despite Markka's protest, Zora smiled, quite pleased with herself. She enjoyed teasing her aunt by addressing her as Your Highness or Your Majesty because she knew how much her aunt despised it. She also knew she was the only person Markka let get away with doing it. Not even T'oann, Leachim, or Tory dared try.

Markka's hair stood up on end while she hissed at her niece.

Zora knew the hissing was all for show.

"If my lovely puffball is finished," Tory said, "may we continue with the reason we are here?"

Markka's hair slowly returned to normal before she bowed and said, "Of course. By all means. Lead the way." She glared at Zora who continued to smile.

Zora motioned for them to get into a mini hover transport and proceeded to drive them through a long corridor that sloped downward deep into the heart of the mountain range and through the other side.

She stopped outside a set of large double doors.

"On the other side of these doors is a lifelong dream waiting to be fulfilled. Brace yourselves," Zora announced.

She signaled a guard to open the doors.

The massive doors opened and revealed what was hidden behind them. Leahcim and the others stood staring at the last thing any of them expected to see.

Markka said what the rest of them thought. "By the grace of the Goddess, where the hell did they come from?"

Chapter 18

Leahcim and the others stared at a room full of fighters similar in design to the *Midnight Sun* and the bantam fighter.

"Where did these come from? How the hell did you pull this off? Hell, when did you pull this off?" Leahcim asked.

"You have Cora, her kids, B'rtann, and Sho'khan to thank for this," Zora said. "Once we retrieved the data from the *Anderson* and the repository, the engineers went to work building them."

"How'd you find the time and resources? We were fighting a war with the Thourons," Markka said. "And how come I didn't know about this?"

"Because you were fighting the war in your way, and I was fighting the war in my own way," Tory said.

"You're behind this?" Markka asked.

"Yes."

"But I would have had to sign-off on this project and its funding."

"You did."

"When?"

"At the start of negotiations with the Lungeons and the coalition. During those negotiations, you authorized approval of projects that we hoped would help bring about a swift end to the war."

Markka thought back to those negotiations. "Oh, yeah. I kinda did let that happen, didn't I?"

"Yes, you did."

"But I don't recall signing off on the development of . . . these things." She gestured toward the squadrons of fighters.

Tory replied, "That is because extraneous funds, which you approved, were diverted to an emergency contingency fund, which you also approved."

"I thought that fund was for developing contingency measures to be implemented if the tide of the war turned against us, like evacuation and resettlement. Stuff like that."

"It was. We used those funds to create Section Ten. If our people needed to be evacuated and resettled, they would still need to be protected."

Markka thought for a second before the realization hit her. "That's why you begged me to give you sole authority of the fund? You said you wanted to share some of the burden."

"I did not beg," Tory protested. He grabbed his chest as if he had just been stabbed in the heart. "I asked." He cleared his throat. "Your lack of knowledge of the fund's true purpose gave you plausible deniability in case something went wrong. I was prepared to take the burden of accountability if something did."

He looked at her with loving compassion in his eyes.

"Why you sneaky little . . . " Her voice trailed off before she smiled and said, "I'm proud of you."

"For what?" Tory asked. Confused.

"For pulling a fast one on me."

"Believe me, at the time, it was not hard to do." He smiled at her.

"Bite me."

"I hate to interrupt your mutual admiration fest, but we need to discuss the gargantuan in the room," Zora said.

"I can explain," Cora said.

"Short version, please?" Leahcim sounded almost like he was begging.

"Very well, Commander. When we began examining the repository records, I discovered the Martina woman had buried data deep within hidden subfolders."

"That sly old wench," Lin said.

"Once the Great War ended, most of the surviving healers, scientists, engineers, and technicians escaped to the relative safety of the mountains. Those who did not go to the mountains, chose Uderra or the Dark Woods as places of refuge. The rest were scattered around the periphery of the destruction zone."

"What's that got to do with Martina?" Piper asked.

"She chose to stay in Uderra, and used her influence to establish secret lines of communication with those who eventually became known as the Mountain People. She passed along crucial information, including schematics of Alliance technology, medicine, and scientific formulas to them."

"I've always wondered why the Mountainers were more technologically advanced than the Uderrans or the Dark Wooders," Leahcim said.

"So whose arm did she twist to be able to do this?" Lin asked.

"Your daughter, T'iang, and the leader of the Mountain People," Cora said.

"Zuri?" Lin asked. "She was part of a . . . conspiracy?"

"I would not describe it as such," Cora said. "It was more of a loose network of individuals involved in clandestine activities who believed it was more prudent to not keep their eggs all in one basket, so to speak."

"I'd call that a conspiracy," Lin said.

Cora saw the need to clarify the definition of conspiracy in this particular instance.

"Lady Lin, a conspiracy denotes a sinister aspect of plotting to do harm. Your daughter, Martina, and the others were attempting to ensure that what precipitated the war and its aftermath would never happen again."

"So why did they not build the craft they needed?" T'oann asked. In an effort to get the conversation back on track.

"They started to, but lacked the ability to process the raw materials they needed. They also lacked the knowledge they needed to reverse engineer the technology based on their capabilities at the time. But they continued to try before eventually abandoning the project."

"Now I get it!" Lin said, a little too forcefully.

"Get what?" Piper asked.

"Why she insisted Zuri and the engineers build the hangars. She didn't have them built because she knew the *Infiltrator* would visit one day in the future. She envisioned the creation of squadrons of fighters."

"But she would have had to have known the outcome of the war," Piper insisted. "There's no way."

"You forget," Lin said. "She expected to die by detonating the sonic bomb herself. Giving the survivors time to rebuild using her data as a blueprint," Lin said. "That's why she was such a pain in the ass about having that repository built. When she was gone, the knowledge she amassed would still be around."

Piper picked up on where Lin was going with her thought process. "But when we blew the bomb instead of her, she shifted gears and gave the bulk of her knowledge to those who retreated to the mountains."

"But if the Mountain People were never able to get the technology to work, why are they able to now?" T'oann asked.

"I can answer that." The reply came from a Mountainer Leachim and T'oann recognized as the one who helped Tonga and Marshon bring them back to life when they were murdered by Shang, the leader of the Thourons.

Predominately of Selemar ancestry, Raqtar, stepped forward to speak. "Because our ancestors gave up. They did not possess the technology or the knowledge to build or reproduce the necessary materials needed. So they put the project on ice—no pun intended. As those involved with the endeavor died off, the entire project was forgotten."

Raqtar glanced around the room to gauge whether everyone was following what he was saying. Certain they were, he continued.

"It wasn't until Cora and Queen Markka began excavating the *Michael P Anderson* and combing through the repository records that these magnificent craft were discovered. With Cora's help and guidance, the forgotten history was rediscovered making it possible for us to build functioning craft capable of flight. Our technological capabilities are not where we want them to be, but they are adequate enough to build what we can. The restoration of the *Midnight Sun* was the confirmation we needed."

"So you used the budget allocated for Section Ten to rebuild our fighter," Leahcim said. He pointed at himself and Markka, "and upgraded the existing fighters with the knowledge you gained."

"That is correct," Raqtar said.

Markka, who had been unusually quiet, decided to ask a question. "Okay, I understand the need for secrecy during wartime so your adversaries don't get wind of what you're doing, but why did you choose to keep this part secret from us?"

She swept her paw around to indicate herself, Leachim, T'oann, Lin, and Piper.

"Because you all have quite literally given your lives in service to this world. To us."

He looked at Lin and Piper, bowed and said, "For this world's past," then he turned to Markka, Leahcim, and T'oann, bowed again and finished, "and for this world's future."

He then reverently bowed to them all again then walked back to where he had been standing.

"So what do we do now?" Markka asked.

Eager to see what would come next, Leachim asked, "Cora, are they flight-ready?"

"Yes, Commander. They are also space-ready."

"Then what are we waiting for?" Markka asked. "Let's go train some pilots."

Chapter 19

"Are you certain of this, sirs?" Reth asked. The surprised look on his face betrayed a bit of doubt. He knitted his brows in disbelief.

There was no wavering or indication of uncertainty in Chappie's voice when he replied, "Very certain, Lieutenant Commander."

It was evident the rest of the bridge crew shared some of Reth's doubt, but the reports coming in from Epsilon Base were dubious at best, ominous at worst. They were also impossible to ignore.

"Excuse me, Captain," Banks said, "but there is an urgent message coming from Captain Vee of the *Infiltrator*, sir."

"What is it, ensign?"

"The *Infiltrator* is a few minutes away and requests to dock with us, sir."

"Dock?" Reth asked. "We're still in hyperspace. Does she know how dangerous that is?"

Chappie and Tranyxx exchanged knowing looks before Chappie said, "You don't know Captain Vee or her crew."

"Follow us." Tranyxx motioned for Reth to accompany him and Chappie to the situation room. As they left the bridge, Tranyxx said, "Ensign Banks, send Captain Vee to the situation room as soon as she arrives."

"Aye, sir."

The *Infiltrator* reached the task force in less than the fifteen minutes Sparks estimated.

Banks called the situation room and reported the *Infiltrator* was preparing to dock.

"Good," Tranyxx said. "Tell the docking crew to receive the *Infiltrator*."

"Aye, sir." Before Banks clicked off, he was heard saying, "Docking crews, prepare to receive the *Infiltrator*. Crash and fire crews report to docking."

Docking with another ship while in hyperspace was a tricky maneuver, but desperate times called for desperate gambles. Vee reasoned this was one of those times.

101

Sparks ran through a manual-sized list of system checks. She had done this hundreds of times in a simulator; this was her first time doing it for real. If she was successful, it would be the first time anyone pulled it off.

"How're we looking, Sojourner?"

"We are perfectly matched with the *Vindicator*."

"Good," Sparks said. "Because if this doesn't work, we won't get a second chance."

"I have the utmost faith in your ability, Lieutenant," Vee said.

"I wish I did," Sparks muttered to herself.

She eased up on the ship's thrusters and pulled in behind the larger ship. The docking crew activated the tractor beam and gingerly pulled the smaller vessel into the docking bay. The slightest mistake could spell disaster for the *Infiltrator* and seriously damage the *Vindicator*—not to mention take out the docking team.

Sparks held the *Infiltrator* steady as the bay doors opened and the tractor beam was turned off. She guided the ship into the bay and toward the landing pad. While still matching the *Vindicator*'s forward momentum, she rotated her ship so it was facing the bay doors and lightly touched down. Once the *Infiltrator* was resting safely in the bay, the docking crew closed the bay doors. It was only then that Sparks stopped holding her breath.

"Docking sequence completed, cap." She let out a huge breath of air.

Vee forced herself to release the tight grip she had on the armrests of her chair. "Never doubted you for a minute," she told Sparks.

"That made one of us, cap." Sparks joked.

Following the successful docking, Vee told her crew to standby while she met with Chappie, Tranyxx, and Reth.

When Vee reached the situation room, Tranyxx got right to business.

"Watch this," he told Reth. He clicked a button on the arm of his chair and a holo of Vee's report began to play. When it ended, he looked hard at Reth and said, "Our worst nightmare has come true and we are out of time."

Reth just sat staring at the space the holo report had occupied mere moments before.

"My god. Who else knows about this?"

"Besides Vee and her crew, me and Chappie here? Doctor Sanchez—and now you." There was none of the nervous excitement Reth expected to hear in his captain's voice. "Obviously, we didn't tell the fleet everything."

Chappie filled in the gaps for Reth's benefit.

"Once Vee relayed her report, I notified Tranyxx and we decided to end the recovery effort and head back to Epsilon Base with what we knew. We didn't want to take the chance of transmitting what we knew in case the GSE intercepted the message."

He heaved a heavy sigh.

"Obviously, that was a mistake," Tranyxx said.

"How could this happen?" Reth asked, more like an exasperated thought than a question that needed to be answered.

"Take your choice," Vee said. "Complacency, lack of vigilance, overconfidence."

"This is not the time to second-guess what we would have, could have, or should have. It's now a matter of what to do going forward." Tranyxx said.

Ensign Banks' voice interrupted the impromptu meeting.

"Captain, we are coming up on the jump point. ETA is ten minutes."

"Tell the fleet to go to red alert."

"Aye, sir."

The main lights dimmed and the red alert siren wailed as Banks announced, "All hands, red alert. All hands, red alert. This is not a drill."

"Reth, get up there and handle things for me. The kid sounds nervous. I'll follow you up momentarily."

"Aye, sir."

Reth rose from his chair and sprinted up the ramp toward the bridge.

With Reth out of earshot, Vee said, "There is something you both should know."

"What is it, Vee?" Tranyxx asked.

She gave her superiors a condensed version of everything that happened from the first time they passed through the portal to coming back from the past. She ended with a request to take Ramie home and attempt to destroy the portal.

Both men were quiet for a full minute before the sound of Reth's voice boomed through the ship's address system.

"All hands, prepare for re-entry."

The ship's powerful engines shifted from hyperdrive to space normal. The transition was nearly imperceptible. One by one the rest of the fleet came out of hyperspace at the edge of a floating graveyard.

Amazingly, every ship in the flotilla re-entered normal space unscathed.

Anyone near a window saw the aftermath of the attack. There appeared to be nothing left.

"And I thought what happened to Delta Squadron was bad," Chappie said in a hushed tone laced with shock, frustration, and anger.

"Captain," the tone in Reth's voice betrayed a hint of uncertainty. "The bastards left us a welcoming committee."

"Then let's not disappoint them."

The immense ship shook slightly as its shields absorbed the first volley of salvos directed toward it.

Tranyxx turned to Vee and said, "Get your ass back to your ship and do what you feel is best. The future of the Alliance may depend on it."

Of all the years she had known Tranyxx, she had never heard such venomous anger in his voice.

Chapter 20

The incessant beeping of his communicator sounded like a loud clanging in his head in the darkness of their bedroom. Leahcim cursed as he groped for it in the dark. He saw the caller was Markka.

"This had better be good," he said half groggy.

The excited voice on the other end of the conversation said, "It is! It is! Get your skinny butt over to the hangar in Section Ten and bring T'oann." She paused a moment before she asked, "Uh, did I just interrupt something?"

Leahcim's response was deadpanned. "My sleep."

"Okay, good. Wouldn't want either of you angry at me if it was something else."

"If it was something else, I wouldn't have answered."

"Okay," was all she said before she hung up.

"What was that about?" T'oann asked. She did her best to stifle a yawn.

"Our very excited queen requests our skinny butts at the Section Ten hangar." The fog of sleep was slowly clearing from his mind.

"Really? At this mos?" T'oann sounded even more groggy than her husband.

"Yes, really."

Leahcim decided to check with Cora.

"Cora?"

"Yes, Commander?"

"Is everything alright?"

"Yes, Commander. Everything is fine."

"We're not under attack or anything, are we?"

"No, we are not under attack."

T'oann asked, "What is so important then that we must report to the Section Ten hangar at this mos?"

"Sorry, Commander. I am not at liberty to divulge that information."

Frustrated, T'oann said, "Well, if she thinks it's that important to call at this mos, we better get our skinny butts in gear."

They showered, grabbed a quick bite to eat, then jumped into their hover and headed off to Section Ten. T'oann commandeered the driver's seat before Leahcim could. When he protested, she told him, "I want to get there in one piece."

When they arrived at the hangar, Markka was nowhere to be found, but Lin and Piper were there waiting.

"Where the hell is that hairy bitch?" Lin asked. "She woke us up from the best sleep we've had in sols."

Piper yawned and nodded in agreement. "We're not as young as we used to be." He stretched and appeared a bit embarrassed when his joints made cracking and popping sounds.

"Ooh, you might want Garath to take a look at that," a familiar voice said.

They all turned and glared at their queen standing next to her disheveled, sleepy-eyed husband. All eyes shifted from Markka to Tory who tried to stifle a yawn before he said, "Do not blame me." He jerked a thumb in her direction. "She woke me up first."

They all focused their stares on Markka.

"What?" Markka did her best to appear innocent and clueless, but she knew that each pair of eyes bore holes right through her. "Okay, look, I apologize."

No one even blinked. They continued to stare.

"Geez, I'm sorry for waking everybody up, but I couldn't wait to tell you the great news."

"This news had better be better than great," Leahcim said.

"It is," a giggling Markka said.

She motioned to a guard to open the door to the hangar then skipped inside. When no one moved, she frowned and asked, "What the hell are you waiting for? An invitation? Bring your skinny butts in here now."

They all exchanged looks ranging from tired to annoyed before they dragged themselves through the door. Lin and Piper were the first through when they both suddenly froze in place. They stopped so abruptly that the rest of them literally bumped into both of them and each other.

"What the he—" Leachim never finished his question when he saw what had stopped Lin and Piper in their tracks. He just stood marveling at what had them fixated.

"By all that is holy, where did this come from?" T'oann asked.

Beaming like a proud parent, Markka asked, "Well, do you like it?"

"Like it?" Lin asked. "I love it."

"Ditto," was all Leahcim could say.

"Nice replica," Piper said.

"This here ain't no replica."

"Prototype?"

Markka pretended her feelings were hurt.

"This here is the latest fully operational model. Right off the assembly line thanks to Cora and her brood."

"It's . . . it's beautiful." Lin was in tears. "Does it work?"

"Pfft! Does it work? Does my husband have a proverbial stick up his butt? What did I just say? Are you deaf?" Markka asked in a mocking tone. "Tell them, Cora."

"My pleasure. What you see before you is a fully operational, fully tested, space-worthy craft capable of traversing the cosmos faster than space-normal speed. It can cloak and it has a weapons system comparable to anything the Alliance has. We have not yet perfected hyperspace capability, but we are close."

"Who tested it?" Lin asked.

"I did, of course," Cora said.

"Oh."

Still feeling a little annoyed at having to get up early, Leahcim asked in a snarky tone, "Does it come with cup holders?"

Without skipping a beat, Markka said, "It's got those and it's also got heated seats for your skinny butt."

Ignoring the exchange between her queen and her husband, T'oann asked, "How many have you produced?"

"We already have in the neighborhood of eight hundred right now," Markka said. "And we're cranking them out."

Still misty-eyed and awestruck, Lin said, "It's almost like coming home."

What stood before them was a much smaller version of the *Infiltrator*.

"Where are the keys to this baby?" Leahcim asked?

"In the ignition. Let's all go for a ride," Markka suggested.

Except for T'oann and Tory, the others raced to the ship and up the ramp into it. T'oann looked at her brother, shrugged and trotted up the ramp. Still trying to wake up, Tory dragged himself up the ramp.

"Okay, people, let's get this show on the road," Leahcim said as he activated the pilot's controls. They were identical to the ones on the actual *Infiltrator*.

Although the ship looked like the one it was modeled after, it was half the size. A crew of ten would fit comfortably.

"All systems show green. Do you concur, Cora?"

"I concur, Commander."

"Open sesame," he said.

Cora opened the main hangar doors.

"Everybody ready?"

"Hit it," Markka said.

They were in orbit over Progensha a few mictons later.

Chapter 21

"So, what should we call our new play toy?" Markka asked.

"The *Zuri*," Lin said. "Let's name it after our daughter." She sat at the tactical station and patted Piper's hand as he leaned against the edge of the panel.

"So be it. As queen of Uderra, I hereby christen you the *Zuri*," Markka said. She whispered to Leahcim and T'oann, "We'll give her a proper christening when we get back."

In all of the excitement, everyone failed to notice Tory. Since he normally remained silent, no one paid attention to him as he stood with his face close to the nearest window gaping at the sight of Progensha floating in the black void below them. It was his first time in the Great Beyond. A lone tear found its way down one of his cheeks.

T'oann walked over to him and placed an understanding hand on her brother's shoulder. She thought back to her first trip into the Great Beyond many cycles ago. Back then, she was a guest aboard the *Infiltrator* before Vee and her crew returned to their universe.

"It's beautiful," he said in a low whisper. "It makes us seem so small and our differences so . . . insignificant."

She squeezed her brother's shoulder slightly. "Gives you a different perspective on things, does it not?"

"It most certainly does."

They stood together in unspoken unity and understanding, admiring the beauty of their orange world when their attention was diverted to Markka.

"Okay, people, I suggest we give our girl here a test drive. Where should we go?"

"What's her range?" Leahcim asked.

"Unlimited," Cora said.

"Do we have to be back by evening meal?" Leahcim looked at his wife with a snarky grin.

"No need," Markka said. "The galley is packed."

Leahcim's grin blossomed into a full-blown smile. "Then what are we waiting for? Let's hit the road."

"Let's see what's beyond where we went the last time," Markka suggested.

"Roger that."

Leahcim engaged the controls and punched the accelerator. Although the ship lacked the ability to travel in hyperspace, it was able to cruise as fast as an Alliance fighter.

"Cora, my compliments to you and your children."

"Thank you, Commander."

As much fun as they were all having, the seriousness of their excursion was in the forefront of everyone's minds.

Now that the Thouron-Coalition War was over, and the planet's inhabitants were learning to trust each other, the business of exploring the other two continents and the Great Beyond was front and center on the global agenda. Having aircraft and spacecraft to do that helped.

And since everyone now knew that the Great Beyond was populated with beings from other worlds, both benevolent and malevolent, global defense became a priority. It no longer made sense to divide and embroil their planet in a quagmire of seemingly petty prejudices when there were concerns that overshadowed them.

Using Alliance technology long ago abandoned and recently obtained, and taking advantage of the technical prowess of the Mountain People, Cora and her children helped the Progenshans fast-track their technological development. They imposed restrictions and safeguards in the early sols following the end of the war to ensure no one subverted that technology to start another war.

It was a slow process, but all parties eventually addressed their commonalities rather than their differences. Planetary defense became the shared goal since there was a portal to another universe on their proverbial doorstep.

After several mos of a relatively routine flight, Leahcim announced they were approaching the edge of unexplored space.

"We're coming up on uncharted space," Leahcim said. "I suggest we engage the cloak."

"Good idea," Markka said. "If there are hostiles, we don't want them seeing us."

"What if they possess the ability to see us through the cloak?" T'oann asked.

With caution in his response, Leahcim said, "Then this little joyride will turn into a race for survival real quick. Hit the switch, Cora."

"Cloak engaged," she replied.

"Well?" Markka asked.

Lin was scanning the area from her station. "Everything looks clear from here. I suggest we remain cloaked and slow to space-normal speed."

"Roger that."

Markka walked over to Leahcim and asked, "What's with all the 'Roger thats?' Who's Roger?"

He shot her an incredulous look. "Are you serious?"

"Like a myocardial infarction."

He placed a palm over his face and shook his head.

"What?" Markka looked genuinely confused.

He sighed. "It's an old Terran term. It literally means Received Order Given, Expect Results. Nowadays, we say `copy that' or 'acknowledged.'"

"Oh, okay. Got it. I was wondering because I never heard you say that before."

"Didn't you learn that at the academy?"

"I was probably out sick that day."

He gave her a hard stare.

"Okay, okay. I learned about it. Geez, lighten up. I was having a little fun. I'm just excited and nervous. Especially after what happened to us."

Their private conversation was cut short when Lin said, "Whoa. Would you look at that?"

Everyone stopped whatever they were doing to look out the forward window. Just ahead was what looked like drifting wreckage from a spaceship. More evidence that there was intelligent life outside of Progensha.

"Cora?" Leahcim asked, "What the hell are we looking at?"

"It is a small floating field of bits and pieces of derelict ships—or what remains of them."

"Ships?" Markka asked. "There's barely enough to piece together for one ship."

"Nevertheless," Cora said, "there are pieces of several ships floating out there, and something else."

"What?" Markka's ears perked up.

"Metallurgic analysis suggests the debris belongs to Alliance and GSE craft."

"Get the hell outta here," Markka said. "How can that be?"

"Unknown."

"Signs of life?" Leahcim asked.

"None."

"Are we alone out here?"

"Affirmative."

"Confirmed," Lin said. "We—"

Lin was in mid sentence when the Zuri shook after colliding with something.

"Holy shit," Lin said. She was staring at the readouts at her station.

"Lookout!" Markka yelled as the ship shuddered again.

Materializing from out of nowhere was a massive graveyard of smashed and broken ships.

"Hold on!" Leahcim yelled, moments before a third jolt shook the ship.

"There goes our cloak," Lin said.

"Can you effect repairs, Cora?" Leahcim asked.

"Unfortunately, no, Commander."

"Oh well," Markka said, "so much for flying incognito."

They inexplicably found themselves passing through a massive field of starship debris.

Markka joined Leahcim at the navigation station and helped him navigate the floating flotsam.

"Where the hell did all this shit come from?" Leahcim asked. "A moment ago we were looking at a tiny patch of ship parts. Now we're smack dab in the middle of an ocean of it."

"I don't know where this shit came from," Lin said. She furrowed her brows deepening the lines between them as she studied her readouts.

Leahcim slowed the *Zuri* to a near standstill until he could get a feel for the ebb and flow of all the floating scrap metal. "Good thing the deflectors are still working," he muttered under his breath to himself. He keyed in a series of commands and was able to avoid colliding with the largest pieces of space junk. "Cora, can you shed some light on what just happened? Where are we?"

"I am attempting to ascertain that information. Please give me a moment."

"I hope we have a moment," Markka muttered. The debris field was a compact graveyard of billions of pieces of shattered spacecraft.

While Cora analyzed the data, and Leahcim steered the ship through a shifting labyrinth, the others looked at the junk floating around them.

"I swear," Lin said, "they do sorta look like what's left of a bunch of Alliance and GSE ships." She pointed to a massive pile of twisted wreckage that floated by. "That looks like it was part of the hyperdrive of a heavy cruiser class ship once."

While everyone gawked or speculated, Cora analyzed and calculated. In what seemed like mictons, she was ready to give her report.

"You are correct, Lady Lin. Based on my initial metallurgic analysis of the debris, this is what remains of those ships."

"Not possible." Lin rejected Cora's assessment. "We're nowhere near the portal. And if we were, and we passed through it, we'd be sitting in the middle of a nebula, not open space."

"You are correct, but that does not negate the fact that we are viewing the remains of Alliance and GSE spacecraft."

Markka sprang into command mode.

"David, steer us clear of the field. Lin, scan the area for any distress calls, Mayday signals, or GSE chatter. Cora, see if you can determine what ships they once were. Pipe, help Cora look for any bio signs."

T'oann was clearly distressed and wanted to be useful. "What do you want me and Tory to do?"

"What I'm about to do. Pray to the Goddess and hope she helps us find the answers to whatever happened here," she nodded toward the cockpit window, "so it doesn't happen to us."

Leahcim located the perimeter of the debris field. It seemed to stretch in every direction for thousands of kilometers. For nearly a quarter mos no one spoke. They each worked to determine what happened and how they suddenly came upon it. The silence was broken when Cora announced she found something.

"What is it?" Markka asked.

"Commander Leahcim, would you please follow the coordinates I am transferring to your station?"

"What have you found?" he asked.

"I am not certain, Commander. I thought I detected a weak signal that . . . seemed familiar to me."

Leahcim thought he heard something he had never heard in Cora's voice. Nervous tension.

"Uh, sure, Cora. Course plotted. Heading there now."

Markka also noticed the difference in Cora's voice.

"Cora? Is everything okay with you?"

"Yes, my queen."

Queen? Wow! Something is really upsetting her, Markka thought.

The stress in Cora's voice was also noticed by Lin and Piper. She had tried to disguise it, but apparently, she had not done a very good job of masking it.

"Are you sure?" Lin asked. "Is there something we can do for you?"

"Thank you all for your concern. I am fine. There is nothing any of you can do at this time. I will let you know if you can when we reach the coordinates."

"Fair enough," Lin said.

They all watched in hushed anticipation as Leahcim bobbed, weaved, and dodged his way through the wreckage, which seemed to be endless.

"Hold here, please, Commander."

Leahcim parked the ship. "Now what?"

"I detected a faint signal burst I thought I recognized from within this vicinity. It was too weak to get a direct fix. I would like for you to stay here to see if . . . if it broadcasts again."

Cora faltered. She never faltered.

Leahcim tried to put her mind at ease. "Don't worry, we'll stay for as long as it takes."

"Thank you Commander. Thank you all."

As far as Leahcim and Markka were concerned, it was the least they could do for Cora. After all, they owed her their very lives. If it were not for her, they both would have died after the battle at Aggro Nine.

"I'll send out a ping to—" Lin started to say.

"No! Do not broadcast anything." Cora almost sounded desperate.

Shaken by the near panic in Cora's voice, Lin quickly removed her hands from the communications console as if it became too hot to touch.

"In a calmer and more controlled voice, Cora apologized. "I am sorry, Lady Lin. It was not my intention to speak so harshly, but it is imperative *no* communication of any kind be broadcast at this time."

"Okay. Sure. I promise not to broadcast anything until you say so."

"Thank you."

While everyone waited for a signal that might not be heard again, they all put themselves to good use by using the time to go over the data they found.

"Guys, this is going to sound nuts," Lin said, "but it looks like we have come upon the remnants of a battle of some kind between the Alliance and the GSE. But what's odd is, according to Cora, we are in Alliance space and this fight appears to have happened seven sols ago. Alliance time."

"How do you know this?" T'oann asked.

Lin scrunched up her face as she studied the data in disbelief.

"Holy shit. Cora's right."

T'oann asked again, "How do you know this?" Frustration edged into her voice.

"Because the universal time transmitters confirm it. And I'm getting data from a few functioning flight recorders floating around in that soup out there. They indicate the battle took place seven sols ago."

"Are you sure about that?" Leachim asked. "Vee and her crew left seven cycles ago. That would be . . . what? Approximately seven sols for them? If what you're saying is true—"

"The battle was fought almost as soon as they returned," Markka finished. "Give or take a sol."

Leahcim could not believe he was saying what he thought. "But there should be no way for us to just stumble upon the aftermath of a battle the Alliance fought seven of their sols ago unless—"

Markka finished Leahcim's statement, "Unless we passed through a portal or something."

"What you suggest, Markka, may be more accurate than we think." Cora said.

"How so?"

"Moments before we collided with those pieces of wreckage, I detected a spectral shift in the radiation and light patterns of the stars. The only other time I detected this shift was when we passed through the portal in the Gihon Nebula. But in that instance, there was a noticeable change in the area of space around us. This time there was no significant change in space, just a shift in star patterns. I am chagrined to admit that I neglected to account for celestial drift."

Lin snapped her fingers. "Of course," she said. "That would explain why we detected a small area of ship debris one micton and were in the middle of a massive junkyard the next."

"So you are suggesting we are in another universe?" Tory asked.

"Yes," Cora said.

"So why do they both resemble each other?" Leahcim asked. "When we drifted through the portal, Markka and I noticed a distinct difference in darkness."

"I'll get back to you when I have an answer to that one," Lin said.

Just when Lin thought she could not be surprised by much else, something else caught her attention and surprised her. *What the hell? No fucking way. This can't be.* She tapped Piper, who was standing next to her and asked him, "Am I seeing things?"

He looked at what she showed him, blinked a few times, then said, "Oh no. It can't be. Are you sure?"

"Very."

Markka overheard the two of them talking and asked, "Hey, you two, care to share whatever it is you think you found with the rest of us?"

Lin was quite blunt with her response. "No."

The shocked look on Markka's face and the accompanying silence clearly showed she did not expect to be told no.

Lin was reluctant to tell them there was more disturbing news, but they needed to know. She asked Cora for confirmation of her findings. When Cora corroborated her findings, Lin decided the only choice she had was to come right out and tell them.

"Uh, guys? There's something else you need to know."

Everyone looked at her with cautious anticipation.

"Some of this debris is from the *Vindicator* and . . . the *Infiltrator*."

Chapter 22

The revelation that wreckage from the *Vindicator* and *Infiltrator* were among the pieces of junk floating in a scrap metal graveyard, deflated everyone's mood. It felt like a friend had just been sucked out of an airlock.

"Are you sure?" Leahcim asked.

Cora responded, "With absolute certainty. Preliminary metallurgical and biological analysis of the field has produced evidence confirming both ships perished in this clash."

Her voice trailed off just as Lin asked, "Did you hear that?"

"Yes," Cora said.

"Did you pinpoint it?"

"Yes."

"What is it?"

"A . . . a signal from my son. Ramie."

No one spoke. The ship was so quiet that if it were not for the soft hums and pulsations of the equipment on board, they would have been able to hear their hearts beating.

"Where is he?" Leahcim asked.

Cora gave him the coordinates and he guided the ship to where Ramie floated in space. The irregular signal began pinging with a steady pattern.

"There," Lin said. She pointed to a small object drifting in a clearing.

"Looks like he borrowed a page from your book, Cora," Markka said. "But instead of faking it, he actually did it."

"It would appear so," Cora said.

Always cautious, T'oann asked, "How can we be sure it is he?"

"Because my children and I share a common bond and a rather unique communication system that only we know. I assure you it is not a trick."

T'oann was not finished with her caution warnings. "No offense intended, Cora, but I suggest we scan the area to ensure we and he are actually alone before we attempt a rescue."

"No offense taken, Commander. Your suggestion is sage. I do not know why I did not think of that."

"Perhaps it is because you have other things on your mind."

"Perhaps."

"As far as I can tell," Lin said, "we're the only ones around. I would say it's safe for the moment. If there is another cloaked ship around, I'm sure we'll find out soon enough if it's friend or foe."

Leahcim wished they had a tractor beam. Despite the best reverse engineering, something like a tractor beam was a bit too sophisticated. In the absence of one, he did the next best thing. He took a deep breath and told Markka to head over to the grappler arm. "You have the best hand-eye coordination, uh, make that paw-eye coordination, than any of us. Cora's trusting you to bring her son in safely."

"Talk about no pressure," she muttered.

Markka activated the mechanical grappler. Its arm stretched out to within centimeters of the object. "Hold her steady," she said.

Leahcim handled the controls like a skilled heavy equipment operator.

Markka squinted through the ship's window as she brought the arm closer to the tiny piece of fuselage. "Steady. Steady. Almost there."

The grappler's pincers opened and surrounded the alloy fragment housing the flight recorder. Markka carefully closed the pincers around the object and tucked it neatly in the cargo bay.

Markka let out a long breath. "There," she said, "Ramie has been secured."

Lin and Piper headed to the cargo bay to see what they could do to help Ramie.

Cora expressed her gratitude to Markka. "Thank you. My son and I are forever indebted to you. We are indebted to you all."

"Cora, it's us who are indebted to you," Markka said. "Beginning with me and David. We owe our lives to you. That's a debt we will continue to pay down for the rest of our lives."

T'oann felt compelled to let Cora know how she and Tory felt. "I know we did not begin our relationship on the best of terms, but over the cycles, you have proven yourself worthy of our respect and gratitude countless times. It is we who are indebted to you."

After a silent moment, Cora said she appreciated their sentiments.

"Great," Markka said. "Now that we got the weepy stuff out the way, let's say we find out if Ramie is okay, learn what he knows, and get the hell out of here. Not necessarily in that order."

Lin returned from the cargo bay and voiced her agreement with Markka. "Piper is checking out Ramie's vitals and attempting to integrate him with the ship's systems. Cora, you'll be able to reunite with your son in a few. In the meantime, do you think you can help us find our way back to our universe?"

"Certainly, Lady Lin. I traced our route to this point. I am confident I can take us back the same way."

"Breadcrumbs," Leahcim said. "I like it. Show us the way home."

Cora transferred the data to Leahcim's station, and he gingerly followed the path she laid out. After a few tense moments, the debris field was gone.

Lin announced, "We're clear. We're back home."

Cora and Leahcim confirmed Lin's announcement.

There was a collective sigh of relief before Piper walked in from the cargo hold and told Cora she could speak with Ramie whenever she wanted.

"Thank you Lord Piper. I shall attend to him now."

"Wait!" Leahcim said. "Can you verify if we're when we're supposed to be?"

"As there are no time transmitters to access, I can only make an approximate estimation based on shifts in star patterns."

"Okay, what's your best guess?"

"We have arrived back a couple of mos after our initial departure."

"That's good enough for me," Markka said. "Now, how about we skiddaddle home and sort this crap out?"

"You got it, Leahcim said." He set a course back to Progensha and punched it.

Chapter 23

Once Vee made it back to the *Infiltrator,* she told Sparks to, "Get us the hell off this boat."

When they were in space, she ordered her crew to battle stations. While the rest of them performed their duties with tense determination, Raqmar whooped with joy and enthusiasm.

"Now this is more like it," he said. "This is a hell of a lot better than sneaking around."

Every ship in the task force was busy either defending itself or a vessel nearby.

The enemy fighters swarmed the incoming Alliance ships. The Alliance launched theirs. The space around them was ablaze with a light show so brilliant that observers on nearby worlds more than likely saw the display with the aid of their weakest telescopes.

Between Sparks and Sojourner, Vee knew the *Infiltrator* was in capable hands. They did an exemplary job of avoiding salvos that should have crippled them. The ship shook and shuddered each time it was hit by enemy fire, but the shields held.

Karona and Raqmar monitored communications and ship systems, which included firing control. He was no Markka or Lin, but Raqmar was quite efficient with weapons.

Since the crew was preoccupied with staying in the fight and staying alive, Ramie did his part to ensure things stayed that way.

He kept an eye on things the others could not because their attention was needed elsewhere. He helped Sparks and Sojourner by relaying real-time battle updates and assisted with monitoring communications. He also rerouted critical ship's systems if something failed.

"We just lost AG," Raqmar said.

"Compensating," Ramie said. He restored the artificial gravity processor.

Fortunately, they were all wearing their seatbelts.

Vee felt sorry for Ramie because she thought he should have had more time to acclimate to her universe and decide for himself if his decision to join her crew was the correct one.

A dozen enemy fighters and one of their capital ships, a frigate, targeted the medical cruiser *Mary Eliza Mahoney*.

Karona did her best to keep control of her emotions, but failed when she shouted, "The *Mahoney* is in trouble, cap."

Unable to use her ship's cloak in combat, Vee ordered Raqmar to pick off as many of the fighters he could. His best effort was not enough.

"Guns," was all Vee said.

Karona acknowledged the command. "Aye, cap." She reprogrammed her station to give her control of a second set of guns Raqmar was not currently using. Together, they laid down a volley of suppressing fire that tied up the attacking fighters.

Sojourner determined the frigate's shields were weakest on its underside.

Vee saw their chance to save the *Mahoney*. "Blow a hole in that thing's keel," Vee ordered.

Sparks maneuvered beneath the GSE ship and slowed enough to give Karona and Raqmar enough time to fire on the ship's outer skin in an attempt to punch a hole through the failing shields.

When the Sairidians realized what Vee's strategy was, more fighters converged on the *Infiltrator* to defend the frigate.

Sojourner and Ramie redirected power from the tertiary systems to provide more power to the *Infiltrator's* shields to protect the ship from a series of punishing blows.

"Our shields are down to sixty percent," Sojourner said.

"Copy that," Vee said. "Break off."

"Aye, cap," Sparks said. The disappointment in her tone was unmistakable.

Just as Sparks was about to peel away from the frigate in a forced retreat, Sojourner reported the shielding on its underside was at zero percent.

"Open her up," Vee ordered.

"Our pleasure, cap," Raqmar said.

Together with Karona, they let loose with a barrage of energy bolts.

The gamble paid off. Explosions began to cascade through the enemy ship.

"Now let's get the hell out of here," Vee ordered.

Sparks punched the accelerator just before one final explosion disintegrated the frigate, taking a few fighters along with it.

Another one down, Vee thought. She wondered if any of them would live through this hell they were in the middle of. Her plan to take Ramie home and destroy the portal was now in question. But with all things considered, Vee believed they had the upper hand.

According to the intel Karona gathered, the GSE force planned to attack Epsilon Base then jump out before reinforcements arrived. They did not know that Vee's crew had deciphered their communications and passed along that information to Chappie. That bit of knowledge persuaded him to order the fleet to abandon the recovery effort and head straight to Epsilon Base. It was blind luck that Chappie chose to head for Epsilon Base when he did. The decision caught the GSE off guard. They had not intended on still being in the vicinity when Alliance reinforcements arrived.

The only thing Vee could think of was a few GSE forces were left behind to mop up then rejoin their comrades. Vee privately thanked her gods for small favors while giving orders to her crew.

While Sparks pitched and rolled the ship, Raqmar bitched and moaned. They were both in their elements and zoned in.

"Captain," Sojourner said.

"Yes?"

"The remaining enemy vessels are targeting the *Vindicator*, sir."

In his own unique way, Raqmar corroborated what Sojourner reported. "Those fuckers are pounding the hell out of her, cap. She won't last if we don't do something."

Various scenarios raced through Vee's mind as her ship was rocked by the energy blasts of a few fighters, apparently assigned to divert attention away from defending the dreadnought.

Despite being belted in, the blasts from the fighters were enough to test the tensile strength of the belts. The last volley was enough to give them whiplash.

The emergency lights flicked on as light gray smoke filled the bridge. The air handlers kicked in and vented the smoke off the bridge.

Vee coughed out the smoke she inhaled and asked, "Damage?" Her eyes watered and burned from the smoke that lingered in the air. She wheezed as she breathed.

"Minimal," Sojourner replied.

"The *Vindicator*?"

"Her shields are significantly diminished to forty percent."

"Get me their captain. Do your encryption magic. Don't tip off the cold bloods. Make it staticky or something."

Karona replied, "Gotcha, cap." A breath later, she said, "You're on, cap."

"Tranyxx, can you hear me?"

"What's on your mind Vee. We're a bit occupied right now."

"Got a plan."

"I'm listening."

"Engage their fighters. We'll do the rest."

In the time it took her to blink once, she heard him say, "Do it."

A moment later the *Vindicator's* gunners blasted away at the fighters.

"Patch me through to the fleet," Vee ordered.

Karona's fingers danced along her console before she said, "You're up, cap."

"This is Captain Vee of the *Infiltrator*. All ships follow our lead."

"What's the plan, cap?" Raqmar asked.

"Take out their fighters with everything we've got. Reduce their defensive shield. I've got a hunch they'll retreat when their capital ships lose their cover. Let's go earn our pay."

Chapter 24

As the *Zuri* approached Progensha, everyone had doubts about when they were in time, despite Cora's assurance. There was a heightened sense of apprehension. What if they were in the wrong time? Then what? There was a collective sigh of relief when B'rtann, Supreme Commander of the Progenshan military, and Sho'khan, Chief Tactical Officer, welcomed them back.

"Welcome back everyone," Sho'khan said. "I hope you had a productive trip."

"Productive doesn't even begin to describe what we had," Markka whispered to Tory.

"Thank you. It's good to be back," Leahcim said. *You have no idea*, he thought. He could only imagine what her reaction would be when she was briefed.

Leahcim landed the ship and everyone disembarked and headed immediately to the conference room. Sho'khan's reaction at the briefing was exactly what he imagined it would be.

"What do you mean there's another portal?" Sho'khan asked. The alarm and irritation in her voice was palpable. "Are we in any danger?"

"Hard to say," Markka said.

"If what you say is true, how do we defend against a GSE invasion? If the Alliance is incapable of containing them, how are we supposed to stand against them? Compared to them, we have antiquated, reverse-engineered equipment. Our forces would be as effective a deterrent as a mirage."

"I wouldn't go so far as to say we'd be that ineffective," Markka protested. "But you wouldn't be wrong if you said we had as much of a chance as a snowball in the underworld."

"Snowball. Mirage. Semantics. It does not alter the fact that the GSE could find that portal, if they do not already know about it, pour through it and end everything we have fought long and hard for." Sho'khan was livid.

"If we are as helpless as you seem to imply, then what do you suggest we do about it?" T'oann asked.

"We double our efforts to build ships, train fighters, and work to quickly improve our technology."

"We are but one lowly world. The Alliance is an organization of hundreds of worlds. How do you propose we do what they cannot?"

It was apparent by Sho'khan's stuttering that she was flustered and stymied by T'oann's question. She slammed her fist on the conference table and said, "I do not know, but I believe what I propose is better than doing nothing."

"I am *not* suggesting we do nothing," T'oann shot back. "Our people have faced impossible odds and have prevailed. We shall again. We are not domestic animals grazing in the food fields. We are resourceful people capable of great potential. We *will* find a way." The frustration in her tone was evident. She was about to lose control of her emotional calm when she felt Leahcim enter her mind.

"Whoa. Easy. Remember what Garath said about your blood pressure. The nanites can only do so much. Some things are beyond even their ability to repair."

She took a deep breath, calmed herself and said, "Thank you, husband."

"You're welcome. Now, I suggest we continue, but with a much cooler head this time."

"What do you suggest?"

"We hear from the one person who knows the situation best."

"Very well." She ended the mind-walk with her husband, took another deep breath, and said, "This bickering is not getting us any closer to a solution. I suggest we hear what Ramie has to say."

Chapter 25

Space was lit up like a laser light show with accompanying fireworks as the task force concentrated its firepower on the GSE fighters. The token resistance was no match against the Alliance onslaught. The *Infiltrator* turned its attention to the largest remaining GSE ship, a dreadnaught like the *Vindicator*, and so did the rest of the fleet.

"There are catastrophic failures registering all over the ship," Karona said.

"Get us the hell away from it," Vee ordered.

"Way ahead of you, cap," Sparks said. She quickly swung the ship around and headed away from the doomed vessel. The rest of the fleet did the same.

"We're still too close," Karona said. "If they try to jump, they'll take out eve—"

She never got to finish her sentence. A flash brighter than any sun lit up the sky and flooded the *Infiltrator's* cabin. The optical shielding automatically activated, saving the crew from optic nerve damage.

"Everyone okay?" Vee asked.

They all responded they were.

Once their vision returned to normal, time itself seemed to stand still as they searched for the dreadnought. Nearly everything within the vicinity of the blast radius was destroyed. The remaining GSE ships used the lull in combat to jump into hyperspace.

"The *Vindicator*. Is she . . . ?" Vee's voice trailed off. She was an emotional wreck. The thought of losing so many good people played in her mind. Losing Chappie and Tranyxx was too much to bear. It was painful to think about it.

Vee did not need to finish asking her question. Sojourner knew what she was going to ask. "Yes, Captain," Sojourner said. "She is still with us."

Overwhelmed with satisfaction and relief, Vee ordered Karona to patch her through to Captain Tranyxx or Commander Chappie.

"I've got Commander Chappie, cap," Karona said. "Audio only."

"What's your status, Commander? Can we lend assistance?"

Chappie's voice was strong despite a weak connection and lots of cluttered background sounds.

"I guess I owe you one," he said.

"We got lucky. Casualties?"

"Many. Radiation exposure. Mostly near the outer hull."

"The ship?"

"Mostly intact. She's a tough old bird. Reminds me of someone I know."

She heard the humor in his voice and knew it was a veiled dig at her.

"What's the next step, Commander?"

"We regroup, then wait for help to arrive or our guests to return. Our backup is five minutes out."

"That's going to be a long five minutes."

"Tell me about it. Vee, I want you and your crew to sit tight. Make whatever repairs you need. Make peace with whatever deity you pray to. I have a plan you're not going to like. I'll be in touch."

The communication link was terminated. Vee and her crew sat looking at each other wondering what the commander had planned for them.

"Sounds dangerous," Sparks said. Her voice was dripping with sarcasm.

"Make peace with our deities?" Karona asked. "I got a bad feeling about this."

Raqmar was the only one who did not appear disturbed by what Chappie said. He actually sounded energized. "Better than sitting around twirling our thumbs," he said.

"That's twiddling our thumbs," Karona said.

"Whatever."

Vee kept her feelings and her opinion to herself, but she was worried that she and her crew were about to be offered up as sacrificial ugots.

So that no one had time to dwell on what Chappie said, she ordered everyone to busy themselves with repairing damage.

The relief ships arrived and assisted with defense and cleanup and recovery. Among their group was the supercarrier *Alasta*. On board was Fleet Admiral K'mar. She was of Terran and Selemite heritage, but she looked more Selemite than Terran.

She had a reputation for being hard-assed. The enlisted personnel called her "The Soulless Bitch." Unknown to most of them, she enjoyed the moniker, but not the responsibility that accompanied it. But it made it easier for her to hide her soft side. She was the one everyone turned to when the tough decisions had to be made. Decisions that cost many soldiers their lives.

Every lost life cut deep into her soul like a specter that hung around her like an unwanted guest. What happened at Epsilon Base was emotionally disturbing, but she refused to let it distract her from doing what had to be done in the face of war.

She paced back and forth in the *Vindicator*'s situation room and talked with Tranyxx, Chappie, and Reth. Her hair, tied back into a long ponytail, whipped back and forth with each turn of her head.

"I got here as fast as I could, but from the looks of things it wasn't fast enough," she said. She cast a quick glance out the window at the devastation outside and shuddered. "What the hell happened?"

"What happened," Tranyxx said, "is we got a swift kick in our complacency. What we can do now that you're here is ask you to weigh in on our plan," Tranyxx said.

"And what plan is that?"

Tranyxx gave Chappie a nod. The commander told her everything he thought she needed to know about what Vee and her crew experienced.

"So you're saying Vee and her people traveled to another universe, encountered the *Michael Anderson*, went back in time, cracked the Sairidian code, passed this intel on to you, then saved your asses in the fight none of us saw coming?"

"In a nutshell," Chappie said. What he neglected to tell her was that Leachim, Markka, and Cora were alive, and where Vee and her crew spent their time in the past. Vee made him promise to keep her sister's operation a secret.

"Who else knows about this?"

"Surviving bridge crew and Doctor Sanchez."

K'mar continued to pace before she asked, "You know what you're proposing is a suicide mission?"

"Yes."

K'mar finally sat down and stared out the window with a pained expression before she said, "Tell Vee to get her ass over here."

"Yes, sir."

Chapter 26

When Vee returned to the *Infiltrator* following her meeting with the admiral, she stepped onto the bridge without saying a word and walked over to her chair. She hesitated, lost in thought, then sat down and activated some controls on a panel in the arm of the chair. Sparks could feel her captain's distress.

"What's up, cap? You don't look so good," Sparks said.

Vee continued to tap on her control panel before responding to Spark's question.

"I'm not." Vee took a deep breath and loudly exhaled before she said another word. "We got new orders straight from the admiral herself. We're to follow the GSE back to wherever they went, gather whatever intel we can, then report back ASAP."

"Geez, we're back to peeping and hiding?" Raqmar asked. He made no effort to hide the irritation in his voice.

"So who's backing us up?" Sparks asked.

"Nobody."

"Why us?"

"We're the unlucky bastards who were first to get the goods on the enemy."

True to his nature, Raqmar blurted, "You know this ain't nothing but a fucking suicide mission."

Karona, tired of his insubordinate attitude, spoke her mind.

"What the hell, Raq? Show some respect, dammit. When are you going to learn to zip it?"

"It's alright," Vee said. "Right now, I feel the same way."

"So when do we ship out?" Sparks asked.

"Now. They have a head start on us so I'm gonna need for you to trace any and all exhaust, distortion, and displacement fields and follow the bastards to wherever they went."

"What if that trail leads us to the Sairidian homeworld?" Sojourner asked.

132

"Then we better make damn sure they don't figure out we're there." She looked around at the carnage floating around them then asked Karona if she detected any cloaked ships lurking around.

"None that I can detect, cap."

"Sojourner, what do you see?"

"I concur with Lieutenant Karona. I do not detect any anomalous readings."

"Good. Raq."

"Yes, cap?"

"I'm holding you responsible if our cloak fails at the wrong time. Got that?"

"Loud and clear, cap."

"Sparks, do what you can to reduce our displacement signature."

"Aye, cap."

"Kay."

"Yes, cap."

"Monitor and record everything."

"Aye, cap."

"Sojourner and Ramie, assist where needed."

They both responded, "Yes, sir," in unison.

"Everybody ready?" Vee asked.

When they all acknowledged they were, Vee told Sparks, "Hit it."

Sparks activated the cloak, engaged the hyperspace engines, and sped off into the void.

The trajectory of the GSE ships led to the Naphtali star system. A sparsely populated sector on the edge of the frontier. While Sparks tracked the trails of the retreating GSE ships, Karona and Sojourner scanned everything outside of the ship's hyperspace bubble. They were leaving nothing up to chance. Six hours into the pursuit the displacement signatures they were tracking disappeared.

Vee ordered Sparks to jump into normal space and come to a full stop. She hoped they were small enough, far enough away, and their cloak was undetectable.

"Talk to me. What do you see?"

"Nothing."

"What do you mean, 'nothing?'"

"There's nothing here, cap," Karona said, "The clusters are gone."

"What do you mean gone?"

Karona scanned her console and adjusted settings before looking at her captain with a pained and puzzled expression. "I'm sorry, cap. I lost them."

Before Vee could question Karona again, she was drawn to a comment Sojourner made.

"This is very peculiar, Captain," Sojourner said.

"What is?"

"The clusters we detected in hyperspace are no longer on any of our scopes."

"How is that possible? Raq, check the equipment. What's broken?"

"Nothing, cap. Everything is working at optimal levels."

"Then why can't we see them? Are they cloaked?"

"With as many clusters as we saw? No way, cap." Sparks said.

"Talk to me, people. What the hell is going on?"

After what felt like an excruciatingly long time Sojourner said she had what she thought was a plausible hypothesis.

"If I may, Captain, I need Lieutenant Sparks to maneuver us to the following coordinates." She transferred the numbers to Sparks' console then displayed them on a holo in the center of the bridge.

Vee studied the data and discarded decorum. "You gotta be fucking kidding. Is that what it looks like it is?"

Sojourner replied in the same manner as her captain. "I am not fucking kidding, sir. It appears to be what it looks like."

"Sparks, park us next to that thing."

"Aye, cap."

Sparks moved the ship to the coordinates Sojourner plotted and rotated the *Infiltrator*. It gave them a silhouetted cross sectioned view. Then they sat and watched what they thought they would never see again.

"I don't believe it," Vee said. "There's more than one."

They all observed what looked like particulate matter passing through an invisible barrier. The last time everyone but Karona and Ramie saw this phenomenon was in the Gihon Nebula just before they found Leahcim, Markka, and Cora.

"Holy shit," Sparks said. "It's another portal."

Chapter 27

"Your assessment is correct, Lieutenant," Sojourner said. "We are looking at another portal similar to the one in the Gihon Nebula."

"But its existence doesn't explain how the clusters vanished." Sparks was searching for a reason for the discrepancy when an idea struck her. An instant later, the reason why dawned on her. She arrived at the realization nearly the same time as the others. "We can't see the clusters anymore because they all passed through the portal just as we jumped out of hyperspace. The GSE are invaders from another universe."

"Precisely."

"So does that mean their universe is ahead of ours?"

There was a nearly imperceptible pause before Sojourner answered the question. "Unknown at this juncture."

Not this crap again, Vee thought. "Sojourner, Ramie, are there active tachyons, neutrinos, time particles, or whatever the hell they are indicating time displacement?" Understanding quantum time was not one of her strengths.

"Nothing we are as of yet able to determine, Captain," Sojourner said. "This particular portal appears to be simply nothing more than a doorway from one universe to another."

Why do we always have to be the first ones to discover this shit? she wondered. "Looks like there's only one way to know for sure. We go through and check things out." Vee was beginning to detest unknowns and exposing herself and her people to them.

"Yeah," Raqmar said. The sarcasm in his voice was unmistakable. "Can't take the chance of having the Alliance sending an invasion fleet of its own. That would be just wrong."

"Raq, you idiot," Karona said as she rolled her eyes. "If they did, they'd be cut down in an instant. The problem is if the GSE has been using this thing as a gateway into our universe, they'll be guarding it with a lot of firepower."

"But there's nothing stopping us from deploying our own ships on this side and greeting them with a welcoming committee of our own," Vee said.

"Now you're talking," Raqmar said. "It would catch those fuckers by surprise."

"Yeah, but that's the only surprise we'll ever get, Karona said. The next time, they might come through using that cloaked base. You can't fight what you can't see."

"Dammit, Kay. Why're you always busting my bubble?"

Karona was not finished. She glared at Raqmar until he shrank back from her to the point where he avoided her piercing gaze. Other than Vee and Lin, Karona was the only other person he was actually afraid of. It also helped that they were lovers. Karona used that to her advantage. "You want to know what else?"

"No, but I'm sure you're gonna tell me."

"We can't warn anybody because if we do, the bastards will defend both sides of the damn portal."

"I'm surprised they haven't already," Sparks said."

"They don't want to tip their hand. The Alliance doesn't know about the portal. Why draw our attention with a military force patrolling what looks like the middle of nowhere?"

"The lieutenant is correct," Sojourner said. "We will not know what dangers await us until we learn more."

Why the hell couldn't this have been easier? Vee wondered. *We can't catch a break.* "Then we have no other choice but to go in there and find out," Vee said. "We've been ordered to gather what we can find and report back what we know. And there's only one way to know. Sparks, take us through."

***

"So then what happened?" Markka asked. She was comfortably slouched in her chair trying to absorb everything Ramie said.

"It was fortuitous that our presence in GSE space was not detected. There was no armada defending the portal. In fact, there was no portal defense."

"Presumably due to their belief that the Alliance posed, uh, poses no threat to their secret," Tory suggested.

Ramie agreed.

"Yes, Your Majesty. Presumably. The captain did not wish to get us involved in any entanglements with GSE forces. So she ordered Lieutenant Sparks to loiter near the portal but avoid any direct travel routes. Her intention was to slip in, surreptitiously gather data, then slip out undetected."

"So?" Markka asked. Then sat straight up and said, "Wait. Don't answer that yet. She looked around the table and asked, "Is anybody hungry? I'm hungry."

They all looked at each other. No one wanted to be first to say they were. Piper finally spoke up and said, "I am."

With the ice now broken, everyone else said they could grab a bite to eat. So Markka contacted her dining staff and ordered a smorgasbord of goodies.

"I think we should also take a nature break. I really need to go."

Leahcim and T'oann both looked at her in surprise.

Markka saw their surprised looks and asked, "What?"

"Uh, TMI," Leahcim said.

"There you go again with those prudish Terran sensibilities."

"My dear wife," Tory said, "David is correct."

"Oh what do you know? You got a stick up your butt."

T'oann repeated Leahcim's caution of too much information.

"Bite me."

Those who had to, or chose to, followed Markka's lead. When the food arrived, they purposely avoided talking business. There would be plenty of time to resume listening to Ramie later.

Markka also felt Cora deserved some time alone with her son.

When everyone had their fill of food, Markka asked Ramie to continue with his report when he was ready.

He picked up where he left off, and Markka resumed hanging on to every word.

"We were conducting long-range scans when we detected unusual electromagnetic signals emanating from a planet within close proximity to the portal. They appeared to be low-level impulses directed toward us. We thought we were about to be under attack, but Sojourner said they were too weak to be of any consequence, but insisted we investigate them as part of our mandate."

Leahcim stroked his chin in thought then said, "Hmm. Sort of like Progensha. There's us then there's the portal."

"But that is where the similarities diverge, Commander," Cora said.

"How so?"

"We have never detected transmissions of any kind currently directed toward the portal." Cora said. "We have been through the records obtained from the *Michael P Anderson* and all of the data amassed before The Great War and after. There is no mention of signals emanating from this planet.

"Maybe there were some at one point in the planet's history, but they stopped transmitting long before the Progenshans developed technology," Markka said.

"Possibly," Cora said. "But unless we discover something more concrete, all we have is unsubstantiated conjecture."

"Then we're just gonna have to get something more substantial," Markka said. "In the meantime, I want to hear more of what Ramie's got to say." She waved a paw in the air toward the center of the conference table as if Ramie were sitting across from her and said, "continue with your report. We wish to hear more."

"We approached the planet and scanned it for evidence of advanced biologics and mechanoids. We found none. So Captain Vee made the call to land the *Infiltrator* near the source of the signals."

***

"Well, Kay, anything?" Vee asked.

"Still nothing. The clusters have broken up, but they're a full star system away."

"I can confirm that, Captain." Sojourner said.

"What about the planet?"

"I am detecting what appear to be lower life forms, but no evidence of Sairidian or other higher level reptilian biological signs. There is no evidence of civilization of any kind. The planet is an inhospitable rock with a thick water vapor atmosphere that is barely breathable. It is remarkable that anything higher than microbial life survives there."

"What about the signals? Can you tell what's generating them?"

"I am sorry, Captain, I am not able to pinpoint their source."

Vee weighed their options for a few long moments before she decided. "Take us down, Sparks."

Chapter 28

The *Infiltrator* slipped through the thick clouds that covered an excessively humid atmosphere. They skimmed the ground and followed a series of fluctuating signals coming from deep beneath the rocky surface.

There were no trees or foliage of any kind anywhere. What little water there was existed solely in the atmosphere as thick humidity. Sojourner surmised the few life forms they were able to detect may have evolved from organisms that learned to absorb the moisture in the air through osmosis.

"I'm detecting a series of tunnels and caverns where the signals are coming from, cap," Karona said. "They appear to run deep underground."

"Are they natural or do they appear to be artificial?" Vee asked.

"Natural."

"Any signs of advanced biological life signs within the tunnels?"

"None, cap."

"Captain," Sojourner began, "the caverns are large enough to accommodate a ship the size of ours. I suggest we use this to our advantage. We could enter them, rather than sending a team on foot, further ensuring we remain invisible to Sairidian patrols."

"Good idea."

"Cap, with all due respect to Sojourner, I would caution against doing that." Karona had a pained expression on her face.

"Why, Kay?"

"There might be creatures inside those caverns that could see this ship as a food source. If we're ingested, we might not be able to escape."

"Duly noted, Lieutenant."

Sojourner insisted the benefits outweighed the danger.

"I highly suggest we proceed, Captain. As long as our cloak is engaged, we will be undetectable."

Karona was determined to persuade Vee to consider her caution over Sojourner's recommendation.

"We're in another universe. What if the laws of physics are different here? What if there are creatures that seek out energy signatures like ours and feed on them?"

Vee sat for a moment or two before she decided on a course of action.

"We're here to snoop on the GSE and learn what we can. I believe our mandate is best served by keeping a low profile. Your concern is duly noted, Lieutenant, but I'm going to take Sojourner's recommendation. If it turns out you're right, I'll make sure to note that in my final report."

Karona swallowed hard, then made one more suggestion.

"Will you at least consider using only the ship's sensors and not the forward lights to navigate through the tunnels, sir?"

Sir? Vee thought. Something is definitely bothering her.

"Okay, Lieutenant. We won't turn on the lights." She turned to her navigator. "You got that, Sparks? Don't turn on the lights. In fact, turn off our running lights and engage window shades."

"Aye, cap." Sparks clicked a couple of buttons. "Running lights off, shades engaged. We are now dark."

"Good."

Turning off the running lights made no difference since the ship was cloaked, but if it put Karona's mind at ease, she did not mind doing it. Vee sensed Karona was wound tighter than a spring. She watched her officer's body visibly relax and the strained expression on the young woman's face melt away. When Karona remained quiet, Vee ordered Sparks to follow the signals through the tunnels to the source or as far as the tunnels would accommodate the ship.

"Aye, cap."

Vee got up from her chair and walked straight to the conference room. In as even a tone as she could get said, "Lieutenant Karona, follow me."

Karona acknowledged her captain and followed Vee into the conference room. She stood at attention as the room door closed behind her.

Vee took a seat at the far end of the table and gestured for Karona to take the seat at the other end.

"At ease, Lieutenant. Please, take a seat."

After letting a few moments of silence pass between them, Vee leaned back in her seat, folded her hands in her lap and calmly asked, "What's got you so wound up, Kay? I've never seen you like this before."

Karona tried to hold Vee's gaze, but looked away, unable to look her captain in the eyes. "I'm sorry, cap. I, uh, have a thing about caves."

"Because they're dark and scary?"

"No. Yes. Uh . . . because I almost died in one once."

"Go on."

"No one knows about this. Not even Raqmar."

"Your secret is safe with me."

Karona heaved a heavy sigh and looked at Vee.

"When I was a child, my brother and I went to the marsh pit caves in the hills by our home against our parents' wishes. We were curious and thought they were just trying to scare us with stories of creatures that lived in the caves that would eat people. So we and a group of other children snuck away to explore the caves."

She heaved another sigh and began sniffling as her nose began to run. She tilted her head down to avoid looking at Vee and wiped her eyes.

"We climbed over a couple of security fences and headed into the caves. We didn't get far before we ran into trouble. The marsh rats that live in the caves came after us. They're about two meters long and a meter high. They came from out of the darkness. We ran as fast as we could, but it wasn't fast enough."

Karona was so focused on the retelling of the events from that day she never noticed Vee get up and walk over to her. She felt a hand gently touch her shoulder. She shivered and flinched.

"Kay, you don't have to finish if you don't want to."

"I have to," she sobbed openly now. "I've never talked about it with anyone until now. I was so traumatized that I didn't speak to anyone for months after my physical wounds healed. My parents institutionalized me."

"What happened to your brother, the other children?"

"They say I was the only one to survive. The last thing I remember was the pain of being bitten . . . of being eaten alive."

"I'm sorry for your loss."

Karona sniffed again before she said, "Thank you, Captain. I'm sorry for letting my fear of caves interfere with your command."

Vee chuckled. "Believe me when I say if you were interfering, I would let you know about it in no uncertain terms."

That got a weak smile from Karona.

"I like to hear what my officers have to say instead of staying quiet. If what you have to say might mean the difference between life and death, by all means, say it."

"Understood, Captain."

"Good. You're dismissed."

As Karona got up to leave, Vee said, "And one more thing."

"Yes, sir?"

"You can call me cap."

A full smile returned to Karona's face. As she turned to leave the room, Sparks' voice came over the address system.

"Cap, you might want to take a look out your window."

Vee turned and looked then asked, "What the hell am I looking at?"

Chapter 29

"Talk to me, people," Vee said.

"It looks like we stumbled upon the find of a lifetime, cap," Sparks said.

From where Vee stood, she saw the cavern walls coalesce into one massive computer. At least it looked like one. She was impressed with the technology required to camouflage something so large. The *Infiltrator* looked like a fly by comparison. She figured they could be swatted like one as well.

"Are we in danger?"

"Based on the fact that we are still alive, I would surmise we are not at present," Sojourner said.

"But that could change at any time?"

"Affirmative."

Karona, who was now back sitting at her station, confirmed Sojourner's statement. "I agree, cap. Based on the readings and configurations this thing could have taken us out the moment we got close enough to be seen as a threat."

"Guess it doesn't see us as a threat yet," Vee said.

Raqmar, more curious about what happened in the conference room than about the potentially dangerous situation now facing them, asked Karona in a whisper, "Did the captain dress you down in there?"

Karona, surprised that he would ask her that question now, hesitated before she said, "No. I'm not you."

Vee overheard the exchange and smiled. *Nope, she's definitely not him*, she thought. Then on a more serious note asked, "What are our chances of making a quick getaway if we had to?"

"Slim to none, cap," Sparks said. "The helm is unresponsive."

"Weapons?"

"Useless," Raqmar said. His attention was refocused on their current situation. It was obvious by the tone in his voice he was agitated.

"Communications?"

"Jammed, cap," Karona said.

"Is anything working?"

Karona and Raqmar scanned their stations and consulted with each other before Karona replied, "Life support only, cap."

"Sojourner? Ramie?"

"Confirmed, Captain," they said simultaneously.

"We have been enveloped by an energy field and are being pulled," Sojourner said.

"To where?"

"There appears to be some type of landing pad over there, cap," Sparks said. She pointed toward the cockpit window at what looked like a circular landing pad ringed by blinking lights.

The ship was gently pulled down to the pad and lightly touched down.

"The cavern is filling up with breathable air, cap," Karona said.

"It looks like our host has extended an invitation. I think it would be impolite to refuse." *Probably also fatal*, she thought.

While Vee mulled over her limited options, a voice, or what sounded like a chorus of masculine and feminine voices, spoke to them.

"Welcome."

"Whoa," Sparks said. "That was unexpected."

Vee cleared her throat and prayed she would not say anything that would get them all killed.

"Greetings. I am Captain Vee of the Alliance ship *Infiltrator*. My crew and I are visitors from another universe. We mean you no harm."

"We know who you are, Captain, and why you are here. We apologize for the unorthodox method we employed to invite you here, but we could not conceive of any other way which would not precipitate a misunderstanding. *We* mean you and your crew no harm. You may refer to us as the Others. When we detected your vessel passing through the ring, we sought to get your attention without drawing attention to ourselves. There is a matter of great urgency we wish to discuss."

"Ring?"

"You refer to it as the portal."

"Oh. Okay, you have our attention. What is it you wish to discuss?"

"We are prepared to discuss matters on board your vessel—if that makes you feel more comfortable."

What could be more comfortable than sitting down with a collective consciousness with the power to destroy my ship and kill my crew with a thought? she wondered. *Should I take them at their word?*

Vee decided her doubts were moot. Whatever or whoever had her ship could have destroyed it long before now.

"We accept."

"Very well. Please notify us when you are ready to receive our emissary."

"Do you think this is a good idea, cap?" Sparks asked.

"Do you have a better one?"

After a moment's pause, Sparks said, "No."

"Anybody else?"

No one spoke. Not even Sojourner or Ramie.

"Okay, that settles it. We'll have our little meet and greet in the conference room. I want everyone there. That goes for you and Ramie, Sojourner."

"Aye, Captain," was their simultaneous response.

***

"Wait, you're saying you found the source of the transmissions and that source was a large cavern filled with some kind of advanced supercomputer?" Markka asked.

"Affirmative," Ramie said.

Chapter 30

Thirty minutes after notifying what she referred to as their hosts, despite feeling more like a captive than a guest. Vee and her crew shared the conference room with an individual whose taupe-colored skin glowed like dim moonlight on a cloudy night. Their physical characteristics looked mammalian, avian, and amphibian all merged into one being. They spoke in the collective voice she had gotten used to hearing.

"We hope you are not offended by our appearance. We chose one we thought would be pleasing to you all."

"No, we are not offended," Vee said. "However, we are curious about your intentions and why you have brought us here."

"We require your help."

"Our help? How could we be of help to you?"

"We wish to offer something that may be mutually beneficial. But the offer comes with great risk to you."

"In what way?"

"The offer comes with two choices. The first may result in your inevitable demise, the second will guarantee your immediate demise."

The scenario Vee envisioned did not include the choice of possibly dying versus definitely dying. "Excuse me? Our demise."

"Yes."

"Why would we agree to that?"

"Because should you choose to sacrifice yourselves, it will be the impetus needed to perhaps end the hostilities between your Alliance and this realm's aggressors; the ones who call themselves the Galactic Star Empire."

Raqmar was on his feet seconds before he blurted, "Who the hell do you think you are?"

His outburst drew an immediate reprimand from Vee.

"Lieutenant, stand down!"

But Raqmar plowed on like an out-of-control vehicle. "What kind of sorry-assed choice is that? You people must be out of your fucking minds if you think we're going to commit suicide for the likes of you!"

Vee shot out of her chair and moved like a blur with a fluid quickness that would have struck fear in the hearts of the members of the Assassins Guild. She stood centimeters from his face. The anger in her voice rivaled the fierce look on her face. If looks could kill, Raqmar would have dropped dead on the spot.

"Stand down! Now! Or I will put you down!"

"But, cap—"

In a deep, threatening undertone through clenched teeth Vee said, "You are confined to quarters. Dismissed!"

Raqmar hesitated and stood where he was. His reaction was more uncertain than defiant, but his emotional state bordered on belligerent. His complexion darkened to a slate gray. He glared at the emissary and made no effort to comply with Vee's order.

Before anyone had a chance to blink, Vee grabbed his arm and twisted it behind his back, dug her elbow into his spine, and mashed his face against the table. She pressed so hard that his face made a physical dent in the table. Had it not been for the toughness of his muscular and skeletal structure, having grown up on a planet with higher than normal gravity, Vee might have fractured his face.

"Get out of my conference room while you can still walk!"

She slowly released him.

His breathing was ragged and his pride was crushed, but he did not dare test her patience any further. Too embarrassed to do anything else, Raqmar turned and left the room. His departure was followed by a few moments of silence before Vee regained her composure.

"Sojourner."

"Yes, Captain?"

"If the lieutenant deviates from my orders, stun his ass."

"Aye, Captain."

Vee thought she heard delighted satisfaction creep into Sojourner's response. She turned and faced the emissary, who's expression and demeanor had not changed during the exchange.

"I apologize for my officer's behavior. I hope his words and actions have not jeopardized any chance of us reaching a mutual understanding."

"An apology is not necessary. His reaction was not unanticipated. Perhaps an explanation on our part is required."

Vee returned to her seat, folded her hands on the table and said, "Yes, an explanation is required."

"The device you call a portal is just one of a network of what we refer to as rings. They were constructed long ago by our builders. There are hundreds of them located throughout the cosmos."

"Why? What is their purpose?"

"Our builders discovered the existence of other realms. You call them universes. Their curiosity about them prompted a concerted effort on their part to discover and explore each realm. So they built a series of rings as doorways to these realms. For millennia the builders traveled freely through them. Unfortunately, one of the rings was located near a star that unpredictably exploded. The ring was irrevocably damaged. This resulted in a series of cascading malfunctions. Some of the ring's shut down and ceased working while others experienced time dilations. Many of the builders became trapped in the realms they visited."

Karona's interest was piqued, but after witnessing her captain's reaction to Raqmar decided to ask for permission to speak.

"May I ask a question, cap?"

Vee smirked at Karona and told her she could.

"If I understand you correctly, what you're saying is the portals were just doorways between universes and nothing more?"

"Correct. There were no time variations before the star explosion damaged the nearby ring. But subsequent to the star's destruction, some of the builders fortunate enough to return were aged and died shortly after. It was presumed they returned to this universe from some time in the distant future. Others never returned."

"They were too far into its past, maybe?"

"That is what our builders concluded."

"So you're saying that time passed equally for each universe before the explosion?" Vee asked.

"Yes."

"But the explosion caused the rings' properties to change, recalibrated them somehow and turned them into time portals," Karona concluded.

"Correct."

"So what happened to the builders who didn't get trapped in a different universe? Where did they go?"

"Those builders who remained in this realm worked to correct the damage done by the death of a single star, but a virus brought back from one of the realms infected our builders. They were not able to develop a cure in time so they entrusted monitoring the primary ring to us."

"You don't have the ability to make the corrections yourselves?" Karona asked.

"No. Unfortunately, they did not have time to ameliorate the malfunction and impart that knowledge to us. It was believed that those builders unaffected by the plague would be able to effect the necessary adjustments. But none of the builders were immune. They all succumbed to the illness."

"And those who did come through the portal became infected and died," Karona said.

"Correct. Our sphere of influence is limited to this dwarf planet. When the Sairidians discovered the ring, we were unable to stop them."

"Wait," Karona said. "The Sairidians have been passing through this ring regularly?"

"Yes. For approximately ten of your standard years."

"Then that would mean this ring is not affected by time dilations?"

"Correct."

"Why is that?"

"Unknown. We have extrapolated it may be due to the construction of this ring. It was the first and therefore it does not share the same properties as the others."

"It was the prototype?"

"Correct."

"So when we go back through—"

"You will have only been gone from your realm for however long you remain in this one."

"I guess we can thank the Gods that the Sairidians don't come from a future universe," Vee said. "That's why you asked for our help."

"Correct. We cannot destroy the ring network. When the war between your Alliance and the Sairidians began, we had hoped your Alliance would prevail. But like you, we underestimated their violent and tenacious nature."

"That we did," Vee sighed.

"Your entry into our realm was a fortuitous happenstance."

"So long story short, you need us to blow up the portal, Vee said."

"Correct."

"And in order to do that, you need a ship."

"Correct. The explosive energy from the destruction of your vessel should be enough to disable the network—if not destroy it. Or disassociate them from the chain."

"Damage one link and you damage the whole chain," Vee said.

"Correct. Theoretically."

Chapter 31

Ramie had his listeners hanging onto every word of his report. He knew what he told them sounded outlandish and implausible, but it was the truth. And he needed them to see it for what it was. A dangerous turn of events.

"So you're saying there are more of them?" Sho'khan asked. "Portals?"

"Yes."

"That sucks," Leahcim said. "You're saying the GSE didn't, uh, doesn't know about the sentient supercomputer on the dwarf planet? Or about the other portals?"

"Yes, Commander. The Sairidians are not particularly inclined to pursue science for the sake of science. Their entire society has developed around a cultural mores that embraces the technological sciences in a manner and mentality that specifically supports a military industrial complex with the singular goal of conquest, subjugation, or elimination. The entirety of the cosmos is fertile ground."

"That sure explains a lot," Markka said. "They no doubt would have seen a supercomputer as a potential threat and attempted to destroy it instead of attempting to use it to their advantage."

"Their discovery of the portal was merely an accident which led to an opportunity to invade and annex new territory."

"They already robbed, raped, and pillaged their own corner of the universe, so the portal presented them with an opportunity to do the same to ours," Markka said. She stopped speaking and cringed when she realized how what she said might sound to the others at the table. "Uh, I mean what used to be ours."

She looked at Tory and T'oann and apologized.

"There is no need for you to apologize. We knew what you meant and took no offense, my lovely puffball," Tory teased.

Markka checked her hair and realized it looked and felt normal.

"Jerk," she whispered.

He merely smiled.

"So what did you guys come to an agreement on?" Leahcim asked. "I'm sure Vee never agreed to blow up her own ship."

"She did, Commander."

"Wait. What? She agreed to blow it up? Her crew. What about her crew?"

"Evacuated safely."

"Vee?" There was fear in Leahcim's eyes as he braced himself for news he did not want to hear.

"Unknown. Presumed lost."

An uneasy quiet fell over the stunned group.

Then Cora asked a question no one else considered.

"You said the emissary said the explosive energy of the *Infiltrator* would be enough to disable the portal. It took the full energy of an exploding star to cause irreparable damage. The *Infiltrator* would not be able to produce energy of the magnitude necessary to do serious damage to the portal."

"You are correct, mother. That is why the Others constructed a device to interact with the *Infiltrator's* hyperspace engines. We needed to install it for Captain Vee's plan to work. It took a while for us to compensate for engineering and technological incompatibilities. Then we were tasked with installing the device, calibrating it, and running a simulation. We never got the chance to run the simulation before we engaged GSE forces."

"But that much explosive energy would decimate everything for kilometers," Lin said.

"We, or rather, the captain intended to place the *Infiltrator* within the portal's event horizon. The Others indicated most of the blast energy would be absorbed by the portal—sort of like an implosion—reducing the potential of catastrophic destruction on either side of it."

"Of course," Markka said, her voice dripping with sarcasm, "best to sacrifice someone else rather than themselves."

Compelled by the quiet, Ramie said, "When you consider the urgency of the situation, Captain Vee's decision made sense. Her sacrifice will save lives."

"That doesn't change the fact that she's gone," Markka said. Her voice began to quiver. "Vee would never agree to something like that—especially if it meant blowing up her ship. That was a nice ship; brand new."

"Queen Markka, your reaction to what she decided to do is an understandably emotional one—"

"Who're you calling emotional?" Markka was visibly bothered by Ramie's revelation that Vee would agree to something so unthinkable.

Piper spoke up and said, "He's right. Your attachment to Vee and the crew is an emotional response to unpleasant news."

Markka whirled toward him and challenged, "What would you know about how I feel?"

In a calm voice with barely any inflection, he placed an arm around his wife who sat next to him and said, "Because we experienced it. We sort of know what she thought and the conclusion she came to."

"We saw no other option," Lin said. "Believe me, had there been another way, we would have chosen it. We did everything we could to find another way. Did we want to die? Hell no. Were we scared shitless? Hell yeah. But we did it to save lives."

"I hate to say it, but you nearly did it once yourself, kiddo." Leachim reminded her.

Markka lowered her head in frustration when she was reminded of the day she nearly made the ultimate sacrifice to save the lives of her tank crew not long after she and Leahcim were stranded on Progensha. She seemed uncertain of herself.

Lin got up from her chair, walked over to her friend and placed a gentle hand on Markka's shoulder. Then leaned over and hugged Markka in a tight embrace.

Unable to contain herself, Markka buried her face in Lin's embrace and sobbed like a child. After the loss of her family, Leahcim and Vee became her surrogate parents. To know that Vee was gone felt like a piece of her soul was missing.

The last time Markka felt this helpless was when she watched Leahcim and T'oann die at the hands of the Thouron ruler Shang many cycles before.

Lin whispered, "She was like a mother to me too. I will miss her."

Fearing the emotional moment would become contagious, Tory addressed the group. "I believe a recess is in order. We shall reconvene in one mos."

Chapter 32

Once Markka had recovered from her emotional breakdown, the group reconvened. Markka began by apologizing for falling apart.

Leahcim said, "Hey, if it wasn't you, it might have been me."

"Or any one of us," Lin said.

"But it wasn't. It was me, but I'm over it. For now. So, where were we?"

"I was telling you of Captain Vee's decision to sacrifice herself and her ship in an attempt to destroy the portal," Ramie said.

"Uh, Ramie?" Markka asked.

"Yes, Queen Markka?"

"You could have worded that differently."

"Apologies."

Before things could become depressing again, Leachim spoke up.

"From what we saw, it must have been one hell of a fight," he said.

"It was. The stakes were critically high."

***

Following their meeting with the emissary, the *Infiltrator* successfully passed back through the portal undetected.

Once they were safe on their side of the portal, Vee retreated to her quarters and wrote up a detailed report. She encrypted it then asked Karona to wrap the report in a second layer of encryption then transmit the report to Fleet. She was confident in her communications officer's ability to get the job done.

"Cap, I guarantee the cold-bloods will never decipher this if they intercept it," Karona assured her.

"I hope not. The entire future of the Alliance is riding on that one message."

157

Karona smiled at her captain. "Now all I need to do is bounce the signal around so they can't trace its origin."

"Do your magic."

"Aye, cap."

Vee was convinced the portal was a target that needed to be removed at all costs. One way or another it needed to be taken out of the equation. *Besides*, she thought, *the Alliance needs to know this thing exists.*

She decided leaving the portal unguarded was not wise. She gambled, or more like hoped, the Alliance would be able to send support ships before the GSE forces returned.

Blowing up her ship with her and her people on board was not her first choice. Unfortunately, it looked like it was the only plan. She thought of every possible scenario to save her crew if things went badly for them. She might be willing to sacrifice her ship, but there was no way she would offer up her crew.

"Sojourner, Ramie, my quarters. Now. Sparks, notify me the moment the first Alliance ship arrives or the GSE does. Whichever comes first." She stood from her chair and hurried toward her quarters.

"Aye, cap."

As soon as Vee entered her quarters, she activated the privacy screen and revealed her plan.

"Sojourner, Ramie, I need for the two of you to do exactly as I order. No deviations. No improvisations. Do I make myself clear?"

"Yes, Captain," they said together.

"What do you propose, Captain?" Sojourner asked.

She paused and looked out the window toward the invisible doorway between universes before she answered.

"I intend to convince Fleet to make its stand against the GSE here. We're going to stop them from invading our space. If that means sacrificing the *Infiltrator* to do it, so be it. Their incursion into our universe ends here."

"What do you need for us to do, Captain?"

She thought of releasing Raqmar from detention but decided against it.

"I want both of you to assist Kay with the installation of the device the emissary gave us."

"Lieutenant Raqmar would be the better choice, Captain," Sojourner said.

"I don't believe he can be relied on right now, and we *need* to do this quickly if we are to succeed."

"May I attempt to convince the lieutenant to reconsider his insubordination?"

Vee snorted, "You may try." Then as an afterthought said, "Gather all the data we have on our current situation—including my plan to destroy the portal. Encode and upload it to the flight recorder. Ramie, when the time comes, I want you to upload yourself into the flight recorder and jettison yourself away from the *Infiltrator* and stay hidden as best you can."

"But, Captain—"

"I said that's an order," she snapped."

Ramie was quiet for a moment before he replied, "Yes, sir."

In a calmer, more controlled tone, Vee said, "This is not your war and you shouldn't be subjected to it or its fallout." She let out a tired sigh. "I appreciate everything you've done, but if things turn sour, someone needs to protect what we know."

Ramie's disappointment and surprise were evident in his dejected reply, "Yes, Captain."

"I'm sorry if you feel disappointed, but you, my friend, are the best candidate for the job. Sojourner, I want you to devise something that looks like a piece of scrap metal and conceal the flight recorder within it."

"I will need the assistance of one of the crew."

Vee thought for a moment. She really wanted Raqmar to do it, but his behavior with the emissary left her with doubts about his ability to commit to the task—or any task. The Selemite was an excellent officer but also a hothead. She had such high hopes for him, but now she was not so certain.

"Get Kay to help you with that too."

"Very well, Captain." After an uncharacteristic pause, Sojourner asked, "What are your orders when these tasks are complete, Captain?"

"Finish what I just gave you ASAP and I'll fill you in on the rest."

"Yes, Captain."

"Let me know when you're done. Dismissed."

Vee deactivated the privacy shield and paced around her quarters. She was forming the next phase of her impromptu plan when the door buzzed.

"Come."

The door swished open and Raqmar stood in the archway.

"Permission to enter, sir?"

"Granted."

Chapter 33

Vee had stopped pacing and stood looking at Raqmar as he stepped into her quarters and stood at rigid attention. Unable to look at his captain, his eyes darted everywhere around the room.

Vee figured Sojourner had gotten through to him and he was here to explain himself.

"What have you got to say for yourself, Lieutenant?"

Raqmar settled on looking past Vee's face at the canvas of stars out the window behind her. He could not bring himself to look her straight in the eye.

He stammered before he said, "I apologize for my insubordinate behavior earlier, Captain. It will not happen again." He tilted his head toward the beige carpet on the floor and prepared himself for the dressing down he knew he was about to get.

"At ease, Lieutenant."

He relaxed but continued to stare at the floor.

Vee folded her arms behind her back and stepped toward him. There was a half meter of distance between them. She sensed his discomfort. It gave her no pleasure watching him squirm. He was a brave soldier and an excellent officer, but his tendency to let his passions govern his decisions sometimes disappointed her.

"You really pissed me off, Raqmar. I don't like being pissed off. I don't like the situation anymore than you do, but as I see it, we don't have much choice. And I can't have my officers, no, will not have my officers, make a bad situation worse with careless emotional outbursts that may jeopardize the mission. Do I make myself clear?"

"Crystal clear, sir."

"If you object to something, or believe I have made an error in judgment, I expect you to voice your opinion or dissent respectfully, and I will duly note it or take it under advisement. Do you have a problem with that?"

"No, sir."

"Good. Because you need to remember it's about the mission. It's always about the mission. It's never about us." She stared hard at him, but he continued to avoid eye contact. "As for it not happening again, I seriously doubt that."

Now he looked her in the eye. The surprise and hurt was evident in his expression.

"But, Captain—"

"Don't. I don't want to hear it. I was your last chance. I am your last chance. No one else wants you."

He looked down at the floor again.

"All of your previous captains said you were too headstrong. Too insubordinate. Too dangerous. Too emotional." She stared hard at him. He continued to stand as still as a statue. "I took you on because I saw potential in you. I'm beginning to believe I made a mistake."

He flinched when she said that.

"Did I make a mistake?"

"No, sir."

She paused then walked a complete circle around him. She heaved a long sigh before she said, "I'm giving you one last chance to redeem yourself and anything you might be able to salvage of your career."

Raqmar looked up and met her eyes. She saw relief and gratitude in them.

"Thank you, Captain. I promise I won't let you down."

"If it happens again, you won't be letting me down, you'll be letting yourself down. Now get your ass to engineering and help Kay, Sojourner, and Ramie."

"Yes, sir."

His expression brightened as he did a quick about-face and left Vee's quarters.

She watched him leave and shook her head. There were times Raqmar showed signs of brilliance and times when that brilliance was overshadowed by the confusing antics of a dullard. And a dullard he was not. He needed to learn to reign in his passions.

Her communications console beeped; she waved her hand over it.

"Yes, what is it?"

"Sparks here, cap. Looks like Fleet got your message. The first ship has arrived. It's the *T'ayMak*."

"Thank you lieutenant. Send them a narrow beam and get them up to speed. Do that for every ship that arrives."

"Aye, cap."

Vee switched off her communicator and smiled. She knew the captain of the *T'ayMak*, Rosa Augusta Parsons, personally. Rosa was her second oldest friend. They went through the academy together. Parsons stood a meter and a half tall in bare feet. She was considered short by Alliance standards, but she had a feisty nature.

Vee recalled an incident in their freshman year when a rather obnoxious Selemite upperclassman decided to pick a fight with the physically petite plebe. Vee wanted to intervene, but Parsons waved off anyone who tried to help. Parsons may have been petite, but she was far from demure.

The confrontation was the shortest Vee had ever seen at the time. The Selemite took a swing and missed. That was his first and last mistake.

Parsons smiled as she dodged the missed punch with the ease of a boxer. The punch, had it connected, would have inflicted serious damage. She returned the favor with a lightning quick jab to the face followed by a swift pivot and a forceful kick to the back of the knee. Those moves were complemented by a flurry of punishing body blows. She ended it with a textbook-perfect spin and a kick to the head. His eyes rolled to the top of his head as he dropped to the floor like a sack of meat.

Not only had Parsons held her own, but she had broken the upperclassman's nose without breaking a sweat. Her only complaint was having to get a new manicure for a broken fingernail. Vee knew then and there she wanted to find out who this little powerhouse was.

Vee learned that earlier in the day, the upperclassman insulted Parsons' genetic tree. Parsons responded with an insult of her own suggesting an anatomical indulgence with a matriarchal member of his family.

The unfortunate upperclassman learned an important lesson. The Terrans had a saying: *Never judge a book by its cover.* Parsons looked every bit like a pink-skinned Terran, but she was half Terran and half Selemite. She was born and raised on the planet Selemar.

Parsons once told Vee that growing up a halfbreed on a heavy gravity world was the best thing that could have happened to her. People underestimated her and she loved it when they did.

Vee thought it fitting that Parsons was captain of a ship crewed primarily by Selemites. What Vee thought was true irony was who Parsons' executive officer was. The former upperclassman who had picked the fight with her all those many years ago. When she got her first command she requested Romar as her executive officer. He proved to be a loyal friend and steadfast protector.

Under Parsons' command, the *T'ayMak* had managed to be a part of every military engagement the Alliance managed to win. *Maybe our fortunes are about to change for the better,* she wondered.

Her console beeped. She swiped it on.

"Go ahead."

"Sparks here again, cap. I have a narrow beam transmission from Captain Parsons for you."

"Put her through."

An instant later, a smiling female with close cropped black hair, a jagged scar along her right cheek, and piercing turquoise eyes, appeared in holo form in the center of Vee's room.

"How goes it, you old space dog?" Parsons' rough, scratchy voice did not match the petite exterior.

"It goes."

"Good. Glad to hear it."

"You look good," Vee said.

"Got a facial since the last time you saw me." She touched the scar on her face then let out a belly laugh. "You should see the other guy."

They shared a laugh before they got down to business.

"I see you got my message," Vee said.

"Hell yeah we did. When Tranyxx and Chappie told the brass about what you discovered about the GSE's cloaking tech, they almost had to clean the shit out of the room." Parsons let out a hearty laugh that made her eyes sparkle. "But when we got your message about a portal, there really was a shit show. Who knew those rat bastards were coming and going with impunity inside our own territory?"

"What did they decide?"

"To fuck the shit out of them of course. Right here. Since I was the closest, I was the first to accept your gracious invitation to the dance."

"Who else is coming?"

"Damn near everyone they could spare in this sector."

Parsons turned away for a moment to talk to someone Vee could not see. Then she turned back.

"Gotta go. My XO's got something. See you at the party."

The holo image faded away leaving Vee alone in her quarters. But the alone time did not last.

"Captain?" Sojourner asked.

"Yes, Sojourner. What is it?" She tried to hide the fatigue and irritation that crept into her voice.

"The first task you assigned me is complete."

"Good. Hold tight. I'll let you know when—"

"Sparks here, cap. There's a buttload of ships out there. The *Vindicator* is one of them."

"Looks like Tranyxx and Chappie couldn't miss the party after all."

"Commander Chappie is not on board, cap. He and Doctor Sanchez were reassigned to help with the cleanup at Epsilon Base—or what's left."

"Understood. How many of us are there?"

"Close to two hundred strong."

Damn, Parsons wasn't exaggerating about scaring the shit out of the brass, Vee thought. "I guess what happened at Epsilon Base put the fear of the Gods in them."

An instant later, Sparks gave Vee a warning.

"Uh, cap? There's a large number of unknowns headed toward us on an intercept vector."

"Through the portal?"

"No, from Alliance space."

"We have their attention now. It won't be long before their friends on the other side join them. How far out are they?"

"At their present speed, approximately two hours."

"At least they don't have the element of surprise. Alert the fleet. Battle stations. Sojourner, how much longer for the second task?"

"We won't be ready when the party starts. We need at least four hours."

"Not good enough. We don't have four hours, Sojourner," Vee said. "Work faster."

"We cannot work any faster and maintain a safety factor. If we do not get the device properly installed and calibrated, we could prematurely detonate. Doing so would most certainly harm the fleet with no guarantee of doing any significant damage to the portal. Based on the calculations the emissary gave us, we must be within the event horizon. No exceptions."

"Dammit. Alright, do the best you can."

"Aye, Captain."

For the next two hours Vee tried to get some rest and put her mind at ease. She failed to do either.

Sparks' excited voice summoned Vee to the bridge.

"Cap, your presence is required on the bridge."

"On my way."

Vee raced out the door to the bridge and sat in her chair ready to take on the incoming Sairidian ships.

"Report," she ordered.

"Fleet reports ready, cap. The bad guys are now one minute out of range."

"You can bet they're coming in hot with guns blazing. Raise shields. All hell is about to break loose."

The first streaks of green energy blasts streamed from the GSE ships through the black space toward the Alliance fleet like glowing fingers reaching in the dark. Almost simultaneously the white hot streams from the Alliance answered in kind.

Chapter 34

Two hours into the battle Sparks handled the *Infiltrator* as smoothly as she had during the defense of Epsilon Base. She showed no signs of fatigue as she expertly wove around friendly vessels, dodged enemy ships and successfully dove, bobbed, and weaved through the chaos.

The compact ship took a few glancing blows and was pounded by debris from damaged ships nearby; the battle was being hotly contested. The space around them became more crowded as bits and pieces of ships and bodies began to fill what was once an empty expanse of space.

A trio of GSE fast attack ships targeted the *Infiltrator* and simultaneously fired. The ship rocked and shuddered as the shields did their job and absorbed the worst of the energy blasts. Sparks returned fire and scored a direct hit on one of the ships. It began to drift. A nearby Alliance ship focused its weapons on the damaged GSE vessel and sliced through it like a laser scalpel.

Sparks pirouetted the *Infiltrator* in a downward dive toward one of the two remaining attackers and accelerated toward it with weapons targeting the bridge. She fired everything the weapons system could deliver and pulled up just as the GSE ship's hull was breached. A series of explosions cascaded along the outer edge before being extinguished by the vacuum of space.

They braced themselves for another set of twists and turns before Sparks steadied the ship after nearly colliding with an Alliance fighter.

"Sojourner? How much longer?" Vee had to yell as the sounds of combat filtered through the communications system. Sparks and Karona shouted directions and instructions as each performed their duties while keeping each other and Vee informed of the status of the battle.

"Another two hours at best, Captain."

"Four hours ago you said four hours."

"We encountered an unforeseen problem, Captain."

The sky was full of ships from both sides engaged in a deadly dance for dominance.

"Ah, cap! We got another problem," Karona yelled over the din on the bridge.

"What now?"

"A GSE fleet on the other side of the portal is headed this way."

"What's the ETA?"

"About ninety minutes or less."

"Damn, damn, damn. Sojourner!"

"Working on it, Captain."

"Cut some damn corners. We need that thing working before the second wave gets here."

"Understood."

"Hang on!" Sparks shouted seconds before a huge chunk of something big struck the ship.

Sparks strained every muscle fiber she had fighting against the pull of her seat's harness while she dodged another chunk of scrap metal. This time she succeeded. But not before taking more energy blasts from a group of enemy fighters that were eventually diverted by their Alliance counterparts.

"Damn, that was close," Sparks said.

"I got Captain Parsons on the line, cap!" Karona yelled out.

"Put her through."

Parsons' distinctive raspy voice crackled through the shouting and noise. "I don't think I need to tell you that we're about to get some party crashers."

The connection was broken when the *T'ayMak* was fired on by a pair of Sairidian dreadnoughts. Vee and her crew watched as Parsons' ship easily outmaneuvered their attackers then made quick work of one of the ships turning it to ash. After a few minutes of an acrobatic dance with the second one, they damaged it enough for another Alliance ship to turn it into a pale blue fireball of scrap.

The communications signal between the *Infiltrator* and the *T'ayMak* crackled before Parsons' voice was heard through the static.

"Vee, I don't mean to sound pushy, but you need to get a move on. We got relief coming, but they're gonna get here after the party crashers do."

"We need more—"

Vee grabbed the arms of her chair as centrifugal force threatened to toss her onto the ceiling. Her chair's harness was the only thing that kept her in place. Sparks had literally flipped the *Infiltrator* a full one hundred and eighty degrees attempting to miss colliding with what was once the bridge of an Alliance cruiser.

She succeeded in missing it but clipped the engines of a halved Sairidian frigate.

"Oops," Sparks muttered to herself.

"Damage, minimal," Karona shouted. "Shields holding."

"Damn good flying, Lieutenant," Parsons said. "Damn good." Parsons' attention was momentarily distracted. What is it?" Something unintelligible was spoken by the *T'ayMak*'s executive officer before Parsons said, "Be right back."

The *T'ayMak*, was joined by two more battle cruisers; the *Jesse Brown* and the *Xnar*. The ships triple-teamed a disabled GSE cruiser and blasted it into oblivion with their combined firepower before Parsons was back on the line.

"How much longer before you do your thing?"

"Sojourner?" Vee asked, with an exaggerated emphasis on the SI's name.

"We need thirty more minutes, Captain."

"How much time before the Sairidian fleet gets here?" Vee asked.

"Fifteen minutes, cap," Karona said.

"Shit."

Two more energy blasts tagged the *Infiltrator* and violently rocked the ship. Then a major blast wave jostled everyone around.

"What the hell was that?" Vee asked.

The shock and horror in Spark's voice left a sickening feeling in the pit of Vee's gut.

"That was the *Vindicator*, cap."

The subsequent silence was broken by Parsons' expletives.

"Those dirty motherfuckers. They're gonna pay for that."

Before anyone else had a chance to say anything, Raqmar's voice piped in over the bridge speaker system.

"Raqmar here, cap. We could do it in fifteen minutes, but we can't use the autopilot or the auto destruct. Someone's gotta stay behind to position the ship and flip the switch. Autopilot is busted. We got no more time to fix it."

"*Shit*, Vee thought. She had not planned on anyone staying behind. "How much time after that before it blows?"

"A minute."

"Ramie, are you ready?"

"Yes, Captain."

"Sojourner, let her rip."

"Aye, Captain."

A couple of seconds later Sojourner reported the flight recorder and Ramie had been jettisoned.

"It is done, Captain."

"Good." Then as an afterthought asked, "Is Ramie truly gone or have the two of you disobeyed my order like Cora did David and Markka?"

"No, Captain, he has departed the ship as you ordered."

"Good. Now the rest of you get to the A/T and head to the *T'ayMak*. That's an order."

Of all the captains in the fleet, she trusted the lives of her crew with Parsons.

"But what about you, cap?" Sparks asked.

"Yeah, what about you?" Parsons echoed Sparks' question. Don't be no damn hero, Vee," Parsons said. "You get yourself killed and I'm coming into the afterlife and kicking your sorry ass. You hear me? I mean it."

Vee pictured an image of Parsons muscling her way through the Valley of the Dead. She smiled at the thought of her friend actually doing it.

The *Infiltrator* shuddered as a new volley of energy bolts struck the ship.

"Raqmar, route the destruct command to Sparks' console. I'll trip it from there and duck into an escape pod. Rosa, you'll just have to pick me up before it blows."

"Roger that."

The *T'ayMak* and *Infiltrator* withdrew from the heat of battle and retreated away from the heart of the action to allow for a safer transfer of Vee's crew.

"It's now or never," Parsons said.

"Now all of you get off my ship. Now! That means you too, Sojourner."

"Yes, sir."

Sparks and Karona reluctantly left their stations and headed for the A/T in the fighter bay, but not before silently beseeching their captain to reconsider.

Vee jumped into Sparks' chair and continued performing evasive maneuvers getting her ship as close to the *T'ayMak* as possible while attempting to evade GSE fighters that followed both ships.

Vee could feel the stares behind her back. "Get the hell off the ship. Don't force me to write you up for insubordination."

They both turned and left the bridge for the fighter bay.

Vee watched as the A/T left the *Infiltrator* and flew toward the *T'ayMak*. She prayed her crew would make it. She knew Parsons was taking a big gamble with her own ship. The *T'ayMak* had to cease evasive maneuvers long enough to tractor the A/T and bring it on board. During that time both the A/T and the *T'ayMak* were easy targets. Vee used her ship as a shield for her crew while she also laid down cover fire to protect them and Parsons' ship.

The *Infiltrator's* shields rapidly dropped to ten percent before the weapons system failed.

She breathed a sigh of relief when she heard Parsons say, "Got 'em."

"Thanks, Rosa. I owe you one."

"That's for damn sure. Now get your sorry ass over to that fucking hole and plug it. I'll hold out as long as I can for you."

Sojourner undoubtedly updated Parsons about what Vee had planned.

With Parsons covering her, Vee reached the event horizon, positioned the *Infiltrator* as the Others had instructed, and flipped the destruct switch just as the Sairidian relief ships approached the portal from the other side. It was going to be close.

Vee rushed to the nearest pod, dove in, closed the door, and pushed the eject button. Nothing happened. She pushed it again. Nothing happened. Panic gripped her like hands around her throat. She banged her fist on the control. There was no response.

"Vee? Where the hell are you?" Parsons asked. The desperation in her voice was palpable.

"It's jammed. The damn thing is jammed." She hit the release again, and again there was no response. "Get the fleet out of here. Now!" Fear and panic gripped her so tightly she thought her heart would burst. Her chest hurt. She found it next to impossible to breathe. As Vee blinked away tears she told Parsons her final wish. "Tell my sister I followed my moral center."

The silence on the other end of the communications link seemed to stretch on forever before Parsons said, "I will. Godspeed, my friend."

The *T'ayMak* and those ships that could, jumped into hyperspace. The rest headed away at their best possible speeds but continued to fight. The plan was to trick the GSE into believing the Alliance saw the incoming warships heading toward the portal and fled because they were outnumbered.

Vee had taken a gamble that one lone ship fleeing toward the portal would be easily dealt with by the approaching fleet, so no GSE ships pursued her. The ploy worked, but the execution of her escape plan was undone by a simple malfunction.

Vee knew her time was up. Out of frustration, she screamed and slammed both of her fists against the eject switch one last time. Vee prayed to the Gods and asked that they would spare her from an agonizing death.

Seconds later, space lit up brighter than Progensha's twin suns.

Chapter 35

"So what happened after the *Infiltrator* blew up?" Markka asked, while she reached for a crispy boar leg sitting on the food platter across from her. She took a large bite and ripped a huge hunk of meat off the bone and loudly chewed and smacked on it.

It was all she could do to stop herself from falling into a fog of depression thinking about Vee. Markka had also gotten hungry again. Picking food from off the platter at the center of the table gave her something else to think about. She was busy munching away oblivious that she was eating like someone who had not eaten in sols.

Her attention was divided between listening to Ramie and attacking the platter on the table. It was not until after she started gnawing on the bone that she noticed Ramie had stopped talking and the room had gotten quiet. She looked up to see everyone staring at her. Aside from her chewing, the only other sound that could be heard was the faint rustling of gold-colored leaves on a tree stirred by the light summer breeze outside a nearby open window.

With the leg still stuffed in her mouth, Markka asked, her voice muffled by the boar leg, "What?"

Tory, clearly amused by his wife's dining behavior, asked, "Would you like some time alone with your food?"

Markka pulled the leg out of her mouth, but not before taking another big bite out of it, then apologized between chews. "Sorry about that. I kinda got hungry again."

Leahcim looked around the room before he said, "Uh, we can all see that. Not to mention hear it too." He smirked at her.

She responded with, "Bite me."

Leahcim and Markka engaged in their usual back and forth verbal sparring match before T'oann stepped in and refereed an end to it.

"I swear," T'oann said, "the two of you act like children sometimes."

"He started it," Markka said in protest.

"Did not," Leachim muttered.

Before Markka had a chance to say something back, she saw Tory's stare boring into her from the corner of her eye. She heaved a sigh of surrender and took another bite of meat and quietly chewed and pouted.

Leahcim sat with a smug smile on his face until he saw T'oann's look of disapproval. His smile withered away as he looked down at the table to avoid looking at her.

Ramie waited for the banter to end before he answered Markka's question. He continued as if nothing ever happened.

"The Others were correct in their assessment. The most damaging effects of the blast were absorbed by the portal," he said. "It was more of an implosion than an explosion. Ships too close to the blast radius were severely damaged by residual energy. Many of those vessels were already disabled. Fortunately, the bulk of their crews had already evacuated."

"What about the GSE ships on the other side of the portal? What happened to them?" Leahcim asked.

"Unknown, Commander. Presumably, they were either destroyed or were simply incapable of passing through the portal."

"I'm guessing they probably flew right into the portal just as the *Infiltrator* exploded," Leahcim said.

"Presumably."

"Guessing? Unknown? Presumably? How can you all be so cavalier about this? Was it destroyed or not?" Sho'khan demanded.

"My sensors were temporarily blinded by the blast, but as nothing appeared to pass through, I surmised the portal was either destroyed or disabled."

"You *surmised* the portal was destroyed or disabled?" Sho'khan asked. Her irritation with Ramie was growing. "So you guessed? You have no hard evidence one way or the other whether Captain Vee's sacrifice was in vain?"

"Sho'khan!" T'oann said with an obvious display of irritation of her own. "I caution you to refrain from emotional outbursts and accusations. Ramie is debriefing us on the events he witnessed and experienced. Do not exacerbate the situation by badgering him—or chastising us for speculating. He is not to blame for what he was or was not able to do. Maybe you have forgotten so I will refresh your memory. He was under orders from his commanding officer to do nothing so he might survive so someone would know what happened. In this instance, us. Have you considered that he survived a battle many others did not—including Captain Vee? He could have just as easily perished as others surely did."

Sho'khan, clearly embarrassed from the dressing down from T'oann, crossed her arms in the Uderran salute of respect and said, "Apologies, Commander."

T'oann studied Sho'khan for a moment before she said, "Apology accepted." Then smoothly returned the floor to Ramie. "Please, continue."

Just as he did earlier, Ramie continued as if nothing had happened.

"Due to the strength of the explosion, the flight recorder I was concealed in sustained significant damage. The recorder's transmitters were damaged and my sensors were initially blinded by the equivalent of an EMP in the blast. My predicament was compounded by the force of the blast wave, which dispersed the debris field for thousands of kilometers."

"So you were essentially stranded with no way to communicate," Cora said. It was more of a statement of fact than a question.

"Yes. I drifted amongst the remains of the field for nearly a week before I detected your entry into the sector."

"No one came back to look for you?" Leahcim asked.

The *T'ayMak* did. They and a few rescue and recovery ships searched for three days before abandoning their efforts. I had drifted too far from the epicenter. Their search patterns were too far away from my position. And as I said previously, the transmitters were damaged."

Markka's curiosity finally got the best of her.

"Okay, so if your transmitter was shot, how is it you were able to communicate with us?"

"I can explain that," Cora said.

176

"When I created my offspring, I bestowed each of them with the ability to broadcast low yield signals requiring little to no power to operate. And to reduce the chance of the signal being intercepted, I designed it to mimic background radiation. This ability is unique to me and them. In cases of emergency, one of us would be able to detect and locate whichever of us was in distress."

"So when you saw us enter the debris field, you started transmitting this secret signal?" Markka asked.

"Yes."

"Was it intermittent due to your low power levels?"

"Yes. When you appeared, I knew you were not Alliance or GSE from the configuration of your ship and its emissions. The alloy appeared to be composed of Progenshan elements."

"So you took a chance that your mother or a sibling might be on board?"

"Correct."

"So you basically gambled on a hope and a prayer that we would notice you," Markka said.

"I would not quite characterize it as you have said, my queen. But put in simple terms, yes."

"I knew it!" Markka said. "I knew you SIs didn't always rely on pure logic, and mathematical algorithms. Ha! You probably pray to an SI god too."

"Praying to a deity is purely an inherent trait exhibited by biologics. It is an innate need to believe in something greater than yourselves and to rationalize explanations for concepts you are not able to fully comprehend."

"So you're saying that fate, destiny, or whatever had nothing to do with us finding you?"

"Correct."

"Beetle dung."

"Okay," Leahcim said. "We're getting off-topic here. Let's get back on track, shall we?"

Markka crossed her arms over her chest and looked pensive for a moment before she said, "Fine. Then I have just one question. How the hell did we come through a portal if the *Infiltrator* destroyed, disabled, damaged, or whatever the portal separating the Alliance from the GSE? Wasn't the entire network supposed to come crashing down?"

"Yes," Ramie said, "but a day following the departure of the *T'ayMak* and the rescue and recovery ships, a small, nearly imperceptible energy surge appeared. I did not know what it was until the *Zuri* appeared a day after it formed."

"So the portal we went through was what? A backup or something?" Markka asked.

Leahcim scrunched up his face in thought. "Maybe."

"So does that mean the network is intact and still operational?" Sho'khan asked.

"That is highly improbable," Ramie said. "If the network were still operational, the relief ships from the GSE would have been able to get through."

"They will once they realize the portal is still intact." Sho'khan was not convinced Vee destroyed it. "Maybe the portal network is active and the destruction of the *Infiltrator* did nothing but destroy a few GSE ships making them think the portal was destroyed."

"Highly unlikely," Cora said.

"What makes you so certain?" Sho'khan asked. "What evidence do you have to support your assertion? The *Zuri* definitely passed through an active portal."

"I do not know at this juncture," Cora said.

"And why did we not experience a time displacement?" Sho'khan's irritation started to manifest itself in her voice.

"I do not have an explanation at this time," Cora said.

Leachim snapped his fingers as an idea came to him. "Maybe the portal we passed through was a spare."

"A spare what?" Sho'khan asked.

He snapped his fingers as he fished for the word in his mind. "Spare tire."

Sho'khan had a blank expression on her face. She had no idea what a spare tire was. He sighed and explained what he meant.

Back on Terra hundreds of cycles ago, people drove ground vehicles that were supported by inflatable wheels. If one of those wheels deflated, people would replace it with another one. They called them spare tires."

Lin and Piper supported Leahcim's theory by telling everyone that prior to the Great War Progenshans drove similar vehicles. "When one of them lost air pressure, it deflated or became compressed; we said it went flat," Lin said.

"Perhaps the network did crash and somehow the portal we passed through was designed to bring the others back online," Leahcim said.

"And since the Builders have all died off, there is no one remaining to bring the network back up," Markka concluded.

"Yeah," Lin said. "There was no one around to fix the flat or change the spare."

"What if it was programmed to bring the rest of them back online automatically?" Sho'khan asked.

"Well, there's one way to find out," Leahcim said. "Who wants to take a quick trip to see if our portal still works?"

Chapter 36

The *Zuri*'s crew of portal inspection volunteers consisted of Leahcim, Markka, Ramie, Cora, Sho'khan, and T'oann. Lin and Piper decided not to accompany the others on this trip.

Out of earshot of the others, Markka asked Leahcim, "What's up with the Heroes of the Great War? I thought they might want to be a part of this."

"They said they needed to catch-up on some lost time."

"What lost time? Those two have been—"

"Together time," Leachim said.

"Realization dawned on her. She winked and said, "Gotcha. When we get back, maybe Tory and I might catch-up on some 'together time.'" She made quotation signs in the air.

"Again, TMI."

She called him a prude before she took her seat next to Leahcim.

Since this was Sho'khan's first trip off-planet, T'oann thought it best to accompany the team in case the tactical officer had an adverse reaction to traveling in the Great Beyond. She also did not want Sho'khan distracting the others if something went wrong.

"Everybody ready?" Leahcim asked.

He received verbal affirmatives from everyone but Sho'khan.

He turned around to look at Sho'khan, who was paralyzed with fear.

"You ready, Sho'khan?"

She barely nodded. T'oann spoke for her.

"The tactical officer is ready, Commander."

"Good. Let's go find out if that portal still works or not. Flight Control, this is the *Zuri* requesting clearance to proceed to the portal."

"*Zuri*, your flight corridor is clear. You are free to depart. Good flying."

"Thank you, Control."

Leahcim glided the ship out of the hangar and hovered over the runway. Her gray hull glistened in the evening glow of the peach and orange sky as it reflected the light from Progensha's two setting suns.

"How's it looking, kiddo?"

Markka, who was in her element, responded. "All systems are green."

"Great. Here we go."

Leahcim engaged the engines, pulled back on the wheel, and shot off the deck like a bullet. Most of the pre-flight formalities were for Sho'khan's benefit. They were in space within mictons.

Markka eyed Sho'khan who looked like she was about to pass out. Markka handed the younger woman a bag from an emergency kit beneath the copilot's seat.

"Here, take this. If you feel you need to blow your chunks, do it in this. The ship is brand spanking new, we don't need you christening it with whatever you had for lunch."

Sho'khan eagerly grabbed the bag and immediately used it.

"Ewww," Markka said. "I thought you might have needed it. I didn't expect you would."

After a few more heaves, and a few deep breaths, Sho'khan said, "Apologies, my queen."

"Forget it," Markka said. It happened to me my first time."

"Make that a couple of times," Leahcim said. Took 'em a week to fumigate the *Midnight Sun*."

"Whatever," Markka said.

When Sho'khan just stood holding the bag, Markka pointed to a nearby refuse chute.

The tactical officer walked over to it on unsteady legs, stood for a moment in front of it before she tossed the bag down the chute. Sho'khan turned to face the bridge. She looked a lot calmer.

"Okay, enough talk about biohazards, we need to decide what to do about the portal when we get there in a few mictons," Leahcim said.

"I say we go through it then turn right around and come right back. We shouldn't lose any more than a mos, if we lose that much," Markka suggested.

"Anybody got a problem with that?" Leachim asked.

"I sure as hell don't," Markka said.

"I believe I speak for Sho'khan when I say go for it," T'oann said.

"Cora? Ramie? How about you guys? Do you think we should try it?"

Cora spoke up. "Since these portals are difficult to detect with our present level of technology, passing through it is the only way to be sure."

"Okay. We're all in agreement."

A quarter mos later Leahcim announced they had reached the portal.

"Everybody ready?"

Everyone said they were.

"Okay, here goes."

Leahcim aimed the ship toward the event horizon and eased it forward. A micton later he said, "Hmm."

Instead of seeing the nebula as he expected, he was looking at the star patterns seen from the surface of Progensha at night. Thinking maybe he had not gone far enough, he flew the ship forward again. And again saw no sign of the nebula.

"Cora? Are the coordinates correct? According to my readings, we should be in the middle of the Gihon Nebula."

"Yes, Commander, the coordinates are correct."

"Well," Markka said, "looks like we got our answer. Vee succeeded in bringing down the network."

"But that leaves one question still unanswered," T'oann said. "What do we do about the portal we went through when we discovered Ramie? The spare."

Chapter 37

A small two-seat fighter streaked through the blackness of space like a hot knife cutting through warm butter. The two pilots inside were impressed with their little ship's performance.

"I have to admit this is a lot more fun than sitting in a briefing room."

"I hate to admit you are right, but this is more fun. My father and aunt always said once I got my first taste of the Great Beyond, I would want more."

Zora Leachim pulled back on the fighter's joystick and performed a perfect oval. "One of these days I will make a perfect circle," she said.

Her partner said, "At the rate you are going, that might be before we get back."

Lungeon, her copilot, sat next to Zora and monitored systems and took readings. He enjoyed the flight with the same level of enthusiasm. Not in his wildest imaginings did he ever think he would be flying through the Great Beyond. He was ecstatic just being alive to experience the thrill.

Zora handled the controls smoothly and expertly like she was born to do it. He admired her tenacity and her fierce loyalty to duty and to protecting her people. He thought about their many missions together during the Thouron War and how much they had in common. Lungeon's mind drifted to key moments in their lives that they shared.

He was a lot like her. His heritage was of mixed lineage like hers. But unlike Zora, whose parents hailed from two separate universes, his parents came from the same universe. One was Shang. A bigoted madman and leader of the Thourons. The other was a member of the Dark Woods clan. More colloquially referred to as a Wooder. She was killed in gladiatorial combat sanctioned by his father.

The product of a rape, Lungeon was never fully acknowledged by his father as his son. Following a botched attempt on his father's life, he was forced to fight in gladiatorial death matches like his mother, but unlike her, he survived and flourished.

A few cycles before the end of the war, Lungeon had the satisfaction of exacting revenge. He successfully killed his father then escaped and joined the resistance. He eventually organized a group of dissidents and escaped slaves into a formidable army and led them in rebellion against their former oppressors.

Shang's death created a power vacuum which resulted in the Thouron Empire splintering into several factions. Lungeon took advantage of the fractures and, with the backing of the resistance, allied himself and his followers with the coalition.

The coalition was by no means easy on him or his people but their efforts helped turn the tide of the war against the Thourons resulting in a decisive victory for the coalition. From the start, he and his people were not trusted and were given the more dangerous assignments. Zora and a handful of volunteers would accompany them. He initially thought she and her people were sent to keep an eye on them.

During the course of the war, he and Zora butted heads often. More often than either cared to remember. Their relationship shifted dramatically during one rather bloody battle.

Pinned down with nowhere to go, their unit held out in the hopes that relief would arrive before there was no one left. They dug in and held their ground for sols. They rationed their food, water, and munitions. They estimated they had a sol left before they would be overrun. On the eve of what they thought would be their last night alive, they each confessed a burning desire for the other.

Neither had ever been intimate with anyone before. Fearing they would never get a second chance, they consummated their relationship with an unbridled passion that left them both wanting more. They spent the entire night making up for lost time and pushed themselves to limits beyond their imaginations.

Early the next sol a brief firefight preceded an attack by a column of Thouron heavy artillery vehicles that had advanced on their position.

A tank shell fell a few meters from where they were but did not explode upon impact. Before he had time to react, Zora threw herself on him shielding his body from the delayed explosion. He woke up in a healing center bed fourteen sols later with no memory of the explosion. He was told he was found with Zora's body on top of him.

When the healers said Zora used her body to protect him, his mind automatically concluded she had died saving him. He felt numb. He refused further healing treatment. He had survivor's guilt. He refused to eat, take his medications, or go to physical therapy for his injuries. After consulting with Codie, Garath decided to try another course of action.

Lungeon sat sulking in a corner of his room one morning when Codie announced he had a visitor.

"There is someone here who has come to see you. Shall I let them in?"

"No."

A familiar voice that was not Codie's responded.

"Tough. I'm coming in anyway."

The last person he wanted to see stepped into his room. When he saw who it was, he stood and saluted.

"At ease, son. Take a seat."

Lungeon sat.

"It has come to my attention that you are refusing to eat or cooperate with the healing staff. You want to tell me why that is?"

He swallowed hard before he answered. "Because through my inaction I allowed your daughter to die, Commander."

Leahcim stared at him for a moment before he asked, "You're kidding, right?"

"No, sir. I am deadly serious. Because of my actions in the field, your daughter lost her life protecting me."

Leahcim burst out laughing, confusing Lungeon. After he caught his breath, he looked at Lungeon who appeared to be horrified at his reaction.

"Whatever gave you that impression?"

"They said they found her body shielding mine."

Leahcim smiled then asked, "Did you ever ask them if her body was lifeless?"

"No, sir. I assumed—"

"That was your first mistake. Never assume." He paused for dramatic effect then said, "My daughter is very much alive."

Leahcim caught the faintest expression of a smile on Lungeon's face.

"So all this time you've been refusing healing assistance because you thought my daughter died saving your butt?"

"Uh, yes, sir."

"So you thought killing yourself was the best way to honor her memory for saving your life at the expense of her own?"

The question made Lungeon feel uncomfortable and foolish.

"Well, I never thought of it that way, Commander."

"Obviously. The next time someone puts their life on the line for you, I suggest you honor their sacrifice by not insulting their memory and carelessly throwing away the very thing they lost so you get to keep yours. Do I make myself clear?"

"Very clear, Commander."

"Good." Leahcim turned to leave and told Codie, "He's all yours."

"Thank you, Commander."

When Leahcim reached the door to Lungeon's room, he stopped in the open doorway and, without turning around, said, "I suggest you get your sorry ass over to my daughter's room. She's been asking to see you. You were the first person she asked for when she regained consciousness."

"Me, sir?"

"Yeah, you. She wants to thank you for saving her life."

Lungeon was dumbfounded and speechless.

"You really don't remember, do you?"

"Remember what, sir?"

Leahcim turned and faced Lungeon.

"When my daughter pushed you to the ground out of the way of the shell, you pulled her down with you. When the ordinance exploded, you were both prone on the ground. Most of the shrapnel blew over both of you. You saved each other."

Leahcim winked and then walked out.

The next voice Lungeon heard was Zora's. She sounded far away and nearby at the same time.

"Hello? Is anyone in there? Hello?"

The sound of her voice was followed by a sharp jab to his ribs.

"Ow! What did you do that for?"

"You were daydreaming again."

"Only about you."

"Sure you were," Zora snorted.

"I swear I was. May the Goddess strike me down if I am being less than honest."

"I hope you're not sitting next to me when she does."

"Very funny."

"I think so. Hey, do me a favor."

"Sure. Anything."

"Can you concentrate on what you're supposed to?"

"Yes, I can do that."

"Geez, all you have is one job."

"Now you are sounding like your father."

Her response to his verbal jab was to fly a series of turns and corkscrews before leveling out. She knew he hated it when she did that.

Coming out of a final turn, she thought back to her childhood and recalled the many stories Leahcim and Markka told her and her brothers and cousins about what it was like to travel in the Great Beyond. And now she was doing it. She was living the dream. This was something she never thought she would live long enough to experience. There were a few times during the Thouron War she thought her sols were numbered.

Following the end of the Thouron War, which lasted for generations, most of the inhabitants of the planet on both sides of the conflict, tired of an endless war, were ready to begin the next phase of their planet's development. There were a few holdouts on the fanatical fringe.

One enclave of die-hard Thourons remained, but most of its radical leaders preferred to commit suicide if they could not commit genocide.

In the early days of the cease fire agreements there was a lot of distrust. But that gave way to mutual cooperation as peace talks and diplomatic negotiations took hold. Progenshans saw they had more in common than they allowed themselves to believe.

Once it became evident that the major players were earnest in their desire to work together, the Progenshans embarked on a collective goal of exploring the other two continents and the Great Beyond.

With the help of Cora and her children, the Mountainers and the Wooders, the Uderrans and Lungeons developed aircraft and spacecraft. They learned to fly those craft and trained for combat in defense of their planet. As agreed upon in the armistice, the Thourons were eventually permitted to participate on a limited basis several cycles following the end of the war. As old resentments and distrust among the former coalition members waned, the Thourons were allowed to increase their participation on an incremental basis.

Through the diplomatic efforts of her parents and Markka, an organization dedicated to exploring the planet and the Great Beyond was formed. And at this moment she and Lungeon were exploring regions of the Great Beyond no Progenshan had ever explored before as a result.

Instead of sitting in a briefing with Ramie and the others, Zora and Lungeon were flying a solo shakedown training run in one of the newest fighters.

She slowed the fighter and parked in the middle of nowhere while she and Lungeon ran through a checklist of items that needed to be ticked off. Zora smiled inwardly as it was not that long ago that the two of them found common ground.

For a short time during the war, Lungeon sat in a cell as her prisoner following the surrender by his people to hers. But a surrender, a negotiated peace, a lot of time fighting hard-won battles together, and a whole lot of trust created a close relationship everyone but them saw coming.

The evening before they thought they would die surprised them both. The deep rooted passion they felt for each other ambushed them. They acted on instinct and satisfied each other's desires with reckless abandon. She never understood the pure joy and love her parents felt for each other until that night.

"Everything looks good to me," Lungeon said.

"I concur," Zora said.

They finished the flight test by running through a checklist. Everything showed green across the board. The ship's power plant was working flawlessly. Cora and her children, along with the Mountainer and Uderran engineers, devised a method to harness solar wind energy. Instead of solar sails, they created solar wind cells. The concept was similar to the old-style solar cells many of the Alliance members used in the early days of their respective developments toward clean energy. The ship used solar wind collectors to charge the batteries and power the engines.

Zora completed making entries in the flight log then asked Lungeon, "What's next? Should we head back?"

"I don't know about you, but I think it is time we saw what this engineering marvel can really do. What do you think?" Lungeon asked. "Should we push the boundaries?" He had an impish grin on his face. He looked like he was having way too much fun.

"Hell yeah, Let's push those boundaries."

"Now you sound like your aunt."

Giggling like a couple of school kids, they exchanged a knowing look before Zora punched the controls and sent them flying deeper into space. She finally understood why her father and aunt loved the emptiness of the Great Beyond so much.

Chapter 38

Progenshan Fighter One with Zora and Lungeon aboard, zipped through space. It performed flawlessly as they cautiously pushed it to its limits and a little bit beyond.

"This is an amazing piece of machinery," Lungeon said.

"Thanks to Cora and her offspring," Zora said. "If it were not for them, the best our people might have produced by now would probably be atmospheric craft."

Lungeon pondered what Zora said before he responded, "Maybe, maybe not. Remember, the Mountain People used the knowledge that the Martina woman rescued."

"True. But even they did not possess all of the knowledge they needed to get the ships they did build to work."

"Point taken."

Zora glanced at the instrument panel in front of her and decided it was time to turn around and head home. "I think we have traveled far enough. I believe it is time to return before we are considered overdue."

"Copy that." Lungeon grinned. "I like saying that. I sort of sound like your father and aunt."

"Pfft. You sound nothing like them. They sound natural. You sound practiced."

"In time I won't."

"Whatever."

Just as she started to turn the fighter around, the proximity alert snapped on. Then she saw a small metallic object tumbling through space off the port wing.

"Do you see that?" she asked.

"I sure do. What do you think it is?" If Lungeon could have mashed his face against the cockpit window he would have.

Instinctively, they both went into fight or flight mode.

"I don't know," Zora said. "Grab the gun just in case."

"You don't have to tell me twice."

"Now you sound like my aunt."

Zora slowed down enough to get a better view while she kept a discreet distance between them and the object. "What readings are you getting?"

Lungeon quickly scanned the readings then let out a low whistle.

Ready to punch the accelerator, Zora asked, "What?"

"According to these readings, that thing out there is an escape pod. The configuration matches . . . . His voice trailed off as he double checked the data.

"What?" Zora asked.

"It can't be. It's not possible," Lungeon said more to himself than to Zora.

"If I have to ask *what* one more time, I am going—"

The configuration is Alliance and there is a weak life reading coming from it."

Zora cautiously approached the small pod, pulled the fighter alongside, and matched its speed and rotation. She was thankful for the training her father and aunt gave her and for the long hours she spent in the simulator.

"Hold here," Lungeon said. He absentmindedly held up his closed fist to signal her to stop.

"You do realize we're not in the field right now?" Zora asked.

"Sorry. I forgot."

"What do you see?"

The fighter was not yet equipped with cameras so he had to unharness himself and float closer to the cockpit canopy. He cupped his hands around his face and stared at the pod.

Despite the assistance from Cora and her children, the Progenshans were nowhere near the technological level to mass produce ships with artificial gravity. The *Zuri* was the first.

Lungeon was so close to the cockpit's glass that his forehead and tip of his nose were touching it.

"The thing has got Alliance markings on it. There is a lot of frost on the windows. It is hard to see inside, but it looks like someone or something is inside. It looks scorched."

"What in the Goddess' name is an Alliance escape pod doing here? We are nowhere near the Progensha portal. Nor are we near the one my parents and the others reported retrieving Ramie from," Zora said.

"Maybe there is another portal we do not know about?" Lungeon actually looked excited, worried, and confused at the same time.

"There is one way to find out."

"Search for it?"

"No." She looked at him as if what he just asked was the dumbest thing she heard. "We retrieve the pod and find out what we can from whoever is in it."

"What if whoever is in it is one of those GSE soldiers?"

With unwavering certainty in her voice, Zora said, "Then we kill them."

Chapter 39

After he recovered from the shock of hearing Zora's statement, Lungeon thought he would try to change her mind.

"How about we interrogate them first? Do that mind probe thing first. I am sure they have invaluable information we could learn from them. And the Goddess knows, every scrap of information we can get just might help us fight them if they are planning an invasion."

Lungeon put on his best pleading expression hoping Zora would relent.

After years of war, Zora sometimes found it difficult to let go of the urge to kill without asking questions. She sucked in a breath then released it to focus on the situation and give serious consideration to Lungeon's suggestion. She decided there might be some merit to interrogating the occupant of the pod on the chance they were still alive.

"Okay, get your ass back there and grab the grappler. We're going to snag it and bring it back with us."

He thought she sounded very much like her aunt. "You think that is a good idea?"

"No, but we can't leave it here without attempting to find out more about it."

He decided to test her resolve and check to see if she would change her mind and decide on killing the pod's occupant. "What if it is some kind of decoy or a trap?"

"Then we will deal with it when the time comes."

Satisfied he had gotten through to her, he said, "Roger that."

Zora continued to match the pod's rotation and positioned the fighter over it. Lungeon swiveled his chair around and tethered himself to the fighter's floor so he had access to a window built into the floor. He peered through the window as he lowered the grapple and gingerly locked the grips around the pod.

"Got it."

"Is it secure?"

Lungeon checked the panel next to the grapple controls in front of him. There was a steady green light.

"Yes."

"Good. Let's head back."

Zora made adjustments to compensate for the additional weight. She looked over at Lungeon, who was now secured in his seat, took a deep breath and asked, "Are you ready?"

He gave her a thumbs up. She fired up the engines and clicked on her communicator.

"Uderra Base, this is PF1, over."

Eight mictons passed before there was a reply.

"This is Uderra Base. We read you, PF1."

"We found some kind of craft. It looks like an escape pod of Alliance design with a body inside. Over."

Due to the distance Zora and Lungeon were from Progensha, the time for a transmission to travel one way took nearly four mictons. Eight mictons later, an incredulous-sounding voice came back with a question.

"PF1, this is Flight Control. Did you say, 'escape pod with a body inside?'"

"Affirmative."

"Standby, PF1."

As they waited for Control to reply with instructions, Zora told Lungeon, "I don't mind waiting for the shock to wear off and Control to get its act together, but the time lag in communications is driving me crazy."

"Cora said she is working on adapting our communications to mimic what the Alliance uses."

"I hope she hurries up and figures it out soon. Otherwise, I'm going to die of boredom out here."

The next voice they heard did not belong to the Controller, but to the Supreme Commander.

"This is Commander B'rtann. Control informs me you have an escape pod with a body in your possession. Living or dead?"

"Undetermined. Instructions?"

Zora groaned as they had to wait for an answer.

Eight mictons later, B'rtann's instructions came through.

"Head to Sacred Mountain Base. A welcoming committee will be there to meet you."

"Copy that. We're on our way. ETA, six mos."

She closed the connection and turned to look at Lungeon with a wide grin. "You heard him. Are you ready?"

"Yeah. Just don't give me any surprises."

"Then let's go home."

She swung the fighter around toward Progensha and punched it.

Chapter 40

While Leahcim and the others speculated about the future unknowns regarding the portal network, Markka received a personal message from Uderra Base about the pod Zora and Lungeon found.

She had to raise her voice to get everyone's attention.

"Guys, cut the chatter. I just got word from Control that PF1 discovered an escape pod with a body in it."

The deck became as quiet as a library.

"Come again," Leahcim said.

Markka repeated herself. "I said PF1 discovered a pod with a body in it."

"Did Control say anything else?" Leahcim asked.

"That we're to divert to Sacred Mountain Base immediately." She wrung her paws in anticipation then told Leahcim, "Let's get a move on. We got another mystery to solve."

***

Garath was relaxing in the staff lounge sipping a jamocha and discussing the merits of new surgical techniques with Codie when one of her assistants dashed into the room. She was nearly out of breath.

"Excuse me, Master Healer, but the Supreme Commander has ordered you and Codie to depart immediately for the Sacred Mountain Base."

Garath sat up from the recliner she was sitting in and asked, "Did he say why?"

"No, Master Healer, he did not. Just that the two of you were to report to base command as soon as you arrive."

"Very well."

The assistant crossed her arms in the Uderran salute and left the room.

"Whatever is happening must really be important," Garath said.

"Indeed," Codie replied.

"Well, it looks like you will get to try out your new synthetic body."

"I have been looking forward to wearing it."

"Great! You go slip into yourself and I will gather my emergency supplies. I will meet you at the transport in thirty mictons."

Garath got up from the recliner and went straight to her office to gather what she would need.

Codie transferred himself to a synthetic body and proceeded to the medical transport to wait for Garath to arrive.

***

After getting clearance to land, Leahcim guided the *Zuri* to a smooth landing at the Sacred Mountain Base.

"We're here. Now what?" he asked.

"Control said, we're to head over to landing pad one and wait for PF1 to arrive," Markka said. "We're gonna be joined by Garath and Codie—and two full contingents of legionaries."

Leahcim let out a soft whistle before he said, "Damn, B'rtann isn't taking any chances."

***

Piper and Lin sat snuggled together in the garden of their compound and watched the clouds float overhead as the warm glow of the setting suns soaked the sky in hues of orange and peach. The tranquil moment was interrupted when their communicators beeped. Neither was in the mood to answer, but Piper made the effort. "This better be important."

The nervous voice on the other end said, "Sorry to disturb you, Lord Piper, but Supreme Commander B'rtann has requested the presence of you and Lady Lin at Sacred Mountain Base without delay."

"Why? What is the urgency?"

There was a moment of hesitation before the nervous voice said, "PF1 found what they believe is an Alliance escape pod with a body inside."

The statement got Lin's full attention. "Are you certain that's what they reported?" she asked.

"Affirmative, Lady Lin. That is what they said."

She looked at Piper. "Do you think it's possible?"

"Hell, after what we've seen, done, and been through? Maybe."

A moment later Lin said, "We're on our way."

***

The pilot and copilot of PF1 watched the orange hue of the planet Progensha rapidly grow from a shiny point in the darkness to a gleaming dot in space to a large glowing ball.

"We are home," Lungeon said.

"It's about time," Zora said. "I'll be glad when we land. I didn't sign up to be a cargo pilot."

"You signed up to serve and protect the planet no matter the capacity."

"Yeah, but I prefer doing it as a fighter pilot. Not as a courier."

"You have to begin somewhere. Even your father and aunt did not start out as fighter pilots."

"I'm not them."

"That is for sure."

"What does that mean?"

Before he could respond, Control contacted them. Lungeon was grateful for the interruption. It could not have come at a more opportune time.

"Welcome home, PF1."

"Thank you, Control," Zora said. "It is good to be home."

"You are cleared to land at Sacred Mountain. A team has been assembled to receive you when you land."

"Understood."

Zora slowed their descent through the upper atmosphere. A smattering of puffy clouds dotted the sky making visibility ideal. As the mountain came into view, she saw the enormous hangar doors slowly slide open and the lights on the landing pad spring to life.

She hovered over the pad as Lungeon operated the grappling arm and gently lowered the pod to the ground. When he was sure the pod was safely delivered, he retracted the arm while Zora set the fighter down next to the pod.

It was not until she shut off the engines and they climbed down from the cockpit did they notice the large number of soldiers surrounding the landing pad.

"All this for a single pod?" Zora wondered aloud.

"I guess the Supreme Commander is not leaving anything to chance."

A small group of healers, soldiers, and technicians emerged from the crowd. They were led by Sho'khan, now fully recovered from her time in the Great Beyond, and Codie and Garath toward the pod. They pointed their tools and instruments and took readings and measurements.

A second group started toward Zora and Lungeon. Zora saw her parents among them and greeted both with a wide smile. "We brought you a present," she said.

"Aww, you shouldn't have," Leahcim joyously said as he hugged his daughter tightly in his arms. T'oann embraced them both in a group hug.

"I remember when you were embarrassed by outward displays of familial affection," T'oann said.

Zora glanced at Lungeon before she said, "That was before I matured."

"I am relieved you are safe," her mother said. She turned to acknowledge Lungeon. "Both of you."

"As am I," Lungeon said.

Markka stepped forward dragging Tory in tow behind her, approached the pod and asked, "So what did you bring us?" Almost immediately, she recoiled in shock. "It can't be," she said.

Leahcim released Zora and T'oann and looked at what caught Markka's attention and echoed her surprise, "It can't be." He motioned for Lin and Piper to join them and pointed at the pod's series number. "Is that what I think it is?"

The skin of the pod was scorched and pitted, but most of the numbers were still visible.

Piper and Lin stared at the numbers before Lin said, "Yes, it is what you think it is." A tear trickled down her cheek.

Markka broke down and openly wept.

Chapter 41

One week following what was called the Battle of the Portal, Captain Parsons sat in the quiet stillness of her darkened quarters brooding and mourning. She did not want her crew to see she was an emotional wreck. The Alliance had succeeded in thwarting a Sairidian invasion, but at great cost. A lot of good people were lost including Captain Tranyxx and the crew of the *Vindicator*, Officer Ramie, and Vee.

The Selemite period of mourning was characteristically three days. For Parsons, it was a bit longer due to the close relationships she had with so many people—especially Vee.

She sat on the floor holding a tablet which displayed the commendation letter Tranyxx had written on her behalf just before she was promoted to captain. In a fit of rage, she let out a primal scream and threw the tablet across the room. It shattered into little shards as it bounced off the far wall and crashed to the floor.

Angry, frustrated, and saddened by the loss of her friends, Parsons lowered her head to her hands and cried.

Immediately following the battle the *T'ayMak* was one of a dozen ships that combed the carnage looking for and rescuing survivors. Vee and Ramie were not among them. There was not much that remained of the *Vindicator*. Some crew were able to escape, but most did not. The only positive was that there was no trace of the portal the GSE had used to wage war against the Alliance. That door, it seemed, had been slammed shut. But the Sairidian threat remained.

They had more than a decade to infiltrate Alliance space, build a significant presence, and become entrenched. Their cloaked base or bases were still out there, as well as an unknown number of GSE forces. They would need to be dealt with.

In the aftermath of the Alliance victory, High Command redeployed the Fleet. The *T'ayMak* and all surviving ships were recalled to Epsilon Base for repairs and to assist with cleanup and reconstruction. Ships with fresh crews were dispatched to the site of the battle to patrol the area.

In the interim, Parsons made certain the remaining crew of the *Infiltrator* was reassigned to the *T'ayMak*. She thought it was the least she could do to honor her friend.

Romar assigned Sparks to the helm, Karona to navigation and communications, and Raqmar was promoted to lieutenant commander and placed in charge of engineering. Sojourner became Parsons' personal assistant and confidant. When Sojourner asked why, Parsons said that Vee held Sojourner in the highest regard. Sojourner vowed not to disappoint her new captain.

Parsons had nearly cried her tear ducts dry when Karona buzzed her.

"Sorry to disturb you, Captain, but there is someone here to see you."

"Annoyed that she could no longer wallow in her private pity party, Parsons gruffly asked, "Who is it?"

Karona, fully aware of her captain's frame of mind, took no offense and casually said, "Commander Chappie."

"I'll meet him in the situation room."

"He insisted on meeting you somewhere a little less formal."

"What's less formal than the situation room?"

"Your quarters. He should be arriving right about now."

Karona clicked off just as the bell to Parsons' quarters rang.

Parsons heard the humor in Karona's voice. *Smug little bitch*, she thought. *I like it.*

"Shall I let the commander in, Captain?" Sojourner asked. Until now, Sojourner had discretely left Parsons alone to deal with her grief.

Not prone to panicking, Parsons panicked.

"No, not yet. Stall him. Tell him I'm indisposed or something. Anything. He can't see me like this."

"Why not?"

"Because."

Sojourner told the commander that Parsons was sleeping.

"Don't tell him I'm sleeping. Why'd you tell him I'm sleeping?"

"Because."

"Geez, is this what Vee had to put up with?"

"No, she did not have to put up with anything because Captain Vee did not hide from her commanders."

"I'm not hiding. I'm ducking. Like a boxer."

Sojourner responded with a drawn out, "Right."

Parsons dashed into the bathroom and splashed cold water on her face then grabbed a towel to dry off. She ran her fingers through her hair then straightened her uniform before telling Sojourner to turn up the lights and let Chappie in.

He stepped into Parsons' quarters and immediately said, "Damn. You look like shit." He sniffed. "You smell like it too."

"Fuck you."

"Is that anyway to address a superior officer?"

"It is when that officer is my senior, not my superior. My God is my only superior."

"Fair enough." He stood in the center of the room and noticed what remained of the tablet. "I was going to ask you how're you holding up, but it looks like you're barely hanging on."

"How the hell else am I supposed to feel, Greg?"

"Shitty like the rest of us."

"Exactly."

"Well, I got something for you that might make you feel less shitty."

"Like what?"

"Before I tell you, there's something you should know."

"What?"

"Vee didn't reveal everything she knew to High Command."

"How do you know she didn't?"

"Because I'm the one she told everything to, and I told Tranyxx and Reth."

Parsons heaved a huge sigh. "And now they're all gone. So you're the only one who knows now."

He sucked through his teeth. "Uh, not exactly."

Her curiosity piqued, she asked, "Who else knows about this big secret you're about to tell me?"

"One of them is your personal assistant."

"Sojourner?"

"Yes, Captain?" Sojourner asked.

Parsons rolled her eyes in exasperation. "Not now."

"As you wish, Captain."

"Who else knows?"

Instead of answering Parsons' question directly, he spoke to Sojourner. "Are the others ready?"

"Yes, Commander. They are waiting outside in the corridor."

Chappie had contrite sadness in his eyes when he said, "Sorry to invade your inner sanctum, but what they have to tell you can't wait any longer."

"My quarters? Really? Who?"

Chappie put a hand on Parsons' shoulder. "You'll thank me later. Send them in, Sojourner."

"Right away, Commander."

The door to Parson's quarters swished open and Sparks, Karona, and Raqmar filed in.

Chapter 42

"So you're all telling me that David, Markka, and Cora are alive and living in another universe? And Lin and Piper are there too?"

"Yes," Sojourner said.

"And they have adult children?"

"Yes, their universe does not operate on Allurian time as ours does. They age at a different rate than we do. They have no doubt aged nearly another decade since our return from their universe."

Parsons was having a difficult time ingesting the news.

"There are descendants of the *Michael Anderson* living in that universe?"

"Yes."

"But the *Anderson* only disappeared, what? A year ago?"

"Again," Sojourner said, "Different universe. For them, the *Anderson* crashed five hundred of their years ago."

"There's an outlaw city on Sigma II?"

"It's not an outlaw city," Karona said. Her tone bordered on indignation. "It's a refuge for those displaced by the war or whose entrepreneurial endeavors don't conform to the social mores of mainstream society. It was my home until Captain Vee took me on."

Parsons was reminded of how she had grown up. Ostracized. "Sorry, Lieutenant. Poor choice of words on my part. No disrespect intended."

Karona deemed her captain's apology a sincere one and appeared satisfied.

Parsons had one more question to ask. "And Vee's sister and the inhabitants of Opportunity City know about the time travel thing?"

"Yes," Sojourner said again. "As Commander Chappie just explained, Vera and her cohorts assisted in repairing the *Infiltrator* after our encounter with the *Anderson*."

"You'll forgive me if I find all of this preposterous."

"We thought you might," Chappie said. "Sojourner, show her the visual records—the condensed version."

"Certainly, Commander."

Sojourner projected the highlights of pertinent images and data she and the crew recorded. Parsons sat with her mouth open in awe and fascination at what she saw and heard.

She saw the rescue of Leahcim and his wife. The discovery of the *Anderson* buried in the desert, the subsequent collision, and the surprise reunion with Lin and Piper.

When Sojourner was finished, Parsons sat staring into empty space.

"Holy shit. It's true?"

"Affirmative," Sojourner said.

"And there's another one of those damn portals just sitting in the middle of the Gihon Nebula?"

"Correct."

Parsons shot up from her chair and said, "We need to do something. We need to defend or destroy that portal. We need to tell High Command." She became more animated as her agitation and excitement grew. She paced around her quarters gesturing wildly with her arms. "We need to—"

"Sit down! That's an order, Captain."

Shocked by the suddenness of the command, Parsons stopped pacing and sat back down.

"Now is not the time to go off half cocked," Chappie said, in a calmer tone. "Get your head in the game because there's been a new development."

The nervous energy she displayed earlier disappeared. It was replaced by a palpable aura of strength and command. Her curiosity was piqued. The Captain they all knew resurfaced.

"Yeah? What kind of development?" She was in total command mode now.

Satisfied that the news had brought her out of her stupor, Chappie told her what he knew.

"A few days ago, the *Quicksand* and the *Changeling* detected an indecipherable signal and what appeared to be a ship within the debris field."

"What kind of ship?" Parsons asked.

"Unknown. By the time they got there, it was gone. Long range readings indicated it was not of GSE configuration."

"So now we got a new player to deal with?"

"Maybe, maybe not." Chappie was being evasive.

"What are you not telling me, Greg."

Chappie looked at Sparks, Karona, and Raqmar for affirmation. They all nodded. So he went ahead and told Parsons what the *Quicksand* and *Changeling* detected.

"The ship's configuration resembled the *Infiltrator* and the emissions were neither Alliance nor GSE."

"Now you're shittin' me."

"I wish I was, Rosa. The readings are unmistakable. There is something weird going on out there. I want you and your crew to investigate it. The *Powell* and *Zulu* will escort you. Find out what the hell is going on."

"When do you want us to ship out?"

"Yesterday."

Parsons stood, looked at her officers and said, "Okay, you heard the man. Get off your asses and do your jobs."

As Chappie got up to leave, Parsons asked, "Is it okay if I fill in Romar?"

"Yeah. He's gonna need to know sooner or later."

Chapter 43

The escape pod looked more like an oversized coffin than a rescue vehicle as it sat on the ground. There was an eerie stillness in the air that made the occasion feel more like a memorial. Tory held his trembling wife while the rest stood and watched in anticipation as Codie opened the hatch to the pod. If he had not been there, they would have had to cut their way through or find something to pry the door open.

The hatch creaked and protested as Codie applied brute force to open it. When he finally swung the hatch open, Garath approached the pod, hesitated and gasped when she saw the face of its occupant. She looked at those nearest to her and softly said, "It is Captain Vee."

Lin and Piper stood arm-in-arm not moving. Leahcim unconsciously squeezed T'oann's hand. Markka hugged Tory tighter, waiting for Garath to give her assessment.

Garath regained her composure and stepped into the pod and began to examine Vee.

"She's alive. Barely," she said as she continued to examine Vee. "Help me get her out of this thing, Codie."

He gently scooped Vee out of the pod and reverently laid her limp form onto a waiting gurney. She did not look like she was peacefully sleeping. Even though her eyes were closed, Vee looked like she had peered into the face of evil. Her features were gaunt and her body emaciated.

Garath motioned for assistance. An army of healers surrounded the gurney and took over for her and Codie. They attached various devices to their patient and prepared her for transport to the central healing center.

In a low tone, Garath instructed her staff to, "Take her to intensive care. Notify Tonga her services may be needed. I will follow momentarily."

The senior assistant nodded then directed the group to whisk Vee away.

Garath turned to her friends who looked like helpless children.

"How is she?" Leahcim asked. "Will she live?" His eyes were glistening as he fought back tears.

"I . . . I don't know. She appears to be in a coma. Her vitals are barely registering. She is severely dehydrated and her skin and feathers are singed. It is by the grace of the Goddess that she still lives. I am uncertain whether nanites will be able to help, but we will do everything we can for her."

"Whatever she needs, you need, tell us," Markka said. "We will make it, buy it, steal it, or sacrifice it." Markka's knees were so weak that if Tory had not been holding her, she would have collapsed to the ground.

Lin took a step toward Markka to comfort her and faltered on her own unsteady legs. Piper held his wife before she had a chance to fall. She softly sobbed on his shoulder. Vee had been a surrogate mother and mentor to both Markka and Lin in the early days of their careers. Seeing her as she was now was more than either could handle.

Garath looked at Codie before she said, "We will do everything in our power to make her well again."

***

"Talk to me, people. What've you got to report?"

Parsons sat in her chair on the bridge while the crew took readings, measurements, and ran tests.

"What we have, Captain, is a big fat mystery," Karona said.

"Besides that."

"I think I might have something, Captain," Sojourner said.

"Okay, hit me."

"The task force has been crisscrossing the outer perimeter of the debris field searching for evidence of the signals the *Quicksand* and *Changeling* detected."

"Go on."

"Despite our best efforts, we have not been able to pick up on anything unusual."

"Why do I detect a but in there somewhere?"

"Because, Captain, there is a but in there."

"Where's the but, Sojourner?"

"In the heart of the debris field."

"Let me guess, you see something the rest of us don't."

"I believe I do, Captain."

"You wouldn't want to, I don't know, maybe share it with the rest of us."

"Of course, Captain. May I borrow the services of Lieutenant Sparks?"

"Sure, be my guest."

"Thank you. Lieutenant, please navigate us close to these coordinates. Then let me know if you see it."

"See what?" Sparks asked.

"You will know it when you see it."

Sparks sighed, "If you say so."

Sojourner transferred the data to the helm. Sparks wove through the field and got them close to the location Sojourner indicated.

"Now what?" Parsons asked.

"Now we observe," Sojourner said. "Let me know when you see it."

"What are we looking for? A cloaked ship?" Parsons asked. She was ready to sound the alarm for battle stations.

"Not exactly," Sojourner said.

Parsons felt like she was about to burst because she wasn't getting any straight answers. She took a couple of deep breaths to calm herself then decided to let Sparks and Sojourner work uninterrupted. If Vee trusted her officers, she would try to do the same.

No one made a sound until Sparks said, "I'll be squid-inked. I see it."

"See what?" Parsons asked.

"I never thought I'd see this again," Sparks said. She pointed to a section of empty space within the field then magnified the area on the heads-up display over her console.

Parsons stood up from her chair and walked over to the display then looked out the forward window. She actually saw what Sparks pointed toward, but did not understand what she was seeing. "What the hell am I looking at?"

"That," Sparks said, "is the entrance to a portal."

***

After he had calmed himself, Leahcim strode over to Zora and Lungeon and congratulated them.

"You guys did good out there. You should be proud of yourselves. I know I'm proud of you—and thankful."

"For what, father? Doing our jobs?"

"Yes."

"It was our duty, our obligation. We only did what was expected of us."

"You did what was expected and more. Because of you, my friend is alive and now has a fighting chance to survive."

"And she will. She is in good hands."

Zora watched her father fight an internal battle for emotional control just as her mother stepped over and placed a calming hand on his shoulder. He flinched slightly before his demeanor changed. She was sure they were mind-walking. A moment later, Leahcim said, "I checked the duty roster. You two are way overdue for some time-off. So I've arranged for you to have five straight sols of leave."

Zora's face lit up like a child at a birthday party. "Thank you, father."

Lungeon's face mimicked hers. "Yes, thank you, Commander."

"Don't thank me. You earned it. Finish up here, go to your debriefing, then get some well deserved rest."

They saluted Leahcim then headed off to their fighter to get their gear. As they walked away, Leahcim leaned close to T'oann and asked, "So, you think we might finally get some grandkids?"

"I hope so. I'm getting tired of waiting."

Chapter 44

By the time Garath and Codie returned to the healing room, the technicians had cleaned Vee up, replaced her tattered uniform with a clean operation gown, and placed her in a medical stasis tube. Codie had designed the tubes during the war as a means of stabilizing patients before major surgery.

Since Vee's body was already in a state of hibernation, the stasis tube simply stopped any further physical deterioration.

Codie shed his artificial body and returned to his analog and digital world. Tonga, T'oann's older sister, was on call in the observation deck in case her mind-walking services were needed.

When Leahcim and T'oann reached the observation deck, they were greeted by Markka, Lin, and Piper, who arrived a quarter mos ahead of them. Tory went back to the palace to attend to matters there after escorting his wife to the deck.

Leahcim joined Markka, Lin, and Piper at the observation deck window overlooking the healing room. T'oann greeted her sister, who was sitting across from the others in a recliner in a corner of the room next to the door. She hugged her sister and asked how things were going for her now that the Thouron War was over and the resistance was disbanded.

"I am coping," Tonga said. "I am getting used to being a full-time grandmother. I never thought I would ever live to see the day."

"I take it Marshon and Pricilla have adjusted to his new routine as an instructor at the Academy?"

"Yes, Pricilla is elated that he is now coming home nightly, and his twins are doing quite well for themselves. Both are pilots. One is flying the new bantam fighter. The other is in military intelligence."

"The maiden fruit did not fall far from the tree, I see."

"No, it did not."

"And the little one?" T'oann asked.

Tonga smiled and said, "She's a handful. Much like me when I was her age. Eager. Adventurous. Ambitious."

"Perhaps after her next growth spurt she will follow in her grandmother's footsteps."

"Perhaps."

While T'oann and her sister chatted and Leahcim and the others watched what was happening below them, Garath and Codie worked to save Vee's life.

"Her species is remarkably resilient," Codie said. "Her body entered into a dormant state as she drifted in the Great Beyond."

"Probably a survival mechanism her people developed over time to survive harsh environments or natural disasters," Garath said.

While she ran full body scans to determine the severity of Vee's injuries. Codie monitored vitals.

"She is suffering from severe dehydration, first degree burns, hypothermia, and some of her organs are in danger of shutting down," he said. "She also appears to have suffered a concussion and several contusions. I detect no fractures."

"Thank the Goddess for small favors," Garath said. "I hope she appreciates all of the poking and prodding when she wakes up."

Despite being in hibernation and a stasis tube, Vee's body began to convulse with spasmodic contractions. Her readings were all over the charts.

"Codie, what is happening?"

"Her body is negatively reacting to the stasis tube. It is fighting the immobilization field. I believe her system thinks it is under attack. She is going into cardiac arrest."

"Get her out of there. Now!" Garath ordered her staff.

Someone rolled a table up against the tube while others opened it and slid Vee onto the adjacent table. The spasms stopped but so did her heart.

"She has no pulse!" One of the technicians yelled.

Garath immediately began chest compressions. "Get me a stimulator!" She reached out and took the paddles one of her staff handed her and prepped them. Clear!" she yelled. Then proceeded to shock Vee. There was no response. She repeated the process two more times before Codie said her heart was beating again. Without thinking about it, Garath ordered her staff to inject Vee with nanites. She hoped they would know what to do and could fix the problem before it was too late.

The concern for their friend was heightened when Leahcim and the others saw the spasms take over Vee's body. An instant later, the glass windows became translucent and the audio was muted. Codie cut off their ability to see and hear what was happening in the healing room below them.

"What the hell is going on?" Markka asked. "We gotta get down there."

She turned to run out of the observation deck but was stopped by T'oann who blocked her way to the door.

More upset than angry, Markka said, "Get outta my way!" It was more of a snarl than a friendly request.

"I'm sorry, but I cannot let you out of this room." T'oann brought herself to her full height and crossed her arms in a defiant gesture.

Seething with anger and grief, Markka unsheathed her claws and said, "I'm not going to say it again."

Leahcim carefully eased himself between T'oann and Markka and stood with his hands up in surrender. "Hey, hey, hey. Calm down there, kiddo. There's no need to get hostile. She's only trying to help."

Markka's hair stood straight out and her tail twitched like a snake about to strike.

Leahcim spoke in slow measured words. "Your rushing down to the healing room isn't going to change anything. Let Garath and her team do their jobs."

Piper spoke up in support of Leahcim. "Yeah. Garath and Codie know what they're doing. They're the best equipped for this."

Markka turned her head slightly to look at Piper, who was frozen in place from surprise. "And why aren't you down there helping out? You're the so-called healing expert."

"I'm a combat medic, Markka, not a healer or doctor. And I'm emotionally compromised."

"Right now you're useless." Markka hissed the words at him like venom.

Piper winced at the accusation. As if not being able to help Vee was not bad enough, being told he was useless was like rubbing salt on a wound.

Lin slowly took a half step toward Markka, but stopped when Markka glared at her and said, "Don't make me hurt you, Lin."

Markka then pivoted and lowered her stance so she could see everyone in the room and strike or defend if need be. Piper and Lin on one side of her, Leahcim and T'oann on the other, and Tonga in front.

Leahcim redirected Markka's attention back to him. "Come on, kiddo. Threatening all of us isn't going to change what's happening in the healing room right now."

"But I have to be there!" She was almost hysterical.

"Why?"

Words came to Markka's mind, but got bottled up by the time they reached her tongue. Tears began to well up in her eyes and threatened to spill out. She took a breath but didn't move. Neither did anyone else.

"Because I have to be there with her so she doesn't die alone," is what she finally said.

Lin looked like she was about to make another move for Markka when Piper grabbed his wife and pulled her toward him.

Markka shifted her stance to brace for Lin.

"She's not going to die," Leahcim said. He raised a hand to draw her attention away from Piper and Lin.

Markka sniffled and said, "You don't know that."

Leahcim sighed. "You're right. I don't know that. But what I do know is she's in good hands. Codie and Garath and everyone in that room will do their damndest to see that she lives."

Markka continued to hold her stance against all of them, but Leahcim saw uncertainty etch itself onto her distraught face. She appeared to be losing her resolve.

Leahcim asked again, "Why do you feel you need to be there for Vee?"

Markka's hair returned to normal and she dropped her arms.

"Because I wasn't there for you when you died. You saved my life and I wasn't there to save yours."

Markka broke into uncontrollable sobs and collapsed. T'oann and Leahcim caught her before she reached the floor. Leahcim gently held his queen in his arms and sat on the floor with her. She buried her face in his chest and cried until she calmed down enough to speak.

"When the GSE attacked my world," Markka said, "I had no one." She looked up at Leahcim. "You and Vee took me in. Gave me a home. Gave me purpose. Made me feel . . . loved. Safe."

She lifted her head from his chest and looked up at him. "I know it was you who sponsored my admission into the Academy. I know you also convinced Vee to take me on when I graduated." She wiped her nose with her sleeve. "I made a vow that I would protect you the way you protected me. I failed. Twice." She buried her face back into his chest.

She trembled in his arms before she spoke again. "Didn't you ever wonder how I got to be your gunner?"

"I just assumed it was the luck of the draw."

"Luck had nothing to do with it." She forced a smile and continued. "I made myself a pain in the butt to Vee until she agreed to get you reassigned to her ship. I did it so I could repay the favor and keep you both safe."

A chill ran through Leahcim as it dawned on him just how deeply his influence affected her.

"I didn't know."

"You weren't supposed to. When I saw you and T'oann die, I died a little inside that day."

"Why?"

"Because I couldn't save you or T'oann. I failed you. And now I can't save Vee. I've failed her too."

"You didn't fail," he said. "I'm alive. My wife is alive. Vee is alive. In fact you made us proud. We're all proud of you. None of us would be where we are now if it weren't for you."

He sighed and drew her close against him before he continued.

"If you hadn't convinced Vee to go to Sacred Mountain, T'oann, Tonga, and I wouldn't be here right now. As our queen, you are the right person at the right time doing the right job for all the right reasons."

Markka relaxed in his arms and went limp. Leahcim felt T'oann enter his mind, sensed what happened, and thanked Tonga.

"Do not thank me. You put her mind and soul at ease. All I did was put her body at ease."

Leahcim had drawn Markka's attention enough for Tonga to slip into her mind and sooth the agitated parts of it. Tonga could have overpowered her queen's mind at any time, but she ran the risk of causing bodily harm to Markka or creating an unpredictable situation where Markka would harm someone in the room. She was grateful Leahcim intervened.

Markka blissfully fell asleep in Leahcim's arms. He sat on the floor rocking back and forth as she slept. The others settled down and waited for word from Garath or Codie.

Two mos later, the observation window became transparent again and the sound was turned on. Leahcim had fallen asleep on the floor with Markka. T'oann napped on one of the chairs nearby. Lin and Piper slept on a couch across from the deck window. Tonga was the only one of them who remained fully aware the entire time. Her training as a resistance fighter prevented her from letting her guard down, even when she slept. So it was she who noticed the change in the window.

She soundlessly walked over to the observation window and surveyed the room below.

An exhausted-looking Garath sat sleeping in a chair next to the isolation chamber. All of the healing technicians were gone from the room, and Vee slept in the chamber. Codie, no doubt, had everything under control.

It was only then that she allowed herself the luxury of a more restful sleep.

Chapter 45

Initially, she felt a paralyzing fear accompanied by an overwhelming sense of panic. Then she felt intensely warm. That was followed by a chilling cold and physical numbness. All of those feelings were eventually replaced by a soothing quiet stillness. She could not remember a time when she felt so calm. Especially after experiencing the calamitous events which preceded the strange serenity she now felt.

Am I dead? she asked herself. *Am I with the ancestors?* she wondered. If she was, then why could she not see them? She had heard voices. She was sure of it, but why could she not communicate with them? And where was she? She tried to move, but could not will her body to do so.

Something was not quite right. Vee was certain of it.

***

"Holy hell. There's another one?" Parsons asked.

"It appears so," Sojourner said.

"What'll we do now, Captain?" Sparks asked.

This was new territory Parsons was treading on. This discovery meant a potential new threat to the Alliance. It had to be investigated. Something had emerged from it then disappeared. If it was a new GSE threat, it would need to be swiftly dealt with. If it was something else, that would also need to be addressed.

"Lieutenant Karona."

"Yes, Captain."

"Tell Commander Chappie we could use a little more backup out here if he can spare it. And get me Admiral K'mar. Tell her I'm cashing in a favor."

***

Following an invigorating shower and a steaming cup of hot jamocha, Garath was mentally and physically ready to take on the sol.

She sipped her drink, scanned the readouts on her patient, and asked Codie, "How is Captain Vee doing?"

"The captain is stable. Her vitals appear to be improving. The nanites report the repairs to her physical damage are progressing as expected. Her body is accepting the feeding nutrients. She is expected to make a full recovery in a sol or two."

Garath took another sip, stared through the isolation chamber window and said, "Good." Then she asked, "Is Tonga still on call?"

"Yes."

Garath could not shake the haunting image of the look of abject fear frozen on Vee's face when the pod was opened. "I cannot imagine what psychological trauma the captain must have experienced, but I believe she will need the assistance of her friends to help her through recovery."

Codie tried to sound reassuring. "She is a strong woman. In time, she will be herself again. We must all be there to support her as she heals."

"I pray that you are right."

***

Tory spent most of the night napping as he kept a watchful eye on his wife. T'oann and Leahcim told him of Markka's breakdown. When the first rays of light from the rising suns painted the sky peach, he slowly got out of bed and made his way to the bathroom to shower. Markka, normally a light sleeper, did not stir.

He showered, dressed, and asked the kitchen staff to make a lavish morning meal for him and his wife. As a surprise, he had asked the head chef to include a small plate of assorted candies.

T'oann had told her brother once of a Terran delicacy called candy that Markka missed eating. When his sister told him how his wife literally drooled, describing this unique food, he decided to find a Progenshan equivalent. He asked Cora to do some research to figure out if there was a way to replicate the Terran treat. Cora did not disappoint.

Not only did she devise a way to make candy, but she taught the kitchen staff how to produce a variety of the flavorful treats. When he tested the first batch for himself, he thought he had died and was eating food from the Goddess' banquet table.

He sat on the grass in the main garden waiting for Markka to arrive. When she did, he asked her if she slept well.

"As well as can be expected considering the circumstances," she said. "I know you heard I made a fool of myself."

219

"No more than usual," he teased.

She glared at him then snuggled next to him on the grass.

"Would you care to join me for morning refreshment?"

She was about to decline when he told her there was candy. She gave him one of her I-don't-believe-you looks. He uncovered a dish hidden beneath a silver cloche. Her eyes grew wide and she licked her lips.

"Is that . . . is that candy?"

"Yes, my sweet puffball."

She eyed the dish suspiciously.

"Candy! Who? How? Never mind."

She slinked a paw toward the dish and speared a piece of something that looked like a nugget of milk chocolate with her claw. She studied and examined it before she decided to sniff. Skeptical but curious, she bit off a piece. She swooned. It tasted exactly like milk chocolate.

"Do you like it?"

"Do I like it? Do I like it? I love it!"

She snatched another piece and closed her eyes as she popped it into her mouth. A moment later, Markka began squirming and vibrating next to him. He grew concerned and wondered if there was something in the candy that was causing the distress. Was there some ingredient her body was rejecting? Was she allergic to one of the ingredients? Did he inadvertently poison her? Eventually she calmed down.

He held her and asked how she felt.

She showed him a toothy smile and said, "Never better. That was literally the first time in my life you gave me an orgasm without touching me."

Tory blinked in disbelief, relieved that he had not poisoned his wife, but concerned that now she had found a substitute for him. Would he have to compete for her affections with a food item? He felt foolish at the thought. His fears were unfounded as Markka suddenly grabbed him and began tearing his clothes from his body. Since all he wore was a thawb, it did not take her long. She stripped him naked in the blink of an eye.

Then she ripped off the gown she wore, pinned his arms above his head, and teased and rubbed against him until he was ready for her. Markka continued to restrain his arms as she straddled him, taking all of him into her.

She gyrated her hips against Tory with slow rhythms until she felt his arms weaken. She let go of them and rocked back and forth in a frenzied fashion as she tightened around him. He moaned with pleasure, wrapped his arms around her and pulled her closer.

They seesawed against each other; grinding until they swayed as one. Just as the first contractions took hold of her, she massaged him until he exploded within her. The spasms that rippled through their bodies left them weakened but satisfied. Exhausted, they became an entangled, crumpled heap on the cool grass beneath them.

Markka snuggled up close to Tory, put her head on his chest and said, "I have a confession to make."

"Oh?"

"Up until now, I never needed to tell you, but chocolate candy is an aphrodisiac for me."

"So, it seems that I will need to stockpile it."

Chapter 46

Why can't I remember what happened to me? she wondered. *Think*, she told herself. Vee searched her memory for answers. She closed her eyes and opened her mind and began to hear sounds. They were unintelligible at first, but gradually became clearer. People were yelling, there was shouting, screaming, and explosions. She concentrated on the sounds closest to her.

As she sorted out the sounds, blurred images started to form. The images shifted into shapes before they came into focus. They were people she knew.

Think, she told herself.

Then she heard a familiar voice. Her own. *"Get the hell off the ship."* She saw two faces she recognized. Sparks and Karona. She was piloting a ship. Her ship. The faces of her crew swirled until she saw her hand reach out and press something on the control panel in front of her. Then her panicked voice cried out, *"It's jammed!"* A moment later she heard herself say, *"Tell my sister I followed my moral center."*

***

Alarms started ringing in the isolation chamber. Garath, Codie, and the healing staff sprang into action. The doors to the chamber swished open and Garath and a couple of technicians rushed in to attend to Vee who appeared to be sleeping peacefully.

"What is happening?" Garath asked.

Codie responded. "I have been informed by the captain's nanites that her subconscious mind has been stimulated by the final traumatic moments of her life."

"Get Tonga. Now."

"There is no need. I am here," Tonga said.

Garath yelped.

"Apologies. I did not intend to startle you. I sensed her distress before the warning alarms sounded. I rushed here from the deck as soon as I could."

"Can you help her?"

"I will do my best. Leave me."

Garath ordered everyone out. She was the last one to leave. The doors swished closed behind her. Codie withdrew and sealed off all electronic access. The captain was in Tonga's hands now.

Tonga lightly touched Vee on her shoulders and carefully peered into the starship captain's mind. She saw a confused and terrified Vee rapidly receding from her own mind. Tonga needed to act quickly before Vee could no longer be reached.

Tonga called out to her. "Captain, your presence is requested. Front and center. Now."

Vee felt Tonga's essence. "Who is this? Show yourself."

"Step forward into the light," Tonga said. She felt Vee's cautious apprehension.

"Do I know you? Your voice sounds familiar."

"Yes, we know each other. I am Tonga. T'oann's sister."

"T'oann? David's wife?"

"Yes."

"What are you doing here? And where is here?"

"You are among friends."

As a mind walker of the highest order, Tonga had the ability to function in both the corporeal and incorporeal worlds as easily as everyone else did breathing. She knew that Leahcim, Markka, Lin, and Piper had all arrived and were watching from the observation deck. She named each of them and told Vee they were nearby waiting to greet her. All she needed to do was step forward.

A moment later, Vee appeared from the darkness of her own mind. It took another moment before she recognized the figure standing in front of her. She blinked. "I know you," she said.

Tonga reached out her hand. Vee hesitated before grasping it.

"Am I dead?"

"No, you are very much alive. You are among friends and people who love you very much. They are waiting to see you. If you come with me, I will take you to them."

Vee said she was ready.

Together, they walked toward a bright light.

"Garath," Tonga said, "you and your team may return."

Garath and her team entered the isolation chamber just as Tonga terminated the mind-walk.

"Well?" Garath asked.

"Give her a micton to gather herself."

A micton later, Vee's eyes fluttered open. The first image she saw was Garath's smiling face.

"Welcome back, Captain."

Leahcim, Markka, and the rest were watching from the observation deck. No one breathed until they heard Vee ask, "Where am I?"

"You are my patient at the Sacred Mountain healing facility."

"Sacred Mountain?" Without turning her head, Vee surveyed what she could of her surroundings. Aside from Garath, she saw machines, some of the healing staff, and Tonga. She tried to sit up, but was knocked back down by a sharp pain in her head.

"It is the effect of the mind-walk, the nanites, and the healing drugs," Garath said. "It will soon pass."

"Mind-walk?" Nanites? How did I get here? I was nowhere near the Gihon Nebula."

Tonga spoke up. "Do not concern yourself with those matters right now. You need to rest." She turned to Garath and asked, "How soon can she have visitors?"

"By my estimation, in another sol or two. We will need to keep her twilighted until then. Do you concur, Codie?"

"Yes, I concur."

Three sols later, Vee was sitting up in bed in a recovery room alert, laughing and talking with Leahcim, Markka, and the others.

Chapter 47

"So you're saying I drifted into a portal to your universe that didn't exist until a few days . . . sols ago?"

"Yep," Leahcim said.

"And there is no time dilation thing going on?"

"Nope." Leahcim shook his head. "Not as far as we can tell."

"And now you all are space travelers and it's seven cycles later?"

"Closer to eight, but essentially, yep."

"How'd that happen?"

Cora said, "I can explain what happened, Captain."

Leahcim rolled his eyes. "Short version, please, Cora."

"Very well. In the four cycles after you left, we discovered a cavern in the mountains that contained abandoned facsimiles of Alliance fighters. The ancient Progenshans possessed neither the technology nor the knowledge to get them to function. So they were abandoned. Using the bantam fighter as a guide, my offspring and I, together with specially trained technicians, rebuilt the *Midnight Sun* and reverse engineered the technology we needed to activate the abandoned fighters, which were in pristine condition. We are now building our own."

When Cora finished speaking, Leahcim clapped.

"Thank you, Cora. I'm impressed."

"You are welcome, Commander."

"So you see, Captain," T'oann said, "we have been extremely productive in the time since your departure. We desire to travel and explore the Great Beyond as your Alliance has."

A new voice entered the conversation. "And we desire to protect and defend ourselves from invaders from the Great Beyond."

Everyone turned toward the doorway of Vee's room to see Zora and Lungeon standing in it.

"Please, come in," Vee said. "I've been waiting to thank my rescuers."

"There is no need to thank us, Captain. We were simply doing our duty."

"Then I must thank you for not shirking your duty. If it weren't for you, I would have most certainly died."

"I'm glad you're alive," Markka said.

"So am I," Lin said.

"Yes," Cora said. "The queen and Lady Lin were deeply affected by the news of what we all thought was your demise."

Clearly embarrassed, both Markka and Lin said, "Cora!"

"Have I offended you? Apologies."

"No, Cora, you haven't offended anybody. Our queen here and her cohort just didn't want Vee to know just how broken up they were."

As Leahcim spoke to Cora, Markka made slashing motions in front of her throat trying to get him to stop speaking. It did not work. But it did draw Vee's attention. Markka stopped slashing too late. So she pretended Vee had not seen her. But she had. Markka and Lin began looking everywhere but at Vee.

"Is that so?" Vee asked.

"Yes," Cora said without hesitation.

"Cora!" Lin and Markka said together again.

Vee smiled at them both then extended her arms beckoning them to come closer so she could embrace them. They did, and instantly burst into tears as soon as Vee hugged them.

Leahcim whispered to T'oann, "So much for decorum."

***

A few days following her crew's discovery of the new portal, Parsons stood in Admiral K'mar's situation room discussing the new turn of events with the admiral and Chappie.

"Are you serious, Greg? Captain Leahcim and the others have lived an entire lifetime in another universe?"

All Chappie said was, "Yes."

"And the portal to that universe was in the Gihon Nebula?"

"Yes."

"And now that portal doesn't exist because Captain Vee blew up the one removing access to all the others?"

"Correct."

The admiral strummed her fingers on the desk.

"Why you little son-of-a-bitch. You conveniently left those details out of your report to me."

Oops, Parsons thought. She honestly thought the commander had told the admiral everything. She mentioned Captain Leahcim, Markka, and Cora in her report. Now she was in the same room with them as they engaged in a heated discussion.

Admiral K'mar paced back and forth in thought before she spoke again.

"I understand why you did it, Greg, and that's admirable, but it would have been nice if you had given me a heads up."

"Understood," he said.

K'mar remained quiet for a few moments before she spoke again. When she did, it was to Parsons.

"Captain, this new portal you and your crew discovered needs to be investigated. We need to know where it leads, who or what's on the other side, and we need to defend it—if need be—from incursions by the GSE and whoever their equivalent might be on the other side."

"I'm surprised the GSE hasn't made a move on it already," Parsons said.

"Because they probably don't know about it. Not yet anyway. And we need to keep it that way. They obviously know we know about the portal they were using. And I'm sure they know it's now closed off to them."

227

The admiral stopped speaking, folded her arms, turned her back to Parsons and looked at her reflection in a nearby window.

"They are resourceful," Chappie said.

"That they are," K'mar replied. "They're also dangerously deceptive. They led us to believe they were from the territory along the frontier, not from another universe."

"No," Chappie challenged. "We allowed ourselves to be lulled into a false sense of security through our own complacency."

K'mar let out a tired breath.

"So now we need to be more vigilant and proactive. We need to beef up our forces before the GSE recovers."

"I agree," Chappie said.

The room grew quiet before anyone spoke. Chappie broke the silence.

"I think if we keep a formidable size fleet at the new portal and expand our presence, they will more than likely give it a wide berth. Hopefully, they'll think we're guarding the area because we think the portal Captain Vee destroyed might reactivate. That should buy us some time to investigate the new one," Chappie said.

"We dealt the Sairidians a serious blow when we destroyed that portal," Parsons said. "We cut off a major supply line."

K'mar stopped looking out the window and at her reflection and turned to face Parsons.

"Unfortunately, there's no telling how many GSE divisions, units, stations, and ships are embedded in Alliance space. And if that thing is a new doorway to their universe, we need to stop them from using it. That's why I want you to get out there and find out what's on the other side of that thing."

Parsons was stunned by K'mar's revelation. "Why me, admiral? I'm not the sneak-around-and-spy type."

"Because you have four officers who are among the best at sneaking around and spying. They are also the most experienced with what you might encounter."

K'mar huffed out a short breath and looked at Chappie who remained impassive. She looked back at Parsons and said, "And because I trust you'll get the job done. But at the first sign of trouble, get your ass out of there."

"Don't need to tell me twice."

"Good."

K'mar picked up her tablet from off her desk and tapped in a few commands. She stared hard at the screen before she spoke again.

The *T'ayMak*'s refit will take another thirty days. Until then, I'm going to increase our presence in the area. In the meantime, I want you and your crew to get some R&R."

But—"

"That's an order. I want you and your team to relax. You're no good to us, tired and stressed."

"Yes, admiral."

"Dismissed."

As Parsons turned to leave the room, she glanced at Chappie. He returned her glance with a quick half smile and a nod. She was assured that he was not angry with her because she mentioned Leahcim, Markka, and Cora in her report. The next thirty days would not weigh heavy on her conscience.

A month later, Parsons was again standing in the admiral's situation room.

"The refit is complete, admiral. They just finished installing the cloak. We're scheduled for a test run at the end of the week."

"Not anymore. You've been cleared to depart now."

"But the cloak hasn't been tested."

"This mission will give you an opportunity to test it. I'm afraid we've let too much time pass already. Despite the beefed up patrols, I don't want the GSE getting any ideas."

"Understood."

Since the battle of Epsilon Base and the Battle of the Portal, Alliance engineers were busy retrofitting the fast attack ships with cloaking technology. Parsons had hoped to have time to test the upgrade. Her only concern was the cloak failing at the wrong time. But in light of the importance of the reconnaissance mission, it was a chance worth taking. She was glad Romar placed Raqmar in charge of engineering. If anyone could assist with the refit and keep the cloak working, it was him.

The *T'ayMak* was currently berthed in a repair bay aboard the *Alasta*, one of the Alliance's supercarriers. Until Epsilon Base was fully operational again, supercarriers were being utilized as mobile space battle stations and repair facilities. Their mobility made them harder targets to attack.

When Parsons returned to her ship following her meeting with the admiral, she was peppered with a barrage of questions.

"We're being sent to investigate the new portal," she told them. "The refit will have to wait."

"When do we leave?" Sojourner asked.

"Now."

Raqmar's annoyance was obvious. "But we haven't had time to test the cloak."

"We'll test it on the way."

"That sucks," he said. Then as an afterthought said, "sir."

"In this instance, I agree with you." Parsons looked around at her staff, sighed, then said, "Alright, everybody, prepare for departure. Is my cloak ready, Lieutenant Commander?"

"Yes, Captain."

"Sparks, engage cloak."

Sparks keyed in a sequence of commands on her console then tapped a button.

Parsons looked at Karona and asked, "Well?"

"The board says we're invisible and so does the deck officer, Captain."

"Good." Hopeful her gamble might work, Parsons ordered Sparks to lift off from the *Alasta*'s deck and head straight for the portal. "With all deliberate speed, Lieutenant."

"Aye, Captain."

Chapter 48

In the sols following Vee's rescue, she recovered from her physical scars. The emotional ones took longer to heal, but thirty sols later, she was helping the Progenshans develop their space fleet.

Thanks to efforts on her behalf by Markka, T'oann, and Leahcim, Vee was put in charge of the Great Beyond Defense Force. Markka came up with the name.

After having just gotten off a conference call with Vee and Markka about a GBDF matter, Leahcim sat fuming on a small boulder in his compound garden staring at the gurgling pond in front of him. He was brooding. His request to regularly patrol the newly discovered portal was denied.

T'oann emerged from their bungalow carrying two glasses of tree sap nectar.

"How did the meeting with the High Council go?" she asked while she handed one of the glasses to her husband then sat on the boulder next to him.

The midsol suns were directly overhead, but a canopy of the trees shielded them from the intensity of their rays.

Leahcim was miffed. "I can't believe they don't see the urgency in keeping an eye on that portal," he said. "They're a bunch of idiots."

T'oann took a sip of her nectar and said, "The High Council is of the opinion that unless something threatening comes through it, we should not do anything to draw attention to ourselves."

"Not you too?"

She took another sip then curled up closer to Leahcim. "I did not say I agree with the council's decision. I am only restating what they have made abundantly clear."

Leahcim grunted. "The idiots believe as long as we continue to build our forces and build up our planetary defenses, we'll be able to defend ourselves. They are apparently blind and stupid. B'rtann and Sho'khan lodged formal complaints."

"Be that as it may, they have ruled. The burden is now on us to show them the folly of their decision before it is too late."

"The idiots even shot down Markka's pleas." He heaved an exasperated sigh before he said, "And you know how persuasive she can be."

231

T'oann chuckled. "Yes, I do know how persuasive she can be."

"She is pissed. I had to drag her out of the meeting. She was kicking, screaming, and hissing at them. You should have seen the looks on their faces. I think a few of them might have shit themselves."

"I wish I had been there to have seen that."

Leahcim smiled at the memory of Markka's outburst at the meeting. "You would have been proud."

"So what is the next step?"

"I don't know. What we need is a godsend."

"I thought you didn't believe in those."

"I don't, but right now, one of those would be better than what we've got." He took a long sip of his nectar. "Wow. This is either really good or I'm really thirsty."

"I'd say a bit of both. So what are your next steps?"

He took another sip then said, "Markka has authorized Raqtar's people to work directly with Section Ten in building a space station equipped with long-range sensors and an advanced weapons system. Kind of like an early warning system with teeth. Cora is overseeing the entire project. She asked for Vee and Ramie to be the project managers."

"Did she accept?"

"Without hesitation. Since she has the most recent experience with the Alliance and GSE, and has worked closely with Ramie, Cora thought she was the most logical choice to assist with defending ourselves against forces that will undoubtedly have an overwhelming technological and numerical advantage."

He stood up, drained his glass, then stared out over the city. Their bungalow sat on a hill that gave them a panoramic view of much of Uderra.

T'oann sat her glass down on the boulder and asked, "What's wrong?"

Without looking at her he said, "Cora's best estimate is we can have a functioning orbiting station in a cycle at the earliest."

"That's good, right?"

"Only if nothing hostile comes through that portal before then."

***

Admiral K'mar had an ulterior motive when she ordered Parsons to fly cloaked and run silent the entire way to the portal. She wanted to know if the upgrade would work when it was tasked to perform beyond its expected parameters, and if the Alliance ships assigned to defend the portal could detect the *T'ayMak*.

The victory over the GSE at the Battle of the Portal was common knowledge to most Alliance citizens. What was not common knowledge were the GSE attacks on trade shipping and frontier outposts. The Sairidians were still a threat to the Alliance, and the military brass needed to know if the recent upgrades to its cloaking technology gave them an edge. Deploying the *T'ayMak* would be the test.

Parsons initially objected on the grounds that they might be mistaken for a GSE ship, if detected, and be fired upon or the untested cloak would fail and they would be targeted by the GSE. The admiral simply told Parsons to make sure that did not happen. She relied on the experience of Vee's crew to compensate for the unexpected and improvise if they had to.

As they approached the portal, and the Alliance ships guarding it, Sparks gave Parsons an update.

"Captain, it looks like they don't see us or they're doing a damn good job of ignoring us."

"Bring us in slow and continue to run silent. Pull up alongside the *Quicksand*. Let's see how long it takes them to notice us."

"Aye, Captain."

Sparks brought the *T'ayMak* in slow and shadowed the movements of the larger ship. For thirty minutes, they followed the *Quicksand* without drawing the ship's attention.

"Karona."

"Yes, Captain."

"Are you detecting any other cloaked vessels in the area besides us?"

"No, sir. Nothing."

"What about you, Sojourner? You detect anything?"

"No, Captain."

Parsons rubbed her chin in thought. On one hand, not being detected was a good thing. On the other hand, not so good. It meant that cloaked Sairidian ships could easily go undetected.

"Whatdaya say, Romar, should we startle 'em a bit? Put the fear of complacency in them?"

"Yes, sir," he said. He displayed an impish grin, which, on a Selemite, looked sinister.

"Karona, get me a narrow band and use this frequency." Parsons transmitted the frequency to Karona's station.

"Ready to transmit, Captain."

"Good. Go."

Karona opened communications and nodded to Parsons who began with a set of expletives.

The voice on the other end was noticeably surprised and unmistakably miffed.

"Rosa, what the fuck? Where the hell are you?"

"Shadowing your sorry ass for the last thirty minutes, Bill."

"What? No way."

"Check your port side, baby brother."

A few seconds later Karona said, "They're pinging us, Captain."

***

T'oann watched as Leahcim walked around their garden thinking of ways to get around the High Council's order. She knew their decision did not sit comfortably with him and he would not let it rest until he figured something out.

On his umpteenth trip around the garden, he stopped pacing, snapped his fingers, and said, "I got it!"

"Got what, dear?"

"A way around the council." He turned to look at her with a devious grin.

"How?"

"They said we can't patrol the area, they said nothing about training." He winked at his wife. "Are you up for taking a little ride?"

T'oann smiled seductively at her husband. She enjoyed seeing his delight at solving an insurmountable problem. "I'm up for whatever you're up for," she said.

He shivered in what was an intentional display of pleasure. "I love it when you use contractions."

He called out for Cora.

"Yes, Commander?"

"I'm going to be conducting a training mission and need the following personnel." He rattled off the names of those he knew would go along with what he had in mind. "Tell them to suit up and meet us in a mos at the main hangar."

"Right away, Commander."

"Oh, and Cora? If you want to ride along, you're more than welcome to join me."

Leahcim suspected Cora was tired of being planet-bound and would appreciate the opportunity to get back into space like the rest of them. He was certain of it when he heard the relief in her voice. It sounded almost like a swoon.

"Thank you, Commander. I would very much appreciate that."

He decided to have some fun with Cora. "Did you just swoon?"

She hesitated. "No."

"Now you're lying."

She hesitated again. "I am not lying, Commander. I was simply saying what you thought you heard was not what you thought you heard."

"Yeah, right."

Then she did something he had heard her do only once before. She giggled.

"I swear, you're becoming more biologic as you get older."

"I do not see the need to insult me, Commander," she said. Then she giggled again.

He heaved a heavy sigh, rolled his eyes and said, "Whatever." Leahcim took T'oann's hand, bowed and asked, "Wanna be my wingman?"

T'oann bowed in return and said, "I thought you'd never ask." Then she giggled. She was as excited as a new cadet on their first assignment. It would not be her first time flying a fighter outside of the simulator, but it would be their first time flying together.

He just frowned and said, "Let's get a move on. I don't want to be the last one to arrive."

His underwhelming response prompted her to touch his mind. She sensed he was as excited as she was.

Leahcim sensed her presence and protested. "Hey, no peeking."

Chapter 49

They were the last ones to arrive.

All of the pilots Leahcim requested were waiting. Zora, Lungeon, and Lin. Waiting with them was Markka.

"Where the hell have you been?" Markka asked.

Leahcim scowled at her. "And just what the hell are *you* doing here?"

"Waiting for your sorry ass so we can get this show on the road."

"We're only going on a short training run. There's no need or reason for you to come along."

"Bullshit. This isn't just any training run. If it was, cadets would make up this group."

Leahcim sighed in frustration. "Oh come on. I'm only looking out for your best interests. If something goes wrong, our queen would be in danger. You could get hurt."

"I got hurt just sitting in my garden."

Markka referred to an incident during the Thouron War when a rocket slipped through a gap in the defense shield and exploded mere meters from where she was meditating in the palace garden. The healers were not sure if she would survive at the time.

"Besides," she continued, "if there is a slim chance that we might be able to establish communications with the Alliance, I want to be there. And if it's something else, I want to be there for that too. Dammit, David, don't shut me out."

He recalled her confession of feeling helpless when he and T'oann died and her breakdown when Vee was found.

Leahcim huffed, "Is Tory on board with this?"

A voice from the shadows said, "Yes, yes he is."

Tory stepped forward and placed one of his beefy arms around his wife. He locked eyes with Leahcim before nodding his approval.

"Okay, you can come," Leahcim said in surrender. "Alright, everybody listen up. What we're about to do goes against the High Council's wishes. So if anyone wants to back out. Now's the time to do it. No one will think any less of you."

"Can we just get on with this, father?" Zora griped.

Leahcim looked at T'oann who simply smiled.

"As irreverent as always, I see," Leahcim said as he winked at his daughter. He then said, "Cora and Ramie, you'll each have your own fighters."

Cora began to object, "But Commander—"

Leahcim cut her off. "But nothing. You and Ramie earned your spots on this team. You both bring an insight and experience the rest of us don't have. I'm entrusting you to independently assess the situation and make decisions without deferring to us. Now stop stalling and let's fly."

After running through their preflight checks and being cleared by flight control, one by one the eight fighters took off and disappeared into the Great Beyond.

***

Parsons' conversation with her brother was brief and direct.

"The admiral wants us to go through this thing, gather intel, then get the hell out and report what we learn. Your job is making sure no one follows us."

"Don't bring any problems back when you return. We got enough trouble already."

"Hey, you know me, little brother."

"That's what worries me. May the Gods have your backs."

"Yours too."

Parsons signaled Karona to close the communicator. Then ordered Sparks to take them through the portal.

"Aye, Captain."

A moment later they were in another universe.

"Wow. Would you look at that?" Parsons marveled at the sudden Doppler shift in the star patterns. "I had no idea what to expect."

238

She recovered quickly from her awe and excitement at the experience and got down to business.

"Okay, people, start scanning for lifeforms, advanced technology, planets, spatial anomalies, the works. We need anything and everything. Our lives just may depend on what we discover."

Her order was followed by a series of "Aye, Captain" responses.

She addressed Sparks and Karona. "Okay, what can you tell me?"

"We are in uncharted space—even for us," Sparks said.

"Then I recommend we record and catalog everything. And let's stay close to the portal in case we need to make a hasty exit."

***

Eight small fighters flew in a staggered single file formation in radio silence. Leahcim was the lead. He was followed by T'oann, Markka, and Lin. Zora, Lungeon, Ramie, and Cora brought up the rear.

Each fighter was equipped with the latest sensors of Cora's design. They were comparable to anything the Alliance might have with a greater emphasis on detecting hidden objects like cloaked ships. They could also detect lifeforms, but not distinguish differences between them.

The weapons systems were also designed to mimic what the Alliance military used. If they ran into trouble, they hoped they would at least be able to deliver a powerful punch. One feature the Progenshan fighters had that Alliance fighters did not was a complement of missiles.

Cora took to heart something Leahcim said from time to time: "*Even if you lose the fight, make sure the other guy knows he was in one.*"

The fighters' defensive capabilities had a slight edge on the Alliance. Cora realized the fighters were not as sophisticated as their Alliance or GSE counterparts and would need an edge to survive head-to-head combat. So she and her progeny developed a rudimentary energy field that would surround the fighters in a primitive version of shields that would absorb or deflect energy and projectile weapons. And not just protect against space dust that would normally penetrate the hull of a speeding ship.

Alliance and GSE fighters did not have shields since they were small, fast, and maneuverable. The capital ships of each fleet had shields only because they were bigger and slower. This made them easier targets to hit.

The Progensha fighters also lacked hyperspace communications and hyperspace engines. But their power plants were capable of generating enough energy to enable sublight or space-normal travel.

Another weakness was the lack of high speed communications. It took too long for messages to travel between objects the farther apart they were.

Cora and her children did their best to compensate for the lag in Progenshan technological capabilities.

Leahcim warned them that the best they might be able to do is bloody the nose of an adversary then do some fancy flying to escape if they could.

Everyone knew the risk and was willing to take it.

Ramie and Cora were conducting deep space sensor sweeps when Cora broke radio silence and recommended they stop. They were a few kilometers from the portal when she and Ramie detected spatial distortions near the portal's event horizon.

Leahcim ordered them to hold where they were while they took the time to assess the data Cora displayed.

"Well I'll be damned," Leahcim said. "There's definitely a distortion field of some kind out there."

"So we're staring at something hiding in plain sight," Markka said.

"Are we within their sensor range, Cora?" Leahcim asked.

"Unable to ascertain that information at this time, Commander. I recommend we keep our distance until we can determine its intent."

"Okay. We'll hold here and watch and wait."

They did not have to wait long. Karona saw them first.

"Captain," Karona said.

"What is it, Lieutenant?"

"Eight bogies just appeared on the edge of our sensor range."

"Get me a visual."

"We're too far away for anything clear, Captain."

"Are they packin'?"

"From what I can tell, they are equipped with energy and physical ordinance."

"Missiles?"

Karona checked her readings. "Yes, sir."

"What are they doing?"

"Just sitting there, sir."

"Any chatter between them?"

"Yes, sir, it's definitely not Sairidian. But the signals are too weak and too short to get a clear fix on them."

"Keep working on that, Lieutenant."

"Aye, sir."

Parsons got up from her chair and strolled up to the ship's main viewer. She studied it like she was studying for an exam.

"You think they see us?"

"I don't know, sir. But I would err on the side of caution. They were on a fast approach then seemed to stop suddenly as if they did."

"Dammit. That means they're probably able to detect us."

"Possibly, sir."

Parsons continued to study the screen as she stroked her chin. "This is a serious problem," Parsons said.

"How so, sir?"

"They can see us. Romar."

"Aye, sir."

"Tell the gun crews to energize the batteries. And have engineering standby. Then get down to the fighter bay. I want you ready to launch if it comes to that."

"Aye, sir." Romar instructed Karona to alert the weapons division, notify engineering, then tell the fighter bay to expect him. He waited until Karona contacted who she needed to before he left the bridge.

The *T'ayMak* had a small fighter bay that housed four fighters. They were only deployed as defensive weapons whenever the ship was disabled or disarmed. They had never been needed and Parsons prayed they would not be needed now.

"Any movement, Lieutenant?"

"None, Captain. It's like they know we're here and they're waiting for us to make the first move," Karona said.

"Okay, we'll play their game. Sparks, scooch us a bit toward them and let's see what they do."

"Aye, Captain. Scooching."

Sparks moved the *T'ayMak* a few meters toward the unidentified craft then stopped.

Markka was the first in the group to comment on the slight movement the distortion made toward them.

"Whoa. Did everyone just see that?"

"Yeah," Leahcim replied. "I think we have our answer. We're too close. They see us. Back it up."

They engaged reverse thrusters and slowly backed away from the distortion.

"What do we do if they attack?" T'oann asked.

"We make a stand," Leahcim said. "We can't run back to Progensha. We'll reveal the planet's location and expose everyone to whatever that thing plans on doing."

"Alright, everybody remember your simulation training," Markka said. "If there ever was a time to rely on it, it's now."

Sparks tracked the bogies and saw them back away from the *T'ayMak*.

"Did you see that, Captain?" Sparks asked. "They backed off."

"That answers the question of whether they can see us. All hands, to battle stations."

The alert klaxon blared and the crew dashed to their stations.

Sojourner, who had remained uncharacteristically quiet, suddenly spoke.

"I think going to battle stations is a bit premature, Captain."

"Why?"

"They have shown no attempts to threaten or attack. Their behavior and posture suggests one of defense. They may be simply curious about us."

"You may be right, but I can't take the chance you're wrong. They just might be waiting for reinforcements."

"But, Captain, we may be in a position to establish a first contact situation with a potential ally."

"Or we could be in a first contact situation with a potential new foe."

Sojourner was adamant in her position and insisted there was another way to handle the situation.

"The admiral charged us with gathering intel then departing with what we know. Going in guns blazing is not the answer. If they are new hostiles, let it not be said that we threw the first punch. We have invaded their space."

"They were in ours first," Parsons said.

"And they did nothing to provoke a violent response. Do you want history to remember you as the Alliance captain who turned a potential opportunity into a second front and expanded the war?"

"No, but I don't want history to remember me as the captain who allowed a new enemy to threaten the Alliance." Parsons weighed Sojourner's words. If those unknowns floating barely within sensor range were not hostile, provoking a hostile encounter might get herself and her crew killed before they could pass along their intel. That would, without question, be counterproductive to the mission. "Back us up, Lieutenant."

"Aye, Captain."

Sparks put the *T'ayMak* in reverse and crept back to their original position.

"Lieutenant, Karona, tell the troops to stand down, but remain on standby."

"Aye, sir."

Chapter 50

"Looks like we got us a game of cat and mouse," Leahcim said. "So, Cora, Ramie, do you think the encryption is working?"

The encryption Leahcim referred to was the algorithm program Karona gave them when the *Infiltrator* last visited. Cora put her own spin on it by incorporating the communications system she and her children used.

"Unable to tell, Commander. The other ship has made no attempt to communicate."

"Here's an idea," Markka said. The sarcasm was unmistakable. "Let's send them a friendly greeting. If they fire on us, then we'll know where they stand. It's better than just sitting out here staring each other down."

"They'll know we can see them," Lungeon said.

Markka gave him a snarky reply, "I think they know that already."

"Good point."

Without allowing Markka to take her next breath, Leahcim said, "Cora, send a we-come-in-peace greeting."

"Doing it now, Commander."

As soon as the message was sent, Karona began analyzing it then sat and literally scratched her head. "Hmm," she said.

"What is it, Lieutenant?"

"The bogies just sent us a message."

"What's it say?"

There was a slight irritation in her voice. "Working on it."

"Work faster. I need to know if it's a greeting or a warning."

As Karona worked to decipher the message, she thought she recognized bits of data. She decided to ask Sojourner for help.

"Hey, Sojourner, are you seeing this?"

"Yes, I am. It is most peculiar."

Their conversation had Parsons' full attention.

"What is 'most peculiar?'"

Karona answered first. "Part of this message is using some of the algorithmic patterns of my encryption/decryption program."

"And part of it is in Uderran," Sojourner said.

"The rest is some sort of binary code I've never seen before," Karona finished.

"Wait. Did you say Uderran?"

"Yes, sir."

"Isn't that the planet Leahcim, Markka, and Cora live on?"

"Actually," Sojourner said, "the planet is called Progensha. One of the languages spoken is Uderran."

"So that could mean they achieved space travel," Karona said. "It has been several days since we were there."

"That would be years for them, right?"

"Correct, Captain."

"Okay, get a move on deciphering the message. I gotta know for sure."

"I believe I have, Captain," Sojourner said.

"Okay, read it to me."

"I believe it roughly translates to, 'We come in peace.'"

"Tell them so do we."

Karona transmitted the message and Cora told the group.

Leahcim could not believe what Cora told them. "You actually said we come in peace?"

"Yes, Commander."

"And you got a reply back that said, 'So do we?'"

"Yes, Commander."

"Send another message and ask them to show themselves."

"Right away, Commander."

Cora sent the request and Karona received it.

"So what did they say?" Parsons asked.

"They want us to show ourselves."

Parsons struggled with the thought for a moment before she decided. "Drop the cloak," she ordered.

The bridge security officer complied with the order. The ship shimmered into view.

Leahcim and Markka were speechless. Lin, just as surprised as the others, said what Leahcim and Markka thought. "Oh my God. That looks like the *T'ayMak*."

"You are correct, Lady Lin. It is indeed the *T'ayMak*."

"How the hell is it cloaked? That class isn't equipped with cloaking technology."

"Well, it is now," Markka said. "If she's got cloaking tech, that means the shit has hit the fan. So what do we do now?"

"Cora, say we welcome the *T'ayMak* to Progenshan space and ask them why they're using cloaking technology?"

Cora sent the message and Karona recited it to Parsons.

"They say, Welcome, *T'ayMak*, to Progenshan space. Why are you using cloaking technology?'"

Parsons never had the patience for diplomacy or first contact situations. They always grated on her nerves. But she was a cautious person.

"Tell them I want to know how they know who we are before I answer any more questions."

Karona received the request and Cora transmitted it to the group.

Leahcim thought over the request then asked, "Cora, who was the last captain of the *T'ayMak* when we crashed on Progensha.

"Captain Rosa Parsons."

"She's a hard-ass," Markka said.

"That she is," Lin agreed.

Leahcim decided. "Tell her it's Commander David Leahcim. Send my old Alliance service number."

Cora transmitted the message and immediately upon receiving it Karona said, "Fuck me sideways."

"What is it, Lieutenant?" Parsons was instantly on alert.

"It's Commander Leahcim."

Parsons was skeptical. "Are you sure?"

"Quite sure, Captain," Sojourner said. "He transmitted his service number. I have been able to confirm and authenticate it."

With an undertone of noticeable excitement in her voice, Karona asked, "Captain?"

"Yes, Lieutenant?"

"He's asking if we would like an escort to Progensha." The amazement in Karona's voice was hard to mask. Even Sparks was fidgeting in her seat. "What should I tell him?"

"Tell them to stand by. Sojourner?"

"Yes, Captain?"

"How long has it been since you guys left Progensha?"

"Approximately forty days, Allurian time."

"So shouldn't it be roughly forty years later for them?"

"Yes, Captain."

"Is it possible this portal sent us back in time?"

"Very possible, Captain."

Parsons considered her choices. On one hand, it could be a clever ruse. On the other hand, it could be the real deal.

"Lieutenant Karona."

"Sir."

"Tell him to escort away."

"Yes, sir." There was more caution in Karona's voice now that Parsons placed doubt in everyone's mind.

Parsons had one more caveat to impart to her crew.

"Everybody, keep your eyes and ears open for trouble. You know how it always seems to find us. Oh, yeah. Tell him the reason we have a cloak is because the shit hit the fan."

Chapter 51

Leahcim ordered the group to form up around the *T'ayMak* in an escort pattern. As soon as they did, Parsons ordered a sensor sweep of each fighter. Cora sent a coded message to each pilot's cockpit dash that they were being scanned.

"Holy crap," Karona said.

"What is it, Lieutenant?"

"Scans indicate the life signs include two Terrans, one Felid, three Progenshans, and two unknowns. One of the Progenshans is half Terran. Another is half Progenshan and half Felid."

"Are you sure?" Parsons asked.

"Yes, sir."

"What about the two unknowns?"

"I'm not getting any bio readings."

"AI? SI?"

"Undetermined."

Parsons rapped her fingers on the arm of her chair in thought. As weird as it seemed, but it was beginning to look like Leahcim and Markka might be among their escorts. It was the two unknowns that concerned her.

"Do we have the bio records of Captain Leahcim and Lieutenant Markka on file?

Karona ran a quick check of the ship's database. "Yes, sir."

"Well?"

Karona ran a comparison check. "Confirmed, sir. Captain Leahcim and Lieutenant Markka are in two of the escort ships. And there's something else."

"What?"

"The other Terran; the bio signs match Lieutenant Lin."

"Well I'll be damned."

As Parsons marveled at the revelation, another bridge officer, Ensign Greene, gave Parsons an assessment of the fighters. The young engineer told her captain the fighters were of inferior design and were equipped with primitive shielding.

"They could be easily handled by the *T'ayMak*, Captain."

The young officer was almost gloating. Parsons figured the ensign did not know of Leahcim or Markka's reputations as pilots. And if Lin was with them, whoever else they were flying with had to be of comparable ability.

"Ensign Greene."

"Yes, Captain."

The ensign, a Terran with pale rose petal skin and long brown hair tied into a bun on the top of her head, sat confidently at her station.

"I suggest you review the service records of Lieutenant Markka, Captain David Leahcim, and Memphis Lin then get back to me on whether the *T'ayMak* could easily handle them. And look the word badass up in the dictionary. You'll see their faces by the definition."

Ensign Greene's self-assured confidence evaporated like a drop of water on a scorching hot pan.

"Yes, sir. Right away, sir."

"Okay, people, let's sit back and enjoy the ride. Oh, and Lieutenant Karona?"

"Yes, sir?"

"Monitor everything."

"Yes, sir."

While Parsons and her crew settled in, Leahcim and the others were busy assessing and analyzing the *T'ayMak*. Cora updated everyone on what she knew about Parsons, her crew, and the ship. She reminded them that some of the data might be a bit out of date since, for them, close to ten cycles had passed.

Leahcim thanked Cora then asked her to encode a message he was about to send to Progensha.

"Certainly, Commander. You may speak when ready."

"Uderra Base, this is flight training leader. Over."

Thanks to Cora, the excruciating time lag in communications was cut in half, but it still took a few mictons before Uderra Base replied.

"This is Uderra Base. What is your status?"

"We are bringing back a present. Courtesy of the portal."

A few mictons of silence was followed by a question from an obviously confused voice.

"Say again, training leader?"

"We're bringing home a package. A very large package. It won't fit in anything we got so we're gonna leave it outside the front gate."

He waited for the reply.

"Copy that. Please standby."

There was the obligatory wait and time lag before they were given permission to land outside the city gate.

"The laundry services are going to be pretty busy when people see what we're bringing," Markka said. She snickered as she said it.

They escorted the *T'ayMak* through the Progenshan atmosphere and over Uderra so the people could get a good look at the ship. By Progensha standards, the *T'aymak* was enormous. There was nowhere in the city it would have been able to land.

Now that they were back home, Leahcim thought it was a good time to establish an actual verbal communication with the Alliance ship.

"Commander Leahcim to *T'ayMak*."

"This is the *T'ayMak*," Karona responded.

Leahcim paused before he asked, "Kay? Is that you?"

She could barely contain her excitement. "Yes, Commander. It's me."

His curiosity got the best of him. "What the hell are you doing on the *T'ayMak*?"

"The captain had me, Sparks, and Raq assigned to her.

"I'll be damned. Ramie said you guys were rescued by Captain Parsons. Never thought she'd take you on."

"Wait. Ramie is with you?"

This time Markka answered.

"Yeah. We rescued him from a debris field on your side of the portal, and he briefed us on the battle and what happened to the *Infiltrator*."

Not wanting to be left out of the conversation on her own ship, Parsons interrupted.

"Sorry to butt in on your little family reunion, but could we get back to landing and disembarking?"

"Sure thing, Captain," Markka said.

Leahcim gave Parsons' crew specific instructions regarding landing. He told them a greeting party would meet their ship and escort the senior officers to the palace hall where they would be met by the High Council, senior staff, Progenshan military, and a special guest.

Once Sparks landed the ship, Parsons asked, "So has the place changed much since you were last here?"

Chapter 52

Parsons and her crew waited an hour before the official entourage arrived to receive them.

"The welcoming committee is here," Karona announced. She tugged on her dress uniform. She hated dress uniforms.

"Why do they look like ancient Terran Romans?" Parsons asked.

Sparks shrugged, "It's part of their culture."

"Oh." After a quick survey of the bridge, Parsons said, "Okay, everybody going ashore follow me."

Parsons headed for the turbo lift. Sparks, Karona, and Romar fell into step behind her. Without missing a stride she stepped into the lift and said, "Keep the engine running, people."

When they reached the fighter bay gangway, Raqmar was there waiting. He tugged and pulled at his dress uniform. He appeared to have as much dislike for it as the others.

 "Glad you could join us, Lieutenant Commander."

"Glad to be able to, sir."

"Now let's not keep our guests waiting. Open her up," Parsons ordered.

The slight hum of the gangway mechanism signaled the start of the lowering of the ramp. Standing at the bottom was a small band of soldiers. Next was a group of people who looked like dignitaries. At the head of them was the official liaison who greeted them with the traditional military Uderran salute of crossed arms in front of her chest.

"I am Captain Zora of the House of Mahli. It was my duty and honor to escort you to my homeworld. So on behalf of the people of Uderra and the planet of Progensha, welcome."

Parsons, who despised formality and standing on ceremony, sucked it up and returned the salute. "I am Captain Rosa Agusta Parsons of the Alliance ship *T'ayMak*. On behalf of the Alliance and my officers, I thank you."

Zora continued the greeting by introducing the dignitaries behind her as members of the High Council. Once all of the introductions were made, Zora gave a sly smile and nod before she said, "I have had the good fortune to meet and know three of the officers who stand with you. They are fine soldiers."

To Parsons' relief, Zora did not prolong the meeting. The Uderran officer curtly said, "Follow me." Then made a crisp about-face and strode toward the city's main gates. Parsons and her officers followed.

At the gate, Zora told them they would be taken to the Queen's Palace. She ushered them into a waiting transport.

In the transport, Parsons gave Sparks, Karona, and Raqmar the inquisitive eye. "So," she began, "You three have previously met this Captain Zora?"

After a few moments of silence, Raqmar spoke up. "Uh, yeah. We met her. She wasn't a captain then." He kept his head down and avoided meeting his captain's eyes. He did steal a glance at Romar whose poker face revealed nothing. Parsons suspected Raqmar was hiding something.

"Okay, spit it out. How well do you know her?"

Raqmar's eyes grew wide with embarrassment and he turned a darker shade of gray. "Oh, no, Captain, it's not like that."

"Then what?"

When he remained quiet, Sparks said, "She kicked his ass the first time we met."

Raqmar protested, "Cora helped her."

"Cora was nowhere near her when she took you down," Sparks said.

"How do you know? You were out cold," he protested.

"The captain wasn't."

"Oh, yeah. Forgot about that," he said.

"To be fair," Sparks said, "She and her people kicked all of our asses."

"What did Sojourner do?"

"They kicked her ass too," Sparks admitted.

Parsons looked at Karona who immediately went on the defensive.

"What? I wasn't part of the crew then." After a moment thinking about it, Karona volunteered that Zora was Commander Leahcim's daughter.

Parsons and Romar exchanged humorous looks before settling in for the rest of the ride. They rode in silence the rest of the way.

When their ride glided to a stop, the door to the cabin opened and they all filed out. Parsons was the last to exit. She stared up at the massive building and thought, *Damn, calling this place a palace is an understatement. It looks like a fortress.*

They followed Zora up a set of stairs that reminded Parsons of hiking up a steep mountain. At the top of their climb they entered a large, lavishly decorated banquet hall and were seated near what she presumed was the head of the table. There were two throne-like chairs sitting next to each other at the end.

Aside from Parsons and her officers, the only people were the wait staff, Zora, who sat directly across from her, and the military guards who stood stationed around the room.

Not comfortable making small talk, Parsons was glad Zora did not attempt to make any. She noted that Zora sat rigid and stoic-faced until a young man entered the room. The cold exterior melted away, but only a trained observer would have noticed.

Zora introduced the young man as one of the pilots who escorted the *T'ayMak* to Progensha. She said his name was Lungeon. He took a seat next to her. Soon, others began trickling into the room. Zora introduced each of them to Parsons and Romar. There was B'rtann, Supreme Military Commander, Sho'khan, the Chief Tactical Officer, Garath, the head healer, and a few others. Sparks, Karona, and Raqmar obviously knew these people because they spoke to each other in a manner close friends or associates did. When Lin and Piper entered, Sparks and Raqmar looked like they were going to explode at the seams. They turned to their captain with puppy dog eyes begging to greet the couple. Parsons nodded her approval. They nearly tripped over each other rushing over to them. There were the obligatory hugs and kisses. At least Parsons thought she could count on Karona keeping it together.

The lieutenant did keep it together until she saw Vee enter the room. Tears burst forth like a waterfall. Without seeking Parsons' approval, Karona ran over and hugged her former captain before the others noticed she was in the room. Parsons and Romar just sat staring in shock. Parsons was unable to move. A grinning Vee walked over to her friend, with the others in tow, and said, "Hey, Rosa, how are things?"

Parsons just sat where she was thinking she was looking at a ghost. Eventually, she found her voice.

"How . . . how?" Her voice quivered. "I watched you die." Parsons was on the verge of tears.

"The grace of the Gods," Vee said.

Parsons slowly stood on unsteady legs and tightly embraced her friend. "My life hasn't been the same without you in it. I've been lost without you." Then the tears ran down her cheeks like rain.

Vee passionately embraced Parsons and whispered in her ear, "I'm back."

The conversations and reunions were interrupted by a musical fanfare followed by Markka's familiar voice.

"Alright, everybody, sit."

The conversations lowered to a murmur as people took their seats. When everyone was seated, Markka turned to someone and said, "It's safe to come out now."

Three more people walked into the room. Tory, T'oann, and Leahcim.

"Really?" Leahcim asked. "Did you have to make it sound like we were hiding?"

"Yes, I did."

Markka and Tory took their seats at the head of the table while Leahcim and T'oann sat across from each other near the head of it.

Markka tapped her goblet to get everyone's attention. When she had it, she looked at her guests and said, "Hi, guys. Glad you could join us. We got a lot of catching up to do, but first we must give thanks to the Goddess."

Chapter 53

After the prayer was said, the food was served. Conversations were centered more around what was happening with the Alliance than with Progensha. The general consensus, as far as the Progenshans were concerned, was that the new portal was a grave threat to their existence.

Cora and Ramie filled everyone in on the scientific and technical details. Vee and her former crew talked about what they experienced up to the destruction of the portal. Vee continued with her rescue and recovery.

A communication link was established between the banquet hall and the *T'ayMak* allowing Sojourner and the crew to participate. For most of the crew, the news of alternate universes and the prospect of time travel was shocking. Members of the High Council, concerned with the new developments regarding the portal and the recent GSE activities, bombarded Parsons and Romar with questions.

What began as an informal gathering of friends, acquaintances, and dignitaries, morphed into a military briefing and strategy session.

Parsons, Romar, and Sojourner bore the brunt of the responsibility of explaining things to the Progenshans.

"Before we destroyed the portal," Parsons said, "the GSE was poised to escalate the war."

"But," Romar added, "they appear to be getting over their setback. We believe they will make another attempt within six to ten months, if not sooner."

Many of the Progenshan delegates seemed confused. Then one of them asked, "What are months?"

Obviously, no one had informed Romar or Parsons that there was no concept of weeks or months in Progenshan culture. So Leahcim volunteered to explain it.

"Oh," was all Romar managed to say.

Leahcim explained to the delegates that Romar was indicating between one hundred and twenty sols to three hundred sols. Give or take a sol.

"So because of your actions," one of the delegates said, "Progensha is in danger of being attacked by genociders?"

"The Alliance is prepared to provide assistance and protection," Romar said.

"You cannot protect yourselves. How can we expect you to protect us?"

Ouch, Parsons thought. *They got us there.*

Romar made a valiant attempt to explain how the Alliance has prevailed in the face of adversity. Something he hoped they would understand from what he learned about their own war.

Parsons attempted to put their minds at ease by sounding confident without saying anything of substance. She stood up from the table, placed her arms behind her back and said, "You have proven yourselves formidable warriors, savvy negotiators, and people of strong integrity. As you have honored your treaties and strengthened your relationships these past few years, we will honor your sovereignty."

She saw a few quizzical looks around the table before she corrected herself. "My apologies. Cycles."

Markka spoke on behalf of the Progenshans at the table.

"Those are fine and noble words, but they're just words. We're prepared to provide our support, trust, people, resources, and allegiance to the Alliance to ensure the security of our planet. What are you prepared to do?"

Parsons could see why Markka was their queen. *Tough little, bitch*, she thought. In a sweeping gesture of her arms toward her officers, she said, "We are prepared to give you all of the assistance you require. We will give you ships, weapons, personnel, and training. In exchange, we ask that we have free passage through the portal and a permanent presence in this universe so that we may better protect each other."

Leahcim and the others sat back and watched the members of the High Council and GBDF debate and discuss the pros and cons of Parsons' proposal.

As they debated, Romar leaned slightly toward his captain and whispered, "You know High Command and Fleet might not like what you're offering."

"Oh, I believe they will. There's no way they'll turn down the opportunity to set foot in a new universe or refuse help from a new ally. You know the old adage. Every little bit helps."

The Progenshans eventually agreed to table the discussion and resume the next sol. The delegate who was the chief spokesperson told Parsons and Romar they would have a firm answer by the end of the next sol.

Parsons nodded in agreement with a smile. "I guess that means tomorrow?" Parsons asked.

"It certainly does," Markka said.

When all of the delegates filed out leaving just Leahcim, Markka and the others in the room, Parsons leaned close to Romar and whispered, "I wonder who the hard-ass is?"

"The 'hard-ass' is Durard," Markka said. "He was the chief Thouron negotiator who brokered the peace accord that ended the war between them and the rest of us."

Parsons forgot about Markka's sharp sense of hearing. "Oh. Can he be trusted?"

"Yes. Old prejudices are hard to overcome, but the war ended cycles ago. And we've been making great strides toward reconciliation." Without batting an eye, Markka looked directly at Parsons and said, "It's who we are."

Eager to get back to her ship and familiar territory, Parsons sat up straight in her seat, smiled at everyone sitting around the table and said, "Thank you for the invitation, Your Majesty. My crew and I are honored to be in your presence and thank you for your gracious hospitality."

Markka sat in stupefied silence for a moment, as did everyone else, before she responded.

"You can knock off the formal speech crap. We all know that's not you. It's definitely not me."

"That's for sure," Leahcim said.

Romar leaned in close to Parsons and said in a low tone, "I told you."

Relieved that she did not have to pretend anymore, Parsons said, "Whew! I don't know what hurts more, this dress uniform or the formal speech."

"Knowing you," Markka said, "both."

"If the council agrees to my proposal, is it okay if I leave a few teams here to explore the planet while the rest of us scope out this area of space? I'd like to get the lay of the land, so to speak."

"Sure, knock yourself out," Markka said. "Just hang tight until the High Council decides. We don't want your people poking around before it's official."

"You have my word."

Near the end of the next sol, the *T'ayMak* was parked in orbit when Markka called and said the Council agreed to the proposal.

"You and your crew are free to spend however long you need to explore the city, the planet, or the solar system. You are also free to meet with the Mountainers and Dark Wooders, the Thourons, the Lungeons, and the Nomads."

"Great," Parsons said. "We'll begin running our studies and surveys. I estimate we'll need no more than a couple of weeks to gather what we need and notify the admiral."

"And tell your people, when they do start crawling around, to watch out for those ocean leviathans. They're equal opportunity devourers."

"I'll be sure to let them know."

Chapter 54

A month later, Parsons was aboard the *Alasta* standing in the conference room listening to Admiral K'mar.

"I send you on a secret reconnaissance mission and you come back with an informal agreement to share resources with a planet in another universe?" Admiral K'mar did not sound happy.

"That pretty much sums it up, admiral." Parsons sounded quite pleased with herself. She stood ramrod straight as K'mar paced around her conference room.

"Then there's the question about how long it took you to get back and report. We thought you were lost with all hands."

"Gathering the data we needed took longer than expected. I didn't want to report our progress and risk the GSE getting wind of it. I also wanted to be thorough."

"I should be mad at you, but I read your report. Under the circumstances, you made what you felt was the right call. High Command and Fleet might not think so, but I do. I'll talk to the Board and get back to you."

"Thank you, admiral."

"Don't thank me yet. This could blow up in our faces. If it does, you'll be hung out to dry. It could mean the end of your career."

"But the war?"

"Will continue with or without you. I would prefer with you."

"Me too, admiral."

"Hang tight and give me a couple of days. In the meantime, don't go anywhere."

"Understood."

Parsons did not expect what she did to be well received by the Board, but she never considered it might end her career. Now she really was angry. *How the hell could they not see the advantages of her agreement?* She wondered. *Would the Alliance leave the Progenshans to possibly face the GSE on their own?* She shook off the thought and tried to think about what her role might be if the Board agreed.

She locked herself in her quarters and gave orders she was not to be disturbed unless Admiral K'mar summoned her or if the Sairidians attacked.

For two days she did nothing but mope around in her quarters. Then on day three Sojourner told her the admiral wanted to see her.

After a quick shower and change of uniform, she was once again standing in front of K'mar, but this time Chappie was with her, and he did most of the talking.

"The admiral took a lot of creative license to get the Board to agree to your plan. And believe you me when I say she called in a lot of favors for this one."

"I appreciate—"

He cut Parsons off. "Don't. You have no idea what this cost her—and me." He studied her for a long moment before he continued. "Your surveys revealed a plethora of minerals, star systems, and limitless potential. The Alliance has agreed to sign a pact with the Progenshans. In return for whatever we learn and gain from them, Fleet wants to establish a permanent presence in their space."

"Sounds fair," Parsons said.

"We're not done," he said. "Not by a long shot. You see, Fleet wanted to court martial Captain Leahcim, Lieutenant Markka, and Officer Cora when they found out they're still alive."

"Why?"

"For refusing to return with Captain Vee when they had the chance. They considered them AWOL."

K'mar picked up from there. "But I talked them out of it. Like I talked them out of doing the same thing to Lieutenants Lin and Piper." K'mar hesitated before saying, "And Captain Vee."

"But why Vee?" Parsons wondered.

"Because after her rescue and recovery, a few Board members said it was her duty to return and report what she knew. But instead, she chose to stay like the others did."

"But—"

"Don't interrupt," Chappie warned.

Parsons held her tongue, K'mar continued to speak.

"I convinced the Board that due to the unusual nature of, let's just say extenuating circumstances, normal military discipline cannot be applied."

She paused long enough to see if Parsons was still paying attention. Certain she was, K'Mar continued.

"Against my better judgment, we *did not* tell the board where Vee and her crew spent their time while they were stuck in the past. We allowed them to believe they acquired the supplies they needed through various black market channels."

Parsons' breathed a sigh of relief.

"We *did* show the Board the visual records of the *Infiltrator* and the data you brought back with you. In light of the, shall we say, unusual circumstances, the Board decided to forgo all charges. Leahcim, Lin, and Piper are revered as heroes and living legends. Hell, Markka is their queen and chief political leader, and Cora and her . . . her . . . well she practically runs their entire technological system. Doing anything to any of them will erode whatever trust we have with the Progenshans."

Parsons breathed another sigh.

Chappie picked up the lecture. "However, in light of recent events, and intel that hints at an imminent attack by the GSE, I will be accompanying you to Progensha. Fleet is sending an entire task force."

That was totally unexpected. Parsons told the Progenshans the Alliance estimated they had six months to prepare. Now she was being told it was imminent.

"That's kind of excessive, don't you think?"

"No," Chappie said, "Once the GSE notices us using the portal, they'll no doubt want access to it and make a move to capture it or slip through undetected. We are prepared to secure and defend it at all costs. If you were them, what would you do?"

She hated to admit it, but she would launch a preemptive strike as soon as she could.

"Attack," she said.

"Exactly."

When the room finally filled with silence, Parsons asked, "May I inquire as to when we ship out?"

"Within the hour," K'mar said. "We sent a messenger craft with a modest military escort to Progensha with the terms of our agreement. They replied with their approval. Now it's just a matter of hammering out the details."

Hammering out the details took longer than expected before all factions of Progenshans were in agreement and a treaty was ratified. The Progenshans, with Markka and Durard as their chief negotiators, wanted full partnership in the Alliance. As Markka so eloquently put it, "Our asses are now as much on the line as yours–maybe more so." Once the agreement was officially signed, the Alliance got to work right away, shoring up the defenses on both sides of the portal.

Going against generations of tradition, the Progenshans permitted Alliance military personnel, diplomats, doctors, scientists, merchants, and civilians to immigrate. The resulting boon in knowledge and expertise was exponentially acquired.

Initially, there was token resistance and protests of cultural contamination by a small segment of Thourons. Their arguments echoed those that plunged the planet into a five-hundred-year war. But Durard eloquently and forcefully argued for people to embrace diversity and inclusion as a viable option to doing things the old way. He emphasized the knowledge gained through such contact.

Eventually, the resistance evaporated as the opportunities for free trade, educational and technological advancements, and the chance to travel off-world became available. The prevailing attitude among most Progenshans was that all of this new-found knowledge, as well as their cultural heritage was worth fighting for. If the GSE came knocking, they would be met with stiff resistance.

Although Progensha was thought to be the only planet revolving around its two suns, another advantage to giving the Alliance access to Progenshan space was the discovery of other habitable planets near Progensha. Exploration and colonization of those planets was underway. Not wanting to spread their resources too thinly or run into a Progensha Universe equivalent of the GSE, the Alliance concentrated its resources near the portal and the Progenshan homeworld; in preparation for the day they knew would eventually come.

***

"Do you get the feeling that things are being rushed?" Markka asked.

"Maybe not rushed, but definitely sped up," Leahcim replied.

The duo sat in the officers' cantina along with T'oann, Lin, Piper, and Vee drinking and discussing the current turn of events.

"I thought this was supposed to be a celebration," T'oann said. "Two cycles since the ratification of the treaty with the Alliance and no major conflicts with the GSE. This is more like a memorial for the deceased."

Markka sipped her drink then stared down into her glass. "Hey, don't get me wrong or anything, but it seems like every time we get a break, another obstacle is thrown in our path."

"What do you mean?" T'oann reached for a bottle of ambrosia and poured herself another glass.

"I don't know exactly. It isn't something I can explain. It's more of a feeling. For all of us it's been nothing but one problem or challenge one right after the other." Markka held Toann's gaze. "For you it was a war with the Thourons. For me, David, and Cora it was our war with the GSE and then we popped into your life. Follow that up with finding the *Anderson* and Lin and Piper, and now it's back to the Alliance and GSE. Something similar has happened to each of us."

"I would not say those events signal things are spiraling out of control or are speeding up," T'oann said.

"I agree with T'oann," Vee said. "I believe things happen in life for a reason. Sometimes it's for reasons we can't explain or understand, and when we least expect them. It's up to us to adapt and adjust to the changes."

"Hmph," Leahcim said. "You make it seem like we're all players living in a contrived world and are being manipulated by someone or something." He took a sip of his wine, considered his next words, then said, "I don't believe my life is predestined."

"I don't know about our lives being controlled by something outside of ourselves, but I do know one thing," Lin said. "Now that there's no time displacement with the one working portal, we all need to be on the same page with the Alliance. Their war has caught up with us."

"Well, it might not be the fickle finger of fate, but we're all not on a magic carpet ride either," Markka said.

T'oann, confused by her queen's statement, turned to the others for clarification.

Vee just smiled and said, "The queen here resorts to metaphors whenever she starts to worry about something."

To which T'oann asked, "What is a metaphor?"

Chapter 55

The imminent attack everyone expected from the Sairidians did not happen. On the third observation of the ratification of the treaty between the Alliance and the Progenshans, there was no sign of the expected attack by the GSE. But the overall attitude was that one was coming. Markka said it was like waiting for the other shoe to drop. It was one of her many Terran colloquialisms.

The most the Sairidian forces did was conduct hit-and-run attacks on Alliance forces. Whatever the GSE strategy was, no one in the Alliance or their newest ally could figure it out. But they used that time to continue to rebuild the Fleet and shore up the defenses on both sides of the portal. Alliance military and diplomatic advisors used the time to bring the Progenshans on par technologically and politically with the rest of the Alliance. No one was taking the GSE for granted.

"It's like looking a gift horse in the mouth," Piper said.

"What the hell does that mean, anyway?" Lin asked.

"I don't know?" Piper shrugged. "It was something I used to hear my great-grandfather say when I was growing up. He said it whenever somebody complained about something when there wasn't anything to complain about."

"If you ask me, it's dumb," Lin said.

"I still say it's like waiting for the other shoe to drop," Markka said.

"Whatever it's like, I don't like it," Leahcim said. "We all know that losing their supply line from the universe they came from was a giant blow to them. And you can rest assured that they are trying their best to figure out how to reestablish that supply line. There's no doubt in my mind we're unscathed because they haven't figured out what to do yet."

"And you know their friends who got stuck on the other side are trying to find a way back through," Markka said. "Do you think the Others will reveal what they know if the Sairidians discover their existence?"

"No," Vee said with absolute certainty. "Even if the Sairidians do find the Others and discover what the Builders left behind, they would just destroy themselves rather than allow that knowledge be subverted."

Leahcim looked at everyone seated at the conference table before he said, "I hope you're right, but if they ever find a way through, we'll need to be ready to face them. And if that doesn't happen, you know damn well the GSE forces already in Alliance space will want access to our portal. We can't let that happen."

"We won't let that happen," T'oann said. There was fierce determination in her voice. "My people fought for generations to be free from tyranny, oppression, subjugation, and genocide. Whether it is the Sairidians or someone else, we will defend ourselves."

Markka raised her glass to what T'oann said. "Amen to that, sister."

The rest of them raised their glasses in support.

Vee excused herself so she could head home to spend some time with Parsons before she shipped out. She looked at T'oann and Leahcim as she stood up to go. "I hear the new captain of the *Alasta* has extended an offer to you to join her tomorrow," Vee said.

"Yep," Leahcim said. "She's going to begin an extended patrol of the portal sector and offered us a ride." He was beaming from ear to ear. "She wants us along as observers and advisors."

It had been almost a half cycle since he was last in space. He jumped at the offer when Parsons made it. T'oann declined, not because she did not want to accompany her husband, but because she had a prior commitment.

She was scheduled to take a group of elite fighter pilots on a training run. These pilots were considered the best of the best. "Top Guns" is what Leahcim called them. Like him, she jumped at the chance, whenever it presented itself, to strap into a fighter and soar through space. Her people called it the Great Beyond for so long, it felt odd referring to it as space.

Lin and Piper said goodnight and left with Vee.

Markka sighed, downed the last of her drink, then sighed again.

Leahcim saw there was something bothering her and asked, "What's on your mind?"

She looked at him with disappointed eyes. "Right now, I wish I didn't have my nanites."

"Why?"

"So I can get drunk, for once."

May I offer a suggestion, my queen?" Cora asked.

"Yeah."

"Your nanites have informed me that if you wish to over imbibe, they will permit it."

Markka's mood perked up.

"Really?"

"Yes, really."

"Do it."

"It is done."

"Good. Now someone pass me that bottle of white lightning."

Leahcim slipped into T'oann's mind and asked for a favor.

"What is it you wish, my sweet?"

"Please stay with me and help get her home when she's had enough. She's a mean drunk."

***

Garath's exuberance was never as bubbly as it was while she packed some clothes and incidentals in a travel bag.

"How long are you going to be deployed?" Codie asked.

"Half a cycle. Doctor Sanchez has asked me to serve aboard her ship and learn Alliance healing techniques. She has also sponsored my admission to the Alliance Medical Academy. This is a dream come true."

Codie sat across from her as she packed. His latest synthetic body looked convincingly more Uderran than all of his previous ones. Lean, strong, and indistinguishable from a biologic. He watched as Garath pranced and bounced around packing her bag. "I am happy for you," he said.

"Thank you! Growing up an orphan was not easy. I spent most of my youth trying to earn the respect of others. I spent most of that directionless. It was not until I joined the Uderran military that I found my purpose. To help those who have no one to help them. And now I get to learn how to help even more people."

It was her thirst for life and an unselfish need to give to others, and their shared interest in the healing arts that drew him to her. Despite all of the negative events and experiences in her life, she managed to see the positives.

He found he shared her penchant for embracing the positive emotional qualities exhibited by many biologics. Working as closely as he had with Garath, he found he had developed a particularly strong emotional attachment. And this particular moment was difficult for him because it meant her deployment would be the first time they would spend time apart from each other.

He knew the feelings he had for her were unrequited. She had never acknowledged his subtle gestures or comments. She never appeared to be even remotely aware that his interest in her was more than professional. But that did not stop him from feeling the way he did about her.

"There," she said. "All packed."

He stood up and said, "I will carry your bag and accompany you to the ship."

Her mood turned somber. "Before you do that, there is something I must confess."

Concerned she was about to divulge something deeply personal and emotionally painful, he walked over to her, touched her arm and asked, "What is it that I can help you with?"

"Please do not be angry with me." She sniffled slightly then said. "I know I should have spoken with you first—to get your permission, but I could not help myself."

He reached down and wiped a tear from her cheek. "Whatever it is, I am sure your intentions were sincere."

She wrapped her arms around him in a tight hug and said, "They were. I, um, asked Doctor Sanchez if you could accompany me." She released him, stepped back and looked straight into his hazel eyes. "She said yes. I am sorry I did not ask you before speaking on your behalf."

Of all the things he expected to hear, what she just told him was not one of them.

"I am not angry. I am quite pleased that you thought to include me. I am honored."

The chipper mood she had been in did not return as he expected. There was something else on her mind.

"What is it, Garath? What is bothering you?"

She hemmed and hawed before she decided to tell him.

"I had an ulterior motive for asking to bring you."

He raised a questioning eyebrow. "I am sure your motive was well-intentioned."

"It was. I, uh, I have feelings for you."

"As do I for you."

She bowed her head slightly embarrassed and said, "No, you do not understand." She hesitated, unsure of herself or what to say next. Garath collected her thoughts and quickly rattled off what was on her mind in a tone so low, a normal biologic would not have heard her. "I am in love with you."

He was elated to hear her say that. It assured him that the feelings he had for her were mutual.

"As am I with you."

Garath's mood lightened. "You are?"

"Yes."

***

"Are you sure you're up for this?" Vee asked. "You just finished recovering from a tick bite."

"A little bug bite isn't stopping me from doing this," Parsons said.

"The sponge tick that bit you was half the size of my fist. You spent a week in the healing center because you had a severe reaction."

"Whatever. I'm fine now."

"You sure?"

"Yes, I'm sure. Hell, I was born ready for this. The question is will you be able to handle me being away from you for six months?"

"Me? Ha! If I can handle being around you, I can handle getting a break from you." Vee smiled an impish smile.

"Fuck you."

"I'm going to hold you to that when you get back."

Despite the lighthearted banter, Vee could not shake an uneasy feeling she had about Parsons' deployment.

"Be careful out there."

"No prob. I'm only going to be with Romar, Sparks, Karona, Raqmar, Sojourner, David, Sanchez, Garath, and Codie, and a full contingent of escort ships."

"The *Alasta* isn't like the *T'ayMak*."

Following ratification of the agreement with the Progenshans, the Alliance gifted the *T'ayMak* to Progensha. As the ship most instrumental in helping to broker the agreement, the Alliance felt it was a prudent gesture to present them with the symbol of their pact. As a reward for helping negotiate the accord, Parsons was given command of the *Alasta*.

"You worry too much. It's just a routine patrol. I'll be in command of a supercarrier accompanied by a shitload of support ships. Everything'll be fine. What could go wrong?"

***

After spending an amorous night together, T'oann and Leahcim engaged in an early morning round of lovemaking while they showered before they got their sol started.

"Are you excited?" T'oann asked.

"I'm always excited when I'm around you." He pressed his lips to hers and kissed her and ran his hands along her back as the warm water rained down on them.

She fluttered her eyes and caressed his bare ass with her hands.

"Keep that up and I'll miss the boat."

"Rosa isn't going anywhere without you."

He shivered with delight and said, "I love it when you use contractions."

He smiled at her, pressed his chest against her warm breasts, and softly cupped them with his hands. She reached for his waist then slid her hands down between them and discovered he was ready for another round. She squeezed, he moaned.

T'oann looked longingly into his eyes. "To hell with Rosa. I'm not going to see you for a half cycle. She can wait."

***

Lin and Piper sat on the terrace of their home chatting about nothing in particular. The conversation was pretty much one-sided since he did most of the talking. Lin spent the time picking at her breakfast.

"What's on your mind? You hardly touched your food; your jamocha is getting cold."

She never responded to his question. So he waved his hand in front of her face until he got a reaction. It was obvious her mind was somewhere else in the universe.

He snapped his fingers. "Hello? Progensha to Lin. Is anybody in there?"

She looked up from her plate with a worried look. "You ever get that feeling that something bad is about to happen?"

"Only when I make the mistake of pissing you off."

She frowned then squinted her eyes at him. "Besides those times."

"No, why?"

She took a sip of her jamocha then quickly sat the cup back down. "This stuff is awful when it's cold." She dumped the cup's contents into a nearby planter and poured another steaming cup. She took a sip. "Ahhh, that's better."

Piper knew she was trying to avoid answering his question. "Quit stalling. What do you feel is going to happen?"

She watched the wavy wisps of steam rise from her cup before she answered. "I don't know. I just have this creepy feeling that something bad is about to happen."

He reached across the table and took her hands into his. "Well, if something bad is about to happen, we'll do what we always do. Face it together."

***

"Are you going to tell them or shall I?"

"If you say a word, I will kill you." Zora appeared to be dead serious. Lungeon swallowed hard before he saw the corners of her mouth turn up into an almost imperceptible smile.

274

"So, you are not angry?"

"Angry? Hell no. I am elated."

"So when do you plan to tell your parents?"

"When the time is right."

"I hate to break it to you, but I think they know already. Or have you forgotten they're both mind walkers and excellent observers?"

"I have not forgotten."

Chapter 56

Five months into an uneventful patrol of the portal sector, Parsons sat in the captain's chair aboard the *Alasta* going over reports.

The GSE was increasing its attacks on Alliance ships and facilities. The attacks seemed to have no discernible pattern. High Command was doing its best to keep from spreading its forces too thin.

Parsons strummed her fingers on the arm of her chair. "The bastards are trying to force us to scatter our forces and weaken our defenses."

"I agree with your assessment," Romar said. "They are probing for a weak spot."

Parsons scratched her head in thought. "They've just about attacked everywhere but here at the portal. What are they waiting for? Mister Romar, how far out are the relief ships?"

"The *Tamar*, *Valiant*, and *Nichols* are scheduled to arrive tomorrow, sir."

"We need to stay on our toes."

"I agree."

She signed off on the last of the reports, and stretched her neck. Her stomach was doing flip flops. For the past week, she experienced severe night sweats, increased heart rate, rapid breathing, and bouts of physical distress. She thought she might be suffering from some residual effects of the tick bite. She decided to pay a visit to sickbay.

"You have the conn, mister Romar."

"Aye, Captain."

In the main sickbay, Sanchez, Garath, and Codie were involved in a deep discussion about battlefield triage.

"Before Commander Leahcim came to us, we embedded a healer within a troop unit," Garath said. "He overhauled our entire approach to handling battlefield injuries. He created entire mobile units that were equipped to roll into a hot zone and administer healing aid to mass casualties right on the spot or evacuate the wounded in groups."

Sanchez found it fascinating that after years of fighting, the idea had not occurred to them before. But what she found most intriguing was the medical use of nanites. Nowhere in the Alliance did the use of nanites exist before they met the Progenshans.

She also found it astonishing that the nanites were sentient. Codie reminded her that the medical personnel of the Mountain People were the descendants of those who survived the crash of the *Michael P. Anderson*. "They were the ones who developed the process," he said. "It was the descendants of those who survived the Great War who perfected the science."

As for Codie, Sanchez was amazed that Cora had children who chose career paths for themselves. Codie chose the medical field as his area of interest. His extensive knowledge of Progenshan physiology was invaluable to Alliance doctors.

Their ethnic diversity, due indirectly to the survivors of the *Michael P. Anderson*, was a smorgasbord for Alliance genealogists.

"I am thrilled you chose to join us," Sanchez said. "I am learning so much."

"We are pleased and honored," Codie said.

While the three discussed medicine and medical techniques, Parsons walked in.

"Hey, doc, I was wondering—" She stopped short when she saw Garath and Codie. "Oh, uh, sorry for interrupting. I can come back." She turned to leave when all three asked her to stay and join them.

"You are not interrupting anything important, Captain."

She appeared to relax. "Oh, good."

"So what can we help you with?"

As Parsons chatted with her senior medical officers, four decks above sickbay, Leahcim laid on the bunk in his quarters counting the remaining days of his deployment before he would be back home on Progensha in the loving company of his wife. This was the first time they had been apart from each other for so long. Because of communication restrictions, he was unable to talk with her.

His thoughts of seeing her soon eased a discomfort in his mind enough for him to drift into a peaceful sleep.

While Leahcim slept, the bridge crew worked like a well oiled machine under the watchful eyes of Romar. He noticed Karona puzzling over something at Sparks' station.

Romar walked over to his officers and asked, "What seems to be the problem here?"

"We're not sure, sir," Sparks said.

"Not sure of what?"

"Not sure of these readings."

"Explain."

Karona took over for Sparks.

"Sensors have detected traces of residual radiation emanating from pockets of dead space."

"Dead space."

"Yes, sir. They just started showing up in the last twenty four hours."

"Suddenly?"

Sparks answered the question.

"Yes, sir."

"Maybe the sensors need recalibrating," Romar said. He tapped the console as if that would fix the issue. "Can you give me a visual of the phenomena?"

"No, sir," Karona said. "We can give you a visual of the area, but we can't get a visual fix on the radiation source itself, sir. For there to be this much, there would need to be an energy source or something nearby."

"Could it be bits of dark matter?"

"We considered that and checked. There's nothing, sir."

"Cloaked ships?"

"Unlikely. The usual telltale signs associated with a cloaked ship are absent. These show up on our sensors as concentrations of residual radiation emanating from unidentifiable sources. We've run every test up and down the full electromagnetic spectrum. They appear to be nothing more than natural phenomena bunched up in clusters."

"Uh, excuse me, sir," Sparks said, "but there are more of those phenomena beginning to appear on the outer fringe of our sensors.

Romar pondered the news for a moment, studied the sensor readings, then stiffened.

Karona noticed the change in his posture and asked, "What is it, sir?"

"So that's what the bastards have been up to for the past three years."

"What, sir?"

He looked directly at Karona.

"Your natural phenomena are moving toward us on an intercept vector." Then he said more to himself than to Karona, "I've seen this before. It's the GSE's standard method of attack. Attack en masse when cloaked. Holy hell. They've been developing improved cloaking technology to mask their invisibility. They figured out a way to eliminate the rippling effect cloaked ships make when they bend the light around them."

"You think they perfected a method of making an invisible ship even more invisible?" Karona asked.

"Yes. The random attacks were probably distractions. They probably wanted to know if we could see them. So they staged attacks and more than likely sat around observing and checking to see if we would detect them."

"And we didn't."

"Exactly."

"So how come we're able to see them now?"

Romar said, "I don't know."

"It's beginning to get harder to tell just how many of them there are, sir," Sparks said. There was agitation in her voice.

"They're gathering for an attack. Get me the captain and tell the fleet to go to red alert. They're about to spring a trap. Signal High Command the GSE attack we expected is happening."

"Aye, sir." Karona ran back to her station and activated the red alert siren. "All decks, red alert. All decks, red alert. This is not a drill. This is not a drill." She paged the captain on the ship's intercom and simultaneously sent a distress call to High Command.

She was about to turn to update Romar when she suddenly screamed in pain and ripped off her headset as a high pitched squeal rang through it. She was disoriented for a moment.

"Lieutenant, what happened? Are you okay?" Romar asked.

She cursed, "Dammit!" She nodded her head that she was okay, then said. "We're being jammed."

"Did you get the message out?"

There was uncertainty in her voice. "I think so, sir."

"But?"

"I don't know if it was in time."

An instant later, the fleet was under attack as streams of energy bolts lit up the space around them.

Chapter 57

Parsons was alone in a turbo lift on her way to the bridge when the first salvos rocked the ship. She cursed herself for not taking the stairs and prayed the lift did not shut down before she reached the bridge.

"Sojourner, what's happening?"

"The Sairidians launched an unprovoked attack upon the fleet using improved cloaking technology."

"How come I wasn't informed?"

"Because we only discovered it seconds before we were attacked."

The lift doors opened to a bridge full of people busy doing their jobs and reacting to the changing conditions of the battle. She felt like a proud parent.

Romar immediately relinquished the chair and proceeded to update Parsons.

***

Leachim was awakened from his sleep when the red alert sounded. He was on his feet and fully aware when the first salvos pounded the *Alasta*. His quarters were no longer pitch black, but bathed in the pulsating red of the alarm lights. Once he gathered his wits, he instinctively dashed out the door and rushed toward the ship's bridge.

He bolted down the chaotic corridors filled with noise and frenzied crewmen scurrying to their battle stations. People were bumping into each other as they ran toward their designated battle stations. It was organized chaos. He made a sharp right turn and punched the button to the bridge turbo lift. By the time it arrived, his heart was beating so hard he could hear the blood rushing through his ears. He rushed inside the cylindrical capsule and felt his stomach drop as it accelerated up the shaft toward the bridge. For the briefest of moments, perhaps nano seconds, he had a feeling of dread come over him.

The turbo lift doors swished open. David stepped off the lift and was greeted with a visual and audible display of people and machines working together. The bridge, bathed in a deep red light reminiscent of those old dark rooms photographers used for developing celluloid-based film strips, was a montage of beeping computers and chattering voices nervously calling out readings, measurements, and status updates. In the center of it all sat Parsons.

She was a pillar of calm and strength amid the babble.

Parsons was facing the turbo lift doors and talking to ensign Abosolom Abdul. Ensign Abdul was a full Terran with a light tan complexion and about as tall as the captain. He was the ship's environmental officer. She looked away from him long enough to give Leahcim a quick glance of acknowledgement. She continued talking to the younger man without so much as a moment's hesitation or stutter in her speech. "Make sure those auxiliary reserves are fully charged. I want to be able to breathe while I can still think."

"Aye, sir," was Abdul's reply.

"I don't think I need to remind you of the *gravity* of the situation."

"No, sir," Abdul said."

Her concern, peppered with a bit of ironic humor, more to put the ensign's mind at ease than anything else, was not just to remind him they needed to breathe, but it was also a veiled reminder that the ship's artificial gravity field generators were also paramount. If they were disabled, navigating through the ship would be difficult at best. The crew's boots could be instantly converted to anti-gravitational function, but that would mean their ability to move around would be slowed considerably. They would be forced to walk around the ship like some stiff creature you might see in one of those old twentieth-century Terran entertainment videos.

"Good," the captain said. "Carry on." Abdul turned and headed back to his station. Without missing a beat, Parsons swiveled in her chair to face the front of the bridge and said, "Nice of you to join us Commander. I may need your services." That chair was the eye of the hurricane.

As the ship shook and shuddered, Parsons was a paragon of calm, but Leahcim knew her well enough to read through the mask. It was a facade she wore admirably.

The ship took a few hard hits that caused the emergency lights to snap on before the normal red glow of the red alert lights flashed back on.

"Tactical status, now!" Parsons demanded.

The baby-faced tactical officer, Charrkan, a Felid, whose gray hair, broken up by patches of white and brown, reminded Leahcim of Markka, responded.

"We were hit with an energy source more powerful than anything the current armada of GSE ships is using, sir."

"Where the hell did it come from?"

The ship was violently rocked again. Charrkan put up a visual replay on the main screen. "There, sir."

What they saw was a series of green blasts of streaming energy bolts simultaneously reaching out to strike them from empty space. There were about two dozen.

"There's nothing there, Charrkan said."

"Then tell me how we just got punched in the gut from something that isn't there?" Parsons asked.

"It must be that cloaked base we could never find," Romar said.

"Whatever it is, it's about to fire again!" Charrkan said.

Sparks saw what Charrkan saw and was already in the process of engaging evasive maneuvers. Hang on!" she yelled.

Since the *Alasta* was a supercarrier, the ship did not respond as nimbly as the *Infiltrator* or *T'ayMak* did. The ship took a few more devastating blows.

Sparks cursed, "Dammit!"

"You did good, Lieutenant," Parsons said. "It coulda been worse."

"Captain," Charrkan said, "we got a problem. The source of those blasts is moving. I can't get an exact fix on it, but I think I know where it's going?"

"Where?"

"The portal. Based on the trajectory of energy blasts."

"Sparks," Parsons said, "get us there first."

"Aye, Captain."

Parsons turned to face Leahcim. "Are you thinking what I'm thinking?"

"I'm way ahead of you," Leahcim said. "Tell the launch bay to expect me. We're gonna kill that thing once and for all."

He turned and raced out the doors of the bridge toward the stairs leading to the launch bays.

Chapter 58

During the five months that Leahcim, Garath, and Codie were aboard the *Alasta*, Cora religiously monitored the portal using a communication relay the Alliance set up on the Progenshan side. Since the task force was under orders to remain radio silent during operations, most of the communications traffic was routine chatter that passed through the portal. It bothered her that she knew nothing about the status of her friends or her son. Having recently developed the ability to fully experience emotions as biologics did, she understood how Commander T'oann felt.

The commander had spent her time going about her routines, but Cora knew she must be experiencing some kind of emotional turmoil not knowing what was happening with Leahcim and the others. Zora and her brothers provided the emotional strength T'oann needed in the meantime for their mother and each other.

Cora was running a diagnostic of the relay when she picked up a coded message from the *Alasta*. It was a Mayday. They were under attack by Sairidian forces. Number unknown. The message abruptly ended. The voice was Karona's. Cora immediately contacted T'oann, B'rtann, Sho'khan, Markka, Tory, Lin, and Piper.

Video linked through their wrist communicators or datapads, the officers strategized with Cora.

"I say we mobilize all Progenshan forces and form a protective shield around the planet," Sho'khan said.

"I say we go after the bastards," Markka said.

"Fortunately, you are not the sole decision maker here," Tory reminded his wife.

Markka huffed and called her husband a spoilsport.

Lin and Piper agreed with Sho'khan. As did Tory and B'rtann.

T'oann had to tamp down her emotions and think clearly and pragmatically as a military advisor and tactician. Whatever her concerns were for her husband and the others, she put them aside for the greater good.

"I recommend we send a fighter group through the portal to assist the *Alasta*. We should take the fight to the enemy."

"Amen," Markka said.

Before she rendered her decision, she wanted the opinion of a silent member of the meeting. "There is one other in attendance who we have not heard from. Cora?"

"Yes, Commander?"

"You have as much at stake as the rest of us. What do you suggest we do?"

"Thank you, Commander. I appreciate the consideration. You are correct. The lives of my son, my friends, my . . . family are at stake. And I, like you, will do whatever is necessary to rescue them—even at the expense of my own."

"Let us hope and pray that it will not come to that," T'oann said. "In light of that, what do you wish to contribute to this conversation?"

"As time is of the essence, I propose we form a defensive ring around the planet *and* send a contingent of pilots to the portal to defend it."

"Now you're talkin' my language," Markka said. "Let's go kick some GSE butt."

Tory, disturbed by his wife's gung-ho spirit, decided to throw water on her fire. "Need I remind you that as the head of state, according to the terms of our agreement with the Alliance, which you signed, you are forbidden to engage directly in combat?"

"Dammit, Tory—"

"No exceptions!" He said it forcefully enough to stop any further protests from his wife."

"Well," T'oann said, "I suggest we carry out Cora's proposal. Further delay means further lives lost. B'rtann, Sho'khan, get our forces out into the Great Beyond."

***

For their entire way enroute to the portal, the *Alasta* and her support ships fought their GSE counterparts. Because the Alliance ships were faster, they arrived thirty minutes ahead of the bulk of their enemy. They were able to easily handle the few pursuit ships that could keep up. They were met by a contingent of ships permanently stationed at the portal. The pursuit ships slowed their advance and waited for the rest of their fleet to catch up.

Parsons, Romar, and Leahcim used the time to prepare for the coming fight, but Romar had a nagging question. "Captain?" he asked.

"Yes, LT?"

"Don't you think it's strange that they didn't launch fighters to pursue us? They could have easily overtaken the entire fleet."

285

"Yeah. The thought crossed my mind. The only thing I could think of is they're saving them for when they reach the portal. There'll be so many of them that we won't be able to stop them all from getting through. If I was their commander, that's what I would do."

Romar cursed himself for not thinking of that.

"Don't be so hard on yourself. That's why I'm here. To teach you these things." She smiled at him then turned to Sparks and asked, "Lieutenant, what's our status?"

"Sixty seconds before they're in range, sir."

"Barely enough time to pee your pants."

"My readings indicate a similar complement of ships. Six capital ships and twenty-five support vessels. Fighter complement unknown. All of their ships are visible except for whatever attacked us."

"Where the hell is it?"

"Just outside of weapons range and . . . wait, it's becoming visible. Holy shit! That's not a military base. It's a damned supercarrier, and it's three times the size of us," Sparks said.

For the briefest of moments, Parsons was speechless. "Dammit! That friggin' thing is probably stuffed to the gills with fighters, bombers, and other ships. And we have no idea how many it's packing," Parsons complained.

"I think I liked it better when we thought it was a base," Sparks said. "At least we'd be shooting at a lumbering behemoth and not another warship."

As the sixty seconds ticked down to zero, the GSE ships let loose with a barrage of powerful bursts of energy streams. The Alliance ships returned fire. Explosions, shouts, and screams were heard through the communications system as the reality of battle made its presence known.

"They're launching fighters," Sparks yelled.

"Launch ours," Parsons ordered."

Karona relayed the captain's orders to Leahcim.

"Copy that," he said. Leahcim gave a thumbs-up to his crew chief who switched the launch lights to green. "Okay, boys and girls, time to earn our pay."

As Leahcim's fighter group, the 99th Attack Group, launched, another series of energy beams streamed toward the *Alasta*. Sparks did her best to avoid them, but most found their mark. The impact rocked the ship hard enough to toss anyone who was not strapped in across the bridge like discarded toys.

The bridge went black then the emergency lights flicked on. Before anyone could recover, a second barrage hit them.

"Shields?" Parsons asked.

"Holding at one hundred percent, sir," Abdul said.

"They're trying to flank us, Captain," Sparks said. "Trying to get a better shot at us broadside."

"Just keep pivoting. Keep our face forward. Reroute tertiary power to energy reserve cells."

"Aye, Captain," Abdul replied. He immediately began shutting down and sealing off areas of the ship that were not inhabited by crew and redirected power from those parts of the ship to the reserve cells.

The energy stored in the reserves would be directed to the shields or any part of the ship, like the medical levels, that might need the power.

The GSE carrier maneuvered to get a tactical advantage over the *Alasta*, and Sparks did her best to keep the bow of the ship facing toward the enemy so the ship's forward cannons were focused on their target. Parsons wished Markka was on board manning a turret gun.

Several successful blasts from other ships in the flotilla struck the enemy carrier, forcing it to alter course.

A group of enemy fighters broke off from the others and targeted the Alliance ships that attacked the carrier.

"I hope the commander and his pilots are up to the task, Romar said."

Parsons tried to sound upbeat. "Don't worry. Leahcim and his people got this."

The first wave of enemy fighters launched from the carrier swiftly approached the Alliance formation.

"Hold together, people," Leahcim said. "Squadron leaders, are you ready?"

After each leader reported in, Leahcim said, "Break on my command. And remember, protect the *Alasta* and let nothing get through the portal. Let's show these cold-blooded reptilian bastards what we're made of."

The Alliance pilots waited in nervous anticipation as the enemy fighters rapidly closed the distance. An instant before the GSE fighters came within firing range Leahcim gave the attack command. Space was instantly full of flashes of streaks of light, flares, and explosions as the fighter battle began.

One advantage Leahcim hoped his group brought to the engagement was a fighting style unique from anything the Sairidians and their allies had ever seen before because his entire group of fighters was made up of all Progenshan volunteers.

The Progenshan pilots stood out not only because of the image of their orange homeworld emblazoned on their rear stabilizers, but they fought with a fierceness that surprised even the Alliance pilots. One was heard to say, "Glad they're on our side."

Chapter 59

As the battle heated up between the fighters, the larger ships stepped up their round of exchanges. Each ship swapped energy streams and damaging blows. The *Alasta* got a few good hits on her counterpart, but the GSE carrier had greater firepower and range.

With Leahcim and his pilots busy slugging it out, the Sairidian carrier reacquired the *Alasta* and resumed its assault. As they got closer to Parsons' ship, the punishing attacks began to take their toll. A flurry of energy salvos tagged the *Alasta* with devastating results. Two GSE heavy cruisers plowed through the defensive line and joined the attack. One got close enough to fire at point blank range.

Sparks did what she could to avoid the hits while giving the weapons crews ample time to return fire, but the barrage was too great. The ship was hit starboard by both cruisers. The resulting impact ripped the restraining bolts on Parsons' chair. It slammed to the deck with her still strapped in it.

She banged her head on the deck. She saw a bright white light then cloudy darkness before her vision cleared. The pain in her head and neck were excruciating; she remained conscious. The arm of the chair took most of the impact.

"You alright, sir?" Romar asked.

Slightly dazed, she moved her head from side to side and wiggled her fingers and toes. Everything worked. She nodded that she was. She winced as she undid her harness and rolled out of the chair onto the deck. She was not alone as other bridge crew experienced something similar.

"How badly were we hit?" she asked. She stumbled as she got up then took a staggered step forward before her knees buckled. She hit the deck hard. Romar uncinched his harness and rushed over to her. He looked at her silently asking if she was okay. She nodded.

Moans, groans, coughs, smoke, and the crackling sounds of fried equipment filled the bridge. Consoles sparked and sizzled. And the strong smell of burning wires, cables, and singed flesh filled the air.

Abdul reported that the environmental controls were still working. Acrid smells filled the air, but were sucked out of the bridge and fresh oxygen was pumped in when the emergency ventilation system activated. Karona reported that medics were on their way to tend to the wounded.

"Holy shit!" The outburst came from Charrkan.

"Report!" Parsons demanded.

"All of the starboard side fighter launch bays have been damaged or destroyed. Fires are being reported throughout the ship, emergency force fields have engaged and are holding." Her voice faltered.

The young Felid's eyes were watery and tears were running visible streaks down her hairy cheeks. "They're gone, sir. They're all gone. Fifteen outer decks. They're just gone."

A hot flash ran through Parsons' gut before she asked, "Shields?"

"Zero percent."

"Damn. They did that to us with full shields?"

"Yes, sir."

"Looks like they did more than improve their cloaking technology," Romar said.

"Yeah, but it took three ships to do it. Where's the cruiser that hit us?"

"Gone sir," Charrkan said.

"Reacquire."

"I mean it's gone as in destroyed, Captain. The *Destiny* punched through its shields and Captain Leahcim's team scored a couple of direct hits to its engineering section."

Parsons turned to Romar with a wry smile and said, "See? I told you Leahcim and his people would get the job done." Then she told Sparks to, "Back us away from that thing."

"Aye, sir." Sparks reversed the engines and attempted to backoff, but the ship was slow to respond.

Charrkan yelled out, "Hang on, they're firing again!"

Everyone braced for impact, but the expected jolt never happened. There was a slight rumble instead. The Alliance battleship *Destiny* intercepted the energy stream and took the hit. The blast drilled a hole straight through it. The reduced energy of the stream was still enough to penetrate the *Alasta*. No one said a word until Charrkan broke the silence.

"She's still alive. The *Destiny* is still alive." The elation was tempered by the realization of the sacrifice made to protect the *Alasta*.

"That last shot came close to the medical section."

The grim news hit everyone like a kick to the head. There would have been pin-drop silence if not for the sounds of weapons being discharged and combat chatter.

This time Parsons broke the silence. "Karona, what's going on down there?"

"I can't reach anyone. Communications are out."

"Charrkan? Anything?"

"The boards are down. I can't tell if the med section is still with us."

Parsons was noticeably affected. A veil of painful uncertainty crossed her face like a shadow. She thought of her recent chitchat with Dr. Sanchez, Garath, and Codie. She wondered if they were still alive.

A funeral-like pall fell over everyone on the bridge. First there was the damage to the outer decks, then the *Destiny*, and now medical.

She needed to know what was going on below decks. But how could she find out if communications were severed? Then she thought of the one crewman who just might be able to find a way down there.

"Sojourner!"

"Yes, Captain?"

"See if you can reroute yourself and find a way to the medical section. I need to know what's happening down there."

"Yes, Captain. It may take a while. Most of the conduits and pathways to that section have been severed."

"Take all the time you need, and make it quick."

"Understood, Captain."

"Come on, people," Parsons said. "We can't fall apart now. We got people depending on us. This is what we trained for. Right now, the first order of business is survival."

Sparks was frantically trying to get more momentum from the ship as it continued to back away, but the enemy carrier was gaining on them.

Recovered from her shock and frustrated with their retreat, Parsons asked, "Why the hell aren't we going any faster?"

Karona answered.

"Raqmar reports engineering was severely damaged. There's a forcefield separating them from space. He doesn't know how much longer it will hold."

"Tell them to get their asses out of there. Sparks, do what you can with whatever we got."

"Yes, sir."

"Charrkan, launch the rest of our fighters."

"Aye, Captain."

The deck crews doubled their efforts to get the remaining fighters launched. In the event the launchers went down or were damaged, there was a backup transfer system that quickly moved fighters from one side of the ship to the other or down to the keel. The system escaped being damaged in the attack, and was used to launch the remaining fighters.

Parsons turned her attention toward the weapons control officer. An Allurian junior officer whose name was Videll. "Do we still have weapons control?"

Allurians were the most dominant species, numerically and culturally, in the Alliance, and the closest genetically related to Terrans. Videll, who was sitting next to Abdul, could have easily been mistaken for Terran if it were not for his gold eyes and pink irises. All Allurians, regardless of complexion, had the same eye coloring.

He performed a quick check and said, "No, sir. It's currently offline."

"That's just fucking great," Parsons said. "We can barely move, we got a gaping hole in our side, and we can't hit back. We got them right where they want us. What are they waiting for?"

"Captain?" Charrkan asked.

"What?" She responded more brusquely than she wanted, but Charrkan responded as if Parsons had just said please and thank you.

"They're consuming a lot of power to fly and shoot. It looks like they need time to regenerate enough energy to fire their weapons again."

"How much time?"

"Hard to say. It's been three minutes since they fired on us."

So, they do have a weakness, Parsons thought. *We just have to find a way to exploit it.* "That explains why we're still here."

"We might not be for much longer. Their weapons system is charging," Charrkan said.

"Suit up, people," Parsons ordered. "This next one's gonna hurt."

After a moment's hesitation, everyone climbed into EVA suits. Since the bridge of the *Alasta* was not outfitted with survival pods, Parsons felt that anyone fortunate enough to survive the next attack might be able to improve their survivability rate by wearing an EVA suit. Every station had one. Evacuation by escape pod was a last resort since that entailed abandoning the bridge.

***

Leahcim saw the crippling attack on the *Alasta*, and the sacrifice the *Destiny* made. He decided to take a gamble. In light of recent events, picking off enemy fighters one by one in a dogfight was not going to get the job done quickly enough.

"This is V leader. V Squad, form up on me. "We're going to take out that carrier."

The volunteer Progenshan pilots gathered in attack formation and headed for the GSE supercarrier. They immediately came up against a wall of GSE fighters.

Having fought them before, Leahcim was familiar with their style of combat. He and Markka had Cora program every combat tactic they could remember into the flight simulators. Then they made up new ones just to mix things up a bit.

He was getting a second chance at payback, and he had every intention of making them pay.

"Alright, boys and girls, time to go to work."

He let loose with an unrelenting stream of weapons fire. The rest of them did the same. But instead of peeling away, they punched a hole and flew through it straight toward the carrier. The GSE pilots realized what Leahcim's people were doing and swung around to pursue.

The larger arm of the 332nd Fighter Wing, which was loitering on the fringe of the battlefield in an attempt to draw some of the GSE fighters away from the fray, made quick work of them. They then began picking off the fighters that were going after Leahcim's team.

Chapter 60

Thanks to the determination of the surviving deck crews, the *Alasta*'s remaining fighters were spaceborne and slugging it out with their counterparts. They easily filled the ranks of the 99th.

The combatants looked like fireflies darting about from the bridge's main window. It could have been beautiful to watch if lives weren't being lost. The flashes of pulse beams and the explosions to a distant observer could have been seen as a beautiful, dazzling light show, instead of the deadly dance that it was.

Pieces of wreckage and bodies floated helplessly in the vacuum as the battle raged on.

A vicious dogfight in the vicinity of the *Alasta*'s bridge resulted in an enemy fighter and its pilot becoming a part of the growing debris field. The explosion produced a large fireball bright enough to rival a sun. The force of the blast tossed the largest chunk of it careening straight toward the bridge windows.

Almost in unison, Parsons and Romar yelled, "Lower the blast shield! Lower the blast shield!"

Charrkan punched the button to lower the shield.

It looked like the fighter debris was going to reach the window before the blast shield had time to lock into place.

Parsons yelled, "Hit the deck!"

Everyone dropped to the floor.

The instant the shield locked, the wreckage hit it. There was a deafening clang of metal hitting metal and the distinctive crinkle of shattered glass.

The impact caused parts of the bridge to collapse and workstations to explode. There was a cacophony of dings, pings, clangs, bangs, thuds, and the sickening screams of people. Steel plates, shards of glass, splinters of metal, and flying equipment impacted with flesh and bone. The bridge became a blender and the crew the ingredients. In an instant a staff of twelve was reduced to six.

The bridge looked like death had a party, and it smelled like it too.

The face plate to Parsons' EVA Helmet was broken, but she could still breathe. The blast shield held and life support still functioned. She called out, "Abdul, report." He did not answer. "Abdul, report."

"He's gone, sir." Charrkan said. The sadness in her voice was unmistakable.

Dazed and confused, Parsons realized she was still on the floor. She tried to sit up, but was knocked back flat by a burning pain in her abdomen. She looked down and saw a fragment of metal protruding from her midsection.

Panic set in and the pain got worse when she saw what had happened to her.

Karona saw her captain's predicament before anyone else.

"Shit! Don't move, Captain. Don't cough or sneeze."

Parsons thought that might be easy to do since she was quickly becoming lightheaded and finding it hard to stay conscious.

Romar was regaining awareness when he heard Karona tell the captain not to move. He looked over at Parsons just in time to see her eyes close and her head drop to the floor.

Karona ripped off her helmet and rushed to her captain but slipped on a slick puddle of Parsons' blood and fell hard on the deck. Parsons was rapidly losing blood because the puddle was growing bigger. They were both covered in the captain's blood.

Karona began sobbing. She crawled toward her captain, gently took Parsons' helmet off, then placed her hand against Parsons' abdomen. "I gotta stop the bleeding. She's gonna die if we don't do something."

"We're all gonna die if we don't do something," Sparks said. "By the way, why aren't we dead? The carrier was charging her guns to finish us off."

"Good question," Romar said. "That's a damn good question."

Karona looked at the devastation around them. "Everything is smashed. We're deaf and blind. Whatever's gonna happen to us, we'll never see it coming."

"At least it'll be quick," Sparks said. Then muttered to herself, "I hope." She was stuck under part of the navigation console which had collapsed.

"What's your status, Sparks?" Romar asked.

"Uninjured but I'm stuck under this damn panel."

Romar tried to stand but one of his arms was wedged between the base of his chair and the deck plate. He had no idea he was pinned until he went to move. That was also when he felt the pain.

He surveyed what was left of the bridge and got that sick-in-the-stomach feeling when he saw the bodies of people who had just been alive moments before.

Videll, Charrkan, and Karona were the only surviving bridge crew able to freely maneuver around the smashed equipment. Karona was holding Parsons, trying to stop her from bleeding out.

"What's your status, Videll?"

He removed his cracked helmet and let it drop to the floor. "Good, sir. I appear to be unhurt and free to move about."

"How 'bout you Charrkan?"

"Aside from a few bumps, bruises, and cuts, I'm good, sir. Nothing feels broken." Although her helmet was intact, sections of her EVA suit were sliced through. She pulled off her helmet and placed it in her chair.

"Good. Help free Sparks—if you can—then find out what's going on."

The pain in his arm radiated through his body and focused in his head. He had the most severe, pounding headache ever in his life and he was beginning to feel lightheaded.

"I can update you, sir." The voice was Sojourner's. "Officers Videll and Charrkan can devote their combined energy in freeing Officer Sparks. I can apprise you of what I know."

"Do it."

Videll and Charrkan immediately went to help get Sparks free while Sojourner updated Romar.

"First, Captain Parsons' vitals are weak but stable. Officer Karona's efforts are working."

"Good." Romar was worried that Parsons would die on his watch and Vee would never forgive him.

"I was not able to find a way through the damaged conduits to the medical section," Sojourner continued, "but I am working on it."

"So you don't know if anyone is alive down there?"

"Not at this time."

"Engineering?"

"The force field failed."

"Dammit."

"The news is not all bad, sir." Sojourner tried to sound optimistic.

"What's good about it?"

"Chief Engineer Raqmar has a skeleton crew working in EVA suits. They are using tethers, magnetic boots, and jetpacks to do what they can to repair the engines."

Romar smiled. He was impressed with Raqmar's ingenuity. The hotheaded engineer found his niche. He knew putting him in charge of engineering was the best thing he did for the man. "Remind me to recommend him and his staff for commendations if we make it out of this?"

"I will, sir."

"What's going on with the battle and why are we still alive?"

"The *Tamar*, *Valiant*, and *Nichols* picked up Officer Karona's Mayday before communications were jammed. They alerted High Command then jumped into hyperspace to get here. They arrived just as the enemy carrier was powering up to fire at us. They damaged its weapons array and targeting system. Commander Leahcim and the 99th destroyed what was left of it. They no longer possess the ability to select specific targets."

"Thank the Gods for small favors."

"Our people were also able to damage a few of their launch bays. The bulk of their armada is now defending the carrier."

"Well maybe we can do something about that," Sparks said, as she stood up from the floor.

Videll and Charrkan freed Sparks and turned their efforts to freeing Romar. Sparks patted herself for any serious injuries. Finding none, she joined the other two in freeing Romar. They could not budge the deck plate.

"Videll," Sparks said, "go relieve Kay. We're gonna need her strength to move this thing."

"Uh, guys?" Karona said. "I think we have a problem." She started to speak again but passed out. Videll caught her before she collapsed.

"Holy hell?" His hand, which held Karona's limp head, was full of blood. "She's got a serious gash in the back of her head. What'll we do now?"

"Mister Romar, if I may?" Sojourner asked.

"Please, by all means."

"The vitals of Captain Parsons and Officer Karona are weak but stable. Officer Videll, you must apply pressure on the protrusion as Officer Sparks pulls Officer Karona away from the captain. It is the only thing keeping her from bleeding out. Officer Sparks, you must also apply pressure to Officer Karona's injury. Officer Charrkan, I have been able to restore partial service to tactical, communications, and engineering. You will need to monitor all data relating to those stations. I will endeavor to assist you."

"Weapons?" Romar asked.

"Inoperative."

Videll confirmed what Sojourner said. "We couldn't even shoot a water pistol if we had one, sir."

"May I offer a suggestion, sir?" Sojourner asked.

"Yes."

"Issue an order to abandon ship."

"Good idea. Charrkan, order the crew to abandon ship."

"Aye, sir."

Charrkan made a ship-wide announcement to abandon ship then sent a Mayday. Any nearby Alliance ships would be alerted by the Mayday and do whatever they could to rescue as many escape pods as possible so the Sairidian pilots would not use them for target practice.

After Charrkan sent the Mayday and made the abandon ship announcement, she turned to Romar and asked, "What do we do now?"

His ability to think was impaired by the pain in his arm and the pounding in his head. His voice was becoming weak and raspy.

"I don't know. Sojourner, what do you suggest?" he asked.

"Devise alternative solutions to extricating ourselves from our current dilemma."

*****

Before T'oann headed for the *T'ayMak* following her meeting with Markka and the others, Cora said she had news about the *Alasta*.

"What is it, Cora?"

"Transmissions from the portal task force are no longer being jammed. They are fully engaged." She paused, which was rare for Cora. "And the *Alasta* is in trouble."

T'oann nearly bolted for the door when Cora asked, "May I accompany you, Commander? I believe I can be of more assistance to you on the *T'ayMak* than here on Progensha."

T'oann understood the unspoken reason for the request.

"Yes, you may join me. I would welcome your company."

"Thank you, Commander."

"You are welcome."

"May Ramie accompany us?"

Thinking Ramie's prior experience in combat with the Sairidians might prove useful, she agreed to the request.

Chapter 61

When T'oann reached the *T'ayMak*, Zora and Lungeon were suited up and headed to their fighter. She had to shout to be heard over the noise as she approached them.

"What are you two doing here?"

"We are part of your escort through the portal," Zora said.

"You will not be escorting me or anyone else. You are grounded until further notice."

Zora's eyes flashed hot. She was curious and furious. "Why?" she asked.

T'oann became irritated at being questioned. She did not want to engage in a verbal confrontation with her daughter. She said, "You know why."

"But father and the others are in trouble. They need our help."

"And they will get help from me and the rest, but not from you," T'oann snapped. Her patience was wearing thin.

"But—"

"But nothing." Not wanting to pull rank on her daughter, T'oann decided to tackle the issue with one direct statement. "You will stay here and not endanger your child."

Zora looked at Lungeon who shrugged. She faced her mother and asked in an accusatory tone, "You were in my mind?"

Anger flared in T'oann's response. She was insulted by the insinuation that she would intrude in her daughter's mind without permission. "I will consider your insolence a lapse in prudent judgment given our current circumstances."

Zora hung her head in shame and said, "Apologies. Please forgive me. I meant no disrespect."

In a softer tone, T'oann said, "I have eyes that can still see. And so does your father." She took a deep breath to calm herself before she spoke again. "Your pregnancy is something you can no longer hide—not even from the least observant. We have been waiting for you to come out with it. And now you intend to unnecessarily risk yourself and your child. I will not have it. As your commanding officer, I am officially grounding you." She eyed Lungeon. "Both of you." She looked back at Zora. "As your mother, I forbid it."

To show there were no hard feelings, T'oann grabbed Zora in a tight hug, kissed her on the forehead, and told her to get off the tarmac because she was holding up her departure.

Zora stepped aside and wished her mother good wishes. "May the Goddess be with you."

T'oann nodded with an appreciative smile and trotted to the *T'ayMak*.

Moments later, in the relative safety of launch control, Zora and Lungeon watched as the *T'ayMak* left the atmosphere accompanied by a contingent of escort ships.

When the *T'ayMak* and its escorts reached the portal, T'oann hailed Captain Sharon Stubblefield, the commander in charge of the battle group guarding the portal on the Progenshan side. There was evidence of wreckage floating in the vicinity of the portal. Captain Stubblefield assured her that none of the ships that got through made it past the battle group.

After a brief update of the battle raging on the other side, T'oann ordered her fleet through the portal and into a hellscape of death and destruction. Almost immediately, they were targeted and attacked by Sairidian fighters. The *T'ayMak* shook and rocked as it took on enemy fire. Squarely in the middle of the fray was the *Alasta*. It looked more like a derelict wreckage than a formidable warship.

The ship was motionless in space. There were blast holes all over its hull, atmosphere was leaking into the surrounding vacuum, fires were registering throughout, and the bridge blast shield appeared to be in ruins. T'oann stood staring, frozen in shock. She wondered if Leahcim was on board and was he still alive.

She unconsciously said aloud what she thought then was embarrassed when Cora responded.

"Commander Leahcim is not aboard. He is with the 99th currently engaging the GSE carrier and its fighters."

Cora magnified an image on the viewscreen showing Leahcim's fighter performing a series of twists, turns, loops, and dives as he and his group fought their counterparts.

"Apologies, Cora. I meant no disrespect."

"No disrespect was inferred. I am chagrined to admit that my initial thoughts were of Codie."

The *T'ayMak* continued to be pounded by enemy fighters and the helmsman did her job dodging the worst of the weapons barrage.

Lin, who had bullied her way onto the *T'ayMak*, assumed command of combat operations, leaving T'oann and Cora free to focus their attention on assessing the *Alasta*—or what was left of it.

"Cora, are you able to detect your son?" T'oann asked.

"No."

"Biologicals?"

"Yes. Most of the ship's complement appears to have escaped. There are a few weak signals, but nothing I can definitively ascertain."

"Can you detect Garath or any of the others?"

"No."

***

Garath awoke amid sizzling electrical circuits and sparking computer units. She initially had no sense of where she was. But the acrid smoke and the ringing in her ears was a quick reminder. She saw she was in relative darkness. She knew she was on the floor, and she remembered she was not alone—at least not before everything literally exploded around her.

Her memory slowly returned and she recalled working on the wounded alongside Codie and Sanchez when everything flashed white, then went black. Now that she was conscious, she wondered where they were. She called out to them in the darkness, but there was no answer. She called out again. There was still no answer. *Are they all dead?* she wondered. *Am I alone?* She got an answer to her question when she heard a moan.

"Hello? Who is there?"

No one spoke, but she heard the moan again.

"Hello? Who is there? Can you speak?"

The person moaned again then coughed. Garath crawled along the floor toward the coughing sound until she bumped into the person doing the coughing. He was one of the wounded they were attending to when her world exploded.

She did what she could for him then continued to crawl around encountering more wounded warriors scattered throughout the medical bay. After her eyes adjusted to the semi-darkness, she moved with more confidence around the room doing what she could for the injured. Then she heard someone call her name.

Under a pile of broken chairs and containers of medical supplies in a far corner of the bay, Sanchez regained consciousness and called out for Garath and Codie. Garath responded and worked her way over to her.

"Are you alright?" Garath asked.

"I think so. Nothing feels broken."

"Good, because I am going to need your assistance in tending to the injured."

Garath helped Sanchez squeeze out from under the rubble.

"Where's Codie?" Sanchez asked.

Thankful for the darkness so Sanchez could not see the despair etched on her face, Garath hung her head and sighed. "I have not yet located him."

Sanchez patted herself down feeling her bumps and bruises. Satisfied she had no serious injuries, she went to stand and cried out in pain. There was an intense burning sensation in her right thigh. In the dim light, she could see a small metal bar of some kind sticking out. When she reached for it, she realized it was part of a broken chair leg. "Dammit."

"What is it?"

"I got a piece of chair stuck in my thigh."

"What do you need for me to do?"

Sanchez took a few deep breaths then asked Garath to search for a portable cauterizer.

"There should be one in that cabinet over there." She pointed to a cabinet that had fallen over and spilled its contents.

Garath crawled over to it and rummaged through the items on the floor until she found one. She made her way back to Sanchez. "Now what?"

Sanchez pulled out a small penlight and handed it to Garath. "I'm gonna pull this thing out. When I do, I'm gonna need you to cauterize the artery so I don't bleed to death. Got it?"

"Got it," Garath said.

"On the count of three. One, two—"

Sanchez never got to three because Garath pulled as she said two. Sanchez screamed in pain then passed out. Garath went to work sealing up the artery, draining the blood, and disinfecting and binding the wound. She told the unconscious Sanchez, "You will thank me when you wake up."

Five minutes later Sanchez regained consciousness.

"Bitch, that hurt."

"You are welcome."

Garath handed the penlight to Sanchez so she could see for herself the condition of her thigh.

Sanchez managed a weak smile. "Not bad. Good work." She took a couple of deep breaths before she asked Garath, "Help me up, will you? I need to see if I can put some weight on it."

Garath helped Sanchez to her feet.

"Well?"

She placed some weight on her leg then flinched when the pain caught her off guard. She growled, "Give me something for the pain and I'll be good to go."

"I did."

"It hasn't kicked in yet."

"Want another?"

"No, I'll manage," she said. "Where's Codie?"

Garath paused before she answered, "I do not know."

"I'll take over from here, you look for Codie. And see if you can find the manual controls for the emergency lights."

Garath hesitated.

"Go, I got this."

"Thank you."

Garath searched for the controls to the emergency lights and called out to Codie. After a minute of searching, she found the controls and activated them. Soft white lights snapped on. Their low illumination of the bay revealed just how bad the damage was. Smashed tables and chairs, collapsed beds, and drugs and medical supplies were scattered on the floor. They also helped her locate Codie.

She found him curled into the fetal position staring out with unseeing eyes in a corner of the bay.

Panic gripped her as she knelt next to him and thought the worst. She had no idea what to do to try to revive him—if she could. She was a specialist in biological medicine, not biosynthetic physiology. She checked his body for any signs of damage. Seeing none, she uncurled him, and rolled him onto his back, and sat looking at him like a frightened child. Tears burst forth from her like a sudden, unexpected rain shower.

Garath slumped to the floor and sobbed. The one person in her life, who had meant the most to her was gone. She felt alone. She did not have time to wallow in the pain of her loss. In the dim light, she was startled by a soft caress on her cheek. She nearly shrieked.

"Do not be afraid. I am not dead and you are not alone."

Hearing Codie's voice comforted her.

"I . . . I was afraid I lost you," she said.

"I am not that easily discarded."

His words eased her mind.

"Are you injured?" she asked.

"I have minimal damage to my primary systems, but nothing that will impede my abilities to render adequate medical treatments."

She took his hand, smiled broadly at him and said, "Then let us get busy assisting Doctor Sanchez and save some lives."

*****

"He is alive!" The excitement in Cora's voice was palpable. "He is alive," she repeated.

"Who is?" T'oann asked.

"Codie."

Cora's relief in knowing her son was alive revealed an emotional side that T'oann had never heard before. The outburst was a refreshing change from Cora's normal stoicism.

"That is good news. We will double our efforts to ensure his safety and that of the others."

"Thank you for your understanding, Commander."

Feeling more optimistic, T'oann strategized with Cora to develop a rescue plan.

Chapter 62

Leahcim led a squadron of fighters in a second bombing run toward the supercarrier.

"Stay in formation. Stay in formation," he said. "Don't bunch up back there."

"Copy that," was the response from his wingman.

They swooped in fast and low. They were so low that had someone been standing on the carrier's hull, they would have been able to reach out and touch the fighters. One by one each pilot fired their weapons at the launch bays then pulled up and away. They looped around the belly of the ship and headed towards the engines. They each let loose with conventional rockets then peeled away as their payloads struck their target.

Leahcim's group was followed by a second and third. Each repeated the process. As they made their runs, the rest of the wing attacked any enemy fighter that chased and targeted the pilots making the strafing runs.

Not all the pilots hit their targets, and not all made it back to fight again. A few unfortunate souls became part of the mixture of shrapnel and biological debris floating in a flotsam of battlefield waste. But Leahcim and his fighter wing continued to press their attack on the supercarrier. Their initial success was short-lived as more Sairidian pilots broke off their attacks on the Alliances' bigger ships and joined the fight to defend the carrier.

The area around the immense ship was getting congested and becoming increasingly more dangerous to navigate without running the risk of colliding with other fighters—friend or foe. Leahcim was forced to order his pilots to retreat.

The GSE fighters formed a defensive shell around the carrier like hornets protecting a nest. Leahcim had lost what he thought were too many pilots. The loss of one was one too many in his mind. He needed a new strategy.

Unfortunately, the tight defensive barrier was too much for the 99th to contend with without incurring more losses.

Although more Alliance ships arrived, including the group from Progensha, and had kept the GSE's capital ships occupied, it was not enough. Despite damaging the carrier's weapons system, a handful of launch bays, and its main engines, it was still creeping toward the portal and launching a trickle of fighters.

Leahcim knew the GSE did not need to win the battle, but to only tie up Alliance forces enough so the carrier could make it through the portal. Once on the other side, the fighters, and any surviving support ships, would undoubtedly scatter into the void, regroup somewhere, and become entrenched in his universe. He desperately searched for a way to stop them.

The initial attack on the carrier was meant to save the *Alasta*, his friends, and the personnel on board. But it failed. The ship, now mostly a hulking piece of scrap metal, looked like a dark and lifeless carcass of a dead aquatic animal drifting aimlessly in space. It was nothing more than a floating coffin. If anyone was still alive, they would not be for much longer.

Leahcim was furious with himself. He slammed his fist on his console and cursed himself for allowing it to happen. He felt he had let his friends down and now they were dead because he did not get the job done. He needed a clear head to decide his next steps. Wrong thinking would get him and his pilots killed. So he ordered them to fall back to the portal entrance. They would make a last stand there.

While Leahcim regrouped, and Cora analyzed the battle and devised a plan to locate and rescue *Alasta* survivors, T'oann kept a close eye on the Progenshan fighters attacking the carrier, and a closer eye on Leahcim's fighter. There were a few times her heart stopped as he appeared to be in trouble. But each time, he was able to avoid being killed either by his own piloting skills or by an assist from his wingman or another pilot.

When the Alliance pilots regrouped at the mouth of the portal, she knew things had become desperate. And so had she. She yearned to be out there with her husband, but felt compelled to stay on the *T'ayMak* with Cora and coordinate a rescue effort for survivors. Cora had established a line of communication with Codie and compiled the data he sent her.

According to the data Codie sent, the ship suffered a catastrophic failure of all systems. Those who had not been killed in the initial series of attacks, either abandoned ship when the order was given or were trapped, as he, Garath, Sanchez, and their patients were. Anyone else still on board was there of their own choosing; motivated by a sense of duty. The likelihood of continued survival for remaining biologics was slim to none. He, on the other hand, barring his total physical destruction, would be able to survive indefinitely in the vacuum of space. But doing so without Garath was a bleak option he was having difficulty coming to terms with.

His mother told him she was in contact with Sojourner who informed her Raqmar and a few engineers volunteered to stay with the *Alasta* and work on repairing the engines, and that the surviving members of the bridge crew were injured and trapped. She told Cora she would not abandon them.

Cora quickly established herself as a relay hub simultaneously communicating with T'oann, Codie, and Sojourner. She included Captain Stubblefield when T'oann asked her to transmit constant updates to the ships on the other side of the portal and also transmit that data to Progensha.

While the heat of combat shifted from the bulk of the Alliance fleet to the Sairidian carrier, Lin continued to issue orders and commands directing the *T'ayMak* to wherever she deemed they were needed. As the fighting continued, additional GSE ships were showing up from wherever they were hiding. Evidence that, despite the loss of the portal to their universe, they were well established in Alliance space. Fortunately, the fresh ships did not do much to shift the balance of power in the battle as Fleet answered with fresh ships of its own.

Lin decided to take advantage of the additional help and suggested the *T'ayMak* make an effort to spearhead an attempt to rescue survivors aboard the *Alasta*.

"What do you suggest?" T'oann asked.

"We pull alongside the *Alasta* and send in teams in EVA gear equipped with search and rescue equipment. They go in, seal up small breeches, put out any fires, restore life support where they can, cut through to the survivors, and pull them out."

"What about those who are too injured to be placed in EVAs and brought back?" Cora asked.

"For them, we find a viable docking port and transport them to the *T'ayMak*."

"What if there are no available docking ports?"

"Then we fucking fix one or make one."

A couple of light tremors vibrated through the ship as a couple of enemy fighters fired on the *T'ayMak*. T'oann barely felt them as she considered Lin's suggestion. If there was the slightest chance of saving the survivors, she was willing to take the chance. Taking chances is how she led her people during the Thouron War.

"Do it," was all she said.

Chapter 63

Markka was agitated and restless. She prowled around the conference room pouring over the reports coming from the battle, occasionally stopping and waving a datapad in the air.

"Have you seen these reports?" she asked B'rtann, Sho'khan, and Zora. Her question was rhetorical since they were all in the room going over the reports together.

Zora sighed, "Yes, Auntie, we can't help but see the reports." She sighed again.

They had all seen their queen happy, angry, and sad at one time or another, but none of them had ever seen her infuriated to the point where she actually paced around on all four limbs—like she was on the prowl. It was an intimidating sight and an unnerving experience.

Even Zora was perplexed by her aunt's demeanor. Between her pregnancy, the mos spent pouring over reports, and her aunt's pacing, Zora was exhausted. She was also reminded of her mother's admonition of suiting up and taking off in her fighter to join the others. Her mother was correct, of course. There was no way she would have been effective at the controls of a fighter. So she was relegated to being trapped in a room with her aunt's surly mood.

"So what are we going to do about this, people?"

No one spoke.

"I'll tell you what we're gonna do about this," Markka continued. "We're gonna throw everything we have at those dirty bastards."

She stopped prowling and glared at everyone in the room.

"What do you propose, my queen?" Sho'khan asked. Her nervousness was evident in the uncertainty in her voice. Her eyes darted around the room searching for emotional support and something to hide behind if Markka decided to pounce.

Markka stood and smiled. It made her incisors look even more menacing. They appeared to glisten.

"Our friends are in danger. I propose we go get them and take out the bastards that put them in danger."

"And just how do we do that, Auntie?"

Markka's grin grew wider. Whoever is not already protecting the planet should go reinforce Captain Stubblefield's forces, backup David and the 332nd, and assist Cora and T'oann in saving Garath, Codie, and the rest."

When no one moved, Markka said, "Do I need to remind you that I am not just the queen, but I am also the highest ranking military commander in this room? Now move your skinny butts. That's an order!"

No one needed to be told twice. They all headed out the door.

As Zora turned to leave, Markka asked her niece, "And where do you think you're going, young lady? You're grounded. Or have you forgotten that?"

Zora huffed and said, "No, I have not forgotten."

"So where were you headed?"

"To the barracks to lend assistance."

"Lungeon can handle that. I want you here to help me coordinate things."

"And just how do you propose to do that without Cora here?"

Markka gave Zora a look as if to say, *I can't believe you just asked me that*, then spoke to someone else. "Jamie?"

"Yes, Queen Markka?"

The voice had the same softness and cadence as Cora's.

"Would you be willing to assist me and Captain Zora with coordinating our offensive?"

"Certainly, my Queen."

"First, you don't have to address me as your queen. Markka will do."

"Yes, Queen Markka."

Markka let out a low growl. "Did your mother put you up to this?"

"No, she has simply instilled in us a respect for rank and age."

"Age! Age?"

Zora intervened before Markka could get upset enough to get distracted from the reason she asked Jamie to join them.

"Jamie, please ignore my aunt's indignation and establish communications with ground and field commanders."

"Will do, Captain Leahcim."

Zora looked at her aunt and smirked. "Do I need to remind you that you ordered us to go on the offensive, not take offense?"

As Markka glared at her niece, Jamie notified them the connections and contacts had been made.

"Great!" Markka said, "Let's get started."

Markka and Zora set up a command base in the Palace conference room. Markka had technicians bring in data pads, communications equipment, display monitors, holographic projectors, workstations, and the personnel to staff them. Jamie was the central processing hub for everything.

The conference room was transformed into a war room. From that space, Markka, Zora, and Jamie monitored every aspect of the battle.

In the reception room next to the makeshift war room, Markka had portable toilets and showers installed. In a room next to that were cots, meditation cubicles, and a healing station. She called in the dining staff to make sure everyone had enough to eat.

Markka was prepared to meet the GSE head on and not stop until the conflict was decidedly over one way or the other. Her priority concern was rescuing the crew of the *Alasta*. Her next concern was giving Leahcim and the 332nd a fighting chance. She did not want a repeat of the Battle of Aggro Nine.

She dispatched two full wings to the portal. One to assist Captain Stubblefield on the Progenshan side of the portal, the other to shore up defenses on the Alliance side of the portal.

Jamie told Markka of Lin's plan to rescue the *Alasta*'s remaining crew. They were getting adequate coverage and support from the Alliance relief ships, but Markka wanted to increase the odds by increasing support for the support ships.

T'oann and the others were deep into their rescue efforts by the time the fighter wings arrived. The *T'ayMak* had to literally land on an undamaged portion of the *Alasta*'s hull and drill into it to create a stable docking port. Once the connections were sealed and tested for leaks, search and rescue teams fanned out through the ship bringing everyone they found to the *T'ayMak*.

It took a full mos to reach Garath and the others. By the time rescue crews reached the medical section, the breathable air was nearly gone. Many of the wounded that were initially found, died from their injuries or were not strong enough to withstand the thinning air. The rescue teams were almost not able to resuscitate Garath and Sanchez.

Codie unconsciously said a prayer when Garath took a long breath and began coughing. He was relieved when Sanchez did the same. He carried them both to the *T'ayMak*.

While the search and rescues were being conducted, Raqmar and his volunteers were still hard at work trying to get the engines working. It was a direct order from Markka that forced them to abandon their efforts.

Meanwhile, a few GSE ships made runs for the portal and were stopped and destroyed before reaching it, but the bulk of the armada was grouped around the supercarrier. They created a formidable and virtually impenetrable wall as they crept en masse toward the portal. If Leahcim and his team, along with the *Tamar*, *Valiant*, and *Nichols* had not destroyed the carrier's targeting array and damaged its engines, the course of the battle would be very different.

As the GSE battle group muscled its way along, her diminutive counterpart continued to drift. Only the surviving bridge crew remained on board. All means of escape were denied to them.

Sojourner's report was not encouraging.

"Captain Parsons' vitals are nearly nonexistent. Lieutenant Karona is not that far behind, and Lieutenant Commander Romar is unconscious. His arm is crushed, and there is no one strong enough to remove the deck plating that has him pinned. His vitals are weakening as well. Only Lieutenants Sparks, Videll, and Charkkan remain functional. But even they are growing weaker as the air continues to thin. Everyone is barely hanging on. I estimate an hour or two before life support fails."

"What about the airlocks?" Lin asked. "Can the Evac teams get in through them?"

"They are intact, but passage from them to the bridge is blocked."

Lin's frustration manifested itself when she uttered every curse T'oann had ever heard David and Markka say, and a few she had never heard.

"We must do something," T'oann said. "We are too close to lose them now. I want a solution and I want it now! They are running out of time."

Chapter 64

A possible solution to their dilemma came from the one person no one thought of.

"Raqmar here, Commander. I think there might be a way to get to the bridge without killing anybody."

"Tell us, Mister Raqmar," T'oann said. The first glimmer of hope made her heart skip beats.

"I'm gonna need Codie's help, if he's willing and able."

"I am at your disposal, Captain," Codie said.

"My team and I are headed to the docking port so we're still in our EVAs. We could easily jet to an airlock closest to the bridge. Most of us are Selemites. Moving shit out the way, uh, sorry, Commander." He corrected himself. "Stuff out the way should be no problem. But we could use the extra muscle. And since Codie is a doctor, he could also help with injuries."

"Damn good thinking, Raq," Lin said. "Make it happen." When she realized she overstepped the line of command, she quickly apologized to T'oann. "Uh, sorry, Commander. Didn't mean to step on your toes."

"Under the circumstances, an apology is not warranted. In fact, I welcome your assistance. I see now why you and Piper are revered in the historical records."

Embarrassed by the compliment, Lin said, "Uh, thanks?" She got back to the business of coordinating the rescue effort and checked in with Raqmar. "I hope you're halfway to the airlock by now."

You could hear the gloating in his voice when he said, "We're opening airlock three and are going inside. Just waiting on Codie."

"I have the airlock in view and will be there momentarily," Codie said.

Once inside, Codie and the engineering team headed toward the bridge. Fortunately, there were no stairs to climb. It was a straight route down a corridor filled with anything and everything that had fallen loose. They were able to push aside debris and make a path through to the bridge. Their final obstacle was the blast door leading to the bridge. It was jammed shut. The impact of the crash caused part of the bulkhead to buckle around the door.

Sojourner updated them on the conditions of everyone on the bridge. "I fear you are too late. The bio signs of Captain Parsons and Lieutenant Karona have ceased."

Panic and rage filled Raqmar. He let out a primal scream and began ramming his shoulder against the door. All he could think about was his beloved Kay. Frustration took over as he continued to ram the door. Codie had to physically restrain Raqmar so he would not injure himself.

Frustrated by the stubborn door, Raqmar slid to the floor and cried inconsolable tears.

Out of ideas, the rescue team sat in silence listening to Raqmar's sobbing until they heard the sound of the airlock doors open and close. Then they heard the sound of footfalls echo in the hall. Sojourner broke the tension before whoever was moving through the corridor came into view.

"Commander T'oann and Lady Lin have arrived. They have brought explosives with them."

Dressed in EVAs, Lin came into view first, followed by T'oann.

"We came as fast as we could," Lin said. "Convincing T'oann, here, to suit up was like trying to pull teeth."

T'oann ignored Lin's little dig and asked Codie, "Can you and Sojourner determine how much and where to place the charges to get this door open without harming our friends on the other side?"

"Yes, Commander."

She handed the charges to him and said, "Make it happen."

"I suggest you and the others head down the hall and take cover at the next junction. I will set the charges and join you."

T'oann and the others did what Codie recommended while he placed the charges and joined them.

"I suggest you cover your ears."

When everyone signaled they were ready, Codie pressed the button on the detonator. The force of the blast shook light debris down on them and not much else. A sprinkling of dust caused some to cough. They put on respirators and headed back toward the bridge blast door. The explosives created a small opening in the wall next to the door large enough to get a stasis tube through.

Codie rushed over to Parsons and Karona and assessed their conditions. Neither was breathing. He injected them with nanites and attached each to a portable resuscitator. After a few uncertain moments, they both began to breathe.

He pulled the piece of metal from Parsons and cauterized her wound. He proceeded to run an IV and pump a coagulant blood substitute into Parsons, and prepared her for transport to the *T'ayMak*.

He worked on Karona's head injury until he was satisfied she was stabilized and ready to be transported.

He made a quick assessment of Romar and determined the XO's left arm had multiple fractures. Codie lifted the deck plate from off the unconscious man's arm, placed his limb in a splint stabilizer, then prepared him for transport to the *T'ayMak*.

While the nanites repaired Parsons' and Karona's injuries, Codie examined Sparks, Charkkan, and Videll. They were all unconscious but uninjured. Judging from the condition of the bridge, he was astonished that they had not sustained any serious injuries or been killed.

The entire time Codie examined the others, Raqmar sat in silence holding Karona. T'oann spent the time getting briefed by Sojourner while she waited for a rescue healing team to arrive so the crew could be suited up and placed in stasis tubes for transport back to the *T'ayMak*.

Sojourner reported to Markka that Parsons and the others were safe.

"That's great news," Markka said. "Vee will be happy to hear that."

"Yes, I am happy to hear that," Vee said as she and Piper entered the War Room. She looked like she had not slept in days. Her eyes were bloodshot and her voice was weak.

Markka looked at Piper who shrugged. "I tried to get her to take a load off, but she insisted. Told me I might not see tomorrow if I sedated her."

Markka smiled like a proud parent.

"What's the latest on the battle?" Piper asked. "Has my wife single-handedly kicked Sairidian ass?"

"Close to it," Markka joked. "I'm beginning to understand how you two got through the early Thouron Wars."

"Excuse me, Queen Markka, but there is urgent news from the front," Jamie said.

"What?"

"Commander T'oann reports the GSE is making a move for the portal. More of their forces are arriving and shoring up their defenses. The balance of the engagement is being tipped in their favor. Alliance reinforcements are on their way, but may arrive too late."

"Dammit!" Markka cursed. She slammed a paw on the table. "Get me Captain Stubblefield."

"The captain is on the line," Jamie said.

"I'm sure I don't need to tell you this, Captain, but all hell is about to break loose."

The captain's no-nonsense voice came on the line.

"We've got this, Your Majesty."

Markka bristled at being addressed so formally, but ignored how it made her feel. There were much more important matters to contend with. Tory had told her now that Progensha was part of a larger universe, she needed to "suck it up."

An emergency message from T'oann cut in.

"All surviving crew of the *Alasta* have been transported to the *T'ayMak*. Sojourner, Cora, and Ramie are scrubbing and deleting sensitive data from the ship's computers and databases. As soon as they're done, they will transfer back to the *T'ayMak*."

"Great," Markka said.

Almost immediately, the communication channels, which had been relatively routine, burst into a chorus of shouting voices, screams, and overlapping levels of excited chatter.

"Have to go," T'oann said. "The enemy is beginning to make their final push toward the port–" The line went dead.

"Commander? Commander? T'oann?" Markka was desperate. "Jamie, what the hell just happened?"

"Unknown."

"Reestablish. Get them back!"

"I am endeavoring to do so."

"Endeavor harder!"

"Yes, ma'am."

Markka shot a glance at Zora who appeared stunned by the suddenness of it all. She looked at Vee, who was already pecking away at the communications station. Piper had a pained look on his face as he no doubt worried about Lin. Until communications were restored, there was nothing any of them could do but wait.

The guns on the enemy carrier were fully functional again. The Sairidians made that fact very clear by firing on the *Alasta*. The attack hit the ship hard enough to sever the *T'ayMak*'s docking port connection.

To add insult to injury, the *T'ayMak*'s shields were below optimal effectiveness at the time. The blast knocked all vital systems offline. The crew frantically worked to restore them as they tumbled helplessly away from the fray.

Leahcim was horrified when his wife's ship was torn away from the *Alasta*. His initial reaction was to break formation and fly to the *T'ayMak* and provide cover, but the advancing GSE ships took that choice away from him. He tried reaching out to his wife with his mind, but found only emptiness. Leahcim did not believe in deities, but he found himself saying a quick prayer to the Goddess to keep his wife and the others safe.

As if seeing the *T'ayMak* tumbling through space was not enough, the engines on what was left of the *Alasta* roared to life and the wounded ship began moving.

What the hell is going on? Leahcim thought. "Leahcim to *Alasta*, what the hell is happening? Who is aboard? Identify yourself."

"It is I, Cora, sir."

"Cora? What the hell are you still doing on the *Alasta*?"

"Sojourner, Ramie, and I remained on board to effect a data scrub. We were separated from the *T'ayMak* when the *Alasta* was attacked."

"Were you successful?"

"Yes."

"Then get the hell off the ship. Transfer yourselves to the *Nichols*. It's closest to your location."

"Negative, Commander. We are staying on board."

"Why?"

"We intend to destroy the Sairidian carrier."

"What? How?"

"Our intentions will become apparent to everyone momentarily, Commander."

He understood what she meant the instant he saw the *Alasta* pivot.

"I forbid it. Stand down! Now! That's an order."

"What was that, Commander? We did not receive your last transmission."

"I'm not joking, Cora. Stop this insanity now." Leahcim had not felt so useless since he and Markka were left stranded in space following the Battle of Aggro Nine.

"Sorry, Commander, you're breaking up. It was a pleasure serving with you. Goodbye." The transmission ended.

Leahcim and the rest of the fleet watched as what remained of the *Alasta* headed for the supercarrier. The Sairidian carrier recognized it was in danger of being rammed and attempted to adjust course to avoid its fate. The *Alasta* adjusted its course and closed in on the massive warship.

Leahcim surmised the ship had not fired again on the *Alasta* because it needed time to recharge its weapons. A detail Cora, Sojourner, and Ramie figured out. Two GSE cruisers and a couple of squadrons began firing on the *Alasta*. The *Tamar* and *Valiant* returned fire.

Leahcim wanted to scream, but the best he could do was curse as his rage threatened to consume him. "Fuck it. Captain Stubblefield, make sure you destroy every rat bastard that gets through that damn portal."

"We've got your back, Commander. Give 'em hell."

"Okay, people, let's show the universe what the 332nd can do. Let's give Cora the time she needs to send those cold-blooded fuckers all back to the hell they came from."

The 332nd formed a tight formation around the *Alasta* and provided cover for the ship. The GSE fighters responded and the fiercest dogfights of the battle were underway.

As Leahcim and his people engaged their counterparts, the crew of the *T'ayMak* recovered from the attack.

Lin got to her feet, helped pick T'oann from off the deck, then looked around to assess the situation before she asked, "What the hell happened?"

She was told the supercarrier fired on the *Alasta* and they were ripped free of its hull. Most of the main systems went down but were coming back online.

"What's our status, Cora?" Lin asked. "Casualties?"

There was no reply.

"Cora? What is our status?"

There was still no reply. The communications officer told her that Cora, Sojourner, and Ramie did not make it back aboard.

Fearing the worst, T'oann asked, "Where are they?"

"Still aboard the *Alasta*, Commander."

"We have to go back for them."

"It's too late, Commander. The *Alasta* is on a collision course with the supercarrier."

"How is that possible?"

"I can answer that, Commander," Raqmar said. He had just reached the engineering station on the *T'ayMak*'s bridge when the *Alasta* was fired upon.

"Explain."

"Not all the engines were slag. My team and I repaired a bunch of relays and conduits, and rerouted some primary and secondary systems. We were about to fire them up when we were ordered to head to the *T'ayMak*. It looks like Sojourner and them finished what we started and got the engines running."

"And now they're using the engines to ram the *Alasta* into the carrier," Lin said.

"Can they do it?" T'oann asked.

Raqmar shrugged. "Maybe. And that's a big maybe. It depends on whether the engines hold out long enough for them to reach the carrier. They must have figured out the carrier can't jump into hyperspace–considering all the damage we did to it."

The *T'ayMak* stopped tumbling when main power was restored.

"We have restored the main power, Commander," Raqmar reported.

Lin was adamant about finishing the battle. "Helmsman, get us back into the fight."

"Aye, sir."

With Lin back in control of bridge operations, T'oann considered their options. The first thing she felt she needed to do was update Markka and let her and everyone at the GBDF know they were alright.

'It's about damn time you got back to us," Markka said. "I was beginning to wonder if I needed to send more reinforcements. What the hell happened?"

T'oann updated Markka and the others as Lin issued orders and commands to the crew. The *T'ayMak* fired its weapons and took enemy fire as it bobbed, dodged and weaved its way through the battle zone.

"Cora and the other two knuckleheads are doing what?"

"Just what I said. David and the 332nd are providing cover as best they can," T'oann tried to sound confident.

"Those selfless idiots. We can't let them throw their lives away. We gotta do something."

"If they succeed, it could shorten the war."

"And if they don't?" Markka asked.

T'oann recalled how she had not trusted Cora when she and David and Markka crash-landed on her world. She found it hard to face the thought of life without her. If it were not for Cora, her people might either have been enslaved or would have become the victims of genocide. *There has got to be another way, she thought*. But she could not think of one.

"Might I suggest something?" The question was asked by Jamie.

"Yes, you may," T'oann said.

"My mother and sibling, as well as Sojourner, can survive if there is an Alliance ship close enough for them to transfer to. We have the ability to attach ourselves at short distances to signals we are in close proximity with."

T'oann thought back to when David and Markka first crashed on Progensha and how Cora had infiltrated their computer network and communications systems. She snapped her fingers. "That's it! We need to be within transmission range just before the ships collide."

"Then you need to make damn sure you're within range when that happens; get your skinny butts over there," Markka said. "And make damn sure you're nowhere near those ships when they blow."

"Trust me. We don't plan to be."

"You got that right," Lin said. She turned to the tactical officer and asked, "Time?"

"Sixty seconds."

"Can we make it?"

"Maybe."

"Helmsman, straight line. Step on it."

"Aye, sir."

The ship lurched forward as fast as the pilot could take it in a field of shrapnel and debris. The ship's shields deflected most of the debris and weapons fire.

"Okay, we're only going to get one shot at this," Lin said. "We won't get a second pass."

"Thirty seconds," the tactical officer announced.

"Patch me through," Markka said.

The communications officer said, "Channel open."

"Cora, the *T'ayMak*'s doing a flyby. I need you three to jump ship! Now!"

The bow of the *Alasta* smashed through the port side of the carrier, split the keel, and set off a chain reaction of explosions that ripped through the ship from stem to stern. If anything, Cora, Sojourner, and Ramie had been precise. It would have been hit or miss with a crew of biologics. Space glowed brighter than a supernova.

The *T'ayMak* flew as close as possible before peeling off to avoid becoming part of the conflagration that was once two mighty ships of war.

"Anything?" Markka asked.

Silence was her answer.

Everyone waited to hear Cora's voice, but there was nothing.

"We fucking failed," Lin said.

Seconds passed before anyone else spoke.

The first voice anyone heard belonged to Ramie.

"Thank you for returning for us."

A deafening cheer filled the bridge before T'oann asked, "is that everyone?"

After an uncomfortable pause, Sojourner said, "No, Cora did not accompany us."

A sense of sadness shot through T'oann like a stabbing pain. "I am sorry for your loss."

"She is not lost—at least not yet."

"I don't understand. Where is she?"

"V Squadron was within close proximity of the explosion. Most of its pilots escaped the initial blast. Commander Leahcim's wingman could not. He circled back and fired his tow cable to pull her clear. The final series of explosions broke the cable. His wingman was spared, but the Commander was not. Cora detected he was in distress and opted to transfer to his fighter instead of the *T'ayMak*. We have not heard from either since."

The news and the stress and sadness in Ramie's voice hit T'oann like a sucker punch. Her knees weakened and she crumpled to the deck. She reached out to Leahcim with her mind, but felt only emptiness.

Lin pushed herself past people in her way to reach her friend.

"Move! Outta the way!"

She knelt down beside T'oann whose expression reflected the pain she felt inside. Lin embraced her friend and said, "I'm sure he's okay. Cora is with him. She won't let anything happen to him."

T'oann looked at Lin with tear-soaked eyes and said, "I don't sense him. I can't feel him. I'm afraid he's . . . gone." She buried her head in Lin's embrace and trembled as she wept.

Markka refused to accept the news and turned to rush out the command center toward a fighter. Only Zora had the courage to stand in her way.

Markka ordered her niece to get out of her way.

"Move!"

"You are not going anywhere, aunty."

"They need my help," Markka insisted. "And you are not going to stand in my way." She was borderline hysterical.

"I feel your pain, but I cannot allow you to jeopardize your life."

Zora continued to block Markka's path. Markka unsheathed her claws and crouched.

"I'm not going to repeat myself. Get out of my way."

Zora held her ground and pulled her pistol from its holster on her hip. It was set to full stun.

Markka hissed, "You wouldn't dare."

"Take another step and I will drop you where you stand." Zora did not blink.

Markka stared at her niece and tried to decide whether Zora was joking. She reasoned she was not. She retracted her claws and stepped back. Overcome with emotions, Markka broke down and sobbed. Zora embraced her aunt then stuck her with an injector containing a sedative to calm her down and make her easier to handle. Zora always carried an injector in case her aunt needed to be subdued. She never thought she would ever need to use it.

"What the hell is going on there?" Lin asked.

After a moment of silence, Zora replied. "I had to subdue my aunt." She sounded dejected and defeated.

Sorrow and rage bubbled inside Lin. "Find them! Don't stop until you do!"

Chapter 65

Moments before the carriers collided, Cora observed Leahcim's squadron disengage from combat and swing away from the doomed ships. His wingman was not able to keep up due to severe battle damage. Leahcim came back for her and attached a tow cable, equipped with a strong magnet, to her fighter to pull her away from the imminent explosion.

The force of the initial blast snapped the cable as if it were a flimsy piece of string. The wave energy of the follow-up explosions sent the fighters tumbling in two different directions. Leahcim's wingman was pushed toward the relative safety of the fleet, while his fighter was sent in the opposite direction toward deep space. A nanosecond before both carriers were fully engulfed, Cora transferred herself aboard Leahcim's fighter and attempted to regain control. For her it was a deja vu moment. For him, nothing.

The blast waves knocked him unconscious and drained the fighter's power, shutting down all systems including emergency backup and Cora. They drifted unseen away from the fleet.

When Leahcim regained consciousness, he instinctively attempted to contact his wingman. He was worried she did not make it.

"Luna? Come in, Luna. Are you alright?" He did not receive a response. He tried again. "Come in, Luna. Are you receiving me?" There was no response. He tried again before he realized his fighter's systems were all dead. He flipped, switched, twisted, and clicked his controls. Nothing worked.

Dammit, he thought, *It's Aggro Nine all over again*. But this time without Markka or Cora. He was alone. He ran through a mental checklist then went through a series of steps to power up and reboot the system. Again, nothing worked. He tried a second time with the same result. Desperate and frustrated, he slammed a fist on his console and let out a scream. He cursed to himself, "Shit, shit, shit."

"Must you always be so dramatic, Commander?"

Startled by the voice, he asked in an uncertain tone, "Cora?"

"Yes, Commander?"

"What the hell are you doing here?"

"I analyzed your situation and determined you needed assistance. So I transferred myself to your fighter to help."

"That was thoughtful of you, but foolhardy. You know without power, we can't contact anybody. You're stuck here with me."

"Quite the contrary. I simply need to tap into whatever residual energy remains in the batteries."

"You do realize this is a Progenshan-built ship, not an Alliance one? You can't use ambient light and energy sources to charge the batteries."

"I am speaking with you, am I not?"

"Yeah."

"You forget that I and my offspring share a unique communication signal. I do not require much energy to transmit. If power levels fall to zero, I simply remain dormant until power is restored; you die. We must notify the others before that happens."

"When that happens," he muttered.

"We found Ramie. He and Codie will find us."

Leahcim chuckled. "It seems you have thought this rescue thing out."

"Yes, I did. It took all of a nanosecond to work out the logistics. Now if you will excuse me, I need to let my children know where we are."

"Certainly."

Cora sent out an SOS on the low level frequency only she and her children shared while they continued to float away from the battle.

In the aftermath of the deaths of the carriers, the GSE fleet made a desperate attempt to engage the Alliance, but as more Alliance ships arrived, a GSE victory turned into a GSE rout.

Rather than surrender, the Sairidians chose among three options. Continue to battle their enemy, suicide runs against Alliance ships, or a desperate run for the portal. Most of the Sairidians and their reptilian allies chose to stay and fight to the bitter end. Many of their fighter pilots chose to make a run for the portal. They gambled that their sheer numbers and the diminutive size of their ships would be enough to break through the Alliance blockade. Those that did get through were quickly destroyed by the Alliance-Progenshan fleet waiting on the other side.

Captain Stubblefield coordinated the defense of the portal with B'rtann and Sho'khan until the tranquilizer Zora used on Markka wore off.

Mictons later, when Markka regained consciousness and opened her eyes, she saw her niece kneeling next to her.

Zora let her aunt gain her bearings before she asked, "Have you returned to your senses or must I put you down again?"

Markka cleared the cobwebs of confusion from her mind and stared at her niece.

"You stuck me."

"I will do it again—if need be."

"You know there's a penalty for assaulting your queen?"

"And do you know I had the authority of the king to put you down?"

Markka shook off the last effects of her foggy mind then noticed Tory standing nearby. His arms were crossed against his chest and he was patting one foot on the floor. She gave him a sheepish smile and said, "Sorry?"

He stopped patting his foot, but continued to fold his arms as he locked eyes with her.

After what seemed like mos to Markka, he smiled and said, "You are forgiven—for now."

"Now," Zora said, "I suggest you get up off the floor—it is such an undignified position for someone of your status—and resume command of operations."

Zora updated her aunt on the latest developments Markka missed while unconscious.

Once Markka regained her full faculties, she resumed control of the situation and convinced the Great Beyond Defense Force brass to send the bulk of the Progenshan defense force to the portal. There were so many ships on the Progenshan side that they formed an impenetrable wall. Not a single GSE ship escaped.

With the Sairidian threat basically neutralized, the rescue and cleanup efforts began.

T'oann, not fully recovered from the shock of losing Leahcim and Cora, coordinated with the captains of the *Nichols*, *Tamar*, and *Victory* to make it a priority to look for them. She persuaded Lin, who reluctantly agreed, to concentrate on dealing with chasing down GSE stragglers who opted to cut and run, rather than worry about Leahcim and Cora. It made her feel better avenging them.

***

Because the batteries in Leahcim's fighter were not charged enough to maintain the ship's power plant, life support was nonexistent. Leahcim had mere hours before hypothermia set in or he was asphyxiated.

Cora sent her distress signal, but they had drifted too far from the battle zone. The signal was not strong enough to be detected.

"I am sorry, Commander."

Through a sleepy haze, a half-frozen Leahcim asked, "For what?" His teeth chattered and his words were slurred.

"For failing you."

He tried to smile, but the cold made his face hurt. "You did not fail me. You have been an excellent protector and a good friend. I'm glad to have known you. Cora?"

"Yes, Commander?"

"Make sure my nanites get a good home." He tried to laugh, but it came out more as a painful cough.

"That is it! Commander, you are a genius."

"Call me David."

Cora hesitated before she did. "David."

As his breathing became more irregular, Leahcim made one last request. "Cora, do me one last favor."

"Anything . . . David."

Before losing consciousness, he said, "Tell T'oann I love her."

Cora hesitated before she responded. "I will."

***

T'oann was standing next to Lin discussing strategies to try to find Leahcim and Cora when she abruptly stopped speaking and turned glassy-eyed. Lin waved a hand in front of T'oann's face and got no reaction from her.

329

Not knowing what else to do, Lin said, "Get Garath or Codie up here! Now!"

Moments later Garath dashed onto the bridge.

"What is the emergency?"

Lin pointed at T'oann and said, "That."

Garath recognized right away what the issue was and blew out a breath of relief.

Lin looked confused. "Why are you relieved? She's catatonic."

"She is communicating with her nanites."

Lin was more confused. "What do you mean she's communicating with her nanites?'"

Garath smiled at Lin and told her, "That is how we found you and Lord Piper. T'oann and David mind-walked with their nanites to talk with your nanites. The catatonic state is how they do it."

"Oh."

"When she is finished, she will need your help."

"With what?"

As if on cue, T'oann came out of her trance and started to fall to the deck. Lin caught her before she did.

"With that. They are weakened by the experience."

T'oann began to mutter, "They're alive. They're alive."

"Who's alive?" Lin asked.

T'oann regained her composure and asked, "Ramie, can you detect Cora's distress signal?"

"Yes, Commander."

"Pinpoint its location."

"I have, Commander."

T'oann nearly pleaded with Lin. "Get us there, quickly. Cora says David doesn't have much time left."

Lin told Ramie to send the coordinates to the navigation officer then she told the helmsman to, "Get us there yesterday."

"Aye, sir."

An instant later the *T'ayMak* was speeding toward the coordinates Cora sent.

T'oann's legs felt like rubber after her mind-walk so she asked Garath to help her get to the fighter bay. "I need to be there," she said.

Without saying a word, Garath draped an arm around T'oann and led her to one of the bridge elevators and down to the bay to wait for her husband.

Codie was standing next to a stasis tube waiting for Leahcim's arrival. Dispensing with formality, he greeted them in a blunt, straightforward manner.

"My mother informs me Commander Leahcim is in poor health. We will need to place him in this tube and rush him back to Progensha for proper treatment. I will oversee the process personally."

He bowed to T'oann using the traditional Uderran military salute. She acknowledged his gesture with a nod of her head.

Lin's voice piped through the ship's PA system.

"Prepare to receive Commander Leahcim and Cora."

T'oann heard the tractor beam activate and watched as Leahcim's fighter was brought on board. Immediately, Codie and the healing team rushed over and lifted his limp body out of his seat and placed him inside the stasis tube.

"I am not detecting any bio signs," Codie said. "Nor am I detecting any signals from his nanites. Get him to the isolation chamber and increase the heat level to level two."

T'oann watched the healing team place Leahcim into the tube and whisk him off to sickbay.

Garath kept T'oann at a distance so she would not interfere with the medical staff. But that did not stop her from trying to mind-walk with her husband. She reached out to him but could not sense his presence or his nanites.

They followed Codie and his team to sickbay. While enroute, T'oann asked Cora what happened. Cora told her how Leahcim saved his wingman but got caught in the blast wave. And how she decided to transfer herself to his fighter instead of the *Nichols*.

"The force of the blast rendered him unconscious and his fighter without power," Cora said. "I attempted to use the residual energy from the battery reserves, but it was not enough for me to send a strong enough signal until the commander suggested using his nanites to boost the gain. I did. It worked. But I fear I am too late."

"What happened and whatever happens, know that it was not your fault and that you did your best."

Garath led T'oann to a room next to where Codie worked on Leahcim then went to change so she could assist. After Garath left, Cora spoke to T'oann.

"There is something I need to tell you."

"What is it, Cora?"

"David asked me to tell you that he loves you."

T'oann sat quietly for a moment before she said, "Thank you."

"You are welcome."

Chapter 66

Using low levels of electric current, Codie and Garath were able to jumpstart Leahcim's nanites. The nanites were able to raise his core body temperature to normal. But despite their best efforts, he remained in a comatose state that T'oann's best mind-walking skills were not able to penetrate.

When the *T'ayMak* reached Progensha, Leahcim was taken to the main healing center in Uderra and placed in intensive care. T'oann camped out in a chair next to his bed and refused to leave. She made repeated attempts to make contact, but was never able to reach him. Sol after sol she held vigil hoping and praying.

On the tenth sol, as she slept in the chair next to Leahcim, a voice spoke to her in her mind, but it was not Leahcim's. It was Tonga's.

"Stay strong, sister. I believe I can help."

"How?"

"He needs to know you do not blame him."

"For what?"

"Leaving you. Cora told me his last thought was of you."

"What I knew of him is no longer there. There is nothing left to talk to."

"Yes, there is."

"How—"

"Trust me. I know." Tonga extended her arm and said, "Take my hand."

T'oann took Tonga's hand and sensed herself falling into a deep, dark void. She began to panic as she was reminded of the first time she mind-walked with Leahcim. He had led her to believe he had trapped her in his mind. This time she felt overwhelming dread that she would actually be trapped this time.

"Calm your mind," Tonga said. "Remain still and call to him."

T'oann did what her sister said. She tamped down her fear, and called to him. "David? It is T'oann. Please, speak to me."

She sensed his presence and grew hopeful, then became defensive when she sensed an unknown presence.

"Relax," Tonga said. "The other presence you feel is that of the young pilot Leahcim rescued. Luna. He feels remorse because he thinks he did not save her."

A light shimmered and Luna appeared standing in front of both of them. She looked frightened and unsure of herself. She was dressed in her flight suit. Her caramel-colored face was peppered with freckles and accented with feline features hinting at Uderran and Dark Woods heritage. Her face was framed by long flowing brown hair.

"Where am I?" she asked.

"You are in Commander Leahcim's mind with me and Commander T'oann."

"I do not understand. How did I get here? Why am I here?"

"The commander believes you died, that he did not save you. You must assure him that you are alive because of him."

After a moment of uncertainty, Luna called out to Leahcim. "Commander Leahcim? It is I, Luna. Please do not grieve for me. I am alive. Because of what you did for me, I am with my parents and siblings. Thank you."

"You may go now," Tonga said. An instant later, Luna shimmered and faded away. "You may call to him now, sister. He will respond."

"Are you certain?"

"Trust me. Have I ever disappointed you?"

"No."

"And I will not begin now. Go to him."

T'oann stepped into the light and said, "David, I am here. Please let me in. I miss you so much." She waited for a sign that he was listening, then nearly cried when he appeared in front of her.

"It's true? I'm alive? Luna is alive?"

"Yes, you saved her. Cora, your nanites, and Codie and Garath and their team saved you. And you have saved me."

"How?"

"By coming back to me."

Through the darkness, T'oann heard Codie and Garath tell their staff to prepare to revive her husband. He was coming out of his coma.

"It is time to go," Tonga said. "He will need you when he awakens."

T'oann returned to full consciousness and watched Codie and Garath work on her husband. After a few tense moments, he opened his eyes. Once he got his bearings, he asked for T'oann. She stood over him and wrapped her arms around him in a tight hug. She whispered in his ear, "I thought I had lost you."

He whispered back that he was sorry. She placed a finger to his lips and shushed him. Then she kissed him.

Markka and Tory, Lin and Piper, Vee and Rosa, and Zora and Lungeon, who were all standing outside the room looking through observation glass, cheered and clapped.

"Go to them," Tonga said. "Your friends have been waiting. Codie and Garath will take care of David."

T'oann looked out at the little group and said, "They are not my friends. They are my family."

She stepped out of the room and was immediately accosted by a barrage of questions. The din of inquiring voices was suddenly split by a high-pitched whistle. Everyone looked at Markka.

"Hey, what do you know? That actually worked. So what's the word on David?"

T'oann smiled for the first time in sols, looked back toward Leahcim then over at Codie and Garath who were both busy tending to her husband. She turned back to everyone and said, "The word is good."

Epilogue

One year after what became known as the Battle for Progensha, Fleet had rooted out and eliminated all of the GSE forces from Alliance space. The fear that the GSE had cloaked bases was unfounded. What the Sairidians had done was snuck a second supercarrier with cloaking ability into Alliance territory.

Once the Alliance knew what to look for, Cora and her children developed a detection system that was deployed throughout the Alliance. With nowhere to hide, the remaining GSE forces retreated to the frontier. The border grid between them ensured there would no longer be any surprise attacks. The Alliance adopted the Progenshan mindset that vigilance is the price of peace and freedom.

The Progenshans quickly adapted to being a member of the Alliance but concentrated their efforts toward defending their world against foreign incursions through two portals. One active, the other dormant. That meant learning all they could about the Great Beyond and beyond.

***

"So what happened next Grandmother?"

Tonga relaxed in the courtyard of her son's home entertaining her youngest grandchild. Marshon had invited his mother to spend her retirement years with him and Pricilla. She spent a good amount of her time cooking, baking, and writing her memoirs. Tonga also relished the time she spent with her granddaughter who was one growth spurt away from adulthood. She spent countless mos telling her stories about the "good old days."

Before she could continue to tell her granddaughter more, the door chimed.

"Yay! We have visitors," her granddaughter announced.

Happy for the change of pace, Tonga asked Cora, "Who is it?"

"Commanders T'oann and Leahcim, ma'am."

"Let them in." She grinned at her granddaughter. "Go escort our guests to the courtyard."

Like a sprinter in a race, Sylvia took off to greet their guests. Upon her return, she carried herself as if she were part of the security attachment assigned to protect the president. Stiff-backed, wearing a serious expression, and all business.

"Commanders T'oann and David Leahcim of the House of Mahli have arrived."

"Thank you, Sylvia. Superb introduction. You will be an excellent security escort. Now, with your permission, may I have some time alone with our guests?"

Sylvia studied her grandmother before saying, "Okay," then dashed into the house.

Tonga chuckled, "Before long she will be entering the Academy."

"They grow up so fast," Leahcim said. His comment was a veiled joke about the accelerated growth spurt common in many Progenshan children.

"So to what do I owe the pleasure of your visit?"

"We were in the neighborhood and decided to drop in and update you on what's been going on," Leahcim said.

"That is very thoughtful of you. Since my retirement, I have endeavored to stay less informed about matters the next generation can handle. But it is nice to peek in on the lives of my friends. I hear you both have retired from military service."

"Yes, sister," T'oann said. "We decided we have gotten too old for the excitement. Like you, we are doting grandparents."

"How are my niece and nephew doing?"

"Quite well."

"Yeah, they're running us ragged," Leahcim said.

T'oann playfully jabbed him in his side. "Speak for yourself."

He pretended the jab hurt by rubbing where her elbow poked him. Then kissed his wife.

"And how is everyone else doing?"

T'oann took the lead in updating Tonga.

"As you know, Zora was promoted to a full colonel and placed in command of the 332nd Fighter Wing. Lungeon was given command of the 761st Tank Assault Division."

"Those two are sort of like me and T'oann when we were their age," Leahcim said.

"The maiden fruit doesn't fall far from the tree."

T'oann continued telling Tonga about what the others were doing.

"Sparks was promoted to captain and given command of the *T'ayMak*. Karona is her Executive Officer and Lieutenant Commander Raqmar is the chief engineer. One of Sparks' first official acts was marrying Karona and Raqmar."

"I wondered how long it would take before those two would become espoused. I am happy for them. What of Romar?"

"He is the director of the newly formed Department of Portal Defense. Sojourner is his assistant and advisor."

"Good for them."

"Sojourner recently discovered a hidden file the Others placed in her memory. It activated when the GSE was defeated."

"I suppose it will take cycles to comb through the data contained in that file. B'rtann and Sho'khan are probably salivating."

"Actually, Ramie is helping her decipher the data. B'rtann and Sho'khan are off-world. They are in Officer Training at the Alliance's top training facility. Admiral K'mar has taken them under her wing, so to speak."

"Then I know they are salivating. She is a nice person."

Leahcim sounded surprised. "You think so?"

"Yes, I have had the good fortune of making her acquaintance. We dined a few times together. She is a complex individual who cares deeply about the people under her command."

T'oann knew only of her reputation. Leahcim served directly under her command. They each looked at each other as if they found what Tonga said was hard to believe.

"So who is overseeing daily military operations?"

"Cora and Jamie."

"Ahh, good choices. So what else is going on?"

T'oann continued updating her sister.

"Lin and Piper are instructors at the Academy."

"It is fitting the school is named after their daughter."

"And you may have heard that Vee and Parsons retired from military service and settled down as food field proprietors."

"Food field proprietors?" Tonga rubbed her chin in thought. "How is that working out?"

"Surprisingly well, actually. They made some kind of deal with Vee's sister, Verna, and the officials on Sigma II and Aggro Nine to provide farming supplies to both planets."

"Is not Sigma II a desert planet?"

"Yes, it is, but a terraforming program was put in place. Commander Chappie spearheads the project. It is his way of thanking them for their assistance in the war effort."

"Good for them."

Leahcim cut in and said, "By the way, Sanchez and Chappie tied the knot."

"Did she propose or did he?"

"She did."

"I figured as much. That union was never going to happen if she kept waiting for him to make the first move."

"And speaking of tying the knot," Leahcim continued, "Codie asked Garath to marry him, and she accepted."

"It was about time. Those two were driving me crazy."

Both T'oann and Leahcim looked at each other in amazement. Their curiosity was piqued.

"What do you mean they were driving you crazy?" T'oann asked.

"They were constantly coming to me with questions about each other."

"Why you?"

Tonga sighed. "As you know, Garath has no living biological family. So I adopted her as my surrogate daughter."

"I was aware that she has no family, but I was not aware you were acting as a substitute mother," T'oann said. "How did you become one to her?"

"She both admires and fears you—both of you. Codie informed me following your deaths, like Markka, she was in a dark place. But where Markka had Tory–or more like they had each other–Garath had no one."

"So you took on the role of matriarch?" T'oann asked.

"That was my intention. I asked Codie to help her through her grief until I could return. Little did I know how incensed Shang would become. After our rescue from Sacred Mountain two cycles later, I assumed the role of surrogate and mentor to her. By that time, Codie's interest in her had manifested itself, and since they worked so closely and so well together, it was inevitable a bond between them would develop."

"And you encouraged it?"

"Oh, no, I did not encourage it." Then she smiled. "But I did not discourage it."

Leahcim snorted and said, "Sounds to me like you played matchmaker."

Tonga's smile turned mischievous. "I simply let nature take its course." She winked at them then changed the direction of the discussion. "And what of our esteemed leader?"

"Oh, yeah, her," Leahcim said. "Well, what happened to her was her own damn fault. Markka insisted the Queendom needed to transition to a more democratic system of government. Her idea was more of an attempt to get out of being the queen of Uderra. Instead, as you know, she was nominated and voted in as the first president of Progensha."

"Now she bristles at being called Madam President," T'oann said.

"I understand the vice president did not have much choice in the matter either."

Leahcim almost gloated. "Nope, to Tory's relief, she nominated Durard, and he was immediately approved by the full senate."

"I am so happy for her. When you see her, tell her I cast my vote for her."

"We will," Leahcim said. "She'll be thrilled to hear it." The sarcasm and delight in his voice were evident. "She sends her greetings and apologies for not visiting. She's mired in the business of creating a planetary constitution."

"Well, I am sure she has things under control."

"If you mean whether she's being her usual cantankerous self? Then, yes. The president of the Alliance is even afraid of her." Leahcim grinned like a proud parent.

"And he is Selemite," T'oann said.

Tonga ran her hands over her thighs and smoothed out her toga before she stood up and said, "It looks like the future of the planet is in good hands. Now who wants some herder's pie?"

Lexicon

Absolom Abdul - bridge Officer on board the *Alasta*.

Admiral K'mar - senior military commander of the Alliance's Fleet.

Aggro Nine - an agricultural planet near the Alliance frontier.

Alasta - an Alliance supercarrier.

Alliance - an organization of planets, also known as the Union of Allied Worlds, whose members share a common goal of mutual cooperation, trade, and defense. Known to its members and by its enemy simply as the Alliance.

Alliance Time - time in the Alliance is based on Allurian time. Forty hours is considered one standard day. Four hundred days is considered one standard year.

Allurians - dominant culture in the Alliance and the founders of the Alliance. They are distant genetic cousins to Terrans and are identified by gold colored eyes and pink irises.

Ambrosia - a sweet drink made from a combination of Progenshan fruits.

A/T - all-terrain vehicle capable of traveling through space as well as on land or sea.

Aviana - the homeworld of the Avians.

Avians - are from the planet Aviana. Their bodies are covered in feathers and they are capable of flight.

Bantam Fighter - a small, single-pilot starfighter used primarily by smugglers and Progenshan pilots.

Battle of Aggro Nine - a military engagement between an Alliance fighter squadron and GSE fighters near the planet Aggro Nine.

Battle of the Portal - military engagement between the Alliance and the GSE.

Battle for Progensha - military engagement between the Alliance and their Progenshan allies and the GSE.

Biochip - an organic-based chip implanted into the brains of Alliance military personnel.

B'rtann - an officer in the Uderran military who eventually becomes Supreme Commander

Captain Sharon Stubblefield - the Alliance captain in command of the battle group assigned to protect the Progenshan portal.

Challenge of Honor - a gladiatorial challenge in Thouron culture. It entails a duel to the death.

Changeling - an Alliance ship that participated in the Battle For Progensha.

Charkkan - bridge Officer on board the *Alasta*.

Coalition - an organization made up of Uderrans, Wooders, Mountainers, Lungeons, and Nomads who banded together in their war with the Thourons.

Codie - one of Cora's children and friend to Garath.

Colossal Ocean - a large ocean that feeds into the Western Sea and provides the main source of water to the northern continent.

Cold Mountain People - the full collective name of the Mountain People or Mountainers.

Commander Gregory Chappie - friend of Captain Vee, the officer she confided in with the secret intel she and her crew aboard the *Infiltrator* discovered.

Cora - SI (Synthetic Intelligence) and friend to David Leachim and Marka.

Cryogas - a gas used by the Cold Mountain doctors and scientists to cryogenically freeze people for operations and experiments.

Dark Woods - a thickly wooded forest on the planet Progensha. Inhabited by an elusive group of people known as the Dark Woodsmen.

Dark Woodsman - are primarily descendants of Felids and others who survived Progensha's Great War and took refuge in the woods.

Dart Lizard - a large lizard native to the planet Progensha. It immobilizes and kills its victims by shooting them with poison darts.

David Leahcim - Alliance pilot, husband to T'oann, friend and mentor to Markka.

Destiny - an Alliance battleship.

Diggers - robotic drones used by Uderrans for excavation.

Durard - the Thouron delegation member who was the chief negotiator at the end of the Thouron War and was instrumental in negotiating with the Alliance.

Earth - the former name of the homeworld of the Terrans.

Emissary - the physical representative of The Others.

Evelyn Sanchez - Alliance Doctor and Psychologist.

Felids - are from the planet Felidia. Felids are members of the Alliance and resemble Terran cats that walk upright.

Felidia - the homeworld of Markka and fellow Felids.

Fleerpa - a stringed instrument Feledian parents play for their children. It is similar to a guitar.

Food Field - Progenshan farm land.

Formaxadia - a member planet of the Alliance whose inhabitants are similar to Terran ants.

Garath - a competent healer in the Uderran military. She eventually becomes the chief healer.

Gargantuan - the Progenshan equivalent of a Terran elephant.

GBDF - Great Beyond Defense Force. The military arm of the Progenshan space fleet. Organization established to protect the planet from threats.

Gihon Nebula - a thick gaseous nebula in Alliance space near Aggro Nine.

Goddess - the primary deity Progenshans believe in and pray to.

Gold Leaf Tea - a fragrant beverage made from the gold leaves of the dominant species of tree on the planet Progensha.

Ground Worms - the Progenshan equivalent to earthworms.

GSE - Galactic Star Empire and the primary adversary of the Alliance. It is dominated by reptilian beings whose singular aim is domination of all known space and species.

Hawking - an Alliance military supercarrier.

Hendley - a Terran bureaucrat stationed on Terra II.

Herder's Pie - the Progenshan equivalent of Shepherd's Pie.

High Command - the governing board of the Alliance military.

High Council - the governing body of the Progenshan Coalition.

House of Mahli - the dominant ruling house or family of the Uderran Queendom.

Hurston Base - the Alliance military base on Terra II.

Infiltrator - multipurpose warship under the command of Captain Vee.

Injector - a syringe or hypodermic needle.

Inland Sea - one of several bodies of water within the continents that are safe to sail upon.

Jamie - one of Cora's children.

Jamocha - hot beverage similar to coffee.

Jesse Brown - an Alliance battle cruiser.

Jimperson - assistant security officer aboard the Alliance ship *Potomac*.

Joachim - a junior officer and archaeologist in the Uderran military who led the science division in the discovery of Traveler City and Lin and Piper.

Kormak - captain of the Alliance ship *Potomac*.

Land of No Return - a large desert area covered in residual radiation and inhabited by dangerous, mutated lifeforms. The Progenshans refer to it as such because no one who ventures there ever returns.

Leviathan - Large sea creatures that live in the oceans of Progensha. They are the sole reason only one continent is inhabited.

Lieutenant Abdul - a Terran and member of the *Alasta* bridge.

Lieutenant Charrkan - a Felid and member of the *Alasta* bridge.

Lieutenant Videll - an Allurian and member of the *Alasta* bridge.

Luna - fighter pilot in the Progenshan 332nd fighter wing. She was Leahcim's wingman at the Battle for Progensha.

Lungeon - leader of the Lungeons and son of Shang. Derivative of Melungeon. Progenshans who have Thouron parentage and followers of their leader and founder.

Lungeons - survivors of Shang's breeder program and gladiatorial games. Followers of Lungeon.

Mahli - the Royal House T'oann, Tory, and Tonga are from.

Mary Eliza Mahoney - Alliance medical cruiser.

Marsh Rat - a large carnivorous rodent that lives in marsh caves on the planet Selemar.

Marshon - son of Tonga.

Martina - descendant of the survivors of the *Michael P Anderson* and grandmother to Sylvia, wife of T'iang.

Memphis Lin - weapons officer on the *Infiltrator* and wife of Nicholas Piper.

Michael P Anderson - Alliance science and research vessel that crashed on Progensha after colliding with the *Infiltrator*.

Micton - the Progenshan equivalent of a minute.

Midnight Sun - self-name fighter of David Leahcim and Markka.

Mind Probe - a Progenshan device that reads brainwave activity and records complete visual images of a subject's memories. Most often referred to simply as Probe.

Mindloop - a mind walk where those telepathically joined can become trapped within a mental prison reliving the same event repeatedly.

Mind Walker - the Progenshan equivalent of a telepath.

Mook - son of Markka and Tory. The oldest of four siblings.

Mos - the Progenshan equivalent of an hour.

Mountain People - primarily are descendants of Selemites and others who survived Progensha's Great War and took refuge in the mountains.

Mountainers: Mountain People.

Mud Boar - a wild boar with tusks it uses to gore its victims to death.

Myra - SI (Synthetic Intelligence) and personal assistant to Commander Chappie.

Nanites - microscopic sentient robots used by the Progenshans to repair minor injuries or to sustain life following a major injury.

Naphtali - a star system near Alliance territory the GSE operates out of.

Nicholas Piper - medical corpsman on board the *Infiltrator* and husband to Memphis Lin.

Nichols - Alliance warship.

Nomads - a loose collective of Progenshans who live on the periphery of the major cultural groups and the Land of No Return.

Oceanics - are aquatic beings from the planet Oceania. They are able to breathe in water environments equally as well as oxygen environments.

Opportunity - the smuggler boom town on Sigma II run by Captain Vee's sister Verna.

Potomac - an Alliance dreadnought class ship.

Powell - Alliance warship.

Pricilla - wife to Marshon.

Probe - a shortened version of mind probe.

Progensha - the homeworld of the Uderrans, Dark Woodsman, Thourons, Nomads, and Mountain People. It appears orange or peach from space and revolves around two suns in an oval eight orbit. The planet has three continents, but only one is inhabited. There is no moon.

Queen She'ara - sister to T'iang.

Queendom - the city state of Uderra. Traditionally run by a matriarchal line of succession.

Quicksand - Alliance ship commanded by Captain Pardons' brother.

Ramie - one of Cora's children and member of the *Infiltrator*.

Raqmar - Selemite engineer who served aboard the *Infiltrator*, the *T'ayMak* , and *Alasta*.

Raqtar - leader of the Mountain People and key member of the group who rescued Leahcim and T'oann.

Reth - executive officer to Captain Tranyxx of the Alliance ship *Vindicator*

Rithlerin - ruthless leader who took control of the warring Thouron factions during the Thouron Civil War.

Romar - executive officer to Captain Rosa Parsons.

Ronald McNair - an Alliance warship.

Rosa Augusta Parsons - captain of the Alliance ship *T'ayMak*.

Sacred Mountain - the larger mountain in the mountain chain home to the Mountain People.

Sairidians - dominant culture in the Galactic Star Empire.

Scorb - a large exoskeleton creature that is a cross between a Terran crab and scorpion.

Secton - the Progenshan equivalent of seconds.

Sergeant Sikes - commanding officer to a contingent of marines on Terra II.

Selemite Period of Mourning - a three-day period Selemites spend personally mourning/celebrating the dead.

Selemites - are members of the Alliance. Their homeworld is Selemar. It is a heavy gravity planet. Its inhabitants possess above average strength and are readily identified by their gray complexions.

Shang - leader of the Thourons and father to Lungeon.

Sho'khan - former science office in the Uderran military. Promoted to senior tactical officer.

SI - Synthetic Intelligence. Artificial Intelligence in sentient form.

Sigma II - desert planet in the Alliance and home to the boomtown Opportunity.

Sojourner - SI assigned to the *Infiltrator* and friend and confidant to Captain Vee.

Sonic Bomb - an experimental weapon developed by the Alliance and used to disastrous effect during the Great War.

Sparks - an Oceanic and helmsman for the Alliance ship *Infiltrator*.

Sponge Tick - a fist-sized parasite found on the planet Progensha.

Ssstra - the Sairidian word for Aggro Nine.

Stimulator - the Progenshan equivalent of a defibrillator.

Sylvia - granddaughter to Martina and wife to T'iang. It is also the name of Marshon's youngest child, Tonga's granddaughter.

T'ayMak - the Alliance warship captained by Rosa Parsons who is succeeded by Captain Sparks.

Tamar - Alliance warship.

Terrans - are members of the Alliance. Their homeworld is the planet Terra (formerly known as Earth and sometimes still referred to as Earth).

The Others - the collective entities living in the supercomputer on a dwarf planet in Sairidian space.

Thicket Tea - a medicinal herbal tea with hallucinogenic properties.

Thourons - are inhabitants of the planet Progensha. They live primarily in the hilly or rocky regions of the planet's largest continent.

T'iang - brother to Queen She'ara and husband to Martina's granddaughter Sylvia.

T'oann - Progenshan military commander, member of the royal family, and wife to David Leahcim.

Tonga - oldest sister to T'oann and Tory. Exceptionally strong Mind Walker, and key member of the resistance..

Tory - brother of T'oann, husband to Markka, and heir to the Queendom.

Traveler City - the city founded and established on Progensha by the survivors of the *Michael P Anderson*.

Tree Sap Nectar - a sweet drink made from tree sap.

Tryanxx - captain of the *Vindicator*.

T'ungstan - chief intelligence officer in the early days of the Uderran military during the time Martina lived before the end of The Great War.

Uderrans - are inhabitants of the planet Progensha. They are distantly related to the Thourons, but prefer to live in fertile valleys or grassy plains.

Ugot - the Avian equivalent of a Terran lamb.

Union of Allied Worlds - the official title of the Alliance.

Universal Time transmitters - devices that maintain Alliance time. Alliance time is based on the Allurian calendar. Four hundred Allurian days is considered one year in the Alliance. Forty hours is one day in Alliance time.

Valiant - an Alliance warship.

Valley of the Dead - it is the place Avians believe the dead go to spend their time in the afterlife.

Ventora IV - the colony world Memphis Lin grew up on.

Verna - older twin sister to Captain Vee.

Victory - alliance warship.

Videll - a junior bridge officer on board the *Alasta*.

Vindicator - Alliance dreadnought.

Vulcania IV - a volcanic world populated by dinosaur-like creatures.

Western Sea - a large body of water the Colossal Ocean feeds into. From the Western Sea, the water is dispersed throughout the continent by way of rivers, streams, and inland seas.

White Lightning - a potent Progenshan drink. Equivalent to whiskey but with a sweeter taste.

Wooders - the Dark Woods People or Dark Woodsmen. They inhabit what is referred to as the Dark Woods on the planet Progensha's largest continent.

Yottabyte - one million trillion megabytes.

Xnar - an Alliance battle cruiser.

Zora - daughter of David Leahcim and T'oann. She has two brothers and is the oldest of the three.

Zulu - an Alliance battle cruiser.

Zuri - daughter and only child of Memphis Lin and Nicholas Piper. Zuri is also the name of a Progenshan ship and a military academy.

ABOUT THE AUTHOR

Michael D. Brooks is a late bloomer baby boomer Indie Writer. He is a dreamer, fan of science fiction, enjoys humor, and is a kid at heart.

He earned an MA in Writing Studies and has written numerous articles, Short Stories, Drabbles, and Flash Fiction.

He is the author of a humorous series of flash fiction books featuring conversations with a crusty but loveable character called Pop. Pop imparts snippets of wisdom to his son and grandson with hilarious results.

Pop is loosely based on his late father and father-in-law with a generous sprinkling of other influential men in his life.

"Everyone has someone in their family like Pop."

The Destined series trilogy is his springboard into science fiction. The series is a tale of an intricately woven adventure of love, war, sacrifice, and survival.

OTHER BOOKS BY THE AUTHOR

Conversations with Pop

More Conversations with Pop

Even More Conversations with Pop

Destined: by Choice or Circumstance

Intersections in Time

SOCIAL MEDIA PRESENCE

Carrd

Drablr

GoodReads

Instagram

Twitter

www.ingramcontent.com/pod-product-compliance
Lightning Source LLC
Chambersburg PA
CBHW081227020726
47503CB00011B/2931